MW01146087

The Alchemist:
Dawn of Destiny

Book One of the
Alchemist Trilogy

L.A. Wasielewski

Copyright ©2018 by L.A. Wasielewski

This is a work of fiction. Names, characters, places, and incidents are either the products of the author's imagination or used in a fictitious manner. Any resemblance to actual persons, living or dead, or actual events is purely coincidental.

All rights reserved. This book, or any portion thereof, may not be reproduced in any way without the express permission of the publisher or author.

Cover design by Gabriela--BRoseDesignz

Find me on:

Twitter @AuthorBebedora

Facebook: @LAWasielewski

Website: lawasielewski.com (Including exclusive color maps, extra web content, and much more!)

Acknowledgements

Thank you to everyone who has encouraged and inspired me during this journey. First, to my **husband and son**, for their support and love even amidst writing tantrums. More thanks to hubby, for being the most incredible and honest editor and sounding board. My test readers, **Quinn Fitzpatrick, April Lewis, and Philip Milbrath.** Your feedback was essential and so very appreciated. Thank you for taking so much of your time to help! **Chris Lewis**, the grooviest map guru around! **Sean R. Frazier**, all-around rad guy, advice-giver extraordinaire, and the source of most of my twitter-related fits of uncontrollable laughter. Buy his books! Also to **Betsy Fong, Natali Heuss, Robin Janney, Katie Masters,** and **Rob Nugent** for their awesomeness in various fields of expertise!

For the Saurus

PROLOGUE

The jeweler's hands were steady and precise.

A white-haired man sat hunched over the well-worn workbench, the dim light of a single lantern the only illumination in the tiny workshop. Thousands of pieces of jewelry had been crafted at this very station, precious gems and gold transformed from raw materials into works of art.

He heated a thin silver rod in a tiny forge, just enough to make it malleable, before bending the glimmering material into a swirling setting. He worked for the better part of an hour, re-heating and twisting the metal until he was happy with the design. Finally satisfied, he quenched the piece one final time in water, steam billowing up around his face.

The village outside his window was quiet, sleeping as peacefully as they could as war ravaged their country. Frost covered the corners of the thin glass panes. He heard movement behind him—a pained grunt—but did not turn to make sure his guest was alright. It was clear the man was injured when he knocked on the door in the middle of the night, but the jeweler's assistance had been dismissed. Instead, the traveler merely handed him a large handful of coins and beseeched him to craft an item of great importance. Who it was for, he refused to say.

Anyone else would have been unnerved by the presence of a mysterious warrior behind them, observing every detail of their work. But the jeweler was confident in his talent and experience, and was unfazed by the scrutiny. He had a job to do, and he was damn sure going to make it perfect—even if his visitor was bleeding all over the floor.

The figure behind him moved closer, leaning over his shoulder. The smell of blood and sweat was overpowering. The jeweler tried not to gag as he offered the piece for inspection. After a moment, the visitor sighed in relief and produced a small pouch from within his cloak. As the leather cinch was opened, the goldsmith felt a tingle up his spine that made his hair stand on end.

"Take it. Please…"

The man's words were pained and desperate. Accepting the stone from the shaking gloved hand of his guest, the lapidary immediately noticed the snow white cabochon shimmered from the inside, emitting its own soft light. He had never before encountered a stone like this. The instant it touched his skin, warmth seeped into his flesh and began tracking up his arm. The power that surged from the gem was intoxicating.

1

The jeweler curled his fingers around the bauble, welcoming the sensation streaming through his veins. Flashes of energy streaked past his eyes. Power, magic, good and evil—eternity. All floating within the gem. Nothing mattered to him in that moment—except the stone.

He snapped himself from the feeling of ecstasy, hurriedly placing the stone on a small velvet cloth. He suddenly felt cold and weak, the aura around him dissipating rapidly. Even though he had enjoyed the feeling of elation and strength, a powerful presence had crept in on his vision, and a haunting voice had projected directly into his mind, sternly telling him to let the gem go. It was not meant for him.

"Please hurry…"

For the first time in his career, his hands shook. He missed the power surging across his nerves. Quickly making his final measurements, he heated the thin silver filaments one last time, and nestled the gem in the setting. He suddenly wanted the newly-crafted amulet—and his guest—as far away from him as possible. The jeweler handed the piece to his visitor, hoping it was the last time he would ever have to touch it.

The soldier lifted the talisman from wrinkled hands and held it close to his face. Only then did the goldsmith turn to look at him directly. A black cloak covered crystalline mail, spattered with blood. The man wore a mask over his eyes and nose, held to his hood with small tacks inlaid with the same crystal as his armor. A glittering crystal sword rested in a scabbard on his back, held in place by red leather straps. Though hunched in pain, the soldier still towered over the aging goldsmith. The man had never shared his name or where he came from, and the jeweler felt he never would.

Soft words in a language the jeweler did not recognize filled the room, the man's lips brushing across the surface of the embedded gem. Mist tumbled from his mouth, the charm greedily drinking the fog like a cheap brew. The jewel glowed brightly as the last of the words reached the jeweler's ears. In an instant, it changed color, the milky white hue replaced by a deep royal purple. The glaring light shining from the stone dimmed, the gem now shimmering from the inside as swirls of iridescent glitter moved within the bauble. The warrior wordlessly pointed to a simple silver chain hanging from a rack above the worktable. Obliging him, the goldsmith removed it from the hook and placed it in his hand beside the newly-created talisman. A weak but thankful smile crossed the blood-spattered face under the eye mask before both amulet and chain were returned to the pouch.

The soldier raised his hand in the air and tracked it down over the face of the jeweler, a whispered incantation causing the old man to slump forward and lay his head on the worktable. In the morning, aside from a headache, he would have no recollection of the events of the night before.

Wrapping his cloak around himself, the warrior stumbled out into the moonless night, blood splattering on the fresh snow.

CHAPTER ONE

"A man chooses his destiny the way he chooses when and where to sleep. The particulars are flexible and up for debate. But it will happen."

--The wisdom of Leeothea Nye, grandmother of Ryris Bren.

"Ryris Bren, do you really think you'd be able to leave without saying goodbye?"

The alchemist turned awkwardly, the sound of the booming voice startling him. He nearly knocked a cluster of bottles from the counter. One of them wobbled precariously on the edge, before gravity took hold and brought it to the ground with a shattering crash. Green liquid spilled into the spaces between the floor stones. The alchemy shop owned by the Brens—Maxxald and his son Ryris—was old, and the potion quickly seeped into the dusty grout.

Hundreds of bottles lined rickety shelves and alchemical ingredients covered every available space. Bunches of desiccated herbs hung from crooked nails hammered into the heavy wooden ceiling beams. Jars of dried flower petals, bottles of preserved insect wings, and dishes of sparkling mineral chips were readily available to the customers who frequented the small shop. The more precious fare, like needle weed and blood mist were locked away in cabinets behind the counter or sealed in display cases as far from the door as possible. If there was one thing Maxx wasn't—it was careless with his merchandise.

Blackthorne Village may have been out of the way on the map, but loyal alchemy lovers from all over the empire chose Bren's because of their expertise, honest prices, and incredible selection. Several hundred ingredients resided within the walls of the store, most carefully harvested by both Ryris and his father. While a great number of them were easy to obtain with a little hard work and know-how, there were a fair amount that took determination and courage. Yes, the Brens had suppliers that would stock them on merchandise from far-off lands. But for the most part, they procured their goods themselves, sometimes at significant risk. Spelunking in dark caves, wading through festering swamplands, trudging through the deep snow drifts of the Screaming Peaks—the pair had done it all.

The Brens had a reputation for being alchemy geniuses. Their tinctures were legendary. Some attributed it to years of study, long hours toiling over bubbling alembics, and grinding their fingers to the bone with a mortar and pestle. Fair and true—but not exactly the case. The two men couldn't explain it, and didn't really feel the need to—but their expertise was so much more than learned. Maybe it was in their blood, their genes. Maxx' mother once called it 'the touch'. A simple, yet very honest description of their skill set. They simply *knew* the right ways, the correct ingredients. They lived and breathed alchemy—it was who they were, who their ancestors had been—who the universe had destined them to be.

It was what Ryris had always envisioned for himself.

As he looked around the shop, he felt great pride in the business, pride in what he and his father had worked so hard to create. He also felt his stomach jump when his visitor bumped a display case as he crossed the door threshold, nearly toppling a thin glass vase containing dried brumble weed. The guest steadied the vase with giant, calloused hands before turning to face the young man. He pointed to the spilled liquid on the floor.

"Now you've done it. Your dad'll have your head for wastin' potions." The door shut, instantly cutting off the blast of cold air. Heavy footsteps approached, the bottles near the entryway clinking together as the weight of the giant man jostled the shelving they sat on.

Ryris smiled and bent over to pick up the shards of glass. His muffled voice wafted up from behind the counter. "It was one of my creations, Grildi."

Grildi laughed heartily as he leaned his elbows on the workspace and peered down over the top. He took off his wool cap, exposing a shiny bald head. "Even worse! Not to talk stink about Maxx, but..." Grildi stopped himself, realizing Maxx may be within earshot.

Ryris grinned as he moved to the end of the counter and threw the broken bottle bits into the fireplace. "We'll soon find out if I have what it takes, right?"

The hulking man's smile faded and his shoulders slumped. "Don't remind me. Keld is too far away."

"Don't go getting weepy, I'll write you whenever I can."

"You know I'm not that good at reading."

"Consider it practice, then. You'll hear my tales of adventure and prosperity in the big city and hone your literacy skills at the same time." Ryris offered an encouraging smile.

Grildi's eyes crinkled at the sides as his lips curled. Grildi Amzod was the self-appointed village security guard, and the residents were happy to allow him the title. Standing just under seven feet tall and weighing more than two average men combined, he seemed perfectly suited for the job—if you didn't know him well. The townsfolk knew him as kind-hearted and fiercely protective over his friends, but outsiders had no idea. And that suited the people of Blackthorne just fine. To any stranger wanting to make a scene or commit a crime, he was a menacing, muscular beast who wouldn't hesitate to snap you in two before throwing you into the Whispering River. That was, when he wasn't batting his eyes at the baker to get a berry pie gratis or cuddling with one of the many village cats. To the people of the town, he was just 'their Grildi'.

Ryris came back from the hearth and slapped Grildi on the forearm. "And no, I didn't think I could get away with leaving before I said farewell."

"Good. 'Cause I'd have to hunt you down and—"

"—toss me in the river." Ryris moved the remaining bottles away from the edge of the counter.

"You think you'd let me do it for old times' sake?"

"Absolutely not! The water's freezing and I can't afford to be sick when I open the new shop."

Grildi pouted and picked at a leather lace poking out of his jacket sleeve. Ryris could tell he was about to get mushy.

"I tell you what, when I come home to visit, I'll bring you a present from the capital." He held his hands out wide in front of himself. "A big one."

"Aye." Grildi reached across the counter and grabbed the young man by the shoulders, pulling him up and toward his body with such intensity that the alchemist thought all the air would be forced from his lungs.

Ryris' eyes bulged as he struggled to draw in a breath, and he wildly flailed his hands against his friend's massive biceps. His words were raspy and urgent as his feet knocked against the backside of the shop's counter. "Gr-Grildi...can't breathe!"

The older man gasped and let go, sending Ryris tumbling backwards onto his rear end. Grildi reached over and extended a giant hand to help him up, an embarrassed expression crossing his face. "Sorry, Boss. Just wanted you to remember me, that's all."

Ryris attempted to catch his breath as he allowed his friend to help him back to his feet. "Don't you worry; you're one person I'll never forget. And who knows, maybe you'll get the chance to come visit." He turned his attention to the dwindling light filtering through the old shop windows. "You'd better get to your nightly patrol. It's almost time to lock the gates."

Grildi puffed out his chest. Ryris knew he took his job very seriously, and would risk his life protecting the village and its inhabitants. As the lumbering man opened the plain hardwood door, he turned to face his friend one last time.

"I'm awful proud of you, boy. Even if your daddy is scared for you to go." He sighed deeply. "And I know your ma would have been proud, too."

"Thank you, Grildi. That means more than you'll ever know."

The man hesitated at the threshold with a silent, sincere smile before opening the door wide, the brisk autumn air rushing in at full force. Grildi replaced his hat and raised his collar around his neck, hunching his back in an attempt to keep himself warm. He waved his hand over his shoulder, the door slamming shut behind him.

Looking to the last drops of the green restorative elixir on the floor, Ryris sighed somberly. It hit him that he would truly be leaving in the morning. He had grown up in the small apartment in the back with his father and maternal grandmother. It had been crowded and never private, but it was *home*. When his grandmother died, the place had seemed so empty, even though it was filled to the brim with books, bottles, and the occasional live alchemical specimen.

He really was going to miss Blackthorne and its residents—especially Grildi. After his mother had been killed, Grildi had taken it upon himself to comfort him as best he could. He wasn't the smartest man and had a slower way about him. But Grildi was kind and caring, and had become a true friend over the years.

Even at twenty years his senior, Grildi sometimes had the mind of a child, and that suited Ryris just fine during his formative years. He would spend his days following the large man around town, jabbering in his ear about alchemy while he accompanied the guard on his duties. They would occasionally venture into the woods, making sure to steer very clear of the deep, foreboding inner forest. The pair would sometimes collect specimens for Maxx, the elder Bren always paying Grildi a fair price for retrieval.

As Ryris aged and his intellect grew, he realized how special his older friend was—and how important to his life he had been. Grildi had always been there for him.

The young alchemist didn't have many friends. All the children his age had been more interested in playing war games in the forest than mixing potions and sorting alchemical ingredients. And as they aged, they grew more and more apart in interests. It wasn't that the other young villagers were unkind to him; they just didn't have anything in common other than place of birth. When they were busy learning the ways of the village lumberjacks or going off to join the army, Ryris' nose had been in books, his hands coated in the grime of alchemy. He was too engrossed in learning everything he could from his father about their trade.

An icy whirlwind snapped him from his thoughts as his father barreled through the door, arms full of various packages. Ryris rounded the counter and scrambled to help the older man before the parcels tumbled from his hands.

"I see you've done nothing but daydream about Keld today." Maxx' voice wafted around the packages.

Maxxald Bren was a salty old man. He had seen his fair share of tough times, and had risen above to make a name for himself in the alchemical world. His own mother, like Ryris', had passed away when he was young and his hard-nosed father had raised him. There had been times their shop—the one they still ran to this day—didn't see customers for months, and this meant their stomachs were never quite full, the coffers holding nothing but dust. Never attending formal school, the elder Bren learned all he needed from his own father, all while toiling away at an alchemist's worktable. He wasn't "book smart" so to speak; he didn't know history or care about the position of the stars. But when it came to common sense and good old fashioned know-how, he had more than a head start on anyone who wanted to challenge him. The alchemical knowledge contained within his head was vast enough to write books from, but he had no interest in adding to the volumes stored in libraries. Wise beyond his already long years, he wasn't one to mince words. If he didn't like you—or what you were doing—he told you as much. He didn't have time to pussyfoot around anyone's feelings.

Ryris grabbed several small pouches from atop the stack of boxes in his father's hands. Maxx' comment had hurt. Yes, he had been thinking about his journey to Keld and the new store, but he knew better than to waste his entire day in the clouds.

"I cleaned the worktable and mixed a batch of base fluid, just like you asked. And, I worked on some recipes to debut at the new location." Ryris' tone of voice was biting.

"…and daydreamed." His father shuffled past him, peering around the side of the packages to make sure there was clear space before dropping them on the countertop with a grunt. "Heavy buggers."

"You should have yelled from outside for help."

Max shrugged off his coat and tossed it onto the counter with exasperation. "I did. Twice."

The young alchemist looked down at the bags in his hand with a sheepish frown. "Sorry. I guess I didn't hear you."

"Daydreaming…" His father grumbled and snipped the thin twine binding the boxes together.

Ryris took the pouches to the worktable and began sorting the contents. The two worked in silence for several long moments. He could feel his father's eyes on his back from time to time, but didn't turn to confront him. As he laid brittle insect thoraces into a bowl, he was reminded by Maxx' huffing that the old alchemist was having a hard time coming to terms with his impending departure. Ryris finally decided to break the ice. "Look, I know you're nervous about me leaving…"

Maxx just snorted, flipped the small sign on the window to read 'closed', and turned down the oil lamps. He then locked the door, jiggling the old bolt to secure it. Grabbing a small wrapped parcel from the countertop, he walked past his son and into the living space behind the shop. "Don't forget to pull the back door closed, or we'll get a draft."

Ryris, his attempt at conversation thwarted by his father's stubbornness, grabbed his journal from the countertop and followed Maxx into their apartment, closing the heavy oaken door behind him. He could instantly feel the chill in the air, and knew the fire had died down significantly. Maxx muttered under his breath and began pumping a small bellows in an attempt to stoke the flames. After a few tries, he swore quietly and stomped his foot. The coals just wouldn't respond.

Sensing his father's irritation, Ryris held his right palm outstretched and concentrated on his fingertips. Seconds later, tiny flames erupted from the ends and merged together into a small ball of fire. He carefully moved toward the hearth, mindful not to drop his fiery cargo. Kneeling next to the fireplace, he blew a puffed breath at his hand and the flame jumped onto the wood. Within seconds, the fire billowed up, licking the bottom of the cooking pot and warming the two men.

Ryris' hand instinctively went to the ornate amulet hanging at his chest, the purple stone warming his skin in response to his actions. His father turned away from the fireplace, arms waving wildly, eyes burning with fury. He grabbed his son forcefully by the shoulders and shook.

"Are you insane?" Maxx' cheeks immediately flushed bright red.

"It's not a big deal. You needed help with the fire and nobody's here but us." Ryris pushed his father's hands down from his arms.

"Not a big deal? Well if that isn't the most asinine thing I've ever heard!" Maxx shook his head in disbelief. "It's not a toy, Ryris!"

Ryris absentmindedly rubbed his hands together, hating feeling like he had to hide. And in reality—*he did*. Magic users, rare in this time, were looked upon as something to be shunned, hidden. People didn't associate with them for fear of being hunted alongside them, courtesy of age-old fear mongering. The Old War had left its mark, even after countless centuries.

"I'm not stupid. I only do it in your presence, and not very often. I'm sorry, alright? It was a mistake."

"You're awful quick forget what happened to people who had that power... to your mother." It was harsh of Maxx to bring up her death, but he needed to hit home to his son just how foolish he had been in his actions.

Ryris clenched his fists at the thought of the man who had murdered his mother. The mayor had labeled it a senseless, random crime, but Maxx always believed it was from the magic. He swore that he never blamed her for her own death—but he

9

was always quick to point out the dangers of magic use in an unsympathetic world. Sometimes Ryris wasn't so sure he completely believed the older man.

Ryris sighed before continuing. "That war is long since over. The people that caused it are dead and gone. Nothing remains of them or their ideals."

"Says you." Maxx scowled at his son.

"I'll be careful."

"I've spent too much time keeping you safe to have you make a silly mistake in the capital. You don't know who's watching."

"I know you're trying to protect me, and I appreciate it."

Maxx' expression grew concerned. "I know there are still people out there who follow the old ways. Your mother's absence reminds me every day."

"I've managed to stay alive and out of trouble for twenty-seven years so far, haven't I?" Ryris tried to lighten the mood.

Maxx just grunted before he motioned to the butcher's block across the room. "Cut up what's left of the potatoes and onions." He dumped a meaty bone into the pot on the hearth, before grabbing a sachet of spices and tossing them in, along with some milk and a hefty amount of water.

As Ryris chopped the vegetables, he was overcome with a sense of nostalgia. This would be the last meal he would prepare with his father for a very long time. He looked around the room, taking note of the dozen or so boxes resting near the back door, filled with his belongings and all the merchandise and equipment needed for start-up. In the morning, everything would be loaded onto one of their carts and Ryris would begin the long trek to Keld. The storefront they had purchased, with an apartment above, was smaller than their space in Blackthorne, but would suit him nicely just the same.

When he was finished, he brought the bowl to his father, who motioned him to dump the vegetables in. "Give it a stir and let it boil."

The older man sat down at the table with a tired grunt, the chair creaking under his weight. He ran a hand through his white hair with a sigh. Ryris followed suit, leaning over and resting his elbows on the tabletop. The two sat quietly for a long moment.

"You said you came up with some new recipes?" Maxx broke the silence.

"I'm not sure they're ready to be tested yet, but I think they have potential."

Maxx fished a pair of well-used spectacles from his shirt pocket and perched them on the bridge of his nose. "Well, let's see 'em."

10

Ryris obliged his father, drawing several pieces of paper from inside his journal. He handed them over with a hopeful smile. "There's two tinctures for upset stomach, and one for night vision."

"Night vision? Awful ambitious." Maxx studied the pages carefully, mumbling to himself as he read. He finally removed his glasses with a sigh and set them and the recipes on the table.

Ryris was instantly nervous. "I know the night vision still needs work, but I think it'll fetch at least four-hundred gamm when it's perf—"

"Looks good to me."

Ryris smiled hopefully. "You really think so?"

"I wouldn't say it if I didn't mean it!" He pointed a finger at his son. "Just remember to set a fair price. I don't want to lose money in the capital. I had to pay an arm and a leg for that tiny building."

Ryris nodded his head in agreement. He and his father had taken an incredible financial risk. They had a safe cushion in Blackthorne, with loyal customers traveling large distances for their services. They had a nice life, with plenty of money in their pockets. Not overly rich by the standards of the Keld nobility, but their well-respected business afforded them some small luxuries that most residents of their village didn't have the funds to enjoy. Never anything flamboyant or over the top, but quality clothes, a vast inventory, and a choice roast every once and a while was all they ever needed.

So, when Ryris brought up the idea of expanding, his father had been quite vocal—and not in a good way. He had named one-hundred and one reasons why another shop was a bad idea. Crime in the city. Financial loss. Having to maintain two inventories. His son being away from home. The list went on and on. Ryris understood each and every concern his father had brought up, but in the end, he couldn't let go of the one thing that drew him to Keld more than anything else.

Independence.

He had been living in the small village since the day he was born. His education happened there, his business training. The only time he saw the world outside their home province was when they went to collect ingredients. True, they had travelled on many occasions, but the journeys had always been brief. And Maxx had always been with him. Always. To Ryris, the ultimate adventure lay far beyond the gates of Blackthorne.

Keld was the biggest prize of them all.

Ryris had been thorough and smart with his arguments, countering every negative from his father with two positives. The crime problem was met with private

11

security and better locks. Financial loss succumbed to a master marketing and sales plan. The inventory issue would resolve itself at both locations over a period of time, with both men restocking through caravans and their own hard work. When Maxx had been in Keld to purchase the building, he even hired a young man to assist Ryris in unpacking and stocking the store, with the option to stay on as part-time help when his son was out harvesting ingredients—surprising the young alchemist with his willingness to be proactive.

They mutually agreed that opening a store in the capital city of Keld would not only be a very lucrative financial decision, but would give the younger Bren a broader view of the world around him. But it also meant Ryris would be on his own, far from home.

The city was big, crowded, and dangerous, Maxx had claimed. He offered to buy his son a weapon—a dagger—to defend himself and their merchandise if he needed to. Ryris just rolled his eyes and told him he was being overly dramatic—then showed him the dirk he purchased from a travelling merchant several weeks prior. It seemed to calm his father's nerves somewhat.

They had been together for his entire life—especially after his mother and grandmother had died. Both had passed away before he reached the age of ten, and now at twenty-seven, there had been a great number of years where it was just them. They had a routine, a good life together—and now it was ending. He knew his father was having the hardest time with that particular situation.

Ryris knew Maxx would be lonely. But there was a fantastic opportunity for both of them at stake here, and they would have been stupid to pass it up. It was something they had to do—for the business, for the family. And Ryris needed to do this for himself. To prove that he could be independent, run a business, and be his own man. He was a damn good alchemist, of that he was certain. This was his golden opportunity to show the world what he was made of.

The elder Bren got up slowly, his knees cracking. He stirred the pot, taking a taste from the old wooden spoon. "Getting there."

"Good, I'm starving. I can't remember if I ate lunch."

Maxx smirked, his face illuminated by the glowing fire. "Too busy daydreaming."

Ryris shook his head with a huff and got up, fetching a loaf of crusty bread from the kitchen shelving. "You never give up, do you old man? Who are you going to pick on when I'm gone?"

"I'll find someone." Maxx pouted. "I suppose I'll have to take on a helper. Probably end up breaking my glassware like a nincompoop."

12

"It won't be that bad. Whoever you hire will work hard, I know it. You'll fire them if they don't."

"Damn right. Lazy bastards." He stirred the kettle. "Then again, I surely won't miss your constant humming."

Ryris joined his father at the hearth, clapping the old man on the back. "And I won't have to smell that stinking work apron of yours. Seriously, when's the last time you washed that thing?"

"Never. And that's the way I like it." His father offered him a spoonful of the stew. Silently agreeing that it had finished cooking, the young man retrieved two bowls and held them out for Maxx to fill. When they were both satisfied with their servings, they sat at the table and began to eat. Maxx didn't wait long to delve into sensitive conversation.

"I suppose you'll be looking for love in Keld?"

Ryris nearly spit his dinner across the table. Wiping his mouth on his sleeve, he tried to hide the instant blush on his cheeks.

"What? It's a perfectly legitimate question. You're a good-looking young business owner with what I'm assuming is a healthy libido."

"I really don't want to discuss my…uhhhh…with you. Ever." Ryris suddenly felt very hot.

Maxx shoveled a heaping spoonful of stew into his mouth. "It's normal to want someone."

"I won't have time, Dad."

Maxx sighed, his tone sobering. He rarely spoke from the heart, so Ryris was keen to listen. "Make time. You deserve to be happy. We've been together so long here, just the two of us—and I know you haven't much of a love life."

"It's not like there haven't been women. But…" Ryris hesitated, tapping his fingers on the tabletop as he contemplated his next response. "…there just wasn't much of a connection with any of them. There was never that spark that screamed, 'this is the one'! I'm not going to settle for someone just because I'm pushing thirty. Besides, the business is more important."

"Nothing's more important than love. You never know when it's going to be ripped away."

"I know." Ryris knew he was speaking of his mother. Although Maxx rarely mentioned it, the death of his wife haunted him every waking moment. Her presence was still felt throughout the home, however, through small trinkets left on shelves and

13

the ornate jewelry box still residing on his father's bureau. They occasionally spoke her name, but both men were unwilling to enter into deep conversation about her. The memories stung too much.

"Then get your arse out there and meet new people!"

Ryris understood his father meant well, and was genuinely concerned for not only his well-being, but his happiness. He internally vowed to at least make a go at pleasing the old man.

"For you, I will."

"No, not for me." He reached over the table and patted his son's hand. Ryris was immediately taken aback—physical affection was not his father's forte.

"For *me*, then."

"Good." The older man withdrew his hand and began eating once more. "Now, enough of this sappy nonsense, let's get down to business. You better have packed that glassware securely…because I'm not giving you more money to replace those beakers if they break before you even reach Keld."

Ryris smiled and let his father lecture him one last time.

CHAPTER TWO

1200 gamm, Onyx mortar and pestle

1600 gamm, Blown glass alembic

200 gamm, aspirated toad vomit, dried and packaged

--Proof of purchase, Eirik's Alchemical Supplies, Keld

Sunlight filtered in through the tiny, frost-covered bedroom window.

Grumbling under his breath, Ryris pulled the heavy down blanket over his head and turned away from the offending light. Wanting to soak up every last second in his childhood bed, he curled into a ball and sighed. He hoped his mattress in Keld wouldn't have lumps.

His mind flittered aimlessly in a state of limbo—not quite awake, not deep asleep. Images, some he recognized, some he did not, jumped around in his semi-dream state. He imagined what the new storefront would look like filled with potion bottles and ingredient bins, tried to envision all the wonderful things he would experience in the capital city. The grand library, theater, and commerce unlike he had ever seen. Maybe he'd even attend a party or two—if he were invited, of course. Perhaps he'd even get to meet the prince. No matter how nervous he was, the dream world offered incredible opportunities with no risk involved...

...Ryris was in a grand ballroom, filled with nobles. Their fingers glittered with diamonds and gold, their bodies draped in the most opulent silks and velvet. Music floated through the air from an unseen source, and the heavenly aroma of fresh pastries wafted into his nostrils. Couples danced, twirling each other around on the polished marble floor. Laughter echoed off the walls and the wine flowed like water. Ryris had never seen anything like it in his life. The guests parted on the dance floor as he walked forward, the men bowing deeply, the women dropping into curtseys. Confused as to why they were honoring him in such a manner, he turned to make sure a member of the monarchy wasn't on his heels.

As he moved, the unfamiliar sensation of heavy fabric sweeping across his legs caused him to look down at his own clothing. He was shocked to see that he was wearing the blue robes of the emperor. Short, worried breaths puffed from his lips. Surely the security guards would be on him in a heartbeat for such a traitorous act.

He tried to rip the clothing from his body, for fear of being imprisoned for impersonating the emperor, but found it pinned directly to his skin. Every time he tugged, searing pain flashed across his flesh. He attempted to scream for forgiveness, that this was all a big mistake—but his mouth wouldn't open. His hands flew to his lips, only to find them sewn shut with metal filaments. Blood dripped down

15

his chin as the party guests laughed and started to dance once more, surrounding him on the ballroom floor. Clawing at his mouth, he grasped at the metal wires and tried to remove them, only to find them tightening their hold.

Ryris fell to his knees, crying and confused. He was mute, bleeding, and utterly terrified. People continued to dance around him, their ornate shoes stepping on the robes spilled out around his body. They didn't seem to care he was even there. The music became louder and louder until he could no longer bear the sound. His hands shot to his ears in an attempt to muffle the excruciating melodies. The guests twirled around him, giving him a wider berth on every revolution. Within a matter of seconds, they were gathered around the perimeter of the dance floor, silently staring at him.

The music stopped, the lights went out. Everyone disappeared.

Terrified, Ryris tried to get up. His legs wobbled and it felt as if his feet were sinking into the floor. Tentatively taking a few steps, he stretched his arms out to find his way. The room was pitch-black and silent. He raised his fingertips to his mouth again, hoping against hope that the metal stitches were no longer there. He was relieved to find they had disappeared.

"H-hello?" His voice croaked as if it hadn't been used in days. The faint taste of blood lingered on his tongue. "Is anyone there?"

Rustling of clothing and the light taps of shoe heels echoed around him. He sensed—beings—around him, but was unsure if they were human. The ground started to rumble beneath his feet and he stopped moving.

"Please…what's going on?"

Mocking laughter erupted from all around. The unseen crowd murmured and hissed, Ryris' suspicions of their pedigree confirmed. They definitely weren't human. He felt the crowd close in on him, claustrophobia quickly taking hold. Within seconds, clawed hands latched onto his arms and back, serpents wrapping their scaly bodies around his legs. They tangled their gnarled fingers in his hair and pulled in every direction, all trying to get a piece of him. He felt as if his limbs were seconds away from being torn from his body. Ryris cried out in pain as his arms and legs stretched to their breaking point.

"Stop!"

His assailants just laughed and pulled harder, their troll-like voices chattering in some unknown language. Ryris' body was now pulled taught, hovering a few feet off the floor. The imperial robes had disappeared, leaving him naked. His skin prickled with goose bumps as the chill air of the room assaulted his flesh. Feeling the strength starting to fade from his body, he tried one last time to wrench himself free from the crowd's inhuman grip. Kicking and screaming, he flailed wildly until he could no longer move. Entirely spent, he resigned to the fact that these hideous creatures were going to kill him.

His body fell limp in their clutches, blood dripping from the hundreds of tiny cuts their sharp nails had pierced into his skin. Taking a deep breath, he just waited for it to be over. He could no longer fight, no longer cry out. He had nothing left to give.

In an instant, a blazing light enveloped him, the creatures hastily dropping his battered body to the floor as they scurried away. In a haze, Ryris turned his head just in time to catch a glimpse of one of their green, scaly bodies, its hooves clicking on the floor as it ran for protection from the light. One of his captors was not so lucky, and had turned to ash as the light burned its body.

The polished marble floor had been replaced by rough cobblestones, scraping against his already tortured flesh. Knowing this was his chance to escape now that the creatures had fled, he tried desperately to move, only to find his body unwilling. He found himself not caring about the strange illumination surrounding him. It wasn't menacing, but not comforting either. Just there.

As he tried to pull himself along the dusty stone floor, he found that his strength had waned to the point where he could no longer move. His energy depleted, he gave up and waited for his fate. His eyes fluttered closed and he let out a shaky breath.

It was only when soothing hands cupping his face materialized from seemingly nowhere did his body begin to relax. It wasn't a conscious decision, but somehow the presence that had taken form next to him comforted his fears, much like when his late mother had reassured him when the imaginary monster in his childhood closet had threatened him. Ryris tried to crack open his eyes, only to find them caked with dried blood. After a moment of struggle, he was finally able to force his lids open—and caught a fleeting glimpse of shimmering crystalline armor glittering in the light from high above…

"*Ryris?*"

His eyes snapped open and he tumbled out of bed, the muffled voice behind the door startling him from his nightmare. It took him a moment to get his bearings. Realizing he was on the worn wooden floor of his bedroom and not in his bed, he blew out a long breath of relief while simultaneously running his fingertips over his bare arms. He was comforted that his skin no longer bore the terrible wounds from his dream.

"*Dream. Just a dream,*" he told himself. "*You need to stop drinking so much asher tea, it's giving you nightmares.*"

He took a brief moment to try and make sense of his vision. The crowd, the terror—it was all confusing to him. And the crystalline armor? He was instantly reminded of the stories his grandmother had told him as a child—tales he hadn't had the time to think about in ages—about crystal-clad warriors of the Old War.

Ryris would listen intently when she spoke, hanging on her every word. Nothing got his attention faster than the stories of incredible warriors wearing crystalline mail, armed with weapons struck from the same shimmering material. When war ravaged the land centuries ago, or so the legend went, there had been a band of elite

17

soldiers who fought on behalf of the entire world. Warriors that commanded armies of citizens who made their last stand against evil.

The myth was the stuff of dreams to the vast majority of citizens. But to Ryris' grandmother it was true history. Yes, everyone accepted that war had happened, but the true cause of the conflict had been lost to the ages. And to most people, the legend of the Crystal Guard was just too fantastical to believe. His father would scold her for filling his son's head with 'nonsense.' But the old woman would stand her ground and keep on telling her grandson the tales.

"This story is important, little one—more than you can fathom at such a young age. Remember what I've told you. It's not just a fairytale—it's our history."

Our history.

Ryris had never been able to figure out what she meant. Most people would assume she was referencing the collective history of the entire world's people. But there had been something in her voice when she spoke those words—an importance she was trying to convey without bringing too much attention to it. When she passed on to the Gentle Reach, Ryris had become deeply enthralled by alchemy, and her stories had, for the most part, gone with her.

"Ryris? Son?"

Stopping himself from daydreaming, he noticed the shadows on the wall had moved, and he flew into a frenzy. Shaking his head to dissipate the last of the strange feelings left over from his dream, Ryris scrambled out of his night-clothes and into his trousers.

"What time is it?"

"Six. Breakfast is ready. Quit dawdling!"

Pulling his shirt over his head, he threw open the door and was instantly hit with the unmistakable aroma of pellick fruit. His father crouched over the hearth, carefully tending to small cakes cooking on a cast-iron griddle resting on the bare coals. A berry within one of them suddenly popped, the juice sizzling on the cook top. Maxx inhaled deeply and turned toward his son.

"About time..." He scooped the pancakes up with his spatula and plopped them down on a wooden platter, before motioning to a few pans. "Grab the syrup and mush off the stovetop."

Ryris obeyed and moved toward the fireplace, the heat soothing his still-cold toes and fingers. The pellick syrup smelled heavenly as he leaned close to the pot, the steam tickling his nostrils. He had to fight the urge to dip his finger into the boiling liquid to taste.

18

"C'mon, boy. The cakes are getting cold!" Maxx sat at their small table, already having served both himself and his son. "And you know I can't start the day without my mush."

Ryris brought both pans to the table, dropping a spoon into each. He piled a generous helping of mush into a bowl, and the old man immediately dug in.

"Don't you want any syrup on it?"

"It was never intended to taste good, only fill your belly."

Ryris shook his head with a chuckle, filling his own bowl. Grabbing the spoon in the thick pink syrup, he drowned his pancakes before adding a healthy dose to his mush. He had never eaten it without syrup, and today would be no different. Without it, the bland breakfast fare tasted like something that came out of the back end of an oinox.

They ate in silence for a few moments, Ryris savoring every bite of his father's famous cakes. Pellick fruit was native to the Northern provinces, and although he had some dried berries to take with him, he knew he would more than likely not taste them fresh for a very long time.

The sound of his father's voice jolted him from his food-induced ecstasy. His tone indicated he was feeling emotional, his words hesitant. Ryris wasn't used to hearing him speak in such a soft voice. Unsure of what was coming, he set down his fork and prepared for—well, he didn't quite know.

"Son, I've been meaning to tell you something. I know I've been hard on you, but I hope you understand why. I just wanted you to be successful. And be able to handle anyone's garbage."

Ryris was stunned. In all his years, he had never heard his father actually acknowledge what a tyrant he had been. There were times where the young man had been reduced to tears under Maxx' scrutiny and high expectations—and the elder Bren had never apologized for his behavior. Tough love, he called it. As a child, Ryris saw it as just his father being mean or expecting far too much from him. Now, as an adult— and because Maxx had just admitted it—he realized that he was doing it out of respect. His father respected him enough to make sure he would be ready for whatever the world threw at him. At the end of the day, all he wanted was for Ryris to succeed.

"I *am* proud of you, even if it doesn't seem that way."

The young man just stared at Maxx, silent.

"Well don't just sit there gawking at me!"

Ryris quietly tried to respond. "I just… I don't know what to say."

19

"I'm not expecting you to say anything." He motioned to his son's plate. "Eat before it gets cold."

And there it was. Words Ryris had never expected to hear from his father. Sure, he knew deep down Maxx had to have been proud—he wouldn't have agreed to let him open a new location so far away if he wasn't. But the words had never crossed Maxx' lips—ever.

"Thanks, Dad. That means a lot."

Maxx just grunted and shoveled a steaming spoonful of mush into his mouth, his attention now focused on the village newsletter in front of him on the table.

The two men ate the rest of their meal in silence. Even though it was brief, Ryris knew Maxx had meant what he said—and that he more than likely would never hear such words grace his father's lips again. And he was alright with that. He considered Maxx' surprise words another parting gift.

"I suppose you'll be trying to get out of washing the dishes now, right? 'Got to leave', 'a bit too much to do' keeping you from your household duties?"

Ryris stacked his bowl and cup on top of his plate before grabbing his father's dishes. His eyes twinkled with mischief. "I'll give you one more lazy morning, old man."

"Lazy? You're one to talk." Maxx drained his tea and tossed the mug at his son, Ryris barely catching it with his free hand. "I'm going to go through your inventory one last time. I can't have you getting to Keld only to find out you don't have an alembic."

As he stood at the washbasin and soaked his hands in the warm sudsy water, Ryris' mind wandered and he became uncharacteristically sentimental. Sure, he had fond recollections of times past and kept a few trinkets from his childhood as mementos, but for the most part he believed that memories were just that—memories. And yet here he was, washing mush and pellick syrup off of dishes he suddenly felt himself missing. A wave of nostalgia swept over him and for a moment, he almost felt as if he were going to cry. This would be the last time—at least for a very long time—that he would help his father around the house. Setting the dinnerware in a small wooden drying rack, he wiped his hands on a thin towel and joined his father, making sure any trace of moisture that may have graced his eyes was long gone.

As he approached, Ryris could hear his father muttering under his breath as he listed the contents of the boxes out loud. Knowing he was checking up on him—again—the young man decided to have a little fun at the expense of the old man, and allow him one last small moment of satisfaction and fatherly know-how. When Maxx' attention was focused on some satchels of herbs, Ryris knelt and covertly snuck a mortar and pestle specifically designed for crushing insect wings out of a box. Setting it on the floor for his father to happen across, he began small talk.

"I packed and re-packed these boxes three times. Everything's there."

Maxx grunted and pushed him off to the side. "You never know. Now let me look in that one."

Ryris obliged his father and moved out of the way, trading places with the older man. Maxx began to rifle through the new box, counting off envelopes of fire wasp wings on his fingers. As he set the pouches aside and began to dig deeper, his grumbling became increasingly irritated.

"Where's that special mortar and pestle for these ingredients?"

Ryris shrugged his shoulders. "I'm sure I put in in there."

"If you've lost it, I'm going to take one of your toes as payment." Maxx scowled as he dug through the box, his ears flushing red as his anger mounted. After a long moment of searching, he shifted his weight, his kneecap bumping the mortar bowl. The elder man immediately grabbed it, waving it in Ryris' face. "Fess up."

Ryris smirked and knelt next to his father. "There's nothing missing, trust me."

"You damn near gave me a heart attack! That thing wasn't cheap!" He shoved the equipment back into the crate and slammed the top closed.

Ryris patted his father on the back and helped him up from the floor. "I thought it would be funny."

"Well you thought wrong." Maxx shuffled away, grabbing both of their coats off the rack near the door.

Ryris instantly felt bad for trying to fool his father. He followed him out into the shop, taking a moment to pluck a familiar-yet-long forgotten book from the shelves on the wall. Crossing the threshold, he found Maxx rearranging bottles behind the counter. Ryris watched quietly for a moment, trying to come up with an apology. He set his book on the countertop.

"Sorry I tricked you. Like you would say, 'stop being a whiny baby and just get on with it.'" Ryris raised a hopeful eyebrow at his father.

Maxx stood silent for a moment before bursting into a bellowing guffaw. "You know, there are times when I think you don't have a lick of me in you aside from alchemical knowhow—and then you go and say something like that." He pointed to the book on the counter. "Where'd you find that old thing?"

Ryris patted the leather cover, adorned with a geometric pattern. "It's the book Gran used to read to me."

Maxx rolled his eyes. "Oh, *that* one. Aren't you a little old for fairytales?"

Irritated by his father's comment, but not willing to push an argument, Ryris simply replied, "So you don't mind if I take it with me?"

"Go ahead. I won't miss it." Maxx turned to reenter their apartment. "I'm going to load the wagon. Goddess knows if I wait for you to do it, I'll die of old age."

Ryris smiled appreciatively and waited for his father to leave. When he was finally alone in the shop, he began circling around, taking mental note of everything there. He ran his fingertips over the worn edges of the ingredient bins, opening one to dip his hands into the fine dust inside. Sighing as he rounded the countertop, he stopped and took a moment to draw in a deep breath through his nostrils. Their shop smelled of dried herbs and flowers, and years of bubbling brews. According to his father, the new storefront had just smelled old and dusty, having been vacant for several years. He wondered how long it would take to ingrain a scent on the place, how much time would have to pass before the workbench would accrue the layer of grunge that fell hand-in-hand with the creation of such wonderful potions.

He moved toward the door and muttered a final, soft goodbye to the shop in which he had learned everything he knew. Closing his eyes for a moment to commit the place to memory, he grabbed his book and headed back into the apartment and into his room, closing the door behind him. He tucked the old, worn book that belonged to his grandmother into his knapsack and sat down on his bed with a sigh. The mattress dipped under his weight and he resisted the urge to wrap himself in his downy blanket one last time. He wouldn't need the comforter in Keld, where the temperature rarely dropped into the frigid zone.

He could hear his father moving boxes out the back door and onto the cart that would carry him to the capital. Maxx had purchased a new horse from the livery in Lullin for Ryris' journey, with the intent that it would also be the young alchemist's transportation once he reached the city. The day he brought her home, the older man had even given it a name—Ass of the East. When Ryris asked the significance of the eccentric name, his father had replied, 'The whole way home, her rear was facing east— and was very *musical*'. Ryris appreciated his father's sometimes juvenile and crude sense of humor.

Ryris briefly contemplated going out to help his father, but he knew the older man's pride would win out over practicality. True, two men could work faster than one, but if Maxx didn't ask for your help then you had damn well better not offer. Instead, he took one last look around his room.

The walls were old and never painted, the exposed brick showing its age with tiny flecks crumbling off and onto the floor. An oil painting hung on the far wall—a rendering of the Imperial Palace in Keld done by his mother before he was born. He used to stare at it for hours on end when he couldn't sleep, imagining what it would be like to roam the halls and gardens. And now, in a matter of weeks, he would be on its doorstep.

Closing his eyes and taking a deep breath, he inhaled the aroma of his room one last time: a mix of fireplace and the incense he burned at night to rid himself of the scent of some of the more unfavorable-smelling ingredients. Snapping his eyes open, he slapped his thighs with determination—a determination to make a new place for himself.

Shuffling outside his door caught his attention once more, although the noise was different from that of his father loading crates. No—this sound was bigger, heavier...

"Ryris! There's something you need to see outside! It's important!"

The young alchemist recognized that voice. Seconds later, Grildi Amzod barreled into his bedroom and, before he could react, had grabbed him from his bed and tossed him over his shoulder. Ryris screamed, banging his fists on his friend's back.

"You had better not do what I think you're thinking of doing, Grildi! I mean it!" A fleeting image flashed before his eyes, one that involved his giant friend plopping him in the icy Whispering River for old time's sake. "If you so much as get within ten feet of that river, I'm not sending you a present from Keld!"

Grildi just laughed as he made his way out into the store, nearly knocking Ryris' feet into a display stacked with fragile potion bottles. Striding through the open door, the large man toted his cargo across the bridge spanning the river and straight into the town square—where the entire village was waiting.

Cheers immediately erupted from the crowd as Grildi eased Ryris off of his shoulder. Two of the town's strongest lumberjacks each held a wooden stake, with a banner stretched between them.

—Safe Journey, Ryris!—

He couldn't believe his eyes. The townsfolk had come out—all of them—and for *him*. He was absolutely stunned. For his entire life, he had been the 'weird' one, the odd man out. Not that he minded, he enjoyed spending time in the shop mixing potions and cataloging ingredients. But he always got the distinct impression that the villagers, especially the ones closest to him in age—couldn't have cared less about him. They were always polite and never mean, but it was clear they all had other things to do than to try and make friends with the strange alchemist with potion-stained fingers.

23

And now, here they were—celebrating him.

Grildi pushed him toward the crowd, the villagers immediately surrounding him. Some patted him on the back; others grabbed his hands to shake them. Everyone smiled broadly, children gathered at his feet and tugged at his shirt. They guided him toward a group of barrels that had been covered by a red cloth, a small layout of local foods spread across the tops.

"We thought you'd like one more taste of home." An older woman, the baker's wife, motioned toward the treats. "And I've packed some up for you to take with—although I'll wager they won't make it to the capital." She winked.

Ryris took in the sight of all the food laid out for him. Fresh pellick fruit, sausage and cheese, a berry pie, and several cakes enticed not only the young alchemist, but the villagers as well. As he approached, he could smell the deep chocolate aroma of one of the tortes. The baker's wife moved ahead of him and cut into the pastry, offering him the first piece.

"I don't know what to say."

The mayor smiled broadly. "We couldn't be prouder, young man. You'll do right by your family name and everyone in Keld will take notice of your talent. Just don't forget about Blackthorne when you're a big-time noble in the capital!" He clapped Ryris roughly on the back.

A craftsman pushed his way through the villagers, holding a wrapped parcel in his hands. Ryris accepted the package, tearing off the tissue-thin paper. As it fluttered to the ground, he exposed a hand-carved tandlewood sign.

Bren's Alchemy ~~~ Ryris Bren—Proprietor

"The mayor commissioned me to make this for you. We all want you to know how proud we are—and hopefully this will be a small reminder of home."

Ryris ran his fingers over the inscription. He would proudly display this sign in the window of the new shop, and it most definitely would be a wonderful reminder of Blackthorne. He was determined not to be sad when he looked at it—it was going to serve as an object of inspiration to make his village proud of what he would accomplish.

"I'll make sure this stays front and center in the window." Ryris smiled out at the crowd. Pulling his watch out of his pocket, he realized that if he didn't leave soon, he wouldn't make it to Lullin before dark. The small town was the first stop on what would be a three-week journey across the countryside.

Ryris didn't notice his father duck out of the celebration moments before, and only realized the man had been gone when he appeared from around the back of the shop with his wagon. All the crates were neatly stacked and covered with a canvas tarp, a lantern hanging from the side to light his way at night. The old worn seat had been padded for the trip, and Ryris was immediately thankful he wouldn't have to subject his posterior to the horrors of the wooden bench for weeks on end.

As the wagon's wheels clattered on the cobblestones of the village square, the townsfolk began to crowd around Ryris once more, pushing him toward the vehicle. They cheered and laughed, yelling congratulatory and inspiring words. The baker's wife tucked a package underneath the covering on the wagon with a smile.

"Wait! My backpack!" The young alchemist tried to push his way back though the throngs of villagers, desperately trying to move toward his house, but their collective strength was just too great and he didn't stand a chance in getting through. Grildi, seeing Ryris' obvious distress, pushed through the people and lumbered into the Brens shop, emerging moments later with not only the knapsack, but something small cradled in his massive arms as well. He barreled through the crowd, the townspeople all too happy to get out of his way.

"Here you go, Boss." He tossed the knapsack at Ryris. "I rescued it."

Ryris nodded his thanks, then pointed to the small cloth bear in his friend's arms. "Where'd you get that?"

Grildi looked down at the old toy in his hands, a sheepish smile crossing his lips. "It was on the shelf in your room. Don't you want to take him with you?"

"Why don't you keep him safe for me?" Ryris moved forward and patted him on the arm.

"You mean it?" Grildi hugged the bear tightly, a massive grin spreading across his face. "I promise I will!"

Ryris wrapped his arms around the large man's torso in one final embrace. "Thank you, Grildi. And not just for taking care of my bear—for being a good friend too."

"Aye." Tears sparkled in Grildi's eyes. "Aye..."

Ryris felt a hand on his back, and turned to face his father. Maxx held out his palm for him to shake, which Ryris gladly accepted. "Do right by our name. I don't want to have to hunt you down to get my investment back."

The villagers laughed as Ryris and his father shared a quick hug. He knew Maxx wasn't a big fan of public displays of *any* affection, and was pleasantly surprised by the sentiment. As soon as it had started, it was over, with Maxx pulling back awkwardly and straightening his waistcoat. In one quick movement, his eyes went to the amulet around his son's neck, and a wizened expression crossed his face as he made eye contact once more. Ryris knew what he meant without his father having to say a word.

"Don't you dare use that magic."

Ryris climbed up onto the wagon, setting his backpack on the seat next to him. Taking one last look out at the residents of the village he now formerly called home, he waved with a swooping gesture and hiked the reins attached to Ass of the East. The cart began to move as the horse's hooves clicked against the paving stones. He took a deep breath of the chill morning air, realizing that by the time he made it to Keld, on the central western coast, snow would more than likely cover the roofs of his village. Autumn in Blackthorne, unlike most other locations in the Vrelin Empire, meant early snow—and lots of it.

He looked back over his shoulder one last time before training his attention forward, shielding his eyes from the bright morning sunlight.

CHAPTER THREE

On shimmering shores,

Beautiful star, Dungannon.

Gem of the empire.

--Haiku by Balthor Yent, poet.

A blinding flash of red illuminated the black chamber.

The craggy, dulled, obsidian rock absorbed the ominous light, leaving nothing to reflect back into the center of the room. There were no windows, and the walls rose high into the vaulted ceiling arching above.

As quickly as the flash had blazed, it was gone, leaving a fine mist hovering in the air—surrounding a kneeling figure. The man hissed a long breath as he stood and straightened his posture. His boots clicked across the stone floor as he strode toward the center of the chamber, complete darkness surrounding him.

He circled a pedestal, his slender fingers ghosting over the smooth surface of the font. It was waist-high, the bowl nestled inside appearing to be bottomless. Tracing the runes emblazoning it, he waited silently in the intense heat of the room.

The man waited patiently, knowing his master would soon contact him. The feeling of power his orders gave him, the sense of pride as he completed each and every task his master bestowed upon him, was something he always treasured. He knew it took time for his master to seek out his information, and even longer for him to be sure they were progressing along the correct path. They had to be absolutely certain in their efforts before proceeding beyond the point of no return.

The temperature in the room suddenly dropped, the man's breath fogging on the air currents as it exited his lips. He welcomed the change, as the oppressive heat was becoming uncomfortable. His mouth curled into a sinister smile as he waited. A blue flame erupted from the nothingness before him. The flickering flames in the font reflected in the black void of the figure's lifeless eyes.

Leaning to peer into the fire, he inhaled deeply, the scorched air tickling his nostrils. He loved that smell—that smell meant power. The man licked his lips in anticipation and waited for his master to speak.

"...another has been found..."

He smirked in the darkness, his face and torso illuminated by the azure flames. It had been ages since a target had been found for him. He excitedly tapped his fingers against the side of the font as he awaited his orders.

"Where?"

"...*Dungannon*..."

The voice of his master floated through the chamber, echoes of the ghostly whisper lingering long after the words stopped. The image of a middle-aged man appeared within the flames, the devotee immediately committing it to memory. He studied the age lines on the man's face, his bushy beard, mustache, and receding hairline. The intended mark stood with a slight stoop, from years of toiling on fishing docks. While still muscular from loading crates of fish day in and day out, his age was evident in his haggard expression. The mysterious man knew he would be an easy target.

"...*leave no trace*..."

"It will be done." His voice was cold and determined.

"...*excellent...you have grown into a fine disciple*..."

The blue flame slipped from existence and the heat returned, leaving him alone in the chamber. He backed away from the now dark font and dropped to one knee.

In a flash, he was gone.

~~~

"You sure you don't want me to walk with you, Felix? It's awful late."

The burly man scoffed and downed the rest of his ale. "What are you, my mother?"

His friend made an obscene gesture before breaking into a wide-toothed grin. "Get out of here, you drunk!"

Laughter erupted from the pub patrons, some thumping their fists on the bar in delight. The fireplace in the corner popped and crackled as the logs within shifted. The malty aroma of beer lingered in the noses of every customer. The bartender worked slowly. He didn't care if he served his patrons in a timely manner, and neither did they. The Barnacle's Breath was a place where people could come to get a frosty mug of ale, a hearty bowl of stew, and good conversation. Years of dirt and debris tracked in on the boot soles of the patrons accumulated in all the corners and under every barstool. Comfortably crowded and always open, the pub was like a second home to many of the hard-working common folk of Dungannon. This was by no means a fancy establishment, and not meant to be graced by silken shoes.

28

Wiping beer foam from his bushy mustache, Felix Hayeward tossed a few coins on the bar and plopped his hat onto his balding head. He clapped his friend on the back as he moved past, waved to his drinking buddies, and set out into the warm night.

Dungannon was a fishing hub on Lake Browal, the largest inland body of water in the Vrelin Empire. The large town thrived on its seafood industry, exporting its haul to the far reaches of the land. The residents also prospered from the throngs of tourists that came year-round to enjoy the fair southern weather. Resorts lined the shores, where the nobility hob-nobbed, and had no qualms about spending money in the countless specialty shops lining the quaint streets. This end of town, however, was rarely frequented by the rich visitors—and the townsfolk were just fine with that.

A thin layer of fog rolled in off the lake as the coolness of the evening took hold of the town. Felix' modest house was on the outskirts of the city center, where most of the dockworkers resided. He lived alone, never finding a wife. His home was simple and comfortable, just big enough for his possessions and his shaggy mutt of a dog, Reginald.

Deciding to take the long way home to walk off his buzz, Felix headed out the far gate. A circle trail surrounded the town, and if he stayed on it long enough, he would eventually wind up right at his back door. He knew if he didn't clear his head before retiring for the night, his hangover would impede his work the next morning.

Taking a deep breath of the night air, his feet crunched on the gravel path leading into the forests surrounding Dungannon. The evening was quiet, save for the distant gentle lapping of waves on Lake Browal. Humming softly to himself, Felix continued on his way, plucking a few sweet leaves from a sapling to add to his morning tea.

A cold breeze picked up for a split second, causing the fisherman to wrap his loose coat tightly around his body. He thought it odd that such a frosty wind would be present on an early autumn night, when winter's cold kiss rarely touched his town to begin with. Somewhat unsettled, he picked up his pace, suddenly very much in a hurry to get home. A twig snapped somewhere off in the thicket, and Felix whirled around, squinting to see better in the darkness. A sense of foreboding fell over him, the feeling of being watched growing with every passing moment.

"Wh-who's there?"

The forest answered with the flap of bird's wings. *"You're being paranoid,"* he thought to himself. *"There's nothing but skellins and deer."* As if on cue, a tiny skellin, no bigger than his hand, scurried out from the underbrush. Stopping directly before him on the path, it sat up on its hind legs, grey fur rustling in the breeze. It hissed sharply before darting off into the forest once again, obviously not feeling threatened by Felix' intrusion onto her home turf.

He began walking again, keeping his brisk pace. Though he knew there was nothing to be frightened of, he still resolved to get home as quick as he could. To sleep longer, he told himself—not because he was spooked. Striding quickly, he came upon a fallen tree. Grumbling, he scowled and began to climb over it. In his inebriated state, it made more sense to clamber over awkwardly than simply go around. As he pulled himself up, he stood and steadied his body, puffing out his chest with pride at his accomplishment. Movement far down the path behind him caught his attention. He swore he saw a dark figure slip into the lines of trees. Once again, a cold chill came over him, and he called out to the specter.

"Look, I'm bigger and stronger than you…so don't try nothin'!"

The forest stayed silent.

"Idiot," Felix mused. *"You're acting like a child. Scared of the dark…you need to quit drinking."*

He jumped down onto the trail and continued walking. As he moved, he became more and more aware of the fog filling in from within the forest. Unnerved, he began to jog, determined to get home in one piece. *"So much for the long route,"* he thought.

Rustling in the forest beside him caught his attention once more, and this time, he was having none of it. His gut told him that someone—or something—was after him. He bolted down the trail as fast as his drunken feet could take him. He stumbled once, nearly falling flat on his face. Realizing that whatever was chasing him was going to catch up sooner or later, he made the decision to leave the road. He darted off into the woods, ducking into some thick underbrush to watch and wait.

Sitting quietly for a long moment, he held his breath—something hard to do while drunk and tired from running. Paranoia consumed him, every noise from high above in the canopy or deep within the foliage causing him to jump. Still crouching, he turned to look further into the forest—and spotted an abandoned shack in the distance. On his hands and knees like a baby, Felix crawled toward the cabin, trying to make as little noise as possible. By the time he reached it, his palms were cut and bleeding from the thorny vines that littered ground.

After he slithered onto the porch, he sat in the shadows for a moment, listening. He thought back to the pub, trying to recall everything he had consumed earlier in the evening. Even though he had a strong buzz going, he wasn't anywhere near as drunk as he had been in the past. Almost convincing himself he was acting a fool, he suddenly noticed the fog had crept in closer from the trail. He scanned the surrounding forest one last time, trying to find some validation for his fears. Glowing red eyes, perhaps? Winged creatures perched in the trees? His mates playing a trick on him? But, when the underbrush in the distance rustled yet again, his decision was made—he was being hunted.

Quiet as a skellin, he moved on his haunches toward the door and tried the knob. Thankfully, it was unlocked. Pushing it open just enough to slip through, he took one last quick look behind him, hoping against hope that whatever was out there had not seen him enter. He quietly closed the door, locking it tightly. The shack was one room, a small kitchenette in the far corner in obvious dusty disuse. An old wooden chest was nestled in the other corner, a large hole in the panels at the bottom. A rickety table and chairs sat against a side wall, covered in cobwebs. Opposite the table, a single bed, devoid of any linens.

Heavy footsteps thumped on the front porch. The wind picked up, rattling the loose boards of the shack wall. Felix dropped like a lead weight to the floor, pressing his body as flat as he possibly could. The windows of the cabin were boarded, so there was no way anyone could peer inside and find him. Snaking his way along the rough floor, he slid underneath the heavy bed frame. A loose nail in the floorboards snagged on his pants, tearing into his leg. He jammed his fist into his mouth and bit down, stifling the instinctive scream.

The iron doorknob turned and jiggled, the lock holding steady. Felix held his breath. He peered out from underneath the bed and waited. The knob grew still once more, the footsteps backing down off of the porch.

Sighing in hesitant relief, he knew he might still be in danger, although no longer immediate. He waited a moment before slowly easing himself out from under the bed. His leg throbbed where the nail had pierced his flesh, the blood seeping through his burlap trousers.

Without warning, the chill returned abruptly, colder than ever. Looking up toward the door, he gasped as he saw a thick white mist emerging from the keyhole. Silently sliding himself under the bed once more, he rolled onto his back to gain better access to his jacket pocket. Fishing a tiny vial from inside, he brought it close to his face and narrowed his eyes to see the label in the darkness.

Invisibility // Bren's Alchemy

A joke gift given to him by a friend a few days before—in case, as his buddy suggested, he needed to make a quick getaway from a female companion—might now save his life. He had never been happier to have cluttered pockets.

He drank the potion quickly, wincing at the terrible taste. The solution worked instantly, and he saw his hand disappear before his eyes, the bottle along with it. He glanced down and discovered that his clothes, too, had disappeared. He set the bottle down and it flickered back into existence. Marveling at the power of a few ounces of liquid, he momentarily forgot about the danger.

Jolted back to reality when he realized he was still hiding under a bed, Felix watched as the mist floated around the cabin. This couldn't be normal fog—'normal' fog didn't stalk you through the forest, and 'normal' fog certainly didn't pinpoint itself through keyholes.

The mist curled around the table and chairs, ghosted over the cooking hearth and washbasin. It ebbed and flowed like waves, moving intricately around objects—studying them, obviously looking for something. It momentarily hovered over the trunk in the corner before seeping inside via the hole in the bottom. A moment later, it reemerged and continued its search. Beads of sweat rolled down into Felix' invisible collar as the fog drew closer.

A scurrying noise from the kitchenette grabbed its attention and the mist zoomed back over to the other side of the room, instantly enveloping a wayward skellin. It screeched briefly before the fog seeped into its nose and mouth, suffocating it. Once the rodent was dead, the fog left the corpse and floated to the middle of the room. Felix was somewhat relieved that it seemed to have forgotten about looking under the bed. But his relief soon turned to horror as the mist brought itself together, growing thicker and darker in color. It soon took on mass, the fog coalescing into a new form. It definitely wasn't human, for it had clawed feet and hands, and a lithe, sinewy body covered in shimmering black scales. It was bipedal like a man—but no man Felix knew of resembled what he saw before him. Fangs jutted from the mouth, the eyes deep and pitch-black. He had never been so terrified in his life.

Closing his eyes for a split second, he mentally chanted a calming mantra and prayed he wouldn't be spotted. He had no idea how long the potion would last, or if it even mattered when it came to the fog-beast. For all he knew, the thing could smell his stinking work boots or sense his sweaty palms.

The monster moved slowly around the room, its clawed toes clicking on the rotting wooden floorboards. They dipped slightly under the weight of the creature, its head nearly touching the ceiling. Hot puffs of steam jetted from the nostrils of the abomination, a low growling purr rumbling from deep within its chest.

Felix watched helplessly, wishing he were back in his childhood home, waking up from this terrible nightmare. And then, much to his horror, he felt a telltale tickle in his nose. The shack was dusty, covered with years of grime. He slowly brought his finger under his nose and held it there, hopeful that the motion would quell what he begged the goddess Oleana to stop.

He sneezed.

Like lightning, the beast was at the bedside, flinging the heavy wooden frame aside like a piece of kindling. Confused when it saw nothing there, Felix knew he had only a split second to act. He did the one thing he was warned never to do.

His fingertips froze, ice crystals forming around his hands. Seconds later, he flung sharp icicles at the beast, aimed straight for the throat. One well-placed icy puncture wound, he thought, and the monster's blood would freeze in its veins. The icicles bounced off the creature's scales and fell to the floor, shattering. To Felix' horror, when he unleashed his magical powers, the invisibility spell abruptly ended, leaving him exposed. Determined not to give up, he channeled his focus as clawed hands grabbed him by the torso, constricting his body so tight he thought he might pass out. Using his remaining strength, Felix froze his hands, an incredible chill moving up his arms. With all his might, he brought his hands up to the monster's face and grabbed the scaly horns atop its head. If he could hold them there long enough, he might just freeze the bastard's brain

The monster suddenly released its grip and let him drop to the ground. Dazed, Felix scooted backwards on his rear end only to find himself backed up against the wall.

"Was that supposed to hurt?" The beast's voice was low and growling. It was as if the monster was laughing at him, mocking him. It moved closer and Felix began to weep.

"Why…?"

The monster towered over him and pointed to his hands. The fisherman looked down at his palms, still glistening with the melting remnants of tiny ice crystals.

In that instant, he realized all the stories were true: people born with magic were hunted like animals. He had never believed the severity of the tales, but kept his secret hidden nonetheless, at the behest of his family. They certainly thought the legend was real—and now Felix realized they had been right all along. There was no escape— he was going to die alone in a ramshackle cabin.

"Crying like a baby…" The creature's eyes were an unsettling black void. Felix had no response but to shudder silently with terror. The beast knelt on one strong knee and leaned in close. Felix turned his head away from the putrid, hot breath coming from the fanged mouth. The monster grabbed his chin and powerfully turned his head back, forcing him to gaze upon its horrible countenance. "I could have killed you the moment you left the city limits. I had hoped for more…fight. Cowering under a bed? Not very sporting."

The creature grabbed him by the throat and lifted him high into the air before bringing him within an inch of its own face. The claws pierced the sensitive skin, drawing droplets of blood. The thick crimson liquid began to run down into Felix' collar. It tightened its grip on his neck, talons stabbing deep into his flesh and puncturing his jugular vein. Blood began to cascade from the wound at an alarming rate.

33

Felix' face flushed as he tried to take in breaths that just wouldn't come. His brain screamed for oxygen, his fingers clawed at the beast's scaly hands. Kicking his legs wildly, he tried desperately to break free before all his strength left him. The small blood vessels in his eyes began to burst under the pressure of his struggle to breathe, dyeing the whites a haunting red.

The beast momentarily loosened its grip, and Felix watched as the face of the creature began to blur and morph, revealing not a monstrous visage, but that of a human. Although the eyes were completely black, Felix recognized the man. He gasped, his eyes bulging wide with shock. The familiar face sneered as the creature brought a clawed hand up and slashed the man's throat.

Dropping Felix to the ground like a rag doll, the monster turned its face back to the horrible form it had taken previously, and watched as blood spurted from the man's neck. He gagged, writhing on the ground as he tried to hold his hands over the waterfall of life essence spilling from his throat. Growing tired of waiting for his victim to expire, the creature leaned down and gnashed at Felix with razor-sharp teeth, severing his head from his body in one fluid motion. It rolled away, coming to a stop in front of the cooking hearth.

Smashing the locked door with its giant clawed hands, the beast threw it aside as it exited. Away from the structure, it turned and—with a simple glance—set the building ablaze. It took only moments for the white-hot flames to reduce the rotting cabin to ash.

Satisfied its work had been completed and no evidence of its—or Felix'— presence would ever be found; it formed into mist once again and floated away through the forest.

CHAPTER FOUR

12 fluid ounces Base fluid, 8 fluid ounces Bitter Nettle syrup, 1 leveled Imperial scoop crushed Archer Crab chitin, 3 fluid ounces Shimmerwort-in-suspension. Wait for sparks to dissipate and stir. Add 3 fresh Slinker Worms. When churning subsides, remove from heat. Bottle immediately, cool overnight in vials.

--Night Vision potion recipe, Ryris Bren

Dear Father,

I've never been so happy to be off of that wagon seat in my life. Travel is an adventure, but my rear end would surely disagree.

My trip was interesting, that's for sure. My itinerary was fairly accurate, and I made it to Keld with two days to spare. That isn't to say the three weeks flew by, but my travel time definitely seemed shorter than anticipated. The weather was fair, although I did spend one night huddled in a cave on the Plains Road as a horrible thunderstorm raged outside. I was soaked to the bone, and I swear I didn't get warm again for days. I even saw a giant, but it was from a distance and thankfully seemed to be heading in the opposite direction. I honestly don't know what I would have done had it approached, but I can guarantee I would have needed new pants.

I will say, I've never had as much trouble crossing the Farnfoss Bridge as I did this time. A few militants had it blocked, spouting some nonsense about taxes and an imprisoned comrade. The army had the entire area cordoned off, so I waited it out in a bookstore. The owner and I had a long talk about some of the strife in Lullin as of late. You forget sometimes, living in Blackthorne, that other places have unsavory aspects to their everyday life. Anyway, the army, shall I say…dealt with the situation…and the bridge re-opened within a few hours. It wasn't wasted time, per se, I picked up some books for the shop.

The Plains Road is still a bear to traverse, those ruts got bigger since last time, I swear. I overheard a merchant say the Transportation Ministry is planning on repairing it next summer, so at least that's something. Still didn't save my back from being jostled into knots.

When I got to the Crossroads Outpost, I sold a few potions to some travelers, and spread the word about the new shop in Keld. Hopefully I can can get some word-of-mouth going and drum up some business.

I was able to collect quite a few specimens along the way. I even ran across an entire field of akko berries, ready to harvest. I couldn't believe my luck. I only wish I could have sent some back to Blackthorne…I know Grildi would have enjoyed them. I managed to dry them out on the back of the wagon as I rode, and of course ate my fair share. I think they'll be a great seller once I get the shop opened.

Dad, you should have seen Keld as I approached on the Golden Road. I've never seen such a beautiful sight in all my life. The sun was setting and I swear it illuminated the palace like it was in a painting. I knew it was going to be big, but I was absolutely stunned. I may or may not have almost driven off the road because I was distracted. Don't worry, the wagon is just fine.

I'll admit, I was immediately overwhelmed by Keld—but in a most spectacular way. My dreams of what I'd encounter were surpassed within seconds. I did get lost trying to find the building, but some incredibly friendly residents pointed me in the right direction. They even invited me to stop back and say hello after I got settled. I've yet to meet anyone unsavory here in the city, although I know it's just a matter of time. Yes, Keld is grand and seems to have streets paved with gold, but I'm not that naïve to think that there's not an underbelly. I'm just planning on sticking to what I know and mingling with good people, and I think I'll be just fine.

The building definitely needed work, like you said. It took me three days to clear out all the cobwebs and freshen up. There was a bit of damage to the hearthstones that looked like it stemmed from years of disrepair, but I found a handyman that fixed it for a very reasonable price. You'd be proud—I actually haggled. The sign maker is coming tomorrow to hang the placard above the door, and the sign from the villagers is already in the window. I've even seen a few people peering in through the glass trying to get a look inside.

I'm shooting for an official opening one week from now. I finished cataloguing the inventory yesterday, and all the shelves are stocked. All the back stock fit perfectly in the cellar. I began mixing solutions this morning, and I'm confident that if I work at least eight hours a day titrating, I'll have a substantial stock of potions ready to go. In talking to some other merchants and citizens, I'm getting the distinct impression that I'm going to need a lot of hangover cures. The people of Keld definitely enjoy their drink. I'm hoping to have a full stock of health remedies, as well as some more specialized tinctures made first, and then I can move onto the more interesting potions like Invisibility and Night Vision. But, knowing me, I probably won't be able to keep myself from doing the "fun" ones first. Those always seem to draw curious eyes and good conversation, anyway.

One of the commerce ministers came by yesterday to ask how everything was going, and to see if I needed anything. He said all our paperwork was in order and I had the go-ahead to open. I know I'll have competition, but I'm confident that our tried and true recipes—and my new ones—will stand out above the other alchemist in town. Our name is known throughout the Empire, and I think the citizens are excited to have me here. I've already had a few people stop me on the street to ask about the store. It's weird being recognized by strangers. It's different at home, where everyone knows you—and you know them. This city is so massive, and it's bizarre to me that folks already know who I am. I hope that's a good sign.

I did end up parting ways with the employee you hired. Nothing horrible, he claimed he didn't have the time to help out like he thought he would. Frankly, I think the work was a little too physical for him. After just a day, he was complaining that boxes were too heavy, his back hurt, and that he was getting blisters on his hands. I fought the urge to show him my calluses and we agreed that this probably wasn't the best position for him to have. I gave him his day's pay—and he was on his way.

I've yet to see Prince Roann or any of the royal family. From what everyone says about the Vrelins, the prince is very personable. The local baker told me that he often comes into the neighborhood just to mingle. He seems like a very down-to-earth man, and I hope one day I can meet him. Who knows, maybe he'll buy something?

There's a great little café around the corner, and I've already become addicted to their meat pies. I do try to cook a lot on my own, and I've already made some great meals, but when the aroma of those pastries wafts around the building and into the windows, it's hard to resist. It's definitely lonely just cooking for myself, but I'm content being on my own.

I've explored the area around the shop quite a bit, and have found a few places that I already can tell will be my favorite haunts. The bookstore a block down had most of the books I needed for the inventory, and the owner was really kind and gave me a discount for being a new shop proprietor. I thanked him and offered to mix a potion for free next time he needed one. And don't get your britches in a bunch...I'll charge him for the second one.

And before you ask: no, I haven't met any women. Well, technically I have, but most of them are elderly and doting—not exactly marriage material. I'll tell you one thing though; I'm going to be spoiled by all these little old ladies. I've already had cookies baked for me, pots of soup left on the back stoop, and one even knitted me a scarf for the upcoming winter. I could definitely get used to the mother-henning.

The weather here in Keld is really nice—most days it's been sunny and warm...a far cry from Blackthorne! It's amazing to me the difference in climate when you cross the continent. It's warm enough here to open all the windows. My scarf-knitting friend told me it might eventually snow here, but not until well into the new year. In the meantime, I'm enjoying all the sun I can soak up.

I can hear you grumbling that this letter has gone on long enough and to get my ass back to work, so I'll take your advice. I hope everything is well back home, and that Grildi doesn't miss me too much. Let him know I'll send a present soon.

Take care,

Ryris

~~~

The carrier bird took off, Ryris' letter tied securely in a leather pouch around its belly. Its majestic wings caught the upper air current and it glided off into the distance, headed toward Blackthorne. He shielded his eyes from the setting sun with his hands and followed the bird's path around the palace turrets until he lost track of it. The early evening air was crisp, the heavenly scent of his new favorite meat pies drifting out from around the corner. Resisting the urge to indulge, the young alchemist inhaled the delicious aroma once more before heading back inside.

Locking the door behind him, he headed to his workbench, already stained from just a couple days' work. He began to crush faerie moth wings in preparation for his next creation, laboring efficiently and humming softy with no one to complain about it. The amulet around his neck swayed across his chest with every thump of the pestle. When thoroughly ground, he divided the bounty into tiny piles. Using a funnel, he carefully poured an equal amount of base fluid into each vial before adding the glittering dust. With the help of a small pipette, he added a drop of tree toad blood and a pinch of desiccated cliff root before capping each vessel. Once all the small bottles were sealed, he shook each one vigorously, the new Agility potion swirling within. The small flecks of pulverized moth wings disintegrated, coalescing into a shimmering green solution. Depositing them into a canister, he set them on the hearth. Sitting near the heat of the dwindling overnight fire would strengthen the chemicals and render them complete, ready for sale.

Stifling a yawn, Ryris winced as he stretched his back, muscles protesting the movement. As he poured a glass of water, he reminded himself to keep from hunching so much. Leafing through his journal as he slowly drank, he located the next recipe he would need. He decided it was time for some fun. The sun had set, shrouding the store in darkness. Ryris turned the flame on his lamp all the way up, bathing the work area in glaring brilliance.

Lighting a small burner under a ceramic crucible, he waited for the intense flame to warm the underside of the bowl. He grabbed a cloth bandanna from the workbench and fastened it tightly around his nose and mouth, knowing better than to breathe in what he was about to create. As soon as he was satisfied the vessel was sufficiently hot, he poured in his base fluid and thick, black bitter nettle syrup. The liquids immediately bubbled up in a furious boil. Even with the filtering mask over his face, he still coughed at the pungent aroma. Ryris then added his pre-measured archer crab chitin and shimmerwort, and the tincture thinned out with a glorious fan of sparks crackling above the bowl. When the mist hovering over the pot dissipated, Ryris stirred the mixture for a moment before dropping in three slimy slinker worms, which were immediately consumed in a froth of corrosive bubbles. He knew his father would have lost his mind at the stench, and more than likely lecture him about proper ventilation. Fanning his hands in front of his body, he gagged and waited patiently for the excited boiling to subside. After a long moment, the bubbling stopped and he turned off the burner.

He let the mixture cool while he prepped his small, custom-made vials. Hand-blown from frosted blue glass, he took a moment to admire their beauty. His father had never splurged for such fancy containers back in Blackthorne, but Ryris decided this potion—his very own Night Vision creation—deserved a vessel that would make it stand out on the shelves. This was Keld. Nobility would be shopping here, and they certainly didn't want anything ordinary.

Noticing a thin, oily film floating on top of the liquid, Ryris carefully dabbed a clean cloth into the solution, sopping up the offending substance. Satisfied it was gone; he dipped a small spoon into the red tincture to sample his creation. The potion tingled on his tongue, a bitter taste lingering for a few seconds after he swallowed.

Even from just a fraction of the estimated dose of the mixture, his vision immediately changed. Everything in the room became illuminated by a blue glow, and he had to shield his eyes from the sudden brightness of his lantern. Smiling with pride, he hurriedly turned down his lamp and doused the flames on the hearth, leaving the shop bathed only in the dim lights from the street.

Wanting to test his potion further, he moved toward the cellar door. He traversed the small corridor with ease, not once fumbling in what would otherwise be total darkness. The door to the cellar was old and the young alchemist had to yank quite hard to get it to budge. Tonight that fact didn't bother him in the least—because he could see without the aid of a candle. The rickety stairs leading to the basement flashed in front of his eyes, burning bright as if he had a lantern in his hands. When he reached the bottom, he marveled at his accomplishment. He could see every shelf, every item clear as day. He smiled broadly in the complete darkness of the windowless cellar, allowing himself an astounded chuckle of pride as he glanced around the room.

"Hot damn!" Ryris' voice echoed off of the old brick walls.

Moving with ease around the inventory, he picked up a jar of pickled bird's eggs and read the label with absolutely no difficulty. A ring of blue enveloped every letter on the bottle, the eggs illuminated by a haunting azure glow. Knowing his father had never even attempted a potion for night vision, a wave of unexpected confidence washed over him—he suddenly felt he had no limits.

Unsure of how long the small dose would last, he climbed the stairs two at a time with exuberance he hadn't felt since he was a child. Not bothering to turn the oil lamp back up, he carefully filled each vial with the liquid, capping the bottles tightly. After he set them all in a sturdy rack to sit overnight, he cleaned his workstation in darkness, the potion assisting him. He scowled when a gloppy blob of leftover ooze from the crucible stuck to his thumb, and he wiped it on his apron with an irritated grumble. Even in the pitch-black, he could see it had already stained his skin. *"The life of an alchemist,"* he thought. *"Stained hands and a filthy apron."*

Suddenly having to squint to see clearly, Ryris realized the potion was beginning to wear off. He begrudgingly lit his lamp again, but left it at the lowest light possible. As he tossed his used equipment into a portable washbasin, he reminded himself to do a proper time test on a full dose before he completed the instruction labels.

Just as he was about to head into the small workshop behind the storefront, he heard a rapping at the front window. He briefly contemplated ignoring it—he was tired and dirty, and probably smelled like burnt emperor's garlic. But, he had only been in Keld a short time, and didn't want to gain the unfavorable reputation of being unaccommodating. Ryris grabbed a lamp, even though his vision was still affected by the tincture he had ingested. He figured it would have been strange to answer the door at night without a light to greet his guest.

A small smile crept over his lips as he saw the wrinkled, kind face of the woman from across the street, enveloped in a fading blue glow. She and her wife owned a small flower shop on the corner, but Ryris knew her real talent was baking. The old woman had already spoiled him rotten with daily deliveries of sweet treats and flowers for his kitchen table. She had insisted on the blossoms and even supplied him with a simple vase in which to display them. According to her, even a young bachelor needed flowers to brighten up his home.

He waved to her through the window, and she raised a covered basket into his view. Ryris set his lamp down on a waist-high oak shelf already cluttered with bottles, and unlocked the double bolts holding the door closed. As he opened it, a rush of warm night air blew in, ruffling his shaggy brown hair. The flame within his lamp danced on the air current.

"Good evening, Mrs. Briarheart."

She placed the basket in his hands and uncovered the contents. "I've been keeping an eye on you, Mr. Bren. Too busy to take a lunch break, are we?"

Ryris looked down at the bounty she had presented to him. Fresh biscuits— still warm—and a small jar of honey to slather on top. Nestled beside them were a crock of chowder, a rosy apple, and a generous serving of sugar cookies. She had even included an embroidered linen napkin. It definitely felt nice to be looked after by a doting elderly lady.

"Now, don't you go eating those cookies first, you hear me?" She pinched his arm lovingly. "And make sure you finish everything, you could use a little more meat on those bones."

"Yes, ma'am." He motioned into the dimly lit shop. "Would you like to come in? I can make some tea."

She dismissively waved her hands in front of her body. "No…you go on ahead and enjoy your meal in peace. It's getting late, and even a handsome young man such as yourself needs a good night's rest."

The old woman was right—he did just want to eat and go to sleep. He had been going non-stop since dawn, and didn't really want to admit he had no idea what time it was. He smiled wanly and sighed. "I *am* tired."

She leaned forward and scrutinized his face in the low light of the lamp. "Your eyes don't look right, son. I think you need sleep more than you realize."

Ryris furrowed his brows confusedly, then wondered if his potion did more than just give him night vision. Suddenly in a hurry to inspect his eyes for himself, he politely thanked his guest for the meal and bid her farewell. She patted his arm and tottered back across the street. He made sure she was safely inside her business before closing and locking his own door.

Forgetting about the dirty equipment in the washbasin, he cast his apron haphazardly on the counter. He rushed upstairs, relying more and more on the light of the lamp. He set his goodie basket and journal down on his old wooden kitchen table and ran into the small washroom. Turning the light of the lamp up as high as it would go, he leaned close into the mirror and pulled down on his right eye, exposing the white and iris completely. Mrs. Briarheart had most certainly been correct—his eyes *didn't* look right. He was thankful she wasn't able to see clearly in the darkness, because she would have very well shrieked at their appearance.

"You idiot..." The young alchemist's voice was low and irritated as he berated himself. "How could you have been so stupid?"

The whites of Ryris' eyes were stained a pale blue, the brown irises cloudy. He blinked rapidly several times, in an attempt to dissipate the effect. He scowled when there was no change in their appearance. Suddenly very nervous his eyes would remain like this forever, he found himself thankful Maxx was nowhere in sight. Surely the older man would scold him for carelessness. Taking a deep breath, he closed his eyes and blew it out as calmly as he could while he tried to figure out his next course of action. Without knowing what his eyes looked like in the first minutes of exposure, there was no way to compare it to his current situation. He left his eyes closed for a long moment while he thought. Leaning back against the wall, he tried to convince himself that it might not be bad to have stained eyes for the rest of his life—it *would* be a fantastic icebreaker in conversations.

When he opened his eyes again, the glass bell of the lamp had just a small trace of the blue halo around it, and it made Ryris feel more at ease. The potion was definitely wearing off. Cautiously leaning forward once again, he peered at himself in the warped mirror. He didn't know if he was imagining it, but it seemed as if the color was fading and his irises were clearing once again.

Deciding to return to the kitchen and eat his meal, he assured himself that it was a minor setback with temporary side effects. He briefly contemplated putting on a

41

kettle for tea, but when he caught a glimpse of the cuckoo clock on the wall, he realized that such a beverage at half-past nine wouldn't be the smartest. Then again, he obviously wasn't big on intelligent ideas that evening, since his eyes were currently tinted blue. Settling on a glass of cool water, he unpacked the basket his friend had prepared.

On her orders, he ate the chowder and biscuits first, setting one aside along with the apple for his breakfast. He scribbled in his journal as he ate, making note of the incident with his eyes. Halfway through the meal, he jogged back to the tiny bathroom to check on the progress of his unexpected symptoms—and was relieved to see that the effects had faded completely.

Finishing the last bit of the incredible chowder, he quickly scratched down the rest of his notes before washing up. He grabbed two cookies from the basket and headed to his humble bedroom with a huge yawn.

Ryris sat down on his bed with a tired sigh and kicked off his boots. They clattered to the floor as he stretched his arms over his head. Shoving one cookie in his mouth, he began to unbutton his shirt with tired, stained fingers. His fingertips ghosted over the silver chain of his amulet, then instinctively went to the bauble, running across the smooth surface of the inlaid cabochon. Throwing his shirt haphazardly to the floor, he suddenly felt too tired to finish changing into his nightclothes.

A warm breeze blew in through the open window, fluttering the simple, thin curtains. The faint aroma of the sea air from the harbor tickled his nostrils. Taking one last look at the palace in the distance before retiring, Ryris blew out the lamp and flopped down onto his bed in an exhausted heap. Light from the moon high above filtered in, illuminating the now dark room.

As he allowed his eyes to flutter closed, Ryris' thoughts went to his father and Blackthorne. In several hours' time, dawn would break in the village. The lumberjacks would be heading out into the forests, ready to harvest the sought-after tandlewood contained within. He could almost hear the babble of the stream that ran through town—the beginnings of what would become the powerful Whispering River further south—and smiled as he wondered if Grildi had thrown anyone in lately.

Sighing contentedly in the darkness, he let sleep blissfully overtake him.

CHAPTER FIVE

His and Her Royal Highness joyously announce the birth of their son and heir to the throne, Prince Roann Artol Welland Vrelin, on the 62nd day of the Summer Season, in the year of the Goddess 724.

--Royal birth announcement sent to the people of Keld

"Pardon me, Your Highness, but the Dean of Whitehaven is here to see you. He said it's urgent."

The regal young man looked up from his desk, littered with papers and books. He knew what his visitor wanted, and he wasn't particularly in the mood to squabble. But, he had a duty to his people as their prince to listen to their pleas, whether they arrived announced or not. Setting aside his quill pen to pinch the bridge of his nose in irritation, he motioned toward the door with a tired smile.

"Send him in."

His attendant bowed and went to fetch the guest. Moments later, the grand door opened again, producing a short, portly man. He huffed as he walked, obviously exhausted by the climb to the prince's office. His cheeks were flushed red, beads of sweat dripping down his face and into his black beard. He held a large leather briefcase in his hand, embroidered with the crest of the university. His shoulders slumped and the tote dragged on the ground as he approached.

The prince stood out of respect, and extended a hand toward a chair in front of his desk. "Please sit, Dean Ebbersley. Would you like a glass of water?"

"No thank you, Your Highness. Just a moment to catch my breath." He coughed into his hand, then wiped it on his pants. The prince furrowed his brows with a wince and sat once again.

"Prince Roann, thank you for taking the time out of your very busy schedule to meet with me." The man dropped his satchel in front of the massive tandlewood desk as he sat, blowing out a huge relieved bellow of air. He wiped his forehead with a lace handkerchief as he spoke. "How is your father these days?"

"As well as can be expected for a man in his condition, Josef. Thank you for asking."

"It's so wonderful that we have such a caring prince, who is willing to devote his life to the affairs of state while his father recovers. You are truly a saint."

43

"Far from it, Dean Ebbersley. Now, what is it you wish to speak to me about?" Roann tried not to grumble with irritation at the man's obvious attempt to suck up to him.

"Straight to the point, that's what I like about you, Sire." He reached for his briefcase, and removed several rolls of papers. The parchment shimmered in the bright sunlight beaming in through the grand fifteen-foot windows behind the prince. "I've come to discuss the university expansion—again."

The prince sighed. He thought as much when his attendant had announced Ebbersley. "Dean, with all due respect, we've already had this conversation."

"Yes, I know, Your Grace. But..." He stood and unrolled one of the documents, raising his eyebrows hopefully at the prince as he motioned to the desktop. Roann begrudgingly cleared a space. "...you see here that we've drawn up new plans that we hope will work for everyone involved. We have found a new site that may solve our housing conundrum. It is much smaller than the original parcel we were hoping to use." He pointed to a spot on the layout.

Prince Roann leaned forward in his chair to get a better look, a loose strand of his long blonde hair not pulled back falling into his eyes. He brushed it aside. After a long moment studying the plans, he sat back with a frown. "This would still displace dozens of people and businesses."

"Yes, Your Highness, but please hear me out." Ebbersley sat down again, the chair creaking under his weight. "Fewer citizens would be inconvenienced with this new construction plan than with our previous proposal."

"Inconvenienced? If even one of my subjects loses their home or their livelihood due to your venture, it's unacceptable." Roann twirled his signet ring around on his finger with his thumb. The sunlight glinted off the central stone with every revolution, reflecting onto the walls and ceiling.

Ebbersley scowled as he shifted his body uncomfortably in his seat. "Our enrollment numbers are falling because we do not have adequate housing for new arrivals. More and more students are choosing to reside at the university well into their graduate work. If we don't have new enrollees, we have far less income."

"Your campus is sprawling, you have plenty of open space. Repurpose some of it. Build up, not out."

Ebbersley scoffed. "Our gardens and common areas are the pride of our university. We couldn't possibly tarnish the beauty of our land with more buildings."

"And so you propose to 'tarnish' Keld instead? The area you want to destroy is filled with historic buildings. One even dates back to the Old War." The prince was growing increasingly irritated. He had actual official state business to take care of, and didn't have the time to scold the persistent dean. Roann sighed exasperatedly. "There have to be other options that don't involve razing subdivisions. What about encouraging the older students to move on? Give them some sort of incentive to relocate off-campus." The prince stared his visitor down. "I will not put my people out on the street."

"I understand you want to please *your people*, Your Grace, but you have to consider the college as well."

"Oh?"

"Don't forget that Whitehaven University contributes handsomely to many official funds."

Roann raised an eyebrow. "Is that a threat, Dean?"

"No, of course not. Consider it more of a polite reminder that the relationship between the university and your family is one of prosperity and friendship. I would hate to see it sullied over something as trivial as student housing."

The prince kept his emotions in check, realizing quickly that if he leapt over the desk and struck the man, it would look bad for his image. Inside, he was seething; absolutely shocked the dean would even so much as hint at a break in their ties. Yes, the university donated to several charities run by the Vrelin Empire, but it hardly gave them the right to make threats.

"Dean Ebbersley," The prince's voice was steady, his tone stern. "If you meet with the city planners—a conference which I am happy to arrange—perhaps they can assist you in utilizing your existing property better."

"With all due respect, Sire…"

"This is my only offer. I suggest you take it before I change my mind and kick you out of this office."

Ebbersley flinched at his tone and nodded curtly before packing his belongings back into his satchel. When he finally replied, his voice was submissive. "I would be honored if Your Grace would be so kind as to schedule a meeting with the city planners…" He lowered his eyes to his hands, nervously wringing them in his lap, before making eye contact once more with the prince. "…and I am terribly sorry if I have offended you in any way with my uncalled-for remarks. I never meant to threaten or posture in the manner that I did. It is extremely unbecoming of a man in my position. Please forgive me."

Roann stood and extended his hand to the trembling dean. Ebbersley accepted the prince's gesture with an embarrassed smile.

"Is there anything else I can do for you, Josef?" The prince retracted his hand, fighting the urge to wipe the dean's perspiration on his pants.

"No, Your Highness. You have been far too gracious with your time as it is."

Roann sat, picked up his quill, and delved back into his paperwork. He didn't look up at his guest again. "Then I trust you can see yourself out?"

"Of course, Grace. Thank you." The stout man scurried away and was out the door in record time.

Only when the dean was out of sight did Roann grimace and look down at his palm, still glistening with Ebbersley's sweat. Gagging slightly, he opened a drawer and took out a handkerchief, feverishly trying to remove the offending substance. After a few moments, his hand was sufficiently dry and he tossed the cloth into the trash can. He would never be using that one again, that was for sure. Looking back to the mountain of paperwork sitting on his desk, he sighed and stood, stretching his aching back muscles.

With a long audible breath, he turned to gaze out at the city sprawling below him. Quickly shedding the irritation the dean had bestowed upon him, he felt his shoulders relax. He loved the way Keld looked and moved. From his perch near the top of the Imperial Palace, he could see the entire metropolis. The buildings sparkled in the sunlight thanks to small inclusions of minerals within the stone. Colorful banners and flags fluttered on the breeze, the scent of pastries from the palace bakery wafted up from below. Streets radiated out from a central park, neighborhoods taking on their own identities and hallmarks. Artisans and entrepreneurs comingled with educators and families, bookstores and bakeries resided alongside blacksmiths and jewelers. The harbor glistened in the distance, merchant ships moored to the commercial docks, pleasure yachts setting sail for an afternoon adventure. Across the expanse sat Whitehaven University, its grand spire rising almost as high as the tower in which he now stood. The massive walls surrounding the grounds didn't allow anyone on street level to peer in, but from his vantage point high above, Roann had an incredible view. The university's gardens were ablaze with autumn color. He understood why Ebbersley and the other deans were reluctant to dip into their precious land to construct more dorms—the gardens were beautiful. But sacrifices had to be made, and Roann wasn't about to force that sacrifice onto his subjects for the benefit of the college.

People surged through the streets beneath him, darting in and out of elegant shops, chasing children, and tossing coins into one of the many fountains that dotted the fine city. Pride swelled in his chest. Roann Vrelin loved Keld, and he felt honored to be its reigning sovereign.

Roann had been born as a late-in-life child to his parents, the emperor Artol and empress Eilith. Having suffered through several stillbirths and miscarriages before he entered the world, they had resigned to the fact they might never produce a viable heir. Deciding to live their lives the happiest they could without a child, they devoted themselves fully to charities, children's activities, and ruling their empire. If they couldn't have offspring of their own, they would find joy in the children of their subjects.

So when, just before Empress Eilith's forty-third birthday, she found herself once again with child, she didn't hold out much hope it would result in motherhood.

Prince Roann was born on a stormy summer night, lightning striking one of the towers of the palace just moments after he arrived. As the fire brigade swooped into action to contain the flames, the empress held her first live-born child in her arms. That night the palace may have lost a turret to fire—but it gained an emperor.

Fiercely protective of him as a child, the emperor and empress did absolutely everything they could think of to shield their precious son from the evils of the world, no matter the cost. But, as Roann grew, he demanded more freedoms and convinced his parents to let him spread his wings more. After all, he would one day rule the empire.

Under the guidance and watchful eye of several exemplary tutors, he had been sculpted into an intelligent and respected man. The young prince stood by his father's side as he ruled, watching and listening so that one day he could emulate the emperor's ways. He knew the importance of the position, the honor and duty that came with the name Vrelin.

Over the years, the prince had grown into a handsome young man with intelligence that surpassed even some of the most seasoned court scholars. No one doubted he would be a great ruler, and would be fair to his people. And when, at the young age of twenty-two, he had taken over the emperor's duties after Artol suffered a massive stroke, the people of Keld—of the entire empire—never had any reservations.

Ten years in, and Roann had increased prosperity, authored peace treaties between squabbling villages, and ensured that every citizen had access to education and health care. If his father had been a beloved ruler—Roann was close to being revered as a god. Everyone loved him—and he reciprocated that affection tenfold. It had been centuries since war had threatened the empire, and there was no doubt that as long as Prince Roann ruled, all would be protected. The monarchy of Zaiterra, on an adjacent continent, respected the prince even more so than they had his father, with peace continuing between the two nations.

Sighing with contentment, he released the silken tie holding his blonde hair back and allowed it to cascade freely over his shoulders. Although he enjoyed the formal dress and posture of royalty, he cherished the times when he could, quite literally, let his hair down. He straightened the short black waistcoat he wore over a light purple cotton shirt. His black leather pants fit snugly, tucked into his black riding boots. It was modest dress for a quasi- emperor, yes, but he wouldn't have it any other way. After all, his father was still legally the ruler—he was just keeping the fires burning for him on the home front. Though hopes of his father's health improving were nonexistent, he *was* still the emperor. Never once had Roann donned the crown or grand robes his father wore so regally—and he didn't plan to until the day his father left the planet for whatever awaited him on the other side.

The prince's stomach growled audibly, reminding him he had forgotten to eat breakfast. He turned from the window and headed toward a small side door in his office, one he knew would take him straight to the private quarters of his family—and a wonderful lunch with his mother. His emerald eyes sparkled in the sunlight one last time as he ducked into the dimly-lit, hidden hallway. The corridor ended at his mother's sitting room, and he could smell the aroma of roasted ham before he even put his hand on the doorknob. Entering the comfortably furnished room, he was immediately greeted by the Empress' attendant, who motioned him to the table, laid out with a grand luncheon.

"You're late, darling." A soft feminine voice filtered up and over a beautiful high-backed chair.

Roann rounded the table and sat next to his mother with an embarrassed smile. "Dean Ebbersley dropped by unexpectedly and I lost track of time. I'm sorry."

"Still wanting to expand the university?"

"As always." The prince leaned over and kissed his mother on the cheek. "I hope you didn't wait too long."

Empress Eilith shook her head, her gray curls bouncing on her shoulders. "Not at all. I've started already, see?" She pointed to her porcelain plate, piled high with meat, cheese, and fruit.

Roann helped himself to the fabulous spread, taking a generous helping of smoked ham. As he buttered a slice of artisanal bread, he focused his attention on the staircase that led to his parents' private apartments. "How's father today?"

The Empress cast her eyes down to her plate. "He...couldn't make eye contact with me this morning. I could tell he wanted to, but..." She sighed deeply.

The prince hated hearing his mother so upset. His father's stroke had pulled the rug out from under the family—and the whole country. Roann had been thrust into the position to not only take over the empire, but to care for his mother as she, in turn, cared for his father. He had never been given proper time to grieve the loss of the father he once knew, and was instead forced to take over the emperor's position while he watched Artol waste away. But, he knew he had to be a pillar for his mother—and his father. Roann needed to succeed not only for the honor of their family name, but for the well-being of the empire as a whole.

"I know, Mother." Roann patted her hand. "Did you talk to Dr. Thal?"

"Of course, dear. I fear Artol's beginning to fade. You should go see him, it would raise his spirits."

"I have meetings with the commerce ministers this afternoon, but I'll read to him after dinner."

"I'm sure he'd enjoy that." She nodded solemnly before changing her demeanor with a great sigh. "Now, what the devil do the commerce ministers want? Didn't you just meet with them last week?"

It was obvious to Roann by the semi-forced smile on her face that she was finished talking about his father. He knew it was difficult for her to come to terms with her husband's ill health, and it seemed to him that she welcomed her time with the prince—when she could allow herself a few moments of normality.

"You know as well as I, the commerce ministers would gladly follow me home at night and talk my ear off about money and politics as I sat in the bath." Roann cracked a wry smile. "They just want to review the last council meeting. I can't be everywhere at once, and Ministers Malgerius and Brymark were gracious enough to take notes."

"Don't spread yourself too thin, dear. You have the ministers because you trust their judgment when it comes to matters of state. No one will think any less of you if you don't make every single decision. Your father certainly didn't."

"Thank you for your concern."

"You're never going to find a wife if you've got bags under your eyes, you know." Eilith quirked a mischievous eyebrow.

"Mother…"

"Don't 'mother' me. It's my right as your birth-giver to want to know when you're going to get married. I don't want to see you devote all your time to your country and forget about your own personal happiness. Being the emperor doesn't mean you have to leave behind the pursuit of a life of your own."

"Believe me, if there was a woman in my life; you'd be the first to meet her."

Thankfully for him, the empress accepted his reply and he didn't have to explain his lack of love interests any further. It wasn't that he didn't want someone by his side, but all the young women who had been "recommended" had never suited his tastes. Had he lived a normal life, he could have pursued love on his own terms, but being the reigning monarch of the most powerful empire in the world left him little time for a personal life.

Roann relished in every moment he could spend with his mother, knowing that she was getting on in life. Yes, she was in good health, but the years had obviously started to take their toll. Empress Eilith spent most of her days caring for the ailing emperor, with almost no time left for herself. Seven years her senior, Emperor Artol had been an invalid for ten years and had become quite a burden. She and Roann would never say that out loud, of course, but his quality of life was definitely hard for everyone to witness.

Mother and son shared the rest of their meal engaged in quiet small talk, with the empress sharing her dislike for one of the new nurses caring for Artol. Knowing that his mother could, at times, be overly critical when it came to her husband's care, the young prince assured her he could remedy the issue with diplomacy and no need for harsh words. The empress agreed, and the matter was closed.

Roann set his fork down on his now empty plate and dabbed at his lips with a linen napkin. "Wonderful lunch, thank you, Mother."

"Thank the kitchen staff, not me." Her eyes hid a yearning sadness for her old life.

The prince stood and extended his hand to the woman, who graciously accepted. Her delicate fingers curled around his strong ones as he helped her stand. She took a moment to look him up and down, before straightening his collar with a motherly smile.

"You're a good man. Your father and I are very proud of you."

"*Everything* I do, I do for the good of the people—and for you." He kissed her cheek softly. "I just hope it's enough."

"It is, darling. It is." Her hand moved to his face, and she gently tucked a lock of hair back behind his ear. "You're the perfect son."

"That's what you think," Roann said playfully.

His mother moved away, her long yellow gown ghosting across the rich wooden floor. The sunlight beaming in from the stained-glass windows in the empress' sitting room cast a playful kaleidoscope on the floorboards. Eilith climbed the stairs to her private quarters, blowing a kiss to her son before disappearing down the hallway.

Leaving his mother to attend to his father, the prince turned heel and left the room, zigzagging down the warm and inviting corridors connecting his family's apartments with the rest of the palace proper. Emerging into a grand central atrium, he glided down the majestic staircase and into the main corridor of the castle, bustling with activity. Workers dusted tapestries and washed floors, ministers darted in and out of small offices busy with the daily goings-on of running a country. A small group of Keld residents followed a tour guide as they wound their way around the main building, mouths gaping in awe of the sheer grand scale. As Roann passed, they all bowed with flushed faces and wide smiles, absolutely giddy that they had actually been in the presence of their sovereign.

Roann felt perfectly safe within the walls of the fortress—within Keld for that matter. If it were his choice, he would never be accompanied by bodyguards. But he understood the need for protection when he left the palace. After all, he was a monarch—and that position wasn't without risk. So it was times like this, inside the castle, that he relished in the fact that he was allowed to roam free.

He walked past the palace chapel, the aroma of incense wafting out from the open door. The prince felt a tickle in his nostrils, and quickly brought his hand under his nose in an attempt to stifle it. His actions too late, he sneezed loudly, startling the cleric inside. The old house priest, Morigar, was on his hands and knees scrubbing the floor in front of the grand altar. A statue of the Goddess Oleana rested on top, staring out into the room. When Roann sneezed, he jumped up, putting his hand over his heart. At the ready to scold whomever it was that had disturbed the tranquility of the holy place, his grumpy scowl turned to a broad smile when he saw the prince standing in the doorway.

"Your Majesty!" Morigar dropped his sponge into a bucket of soapy water. The light streaming in through ornate windows bathed him in a heavenly aura as he walked through one of the light shafts. The smoke from the incense hung heavy in the air, visible even in the dim chapel as it moved on currents, ebbing and flowing across the shafts of light. Moving swiftly toward his sovereign, he held out both hands to greet the young man. "What a wonderful surprise, Highness."

"I'm sorry I startled you." Roann smiled apologetically as he grabbed the man's hands firmly in greeting. "It's that damn incense."

"Language, Your Grace," the friar scolded with a wry grin.

"Sorry...that *darn* incense." Roann winked, then looked past him toward the front of the room. "Why are you washing the floors? Don't you have acolytes to help you with that?"

"It helps keep me young—and in the good graces of the Goddess. Hard work and penance earn one a place at her side in the Gentle Reach.

"If that's the case, your entrance into the Gentle Reach is certain." The prince motioned to the door with a flick of his head. "I must be going, Father. The commerce ministers aren't patient men."

"Indeed they aren't." The cleric pointed to his bucket. "And duty calls. I trust I'll see you at services tomorrow evening?"

Roann nodded with a warm smile as the priest went back to his sudsy work. Taking one last look at the sight before him—the oaken pews, the ornately carved supporting columns rising high into the vaulted ceiling, the intricately inlaid stained glass depictions of Goddess Oleana—he marveled at the grandeur bestowed upon the deity. As heir to the empire, he dutifully attended church with his mother every week, offering his tithe like any other worshipper. However, known only to his parents, the prince had confided in them at a young age that he didn't believe in what the priests taught, but understood the necessity of keeping up appearances. Had anyone asked about his beliefs—he would have been honest with them. It just so happened that no one ever questioned him—and so there was nothing to say. He knew the people of the empire relied on their beliefs in Oleana to bring a measure of happiness and peace to their lives. It was a perfect example of 'what they don't know can't hurt them'. And he had been eternally grateful to have loving and progressive parents that didn't ostracize their child for not agreeing with the state religion. It didn't mean he still didn't find the tales about the Goddess and other deities across the globe fascinating, but he had his own beliefs— and stories were just stories.

Snapping himself from his thoughts with another incense-induced sneeze, he continued on, deciding to take the long way back to his offices via the gardens. Birds chirped and the sweet scent of giant rose blossoms filtered through the air. He ducked under a tree and leaned against the trunk. A breeze picked up and tickled his face. He cherished these times in this sanctuary. No one bothered him when he was here. There were no urgent messages, no meetings, no business. Just nature, quiet and peaceful.

Grateful to have those few moments to himself, he blew out a long breath and decided it was time to get back to work. Inhaling deeply to smell the aroma of the garden one last time, he exited the courtyard and started back toward the offices. His hair flew around his face as a gust of air blasted down the outside corridor, a wind-tunnel effect he had enjoyed in that particular place in the palace since childhood. A nostalgic grin spread across his face as he extended his arms, feeling the wind on his his limbs. Then, as suddenly as it had blown up, the blast of air died down, leaving him standing in the corridor with incredibly messy hair. He quickly smoothed his locks down and secured them with the tie he had stashed in his pocket.

As he pressed on, he hoped the ministers were behaving themselves in his absence.

~~~

Night had fallen on the grand city of Keld.

Prince Roann knocked quietly on the door, not expecting a response. He did it out of habit and respect, knowing the resident of the chamber couldn't physically answer anyway. Twisting the brushed bronze doorknob, he entered.

The room was dimly lit, a single oil lamp sitting on a desk burning on the lowest setting. The heavy curtains were open, held back by ornate golden ropes. The moon gleamed in the sky, flanked by a few high, wispy clouds. Roann found himself mesmerized by the satellite. He often thought that, had he not been born onto the royal path, he would have very much liked to have become an astronomer.

A raspy cough rattled through the room. Roann grabbed the lamp from the desktop and moved next to the giant bed. Setting the lantern down on the nightstand, he pulled a plushy chair close and sat. He reached over to turn the lamp up, illuminating a frail, gaunt face. Wrinkled, bony hands rested across a slowly rising chest.

"Father, would you like some water?"

The emperor opened his eyes and smiled weakly, the left side of his mouth hanging limp on his face. The prince filled a glass from the bedside pitcher and carefully slid his hand under Artol's head. Lifting slowly, he raised the glass to his father's lips and helped him drink. Half of the water dribbled from the useless side of the emperor's mouth, which Roann dabbed away with a handkerchief before taking a seat.

"Well, I almost murdered Dean Ebbersley today." Roann smirked in the dim light as Artol's right eye crinkled with an attempted smile. "I swear, that man is the most persistent bastard on the planet. Of course, he wanted to talk about expansion for Whitehaven again. He actually went so far as to hint at a split between us and the college if I didn't accept his proposal."

The emperor feebly squeezed his son's hand.

"Don't worry, I was very diplomatic. He saw it my way very quickly." Roann winked before sighing. "I suggested a meeting with the city planners. They'll work it all out."

He grabbed a well-worn book from the tabletop and opened it, tucking the leather bookmark behind the last few pages for safe keeping. Roann skimmed his finger down the margin until he found the place he had left off. "Now, where were we? Ah, Queen Beatrix' defeat of the Giant warmonger."

Artol sighed contentedly and listened. Roann found it amusing that the books his father enjoyed most were fairytales. He had to admit, he loved the stories too, even after hearing them multiple times as a child. Roann saw it as a bit of nostalgia for the both of them.

"The evil giant, Nestil, raised his army and began to march onto Beatrix' lands—his soldiers clattering across the plains toting their bone armor and heavy weapons…"

Twenty minutes later, a soft snore stopped the prince. He replaced the bookmark and set the tome back on the nightstand. Standing, he rearranged his father's blankets, making sure the emperor was well covered. Looking at the sleeping man, he sighed. Yes, Roann liked spending time with Artol, reading and telling him about the

53

days' events, but it was difficult to fully enjoy the experience when the conversations were one-sided. It saddened him to think that things would never get better—only worse.

It was times like this, when the old man seemed most at peace, that Roann wished things had been different. The prince dutifully kept a happy façade. Most of the time, he was genuinely content in his life. He had the air of a strong, independent man and ruler, who knew what was best for his people. The citizens of Keld saw a powerful, noble sovereign—and that was what Roann strived to be. But strength can only last so long before it falters.

Nighttime was the hardest.

When his surroundings were quiet and his mind could wander, Roann's thoughts would inadvertently go to a dark place. A place where his anger at his father's condition could be released.

The prince clenched his fists on his lap and let the thoughts flow unimpeded. He knew if he squelched them, if he attempted to push them from his mind before dealing with them—that they would manifest themselves later as a migraine or upset stomach…or worse.

After several minutes of feeling sorry for himself and wishing harm upon whatever had caused his father's condition, he took a deep, cleansing breath and willed the malicious thoughts to flow away. Left in their wake was a sense of calm, and Roann knew he could now continue his evening peacefully.

Tiptoeing from the room out of habit—his father slept like a rock—he closed the door behind him and went to kiss his mother goodnight in her reading room.

~~~

The cool night air was refreshing.

It was evenings like this when the midnight breezes whipped around the tower, that the prince tried to enjoy a peaceful calmness. Roann leaned his weight on the balcony and peered down into the square below, tapping his signet ring on the railing. His hair blew loose around his face, sticking to his lips. He spit a strand out as he ventured further over the side. Feeling gravity begin to take hold, he tightened his grip on the ornate wrought-iron banister, his knuckles turning white. He closed his eyes and listened to the wind whip past his ears. The prince allowed his body to be pushed by the gusts. Only when his fingertips began to lose their strength from his vise-like grip did he back away from the edge. Straightening his vest, he blew out a long breath and moved back to his patio table. Sitting down with a heavy, tired sigh, he craned his neck upwards and gazed at the stars. He let his head fall backwards onto the back of the chair and watched the night sky glitter above him.

He didn't know how long he had been staring into the night, but when he finally sat back up, he cast a glance at the pocket watch hanging from his trousers. It didn't feel like it was just after midnight. Roann knew he should go to bed, knew that he had an early meeting with his advisors in the morning. But his mind was racing. Even though he didn't want to admit that the Ebbersley incident still irritated him—it did. That, coupled with his father's unusually frail condition earlier, left him feeling anxious and unable to sleep.

He got up, stretched his arms over his head, and walked back into his apartment, heading for his study. Sitting in the corner, on a wooden tripod, was a gift his father had given him for his tenth birthday. Roann approached the object and ran his fingers down the smooth barrel, careful not to touch the lenses. He picked it up and carried it back to the balcony, making sure not to knock it against the doorframe.

The telescope was made of tandlewood and silver, the lenses hand-made by craftsmen in Trill. Roann adjusted the height of the stand, then tilted it up toward the heavens. Leaning over to squint through the eyepiece, he trained the sights on the moon, Iyanides. The brilliant satellite drifted across the blackness of the sky. The prince stared at the craters and pockmarks dotting the surface, taking note of his favorite crescent-shaped canyon. As a child, he had named it "The Smile", and it was always the first landmark he located.

He stood hunched over the telescope for the longest time, moving his attention midway through his observations from the moon to the stars dotting the veil of night. Finally having his fill of stargazing, he sat once again in his comfy chair and stared out across the expanse of the city. Within moments, Roann's eyes began to flutter shut. Crossing his arms over his chest for comfort and warmth, the exhausted prince fell asleep.

A shooting star streaked across the sky above the palace.

CHAPTER SIX

Remember to keep your wits about you during festival season! Pickpockets work quickly, and charlatans prey upon vulnerable minds! Please enjoy the festivities safely!

--Notice from the Keld commerce ministry

Ryris loved street fairs.

When he was living in Blackthorne, he would take a day every now and then and travel to Lullin to visit the outdoor market. He'd always return with enough food to keep him and his father fed for weeks, plenty of new ingredients, and the occasional gift for Grildi. Now living in the big city, he had been more than a little excited to see a flyer for a weekend market and carnival tacked to a bulletin board. The corner general store was a convenient place to get his groceries, but he missed being able to engage directly with the farmers. Plus, there were always local treats to be had—and he most certainly wasn't going to resist his sweet tooth, especially on such a beautiful day.

He walked up the busy causeway, an empty basket slung over his wrist and a fruit pasty in the other hand. Children raced past him, a blue balloon whooshing so close to his face that it ruffled his hair. Their mother apologetically patted him on the shoulder as she ran after them, yelling for them to slow down. The kids darted down a side street, the woman frantically waving her arms over her head as she chased after them. Ryris laughed to himself and took another bite of his pastry.

He stopped at a stall, perusing the selection of vegetables. The farmer smiled warmly, his sun-wrinkled face attesting to just how hard he worked the fields. Ryris chose a few dirt-covered potatoes, two giant tomatoes, and a bunch of carrots. The old farmer held up four fingers.

"Only four gamm? You're kidding." Ryris fished a handful of coins from his pocket. "Best deal in town."

The vendor nodded thankfully as Ryris deposited the coins in his palm, then tossed a small parcel of fresh peas into his basket. "No charge, lad. Enjoy them."

Raising his basket as a gesture of thanks, Ryris backed away from the stall, allowing more patrons to fill in after him. He walked further down the boulevard, looking up at the spire of Whitehaven University. Shielding his eyes from the glaring sun, he was amazed at how the steeple glinted in the daylight, tiny crystals in the stone shining like diamonds in the sky. People crowded around him, also taken by the sight of the grand building. They ebbed and flowed down the street, pulling him along for the ride.

Keld was alive.

His entire life he had become so accustomed to Blackthorne and its slower ways. Never had he witnessed the frenetic chaos of the big city—until now. He marveled at the movement of the crowds, the din of the inhabitants going on with their daily lives.

Coming to a small open park, Ryris' attention was immediately captured by two colorful tents, each adorned with flashy signs. They beckoned him to see the wonders of human oddity, and showcased a plethora of spectacular specimens. A woman with horns jutting from her head stood at the door flap taking tickets, bending down once and a while to allow a child to touch the protuberances. Music played inside the tent, and Ryris could hear the startled gasps of the patrons. The alchemist decided, from the look of the "real" horns on the woman's head, that the fifteen gamm entrance fee wasn't worth shelling out and moved on to the next attraction.

Cages sat on the grass, huge beasts and small animals side-by-side. Ryris had always been fascinated by animal life, and this attraction was free—just his kind of entertainment. Strolling past the temporary enclosures, he stayed well back from a juvenile ice wolf. He really didn't feel like losing any fingers today. Creatures roared and snarled at the onlookers and Ryris found himself hoping that the locks on the cage doors were adequate. Moving on, he came to a small penned-in area with baby goats cavorting in play. A woman offered him a handful of dried corn, which he allowed a tiny animal to nibble. Feeling like a child again, he enjoyed the momentary lack of adult responsibilities.

The last attraction in the plaza was another tent, boasting that it contained the "Mysteries of Alchemy." A locked case containing a giant's toe sat guarded by a feeble old man near the door. Intrigued, Ryris decided to pay the ten gamm just to see what all the fuss was about. The tent was dim, display cases and shelves lining the outer walls. A few tables sat in the middle, littered with dishes of dust and beakers of various animal parts. Run-of-the-mill alchemical ingredients, nothing you couldn't find in any respectable alchemist's shop. He made quick work of the exhibit. Near the back, nestled in a corner, sat the main attraction. A large pedestal, a burly guard on either side, housed a massive black sphere. The sign underneath claimed it was a dragon's egg, harvested from the Screaming Peaks. The young alchemist immediately had to stifle a chuckle. Any educated person knew that dragons didn't exist—ever. Mythical beasts taken from children's tales, they were nothing more than nightmare fodder. Still, people crowded around the artifact, clamoring to get a look at the one-of-a-kind specimen. Ryris kept back, having no need to inspect the suspect "egg" any further. One look told him it was a polished river stone from his home region. He finished his stroll through the tent, ducking out the exit flap and back into the sunlight.

Finding his way onto the street, he decided to head back to his neighborhood. Suddenly, Ryris' foot caught on an uprooted cobblestone, tripping him. As he struggled to keep his balance, his basket tipped and a potato tumbled out. Chasing the rolling vegetable off the beaten path, it came to a stop at the base of a ramshackle tent. The canvas was old, the once bright red color faded from countless years in the sun. Glass baubles and jingle bells hung from thin wires across the entrance. The outside light was tremendously bright, and it was impossible to see inside the dark recesses. The scent of incense wafted out, leaving a thin haze of smoke in the afternoon air.

Ryris read the shabby sign pinned to the fabric as he put his escaped vegetable back in his basket. He had never heard of "Spirit Stones" before. The placard implored him to 'listen to the voice of the universe'. He chuckled, and with a dismissive shake of his head, began to walk away. Maxx had always said fortune tellers were nothing more than charlatans preying on the foolish.

But something stopped him. He didn't know if it was curiosity or out of spite for his father, but he suddenly felt the urge to give it a whirl. These people weren't serious—even if they thought they were. Ryris never believed in any of that mumbo-jumbo and was in it purely for entertainment's sake. What harm could come from a bit of good-natured fun? After all, tomorrow he would be officially opening the shop and would have no time to indulge in such frivolous activities. And it was only ten gamm— a downright bargain. He tucked his amulet safely into his shirt, making sure it was covered by the folds of fabric. More to keep the jewel safe from would-be thieves than anything else; he didn't need it to draw any unwanted attention.

The air inside the tent was stale and bitter, numerous pots of incense burning around the perimeter. Candles flickered on tables and shelves, their waxy leavings dripping onto the surfaces. A haggard old woman with a burlap patch over her left eye sat hunched in a chair. Her snow-white hair was pulled up in a messy bun; both ears lined with rings and stud piercings. Her clothes were old, her skirt patched in several places. Once-pristine shoes adorned her feet, but the leather soles had long since worn down to expose the cork tacking underneath. A soft snore rumbled from her lips. Ryris cleared his throat and she jumped. It took her a moment to get her bearings, but she finally acknowledged him with a swooping gesture of her arms.

"Come on in, young man! You seem to have caught me napping, I do apologize. But, you wouldn't begrudge an old woman her beauty sleep, would you?"

"No, of course not." Ryris smiled endearingly.

"What's your name, dear? I can't be tellin' the stars to an unknown—even if he is as handsome as you."

Ryris' cheeks flushed at her compliment. It wasn't like he had never been told he was good looking, but to have an unfamiliar, somewhat shrewish woman say it was something he wasn't used to. He hoped she wasn't trying to come on to him for a bigger payment. After an awkward silent moment, he finally answered.

"...Ryris."

She took in an awestruck breath. "A name I haven't heard in a very, very long time. Do you know what it means?"

Ryris had never given it much thought. Intrigued, he shook his head and shrugged.

The fortune teller's eyes lit up. "Every name has an origin, son. Most are common, but some are ancient and mysterious. Yours is one of honor...and magic."

He had to stop himself from recoiling at her last word and wondered if she would be offended if he bolted out of the tent flap. "M-magic?"

"Very much so. There was a great wizard, long ago, who shared your name. An ancestor, perhaps? An extraordinary name from an extraordinary time. A lofty title, and not one most parents would bestow upon their progeny—given the magical connection."

It was the first time Ryris had ever heard anyone other than his grandmother mention his ancestors, and certainly not on such specific terms. Whether the old woman was full of beans or not was yet to be determined. A part of him wanted her to be legitimate, to actually be able to tell him something about the family that came long before him. He briefly contemplated asking her to forego the session and just tell him about his history—but he realized that it was a very real possibility she was just making everything up. Before he could decide what to do, she slapped her thighs with an exasperated movement.

"Enough about that fascinating old name of yours," she smiled; exposing several missing teeth, before pointing to a ratty pegboard leaned against an oaken chest. "Choose a pouch and let old Zerl have a look at your spirits."

Determined to get some fun out of the experience, the young alchemist decided she was just going through the motions of selling her craft with the mention of magic, and brushed it off as nonsense. Ryris set his basket down just inside the tent flap and inched toward the selection. Several dozen small pouches—some leather, some velvet, some burlap—waited to be perused. He reached his hand out, drifting his finger across the bags. It lingered over the smallest of the bunch, the purple velvet soft against his skin. He sensed the old woman's eyes on him. Plucking the satchel from its bent metal hook, he turned and approached her table.

"Have a seat, dear." She tapped a small bowl filled with silver and gold coins. "Ten gamm and I'll tell you everything you ever wanted to know—and then some."

The young man retrieved a handful of money from his pants pocket and set the proper amount into the wooden vessel with a smile. He took a moment to observe the leather mat atop the table. Covered with strange markings and a language he didn't recognize, he wondered just how she was going to tell his fortune. The mat was divided into sections, each one with a different symbol in the middle. Surrounding each sigil were words and pictograms, faces of angels and demons, images of stars and planets. Ryris was very intrigued.

"Hold the pouch in your hands and close your fingers around it tightly." The woman waited for him to comply. "Concentrate on what makes you 'you', even if it's not something nice. Take deep, even breaths and let the thoughts flow."

Ryris inhaled through his nose and held it for a moment before letting it out. He scoured his mind. *"Think about what makes me 'me'? Alchemy? Intelligence? Good looks? …magic?"*

The old woman closed her eyes and pressed her gnarled fingertips to her temples. A low hum rumbled from her chest as she swayed in her seat. She began to moan as, Ryris concluded, the spirits entered her. He stifled a snort and tried not to laugh. Biting his lower lip, he prayed she'd be done soon—he didn't know if he could take much more without bursting into a fit of laughter. He was glad her eyes were closed. After almost a minute, her eyes snapped open and she threw her arms wide with a gasp, startling the young man. "Dump the stones!"

Doing as he was told, Ryris loosened the cinch on the pouch and emptied the stones onto the tabletop. The malachite pieces, ten in all, rolled in all directions, clattering to a halt around the mat. Ryris leaned closer to get a better look at them. They were all different in size and shape, a symbol etched into the surface of each one, gilded in silver paint to make it stand out.

Zerl inspected the pieces where they came to a rest, humming to herself as she nodded. It took her a moment of puttering before she began to speak. "You're from very far away, aren't you?"

Ryris decided to test her. "Not really. Dungannon…"

"Is that so?" She eyed him suspiciously, leaning closer over the table. Ryris could smell her bad breath wafting toward him. "Because the stones never lie, young man."

Ryris tried to hide his surprise. Perhaps there was more to this racket than he originally thought.

She leaned back again with a knowing hum, smoothing down the corners of the mat. "Mmmm…very interesting. You've got a good pattern. You see this one? You're going to be rich." She pointed at the largest piece, sitting on top of the image of a rising sun.

"Rich? How rich?" Ryris feigned interest and egged her on.

"Very." She tapped a stone resting next to the one that she claimed indicated wealth. "Within the next five years. It doesn't mean you won't have to work for it, but it's definitely coming."

She continued to stare at the stones, drumming her fingers on the side of the table. "I see that you'll have many audiences with the emperor in the coming years. And you'll also inherit a gem mine!"

He tried not to laugh. There was no way that tiny stone could tell her something so specific. But, he decided to get his money's worth and play along—but not without getting a jab in likewise. He made sure his tone of voice was determined and sincere. "Diamond or ruby? Because it makes a difference."

The old woman stopped short and looked at him, puzzled. It was obvious she wasn't expecting such a question. "The stones aren't clear on that, my dear."

Ryris just nodded and waited for her to begin again. After she re-gathered her thoughts, she continued, clicking her tongue sympathetically.

"Sorry to say lad, but this one…" Her fingertip hovered over an oblong stone. "…is not very friendly today."

"Why?"

"It seems you'll have a bout of food-borne illness soon. Better stock up on ipecac."

The young man tried not to roll his eyes. "You can't possibly predict that."

"I just interpret the spirits, son. What they say is their opinion. But I'd stay away from soft cheeses and uncured meats for a while."

"I'll be careful," he replied with a thankful smile. He knew she probably meant well—even if she seemed to be spewing nonsensical advice about brie.

"Ahh, here's some better news. According to this one," she pointed to a jagged stone resting just to the side of the image of a ringed planet. "A beautiful wife. Plenty of time to start saving for a nice ring. A couple of years." She hummed a moment before tapping another piece. "And this one…well then. Do you have a big house?"

"Not really…why?" Ryris leaned in closer. He didn't want to admit that he was actually interested in what she had to say about—whatever she saw, fake or not.

The things coming out of her mouth were things he never thought anyone would say about him.

"Eight children."

The young alchemist spluttered as he held in his laughter.

"Don't laugh, or the universe might give you more as punishment." Ryris couldn't tell if she was joking or not. He decided to keep quiet and let her continue. She cleared her throat and spoke once again. "Now, this is interesting. Do you like to be successful?"

"There are people who don't?"

"Your business ventures will pay off handsomely in the future. I can tell you've got a good head on your shoulders when it comes to finance, and the stones agree."

Ryris was definitely enjoying the session. Who wouldn't want to hear predictions of wealth, success, and love? He could pass on the multiple children, but he figured two wouldn't be that bad. He had always secretly wished for a sister growing up.

Zerl leaned forward to get a good look at a particular stone that had fallen quite close to the edge of the mat. The space in which it lay was more tattered than the rest of the area, and darker in color. An image of a black planet, cratered and foreboding, adorned the upper corner. The old woman's face contorted and she gasped, her hand snapping up to cover her heart.

The young alchemist grew concerned. "Are you alright? What's wrong?"

"I knew this day would come, although I hoped it would pass me by." Her voice was hushed and stern.

"What do you mean?" He shifted uncomfortably in his seat, the air temperature inside the stuffy tent suddenly becoming stifling. Sweat beaded on his forehead.

"Never before has this stone behaved in such a manner, and I've been at this a very long time." She shuddered. Ryris stared at her blankly, not giving her any response whatsoever. Zerl picked up the stone and tossed it onto the floor, as if she couldn't be rid of it fast enough. She spat in its direction. Her voice became cold and monotone, her gaze boring right through him. "You're hiding something."

"Hiding something? Why would you think that?" He made a conscious effort not to touch his amulet, clenching his fingers to stop himself, his nails biting into the soft flesh of his palm. "I'm not hiding anything."

"Yes…it's deep. Life…as you know it…will come to an end." She rubbed her temples and whispered a chant in a language Ryris did not recognize.

The alchemist had suddenly had enough. He didn't know if he was spooked, or angry that this woman would say such a thing. If she was nothing more than a con artist, then that meant she preyed on the vulnerable. Who knows if she would charge extra to rid her customers of the demons she sensed, or sell them a charm to ward off evil. But, if there was even a shred of truth to what she was saying, and she *did* sense something from these mystical stones, Ryris wanted no part of it. He wasn't about to let himself be convinced that some random pieces of rock could tell his future.

He tried to lighten the mood. "I think I'll be just fine. But thank you for a glimpse into my future successes."

She shook her head sadly. "That's the problem with you young people. You don't understand the spirits; you think this is some game…a charade. But they don't lie, son."

"Well, you and I have differing opinions, then." Ryris stood and extended his hand for her to shake, which she refused to accept. The alchemist awkwardly pulled his hand back.

"Keep yourself safe. There is dread looming on the horizon." Zerl visibly trembled, her eyes darting around the tent anxiously. She wrung her bony hands in her lap.

Ryris hastily ducked out of the tent without saying another word. Moving away, he quickly found himself out of the alley and immediately immersed in the crowd—and fresh air. He took a deep, cleansing breath. People had gathered around a musical group that had taken up residence on the corner. A happy-go-lucky man in a jester's costume danced and shook a tambourine, all while singing an absurd song about the dangers of cave bears. His accompaniment, two old men playing lutes, swayed to their own music, tapping their feet in time with the singer's instrument. Ryris lingered for a few moments before moving on; tossing a few coins into the pitcher the musicians had left out for donations.

It was then that he realized he had left his basket of produce behind. He walked back down the dim alley and stopped dead in his tracks.

Zerl's tent was gone.

Ryris stood there, dumbfounded. He knew it had been there no more than five minutes prior. He could still smell the scent of incense lingering in the air. And yet, there was absolutely no physical trace it had ever been there. He turned around and scanned his surroundings, trying to decide if he had taken a wrong turn.

And then he spotted it. His basket, still filled with vegetables, rested on the corner, his sparkling ten gamm payment piled on top.

CHAPTER SEVEN

<u>Oinox:</u> A rarely-seen, medium-sized, hoofed mammal living in the northern mountains of the Vrelin Empire. Brown and white striped hide covers a muscular body, the head is adorned with small bovine horns. Glands under the chin are used for territory-marking, and emit musky oil that lingers for weeks.

--Excerpt from 'Beasts of the Empire', by Pernal Frelk, Biology Professor Emeritus, Whitehaven University

The stench of decay was overpowering.

Light filtered down from a natural skylight high above in the cavern's ceiling. It fought for dominance against the swarm of buzzing flies threatening to black it out completely. The carcass of a large mammal lay in a contorted heap on the floor, the decomposition process hard at work. The beast had wandered into the cave in the last moments of its life. Thick, putrefied blood oozed from the severed artery at the animal's neck, pooling beneath the quickly bloating abdomen. Rotten flesh fell from exposed bones onto the cavern floor, where it was quickly picked up by smaller creatures and carried away to be feasted upon.

The oinox had obviously been attacked by a very large predator. Huge gashes ran across its back, exposing ribs and muscles in a macabre work of art. Another incision had torn its gut in half, rotting intestines spilling their contents out onto the floor. As tiny maggots crawled within the entrails, the entire body seemed to pulse with movement. The skin of the mighty beast undulated as the bugs moved beneath the flesh, threatening to burst through with every passing second.

A stiff breeze blew into the mouth of the cave, momentarily scattering the swarm of flying insects before they regrouped and descended once more on the corpse. An iridescent tooth, hanging on by a thin thread of rotting tissue, finally released itself from the animal's skull and clattered to the floor.

"Hey, a cave!"

"Don't go in there...it smells like somethin' died."

"Scaredy-cat!"

Rocks crunched just outside the cavern entrance, startling a few brer-rats near the body. One nipped at the piece of meat it had been sniffing and took off toward the other side of the cavern. Another rodent immediately jumped on its back, trying to wrestle the morsel away. When two boys appeared, the small animals scattered to the far reaches of the cave, chittering in irritation at the intruders. The kids paid them no mind; they were far too interested in the sight before their eyes. Even the overwhelming stink of death didn't deter them.

"Whoa! An oinox!" The smaller of the two children, just barely ten, approached the carcass. He pinched his nose shut and winced as he darted forward toward the mess.

"I told you something died. Don't touch it!" The older boy yanked his brother back by the collar. "Stay here and let me look."

The younger child pouted and crossed his arms over his chest. "You always get to have the fun! Why can't I look too? Those teeth and bones are worth a lot of gamm!"

"Don't you think I know that? Stay back there and shut up, or whatever killed this thing might come back." The teenage boy pointed sternly at his sibling.

Alix, the younger of the two boys, immediately stopped whining and looked nervously around the cave. Satisfied that he had scared his brother into submission for the time being, Jord moved closer to inspect the bloated body. He gagged at the sight of the maggots infesting the rotting flesh. Picking up a stick near his feet, he poked at the skull, dislodging one of the teeth. It fell onto a pile of others collected just inside the jaw. Jord's eyes grew large as he realized he and his brother had stumbled upon a small fortune in alchemical ingredients.

"Hand me your satchel, wouldja?" Jord impatiently shook his open palm back toward his brother.

"No way! I don't want that rotten stuff in it!"

"You can buy a new one with all the money we're going to make!"

Contemplating his brother's proposal for a moment, Alix finally relinquished his pack. He scrunched his nose in disgust as Jord plucked a few teeth from the gums before collecting the remaining ones on the floor.

The brothers didn't notice that the brer-rats had begun to be less scared of them and ever more curious. They approached in a sprawling pack, soft chatter coming from their whiskered mouths. A brave rat scurried ahead and sniffed at the younger boy's feet.

"Ummm, Jord? We should get out of here." Alix kicked at the tiny rat nipping his shoe. It bolted back to its companions, hissing in displeasure at the child. "I don't think they like us very much."

"Just a minute! This last tooth is really stuck in here good." The older boy was using his thumb and forefinger as a pincer, wrestling with a molar he deep within the recesses of the mouth. He grunted and tugged, finally wrenching the tooth free. He tumbled backwards from the momentum of his actions, scattering the brer-rats once more.

"Can we go *now?*" Alix rubbed his hands over his arms. "This cave is giving me the creeps."

"You're the one who wanted come in!" Jord stood and wiped his hands on his pants, the festering goop from the oinox' mouth congealing on the fabric. "We're here now, so let's explore. It goes back further, see?"

"But it's dark back there!"

Jord took a small torch from his pack before slapping Alix playfully on the back of the head. "Quit being a baby. I'm going whether you come with or not."

The younger child shuddered at the thought of being left alone. He begrudgingly agreed to join Jord, and went out of his way to step far around the body of the animal his brother had just scavenged.

The brer-rats crept cautiously back to their feeding place, keeping one eye on the boys as they began to tear at the rotten flesh. Hunger took precedence over danger. One tiny rat gnashed at a tendon, ripping it from the bone it clung to. A chunk of meat came with, a coveted prize for the small mammal. Its fellow rats noticed the hunk of carrion and started to move in on its position, the prime meat tempting them. Growling and biting, they wrestled for dominance—and their meals. There were more brer-rats than remaining meat, and it would soon be gone.

The small animal growled as a few of its friends tried to give chase. The brer-rat receded into a dark corner, his counterparts having gone back to find their own pieces of carrion. Nestling against the wall, it quickly found itself entangled in dry moss hanging from the rocks. As it moved, the twisted mass coiled tighter around its limbs. The brer-rat used its razor-sharp teeth to chew through the natural rope. But, the harder it tugged, the more tightly entangled its legs became and before long it was hopelessly trapped.

As the rat struggled to free itself, the boys had made their way deeper into the cave. Jord lit his torch with a flint spark. It illuminated their faces in the darkness, casting long shadows across the walls. Soon, they came upon the flailing rodent.

"Hey, that little one's trapped." Alix grabbed the torch from his brother's hand and knelt down beside the creature. The rat screeched and recoiled, but found itself too tightly entangled to escape. "Should we help it?"

"Those things bite! Do you want to get bone rot?"

"But I think it's scared." Alix reached out to the vine constricting the tiny rat.

Jord grabbed him by the shoulders and forcibly yanked him backwards. "Don't be an idiot!"

Alix narrowed his eyes at his brother and stood, clenching his fists. "Don't call me an idiot, *idiot!* You take that back!"

"You're always being stupid! No wonder you fell from the top of the barn last week! And had to be rescued from the river last year!"

"I *said* take…it…back!"

The boys lunged for one another, knocking each other to the floor. Alix dropped the torch and the tiny rodent screeched. Punches flew, feet kicked, and before long the brothers had pummeled each other savagely over a simple calling of names. Jord, trying to subdue his sibling, wrapped his arms around Alix' chest and biceps, holding the younger boy firmly in his strong grip. Alix tried to wriggle free, his feet flailing wildly beneath him.

The torch rolled away from the warring siblings and the flames began to dim as the burning end became coated in dust. In the throes of thrashing, Alix' shoe collided with the cave wall, punching through the brittle stone. Stale, dusty air rushed out of the opening, extinguishing the torch. The sudden darkness stopped the boys' fracas. They lay there, panting in each other's arms, staring at the hole. Letting go of his younger brother, Jord scrambled toward the opening, pushing his body flat to the floor in order to peer inside.

"What do you see?" Alix' voice was a hushed whisper.

The older boy squinted. There seemed to be a dim light source emanating from somewhere inside.

"Something's in here…" He sniffed, his nose wrinkling. "Smells old."

Alix' voice quivered. "W-we shouldn't be messing…"

Jord pushed himself up, sitting cross-legged in front of the opening. He started to remove loose rocks and wall chunks, and after a few minutes, had excavated a hole big enough for both boys to wiggle through. He lay on his belly and motioned for his brother to do the same. "Let's go."

"I'm not goin' in there!"

"You're always complaining that nothing fun or exciting ever happens in our village—what do you think this is?"

"I don't know…" Alix scowled and nervously wrung his hands together. "Pops said if we got caught snoopin' around again, he'd whip us good."

"I don't see Pops anywhere around here, do you?" Jord huffed and snaked his body into the hole, grunting as he pulled himself along. He barely made it through without getting stuck. When he was on the other side, he thrust his hand through the opening and beckoned for Alix with a crooked finger.

The younger boy reluctantly followed, not too happy about going into a strange chamber—but not willing to stay out in the darkness by himself. When he emerged, he found himself bathed in a soft purple light. In contrast to the dark cavern they had left behind, the haunting illumination exposed a completely new environment. No longer were the walls lined with cracks and moss, the floor littered with years of dirt and debris.

No, this room was man-made, meticulously carved from the actual bedrock of the mountain. The walls were smooth and polished, the floor shined to a mirror finish, accumulating only a light coating of dust. Unlit wall sconces hung dark around the perimeter. Jord inspected the lights, hopeful he could ignite any leftover fuel to illuminate their surroundings. He was surprised to find the bowls contained hunks of crystal, with no way he could discern to "turn them on." Never in his life had he seen such lamps.

Centuries had passed since the footfalls of man had last graced the room's interior, but traces of the human creators still remained. Books and potion bottles resided on shelves. Dozens of weapons hung on racks—everything from maces and daggers to intricately carved bows and pole arms. They all appeared to be made of a crystalline material, shimmering in the soft purple glow coming from across the chamber.

"What is this place?" Alix' voice was a hushed, awed whisper. He instinctively reached for his older brother's hand for comfort, even though they had been fighting mere moments before.

"Come on, let's look around." Jord accepted Alix' hand and held it tightly. He knew his little brother was nervous. Alix hesitated for a moment, his brother gently tugging him to finally encourage him forward.

Having no need for a torch in the eerie light, the boys circled the chamber. They stopped at a bookshelf, Jord removing one of the volumes from storage. Leafing through it briefly, he and his brother looked in wonder at the incredible hand-drawn pictures of warriors, mythical beasts, and fantastical weapons. The language was one they did not recognize, so the stories told within were lost on them.

"Those pages are sparkling, Jord! That's not like any book I've ever seen." Alix stared intently at one of the pages, taking the corner in-between his fingers, feeling the smooth texture of the vellum-like paper. "It's so soft! Can we take it with us?"

"Better not. We'd get whooped for sure if Pops found it." Jord set the tome back in its place, trailing his fingers across the spines of the other books as he walked down the length of the shelf.

Feeling braver, Alix moved ahead on his own, before halting in front of a grand rack of weapons. His eyes widened in awe as he gingerly reached a hand out to touch a shimmering war axe, its leather-wrapped hilt embedded with iridescent flecks of minerals. His brother did the same, marveling at the flawless crystal blade. "I've never seen anything like this in my life. Pops sure can't make swords like these."

Jord approached and immediately attempted to pluck the axe from the stand, only to have it crash to the floor. He had obviously underestimated how heavy the piece actually was. His younger brother shrieked and clapped his hands over his ears at the hideous racket.

"You'll break it! Put it back before we get in trouble!"

"Who's gonna tell on us?" The teen scoffed as he strained to pick the axe up and replace it. He struggled to hoist it back into its slot. When it was safely back on its perch, he noticed a small knick in the blade edge. Scowling, he turned the weapon to the side, hoping the missing chunk would go unnoticed by—whomever—looked at it next.

Jord perused the selection once more, this time choosing a smaller hand-axe. Removing it from the rack, he gripped the handle firmly before giving it a test swing. The lighter weight allowed for the young man to whip it around with ease, his brother backing away quickly.

"Now *this* is more like it!" Taking a fighting stance, Jord motioned for his brother to grab the axe's twin.

Alix shook his head. "You're gonna cut your hand off."

"C'mon! It's just like your woodcutting axe back home—only way neater. You have to try at least once." He swung the weapon over his head before letting it come to rest on his shoulder. The boys were no strangers to hand weapons, their father being the town weapon smith.

Alix took the other axe from the stand. The weight was more substantial than his handy wood-axe back home, and the crystal blade seemed to sing as it cut through the air. The boy marveled. "I wonder who made these things?"

"Dunno, but they're old." Jord gave the hand axe one last swing before depositing it back on the rack. Alix followed suit, sad to let the weapon go. Making sure they were both secure, Jord ran his hand over the smooth blade surface one more time.

Venturing near an ornate glass case, Alix peered inside. A grand crystal helmet sat perched on a silver pedestal, the eyes vacant, the material shimmering. He jiggled the delicate handle on the cabinet, only to find it locked tight. Content to just look, he took a moment to admire the glittering accessory. He wondered who might have worn it, or what it signified. Maybe it was a brave warrior—or perhaps an evil one? The face was definitely fearsome and likely scared anyone facing it in battle.

Jord stood in front of a shelf containing dozens of colored glass bottles, labeled in a language they did not understand. He picked one up, watching the liquid slosh within. Alix joined him at his side, reaching for a bottle of his own.

"What do you think's in there?" He tried wiggling the stopper, scowling when it wouldn't budge.

"Perfume, maybe? Or potions?" Jord successfully pried the cap from the vial in his hands and slowly brought it to his nose. Inhaling gingerly, his lips soon curled into a smile. "Smells like mom!" He held the bottle out to his brother, who agreed with his observation. Intrigued, he replaced the cap and set the container back on the shelf before grabbing another. That bottle was dark brown in color, the liquid inside not nearly as thin as the other had been. It stuck to the sides as he tipped the vial. Removing the cork, he sniffed again—and immediately gagged. The contents had obviously spoiled—or perhaps were meant to be horrid-smelling. Either way, he wasn't about to sample it again. Offering it to his brother with a mischievous smirk, the younger boy pushed his hands away with an offended scoff before plugging his nostrils.

"Put the stopper back in! It's stinkin' up the whole room!" Alix coughed with a grimace.

The older boy replaced the cork and set the bottle back in its original place. He waved his hand in front of his face to dissipate the smell.

"You think it was rotten?"

"Maybe. Or it might have been poison. There's an awful lot of weapons in here." Jord pointed to a quiver of crystal arrows. "You could dip the point of one of those in it, or coat the blade of a short sword and that would end your enemy's day real quick."

Alix shivered at the thought. "Why do you think this place is here? I don't recognize any of this stuff."

Jord shrugged. "I honestly don't know. Looks like an armory, maybe?"

"Just think about how much money Pops could make if he could forge this type of weaponry! We'd be rolling in gamm!"

71

"Got that right." Jord looked back at the weapons racks longingly. "But I've never seen this material—ever. Pops has never mentioned anything like it. It's like…"

"…it's forgotten." Alix peered over to the other side of the room and pointed, his voice suddenly nervous. "Jord? Look…"

A low hum permeated the chamber, quiet and unassuming, pulsing like a heartbeat. An object: opaque, crystalline, and man-sized, sat on the floor, producing the purple light that had first illuminated them upon entry. It was draped with flowers, long since dried out. The colors of the petals faded over time, their once powerful scent no longer distinguishable from the stench of stale cavern air.

Jord approached hesitantly. Leaning over, he peered inside. "What *is* this?"

Through the glass cover, he could barely make out the shape of a person. Sucking in a surprised breath, he couldn't believe what he was seeing. He wiped away the thin layer of dust at the head of the container, exposing the interior through the glass lid.

A woman, clad in crystalline armor, laid peacefully, a crystal bow clutched across her breast. Golden hair splayed out from her head onto a satin pillow. Jord couldn't tell if she was dead or alive, but if she were deceased, it was the most impressive example of embalming he'd ever seen. Alix moved next to him and immediately gasped.

"It's a lady!"

Still completely in awe, all the older boy could muster was, "Yeah…" He plucked a dried petal from one of the rose chains lying across the top of the sarcophagus. It disintegrated on his fingertips and he let the resulting flecks fall to the floor.

"Is she dead?"

"I…I don't know." He was captivated by the woman. From her attire, he surmised that she had to be a warrior. The weapon she held resembled the pieces hanging on the surrounding racks. They seemed to be struck from the same material, shimmering in the low light. Her plate mail was crystal and iridescent, glittering from inside the sarcophagus. It matched the style of the helmet perfectly. He wondered how long she had been here—and who had placed her in this situation. He slowly moved from the head of the box to the foot, his fingers ghosting across the smooth lid.

Rounding the front of the coffin, Jord found himself looking down at a series of glowing, inlaid gems. Five in all, they were flush with the glass box in which they were set. He felt compelled to touch them, but stopped short. He figured they were the release mechanism for the lid, or perhaps, if the mysterious woman wasn't dead, the controls that kept her asleep. Whatever they did, he knew better than to disturb them.

"Who do you think she is?" Alix' voice was awestruck.

"Someone important. Whoever did this wouldn't have gone to all this trouble if she wasn't special." Jord suddenly felt very uneasy. Who was this woman? What if this whole room was supposed to stay sealed forever—and they had just undone everything by exposing her? Nervous butterflies fluttered in his stomach. "I don't think we were meant to find her—I don't think anyone was. We should go."

Jord tugged on his brother's sleeve, the young boy reluctantly following his sibling. They backed away from the sarcophagus with reverence. They knew nothing about this crystalline-clad warrior, and whether or not she was deserving of such honor. But, something about her appearance, the room, its contents—told them that she commanded respect, both in her life before, and her existence now.

Quickly worming their way back through the hole in the wall, Jord searched for the discarded torch. He lit the end with his flint. When they had sufficient light to see, the boys carefully piled the rocks back up as best they could to conceal the opening. For extra defense, Jord scattered dried foliage across the stones, draping hanging moss over the craggy surfaces. Inspecting the disguised entrance to the secret room, the teen rearranged the leaves once more before deciding he was satisfied with placement. He grabbed Alix by the arm and led him back through the cavern. They briefly stopped in front of the rotting oinox, leaving quickly as the stench overpowered them.

Once they were out of the cave and back in the fresh mountain air, the boys sat on a boulder, quietly taking in the scenery. A bird swooped high overhead, screeching into the afternoon air. They remained there for several long moments, neither one discussing what they had just experienced. Alix reached into his pocket and pulled out two strips of fruit leather, handing one to his brother. "Jord, we're not going to tell anyone about this, right?"

"Hell no." The older boy tore off a piece of the thick treat with his front teeth.

The young boy spit in the palm of his hand and extended it to his brother. "Swear on it?"

Jord laughed and mirrored his sibling, depositing a giant glob of saliva in his own palm before pressing it against that of his brother. "Swear. We'll keep her safe. Besides, it's not like we'll never see her again. That oinox is a treasure trove, and it's going to take us months to scavenge all the bones."

"What if people get suspicious about where we're finding all this stuff?"

"Then we tell them it's from somewhere else. If they go looking, it's their own problem. We can always sell the stuff to traders coming from the Crossroads Market, so we don't raise suspicions in town."

Alix nodded in agreement as he finished his snack. "We better get home. Those teeth in my pouch are starting to stink."

CHAPTER EIGHT

6 fluid ounces Base fluid, 2 Midnight Beetle carapaces (pulverized), 1 heaping Imperial scoop crystallized bat skin, 2 drops bat blood. Boil carapaces in base fluid for ten minutes. Let cool to room temp. Add other ingredients and shake vigorously before bottling. Sediment will dissolve.

--Recipe for simple healing potion, Maxxald Bren

Keld in the morning was a sight to behold.

The sunlight glinted off the rooftops, glittering stonework reflecting the new days' brightness. The city was already bustling with early-morning deliveries and people heading to work. Children waved goodbye to parents as the school wagons whisked them off to their classes, shop owners readied their storefronts for the business day ahead.

Prince Roann took a sip of his coffee and sighed contentedly. His day had started wonderfully and without incident. He had awoken feeling serene after a good night's sleep, blissfully aware that he didn't have any meetings with cranky ministers or persistent deans. The schedule for the day was light and enjoyable—and he was very much looking forward to setting foot in the city proper. Deciding to take his morning meal on his grand balcony, he watched the city surge beneath him. He daydreamed as the wind whipped through his hair, birds above screeching their morning calls. It wasn't until his assistant's voice snapped him from his thoughts that he returned to the real world.

"Your Highness? The carriage is waiting."

Roann turned to acknowledge the woman. "Thank you, Casmit. I'll be right down."

"Don't dawdle…" She eyed him knowingly and backed away from the doors.

Draining his cup of coffee in one last gulp, Roann wrapped a small biscuit in a napkin for later and stood. Straightening his doublet, he took one last look at his city before making his way to his waiting stagecoach.

~~~

"You'll be making three stops today, Your Highness. The new alchemist, Ryris Bren, has been open for a week now. His shop is already doing quite well, and I've scheduled a visit so you can officially welcome him. He's come all the way from Blackthorne."

74

Roann took a bite of the biscuit he snagged from his breakfast table. "Blackthorne? Far cry from Keld, isn't it? His name sounds familiar, though."

"I believe the emperor was being treated with a potion from Bren's for a time."

"That's probably it." Roann returned a friendly wave to a pedestrian who had greeted him. "It'll be nice to have another alchemist in town, the people need some variety."

Casmit smiled before checking her file again. "Then, you're visiting a preschool in the eastern district, where the children are eagerly looking forward to listening to you read a story and do a small art project.

"Art?" Roann eyed her.

"Yes, art. Perhaps you can make a gift for the empress." Casmit quirked a mischievous eyebrow. "And finally, Mr. Mombert and his wife have invited you for tea. I know you wouldn't normally partake outside of the palace, but they've made several generous donations to various Vrelin charities lately, and it would be a gesture of thanks if you were to spend an hour with them."

"I've heard that Mrs. Mombert makes an incredible chocolate tart. Maybe she'll indulge me." Roann smiled devilishly.

"Your sweet tooth knows no bounds, Your Majesty."

"Now you know my dirty little secret—I'm only doing this sovereign thing for the free cake." Roann winked.

Soon, the carriage came to a halt, and the prince could hear the muffled din of the street outside. Merchants called out their wares to prospective customers all around him. The door opened and he stepped out, immediately hit by the sweet aroma of flowers. Hundreds of individual blossoms lined a display, lovingly tended to by a short old woman, her wrinkly hands carefully arranging a small bouquet. She turned just in time to see Roann exit his carriage. Bowing, the old woman covertly wiped the dirt from the flowers on the hem of her dress. As she rose from her gesture, the prince extended his hand to her.

"Your Majesty, what an honor!" She blushed as he kissed her gnarled hand.

"The honor is mine. Your flowers are stunning." He inhaled deeply. "And they smell divine."

"Please allow me to make an arrangement for the Empress. It will take but a moment."

"I think she'd love some flowers, thank you. I'm going to visit the shop across the street for a while, so you have plenty of time." Roann smiled in thanks, then lowered his voice to a whisper, bending to speak into her ear and offer a friendly hint. "She loves roses. Yellow ones."

The old woman smiled and nodded in understanding.

Casmit motioned for him to round the carriage. "Right this way, Sire."

People gathered on the sidewalks, all clamoring to get a glimpse of their prince. Some waved, others whistled, and they all smiled broadly. Everyone loved Prince Roann, and it showed. He waved back, and called out a general greeting to his people before approaching the wooden door to Bren's. Roann took a moment to admire the colorful bottles and hand-made sign in the front window. The wood was carved with the words, **Bren's Alchemy. Ryris Bren, Proprietor**. He wondered if it had been a gift from home, since a larger and more colorful sign hung above his head. Putting a hand over his eyes to assist in seeing into the store, he could just make out a figure perched precariously on a ladder, feverishly searching for something on a high-up shelf. Content with his window shopping, he allowed Casmit to push the door open, causing a bell to tinkle.

The shop smelled like incense. Roann was immediately hit with the strong scent, so much so that he recoiled slightly. Not wanting to offend the newest shop-keep in Keld, he stifled a sneeze and moved further into the store, his eyes beginning to water. Glass bottles glittered in the sunlight and books lined the shelf in the far corner, already collecting a small film of dust. A row of vases, each containing bouquets of dried herbs and flowers, sat on a low table, hand-made labels adorning the glass. An alembic bubbled behind the counter, small droplets dripping out from the mouth of the apparatus and into a beaker. A green liquid churned within as the flame underneath flickered. Next to it on the countertop sat a tattered journal, well-loved by its owner. The entire shop had such a cozy feel to it, one would have thought it had been here for years.

Roann tried to ignore that he was feeling ever increasingly "off", something not quite right. His skin crawled and he felt as if the walls were closing in on him. A foreboding sense crept through his mind. But, he wasn't about to let some strange feeling sully his visit with his newest merchant, so he pressed on.

"I'll be right with you!" The young man on the ladder had his head recessed back into a shelf, moving bottles and jars out of the way. He mumbled in irritation as he shoved a box to the side, momentarily losing his balance. Catching himself on the shelf, he swore under his breath and continued to dig for whatever he was looking for.

The prince stood patiently, knowing the alchemist had no idea he was making royalty wait. Roann didn't mind too much, even though his stomach was beginning to tumble. He took a calming breath and the nausea subsided. Perhaps the ham he ate with his breakfast wasn't agreeing with him. Turning to look around the shop, he admired a display case filled with ramekins of shimmering dust, each one a different vibrant hue. Hearing scraping to his side, Roann turned back to see the alchemist descending the ladder, a metal box in his hand.

"That thing was really hidden. I almost had to crawl onto the sh—" Ryris turned, the metal box falling from his hands as he faced his customer. His mouth hung open in shock, his eyes wide. "Your Highness! I didn't …I'm so sorry I made you wait, I feel like a buffoon."

Roann smiled warmly, despite his growing uneasy stomach. "Nonsense. I was just admiring these plates of colorful dust. What are they used for?"

Quickly bending down to pick up his fallen cargo, Ryris set it on the countertop before making his way toward the prince. Fishing a ring of keys from his pocket, they jingled as he unlocked the display cabinet. He reached in and removed one of the dishes. "This is monk's dust. It's mainly used in pain relief potions; each color has a different potency. It's harvested from the bottom of prairie ponds as sludge, then dried in the sun." The alchemist pinched a small amount of the substance between his thumb and forefinger and sprinkled it into the air, the glittering grains catching the light of the sun as they fell to the floor.

"I've always found alchemy to be fascinating." Roann extended his hand for the young man to shake. "Forgive me for not introducing myself properly. I am Prince Roann Vrelin."

The alchemist hurriedly put the dish back, neglecting to lock the cabinet again. He firmly gripped Roann's outstretched hand, an excited smile consuming his face.

"Ryris Bren. It's an honor to finally meet you, Your Majesty. I'm humbled that you would visit my shop."

Roann barely heard a word the man was saying. A violent shockwave of nausea flashed over him as soon as he made contact with Ryris' skin. Never in his life had he felt such negative energy. He felt as if he might faint. Steadying himself, he struggled to remain standing and willed himself not to vomit. It was apparent that Ryris noticed something was amiss, because he immediately ended the handshake and grabbed the prince by the bicep to steady him.

"Are you alright? Do you need to sit down?"

The room spun around Roann, Ryris' voice muffled and distant. His assistant ran to his side and grabbed his other arm. They both eased the prince onto a crate in the corner.

"Your Highness, what's the matter?" Casmit's voice was laced with panic, her face flushing with anxiety. She snapped her fingers in front of his non-focusing eyes. "Can you hear me?"

Roann's head began to de-clutter as soon as Ryris released his grasp. The room stopped moving and his vision cleared. His stomach still churned, however, and he thought at any moment he might lose his breakfast. Dismissively waving a hand in front of himself, he tried to get his assistant to relinquish her hold.

"I'm better now Casmit, you can let go." His voice was wispy as he attempted to get his bearings, taking slow deep breaths.

"Your Majesty, what happened?"

The prince turned toward the voice, meeting the concerned face of the newest alchemist in Keld. The young man knelt next to the chair, tapping his fingers nervously on the display shelves at his side.

"I'm not sure. A sudden wave of...I don't know." Roann tried to hide his shaking hands by wringing them together. His mind was a whirling dervish of thoughts. Was he allergic to something in the shop? Perhaps the dust that Ryris had sprinkled into the air just prior to the episode?

Ryris.

A strange thought bubbled in Roann's brain. He tried to make sense of it as his body still reeled from the instant sickness. The horrible wave had only hit as he made skin-to-skin contact with the young man. But why would his body react in such a way to a simple, innocent handshake? The prince covertly looked down at the alchemist's hands, noting the skin was stained red. It was quite possible he had experienced an allergic reaction to something Ryris had been working with before he visited.

"We need to get you back to the palace." His assistant stood, never releasing her grip on his arm. "I'll call Doctor Thal."

"You'll do nothing of the sort. I'll be fine once I get some fresh air." Roann stood on his own, brushing his companion's hand away from his arm with a grimace. "My apologies, Mr. Bren. I'm afraid I'll have to cut this visit short. I don't know what has come over me, and I'm terribly embarrassed."

"No apology needed, Your Highness." The young man walked to the door and opened it, letting in a welcomed blast of warm, fresh air. "Please allow me to mix a solution for you and send it to the palace. It's the least I can do. No charge, of course."

"That's very kind of you." Roann mustered a thankful smile as he crossed the threshold. The sun hurt his eyes. The carriage was waiting for him, door open. He was thankful the crowd had dispersed, the citizens going back to their daily routines. As quickly as he could, he mounted the side of the coach and disappeared into the vehicle, slumping against the plush interior. He immediately pulled the velvet drapes closed.

Casmit followed hot on his heels, slamming the door shut as the driver encouraged the horses to move.

The bumpiness of the cobblestone streets had never bothered Roann before this day.

~~~

Ryris shut the door and stood at the window, berating himself as Roann's carriage pulled away. "Way to go, Bren…"

The old fortune teller's words echoed in his ears, about the world as he knew it changing. Surely once word got out that Prince Roann had become ill in his store, all bets would be off. No one would want to enter a place that nearly killed the prince. He tried to figure out how he was going to explain his move back home to Maxx. Kicking a shelf as he passed by, he grumbled as he headed for the workbench. Even if he was now unsure of what the future held for him in Keld, he was determined to make the best healing potion he had ever created. The prince deserved as much.

He got to work grinding a dried midnight beetle carapace into a fine powder. When he was satisfied it was sufficiently pulverized, he poured the contents of the mortar into a wooden bowl and went in search of his other ingredients. He knew the prince had been dizzy, and therefore more than likely nauseous. A pinch of crystallized bat skin would do the trick in combating both ailments. Now, he just had to find it.

Not completely used to the layout of the new store, it took the young alchemist a few moments to locate the ingredient he sought. He absentmindedly scratched at the skin beneath his amulet, his chest feeling dry. Ryris was taken aback when he withdrew his hand from his shirt and found his fingertips to be sooty. He quickly sniffed the substance and found it had the aroma of singed skin. Pulling open his shirt, he looked down past his chin to inspect the area. Unable to see clearly, he trotted upstairs to get a better look in his mirror. The bell on the door would alert him if he had any customers.

Sunlight beamed in through the bathroom window, allowing him to see unimpeded. He unbuttoned his shirt and drew the fabric aside. His amulet hung across his chest, the purple stone glimmering in the daylight. Lifting the talisman up, he was shocked at what he saw.

A layer of soot, black as coal, covered his skin. It didn't expand out further than the width of the amulet. Never recalling any discomfort or heat emanating from the object, Ryris was thoroughly perplexed. He knew it hadn't been there when he dressed in the morning. Confused, he tried to remember everything he had done—or touched—that morning that would have caused such a strange phenomenon. If the amulet had produced the mark, it surely would have felt hot to the touch. He inspected the charm hanging around his neck, turning it over to get a better look at the back in the mirror's reflection. Nothing had changed. There was no sign of the substance on the piece, no indication that there had been any damage. Thinking for a long moment, he decided that he more than likely touched his chest with sooty fingers after stoking the morning fire. After all, what else could it be?

Shrugging his shoulders, he sighed and returned to the shop. No use trying to figure out something that was probably nothing anyway. Maxx had always accused him of trying to read into situations way more than was warranted, and Ryris decided this was one of those times. Besides, he had a royal tincture to create.

Three hours later, the fresh potion was nestled safely in a box and on its way into the hands of the prince, via royal carriage. Ryris waved after the coach, hoping that the peace offering was enough to mend any misgivings the prince may have developed since their visit. The last thing Ryris needed was to be on the bad side of the sovereign.

~~~

"Roann?"

The prince turned at the sound of his mother's voice echoing from the foyer.

"In the den." He set his book down on his lap and threw his arm over the back of the couch. The thin short-sleeved shirt he wore hugged his muscles. Roann definitely enjoyed his 'civilian clothes', and relished every moment he could relax comfortably without a heavy doublet weighing him down. The empress, on the other hand, never wore anything but beautiful silk and satin dresses, her hair always perfectly coiffed, her makeup impeccable.

Eilith glided into the brightly-lit room, immediately coming to a stop at her son's side. She reached over and put a hand on his forehead. "Casmit told me you came home ill today?"

"It was nothing."

The empress pursed her lips as she leaned closer to inspect his eyes. She finally sat beside him, pressing her fingers to the pulse point on his wrist. "That's not what I heard. She said you were overwhelmed while visiting the new alchemist. That she had to help you back into the coach. *And* that you refused the doctor."

"She's exaggerating. The shop was filled with very powerful aromas. It just got to me." He patted her hand to reassure her. "I've been sitting here in front of the open window all afternoon, and the fresh air has cleared everything up."

Eilith narrowed her eyes, trying to decide whether or not to believe her son. She finally blew out a sharp breath from her nose. "Well, if you really think that's all it was."

"I do." Roann hoped she had been sufficiently appeased.

"Those children at the preschool were very disappointed, you know. And hopefully the Momberts won't reconsider any future donations."

Roann loved his mother, but she was one of the most passive-aggressive people he had ever met. She always tried to stay sweet and respectful, but she was a strong-willed woman and when she was displeased, she let you know it—sometimes subtly, sometimes not.

"Now mother…" The prince shifted his weight on the couch, giving Eilith more room for her flowing gown. "Casmit has already rescheduled the preschool visit for tomorrow morning, and the Momberts are coming for dinner at the end of the week. I'm sure they were more than excited to tell their friends they'd be dining at the palace. They've probably forgotten all about tea this afternoon."

"The whole neighborhood most likely knew within minutes of the courier leaving." The empress laughed and reached to take her son's hand in her own. She squeezed it lovingly. "Are you sure you're fine?"

"Yes. I've put it behind me, and so should you." Roann pointed over to the end table, at a small vial nestled within a box. "The alchemist, Bren, even sent a potion this afternoon to help me feel better."

The empress picked up the bottle and tilted it, the liquid inside sloshing around. "Did you try it?"

"No, but it was a nice gesture. I'll hang onto it in case I'm ever feeling ill like that again. I've heard through the grapevine that he's very talented, and that the shop he and his father ran in Blackthorne has been successful for many generations."

Eilith replaced the vial into the container. "Well then, I suppose there's nothing more to discuss. I'll stop fretting." She stood up, flattening out the creases in her bodice, before she offered her arm to him. "Accompany an old woman to dinner?"

Smiling, Roann set his book on the end table and stood, hooking his own arm around his mother's. "It would be my honor."

~~~

The draperies blew in the wind, the fabric flapping in the dark room. The moon was absent from the sky, having entered its new phase that evening. Atop the dresser, a pristine pink gem sat on a small velvet pedestal, inclusions within glowing brightly, giving the room its only source of light.

A figure tossed and turned in the large bed, a pillow knocked to the floor seconds later. With a start, the man sat bolt upright, raspy and uneven gasps shooting from his lips. Sitting hunched with a hand clasped to his bare chest, he waited for a moment in the darkness, trying to catch his breath.

Roann hadn't slept this poorly in ages. After what seemed like an eternity spent even trying to fall asleep, he was awakened soon after by his racing brain. The prince ran a hand through his tousled hair and sighed. He knew he wasn't going to get any sleep tonight. Throwing the covers aside, he rolled out of bed.

Something still didn't sit right with him about the events of the morning. The more he thought about the incident, the more he thought it most definitely wasn't the scent of the store or the stains on the alchemist's hands. Something was off about Bren himself. Not outwardly, for the young man was chipper and polite. But the moment he made contact with that handshake, his brain had been set ablaze with energy unlike he had ever experienced before. The sensations that coursed through him had threatened to render him unconscious. But why? Sighing with irritation, and with a headache threatening to consume him, Roann decided the only thing he could do in that moment was put it behind him.

Clad only in a pair of sleeping pants, he padded barefoot to the den, not bothering to put on his robe. He lit the oil lamp atop his desk as he sat, and immediately retrieved a sheet of his personal stationery. Dipping his quill into a pot of ink, he began to write.

Dear Mr. Bren,

I want to extend my deepest apologies once again for the incident yesterday morning. I want to assure you that in no way are you at fault for my illness. I am truly sorry I left in such haste, and am looking forward to visiting again in the future. I would very much like to pick your brain about alchemy—it is a subject that I know very little about, and would like to learn. I am confident that your shop will enjoy great successes in Keld, and you will rise to the top of your niche very quickly.

Thank you for the potion you sent to the palace, it will be put to good use, I assure you.

Best regards for the future,

Prince Roann Vrelin

Roann signed his name with a flourish. Satisfied with his communiqué, he set a small tin of wax atop the open mouth of the oil lamp. Folding the delicate parchment into thirds, he waited for the blue sealing wax to melt. When it was sufficiently liquefied, he removed the container to his desk, careful not to burn his fingers on the hot metal. He deposited a large glob of wax onto the folded edge of the paper. Wasting no time, he pressed his signet ring into the quickly cooling blob, making sure the family insignia was properly embossed. The prince set it aside to dry, ready for his assistant to deliver in the morning.

Roann extinguished the flame of the lamp, rendering the room almost completely dark. He turned in his chair and stared out at the horizon.

That morning, he saw the sun rise.

CHAPTER NINE

The martial artists hailing from Zaiterra are not to be trifled with. While trained with great discipline and morals in their hallowed school, they will not hesitate to take your life before you have time to pray it be spared.

--Excerpt from 'On Zaiterra', Eakim Whitehaven, founder of Whitehaven University

~ Six Weeks Later ~

The heavens opened up, and a chilled mid-autumn rain cascaded down over Keld.

Roann stood at the open balcony doors in his parents' bedroom. Every time the wind picked up, tiny tickles of moisture peppered his face. The breeze blew his loose hair around his shoulders. Not willing to venture outside and risk a proper soaking, he closed his eyes and let the mists flow over his body. The darkness of night encompassed the palace. Eilith cried softly behind him. He didn't bother to turn around.

The morning had started out like any other, with Roann tending to his daily duties as acting sovereign. But shortly after lunch with his mother, it became obvious the day was anything but ordinary. It had happened fast, with the emperor's breathing slowing down, his heart rate following suit. Unwilling to open his eyes, unable to take regular breaths. The prince was called away from his office, and told to prepare for the worst.

And, just after nine o'clock, Artol had taken his final, shaky breath. Eilith sobbed—and Roann was silent.

That night, a prince would become emperor.

He stood watching the torrents of water cascade from the downspouts on the parapets. Thunder rumbled behind the palace. Roann knew it was just a matter of time before the brunt of the storm hit Keld. Father Morigar's melodic voice floated through the room as he administered various blessings over his father's body. He did not pay attention to the cleric's hollow words.

Taking in the humid air in one gigantic breath, Roann allowed his lungs to fill to capacity. His muscles burned as his chest expanded. He held the breath for as long as he could, opening his eyes just before billowing out a great exhale. Lightning flashed, and he cast his gaze up toward the heavens, watching as fast-moving clouds churned in the sky. A great crash of thunder followed the brilliance, rattling the antique glass panes of the balcony doors. The prince felt a comforting hand on his shoulder, and realized the room had fallen silent.

"The rites are finished, Your Grace."

Roann didn't turn to acknowledge the figure behind him. He really didn't feel like engaging in conversation with anyone.

"Your mother's attendant has convinced her to get some rest. You should really do the same."

Roann simply nodded with a deep sigh. The cleric removed his hand from Roann's shoulder and stood quietly next to him, watching rain drench the sleeping city. When dawn's light broke over the horizon, the official criers of the Vrelin Empire would flood the streets, and the people of Keld would hear the news they knew was coming, but hoped would never arrive. That morning, Roann would be crowned. The robes of his father would be placed upon his shoulders, and the citizens would look on him for the first time as their true emperor.

"Promise me you'll sleep, Roann…"

It had been ages since the priest had referred to him by his given name. In fact, the only person to really ever do so anymore was his mother. The last time his father had spoken his name was the day of his stroke. His breath hitched ever so slightly as he realized it had been years since his father had uttered a single word. And now, any hope of that ever happening again was gone. The prince finally turned to face the cleric.

"I will. And…" He found himself grasping for words, even if they were simple. His mind was racing: thoughts of funerals, coronations, and life without his father. "…thank you. For everything you've done for my mother this evening. I know it comforted her to have you here."

The old man leaned in and embraced Roann tightly, like a father would his own son. It had been so long since he had felt the embrace of a person other than Eilith. The empress hugged him on a daily basis, but all others refrained from making such intimate physical contact with the prince. He was the sovereign, and it was deemed inappropriate to go much further than a firm handshake. Releasing from the embrace, Roann mustered a thankful smile, just barely visible in the dimly-lit room.

"Tomorrow the people will see you as emperor." Morigar's voice was strong, yet sad. "I know you will make your father proud—you already have. He's watching you from beyond, rest assured."

Roann nodded weakly and turned back to the open balcony doors as the cleric took his leave. Lightning flashed at faster intervals now, the storm bearing down on the

84

city with furious intensity. Wind whipped in through the doors, papers on his father's desk catching on the currents and flying about the room. The stationery rustled around in the corner, falling to the floor as the wind died down once again. The rain shifted direction, and the prince suddenly found himself pelted with giant drops. He hurriedly closed the doors with a grumble, not ready for his silent reverie to be broken. Now he would have to face his mother—and his father.

He knew this day was coming. And yet, now that it had become reality, and he looked upon the lifeless body of the once strong Emperor Artol—he suddenly felt very ill-equipped to carry on. Yes, he had been ruling by himself for all intents and purposes, but at the end of the day, Roann would still go to Artol for approval. The prince had learned his father's silent signals. whether it be a wink of his good eye, a small smile or frown, or a squeeze of the hand. Roann knew that his father understood what he was saying, and wanted to be as present as he could be when it came to the welfare of the nation.

And now—he was truly was on his own.

Making his way toward the slouched figure at the bedside, he hesitated for a brief moment before pressing on. Roann hated seeing his mother in such a state. Eilith was always graceful and poised. Now, she sat hunched over, her shoulders sagging, her head hanging low. Her hair fell messily over her shoulders, her gown un-pressed and wrinkled. She had been sitting there for hours, never leaving Artol's side. And now, even after his passing, she kept vigil over his corpse, unwilling to leave until the doctors came to remove him. In two days, he would lie in state before being interred within the family catacombs. The empress sobbed quietly into her handkerchief. A wedding gift from her beloved groom, the lace was old and stained from years of use.

The sound of Roann's boots on the wooden floor startled the empress, and Eilith turned in great surprise, her red swollen eyes glistening in the flickering light of the bedside lamp.

"Mother…" He took her hand in his, noting the chill on her skin. "You need to rest."

Eilith shook her head and watched him wearily as he knelt beside her. "Not until your father is taken care of." She turned back to her husband, letting go of her son's hand to take his. Staring at him longingly, she cried, tears falling down her cheeks and onto the pink satin of her dress. The droplets darkened the fabric as they soaked in, forming a dotted pattern on her skirt.

"I'll stay." He stood, urging her to follow. Resting a hand on her back, he helped her up, Eilith's legs wobbling as she left her seat. In that moment, his mother seemed so frail. It was as if all the heartbreak and stress of the last decade had finally caught up with her. Leaning down to kiss Artol's forehead, she lingered. She whispered hushed words into his ear. Whatever had been said was private, and not meant for anyone but them.

"Stay until Dr. Thal returns. Please..." Her voice was meek as she moved forward, resting her cheek on her son's chest. Her small arms snaked around his back and she cried into his doublet, soaking the velvet. Roann held his weeping mother in silence, showing no emotion of his own. He had no sense that grief would ever overtake him. Eilith finally broke the embrace and pushed back to look upon her son. She regarded him closely before placing her hand on his face, her thumb wiping a tear that was not there.

Roann licked his dry lips, a small, sorrowful nod all he could muster. Eilith kissed his cheek and moved around him toward the door, patting her husband's foot through the blankets on her way out. A lady-in-waiting took her hand and led her away.

Finally alone with his father, Roann slumped into the chair his mother had just vacated and stared at the lifeless shell in front of him. Morigar's words had been about salvation, honor, and the Goddess. About the Gentle Reach and what lies beyond for Artol. Now, sitting here looking at his father's body, he struggled to find solace in the priest's prayers. Where they were supposed to bring peace to those who heard them, to the prince they brought only skepticism. While Roann had stood at the window listening, he felt himself slip away, into his dark place. As Morigar's voice went on about tranquility and duty to Oleana, Roann had to stifle a curt laugh. It all sounded so silly. His father lay dead before him. An empty vessel, a body that would soon decompose and return to the earth. There had been no ghostly apparition floating up toward the heavens.

He snorted in the darkness, cursing his mother's Goddess. It was something he had done many times since his father had been stricken by his stroke. People always said Oleana had a plan for everything, but Roann found it very hard to believe that it included turning the emperor into a veritable vegetable. If there had ever been a time where he considered following the state religion, his father's sickness had relieved him of the need. The prince knew it was a sham. He knew it was a lie.

He knew there was something out there that was much better.

There had *always* been something better.

A chill ran up his spine, tickling the hair on the back of his neck. He smiled in the darkness, welcoming the familiar feeling. It seemed to know when it was needed. Always comforted by the spectral wind, he closed his eyes and took in a deep breath, relishing in the sudden cold air that enveloped him. In that moment, any semblance of grief abated. In that moment, he knew destiny was close at hand. In that moment—the darkness seeped completely into his soul, never to leave.

Knowing there was no need to cry over his father, Roann sat quietly twirling his signet ring as rain pelted the windowpanes above Artol's deathbed.

~~~

The storms had passed, ushering in a sun-drenched new day.

Citizens of Keld gathered in the grand square in front of the palace. The crowd was unusually solemn, there were no cheers or music. All anticipated the start of the ceremony, although many were having a hard time dealing with the reason they were all called. Sadness mingled with excitement. They had lost a beloved monarch, but would witness the heir finally taking his rightful place after so very long.

The prince had spent the morning in quiet reflection. Having slept more soundly than he had anticipated, he awoke feeling refreshed and ready to accept the destiny his father's death had bestowed upon him. As official ruler, he would see Keld into a new era of prosperity and power. As official ruler—there would be a new dawn.

He ate a small breakfast alone before joining his mother in her apartment. Together, they left the family dwellings and made their way through the palace halls arm-in-arm, guards saluting them with raised swords and shields as they passed by.

Roann stood just inside the grand doorway of the citadel, the sunlight peeking in through the slats of the wooden shutters on the lower windows. It illuminated his golden hair, tied back loosely by a silken thread. His green eyes sparkled, his signet ring polished to a mirror sheen. At Father Morigar's command, the guards on either side of the door heaved in unison, opening the palace to the outside world. The imperial horn brigade blasted the royal fanfare from all corners of the square, signaling the entrance of the heir to the Vrelin throne. Thousands of subdued cheers erupted, and Roann exited for the last time as their prince, his mother on his arm. Dressed in the deep blue hues that had been the defining colors of his family for generations, he held his head high, his shoulders squared. Not once did he squint in the glaring sun. A pair of attendants followed directly behind them, the crown and robes of his late father resting on a velvet-lined litter. The sea of people before him bowed, their movement resembling an enormous wave. The trumpeters ceased, and the square was quiet.

Roann stared out at the people—his people. As he came to a stop at the top of the sprawling stone steps of the palace, he let go of his mother's arm. Raising his hands above his head, he gestured to the citizens to rise once more. The crowd finally bellowed a cry of hail and raised their own arms to mirror that of their sovereign in solidarity. Their prince had given them permission to celebrate. After a moment, they quieted and waited for the ceremony to begin.

Father Morigar moved forward, his robes of office wisping just above the ground. He pressed his hands together to begin the invocation. "Today we come together as an empire to mourn the passing of Artol the Honorable. His devotion to his country was unsurpassed, his love for his family expansive. Oleana is surely honored to finally have such an incredible man at her side. Let us pray she blesses our late emperor as he begins his new life in the Gentle Reach."

Roann tried not to roll his eyes at the mention of the deity, but dutifully lowered his head as the cleric led the citizens in prayer. His words floated around the city center, the people repeating meaningful phrases back to him in unison. After a long benediction, he continued with the ceremony.

"Let us remember that our beloved former sovereign bestowed upon us a great gift—that of his son, Prince Roann. When his father could not, the prince took the helm of the empire and brought even more glory upon our shores. And it is with great honor to every citizen in the realm that today, as you all witness, he will be crowned true emperor."

Pride filled Roann's chest. The country was now unequivocally his, to do with as he pleased. His mother moved from beside him, approaching the litter containing the royal vestments. Morigar assisted her in removing the heavy velvet robe from its seat.

"As the Empress places the imperial robes on the shoulders of her only child, a torch is passed from one generation to another."

Eilith stood on her tiptoes as she draped the royal garment over her son's broad back. The weight of the cloth felt sensational. He felt a gentle touch on his arm through the fabric, and turned to gaze into his mother's eyes. She smiled softly, overcome simultaneously with pride and grief. Roann knew this was his cue to kneel before her.

He dropped to the ground and turned sideways to face his mother, one knee resting on the sparkling stone of the staircase. Morigar moved behind him, retrieving the golden, jeweled crown of the empire. He hadn't seen it in a long time, Artol having no need to wear it in the last ten years. It had been safely locked away in the palace keep, under the watchful eye of the royal quartermaster. And now, it was to be his.

Eilith lovingly cupped her son's cheek before accepting the crown from the old priest. Raising it above their heads for all to see, it shone in the bright sunlight, the diamonds and sapphires gleaming across the expanse of the square. Her voice was strong as she spoke, no hint of sadness.

"Today I crown you, my one and only son, Emperor Roann the First. You shall be known throughout the Vrelin Empire as Roann the Devoted, a title personally chosen by myself as a sign of your devotion not only to your country, but to your family. Wear the crown with pride, son. Rule with honor." A tear slipped down her cheek as she placed the crown atop her son's golden locks. She beckoned him to rise with her delicate hand and presented him to the crowd.

"All hail Roann the Devoted!" Father Morigar's voice was booming, echoing off the masonry of the palace.

"All hail Roann the Devoted!" The crowd parroted the cleric's words back to him, as they erupted in thunderous applause. Trumpeters blared in symphony, ushering in a new history for the people of the empire.

Standing there, the exuberance of the crowd and the harmony of the bugles rattling through his bones, Roann was suddenly overcome with emotion. He would make sure his name would be remembered throughout the annals of history. Stepping forward, he raised his hands to quiet the cheers of his people. They instantly obeyed, a reverent hush falling over the crowd as they waited in anticipation. He hadn't prepared a speech, deciding the night before to speak from his heart as the words came to him.

"Citizens of Keld...people of the realm! Last night my father took his final breath. While we mourn his loss, we must not forget to look ahead to the future. Today I stand before you as your emperor and give you my undying word that the Vrelin Empire will grow even stronger!"

At the back of the crowd, legendary Zaiterran weaponmaster Isum Dran leaned against the side of a tavern, watching the new emperor address his subjects. He studied the young man's body language, unable to clearly hear what he was saying.

The surrounding crowd stood on tip-toes and held their hands to their ears in an attempt to see and hear better. An elderly man pressed a horn into his ear and turned it toward the palace. A young woman tapped him on the shoulder and asked for a recap.

"He says we need to grow stronger!"

The young lady scowled. "Huh? We're not strong enough already?"

"Shush! I can't hear!" The old man turned his horn to the speaking emperor once more. He chewed on his lower lip as he concentrated on Roann's words.

Arms crossed over his chest, Dran kept his eyes trained on the young emperor. His confidence was stellar, his smile broad. He had the air of a man with no care for anyone but himself, even if the people couldn't discern it. But to Dran, it was obvious that Roann had changed. He stroked his thin braided beard, fingers lingering on the single bead knotted at the bottom.

"Now he says 'we need to regain the respect of the world'. What the devil is he talking about?" The old man furrowed his eyebrows and shook his head.

"Maybe you didn't hear him right." The young woman grabbed his hearing horn and re-adjusted it in his ear.

"I know what I heard!" He swatted her hand away.

"What does he mean by that?" Another person in the crowed chimed in.

A blacksmith offered his opinion. "I don't care what he means... just so long as my taxes don't go up."

The crowd around them grumbled in agreement.

"He's going to lead us all to prosperity, you'll see!" An old woman beamed and thrust her fist into the air in Roann's direction.

Isum Dran pushed himself off of the wall with a sigh, having seen and heard enough. He let his gaze linger on the new emperor for a few seconds before turning his back and walking away. Roann's words still carried across the square.

"...We do not know what the future holds, but I ask you to embark on this journey with me—to our collective destiny!"

The crowd exploded with excitement, waving banners in honor of their new emperor. People jumped up and down, hoisted children onto their shoulders to gain a better view. A woman near the front of the group blew her emperor a kiss.

Roann held out a hand to his mother, who accepted the gesture with a warm smile. Together, they looked out at the people.

Roann the Devoted had been born again.

The chill spectral wind tickled his neck once more.

~~~

The sound of metal clanking together echoed down the hallway.

The hour was late, close to midnight. Hidden near the palace's unused dungeon, a cavernous, circular room sat with its door cracked slightly for ventilation. Light flickered from within, the wall sconces blazing brightly. The aroma of sweat lingered in the air.

Two men lunged at each other, wielding blades of incomparable quality. The older of the two swung a mighty longsword, his movements fluid and grand. Moving precisely and with purpose, he carefully danced with his opponent, trying to outsmart him. The younger man taunted his foe, flicking twin katanas in front of his body. Every so often he would use one of the blades to beckon his opponent, tempting him to make his next attack. Their swords clashed time and time again, both men showing no signs of fatigue.

"Is that all you've got, old man?"

The weaponmaster wiped his sweaty brow with the back of his hand before charging at the new emperor with a hearty battle cry. Their blades struck together with incredible force, the young man catching his opponent's sword-edge in-between his dual blades. He flung his arms wide with a boastful laugh, releasing his hold on the sword with a mighty grunt. The weaponmaster was hurtled backwards from the force, his blade knocked from his hand. It clattered to the ground a few feet away from them.

Both eyeing the discarded longsword, the men made a move for it, pushing each other out of the way to claim the prize. Bodies slammed together, long golden hair came loose from its tie. The older man managed to bash his shoulder into the younger man's flank, giving himself a moments' advantage. It was all the time he needed, and he grabbed the sword with ease. A polished metal ring, with a small inlaid crystal, glinted on his finger.

"You might be younger than me ...but I'm smarter!" Isum Dran lunged at Roann.

The emperor parried his mentor's thrusting blade, narrowly missing the sharpened tip. Blowing an errant strand of hair from his face, Roann wrung his fingers tightly around his weapons' hilts and made his own move. Whipping his twin blades around in a furious whirlwind, he steadily forced his way forward, backing his opponent against the wall.

"Smarter? If you're so smart, why did you allow yourself to be cornered?" Roann swung feverishly at the older man, his fervor consuming him. He felt alive, empowered. There were few things he enjoyed more in life than training with Isum. Artol had requested his talents when Roann was a child, and the two had been together ever since. Isum treated the young prince-now-emperor as if he was his very own son— which included swift punishments for not progressing in a manner he deemed acceptable. Roann had endured whacks on the back with fake wooden swords when he didn't listen as a young boy, countless hours of training that left him bruised and bloodied. But in the end, Isum had crafted a formidable warrior in the young man, and his pride showed.

"I let you corner me, you smug bastard!" Isum pushed forward, his blade clashing with Roann's. "The old tactic dictates that you lull your enemy into a false sense of security before delivering a striking blow!"

"Bastard? That's no way to talk to the emperor!" Roann smirked, enjoying banter that, had it come out of the mouth of any other person, would have ended with imprisonment. "I'll have you beheaded!"

Isum snorted, before bellowing out a great laugh. "You'd have to catch me first!" The older man darted around his student, catching Roann off guard. Like lightning, the master had grabbed Roann's wrist and applied a painful pressure pinch on the nerves, causing the young emperor to drop one of his swords. Isum kicked the discarded katana out of the way to prevent his captive from re-arming himself.

Unwilling to admit defeat, Roann roared as he locked his knees to give himself more leverage. Bending his entire body, and using Isum's mighty grip on his arm to his advantage, the emperor flung his teacher over his back, slamming him to the floor. Isum grunted as the wind was knocked from his lungs, wincing as his body made contact with the stone tiles. Roann hovered over him, the point of his sword barely touching the soft skin of his throat.

"I win!" The young man was panting, sweat rolling down his bare back. Strands of hair stuck to his flushed cheeks. But, the look in Isum's eyes told him the older man was nowhere near finished with him.

"Just because you've pinned me doesn't mean you're victorious!" Isum swung his leg up and around, a daring move considering he had a blade at his neck. One wrong move and it would have pierced his throat. He hooked his foot around and tugged at the back of Roann's knee, knocking him to the ground. His sword went clattering to the floor, his hand releasing its grip on the hilt as his body smashed down. Isum laughed heartily as he rolled away.

Roann saw stars as the back of his skull connected with the floor and, for a moment, he thought he might black out. As he recovered from the haze, he decided that this battle would not end in such a manner. There was no way he was going to let Isum brag about besting him like this. Shaking the fog from his head, he struggled to get up. His wits returning, Roann was able to grab one of his swords before his partner could. He lunged at Isum once more, the older man barely having enough time to arm himself.

The new emperor swung at him ferociously, even as fatigue ate away at his muscles. He felt as if he was faltering, but would not give up. The adrenaline of the day wouldn't allow it. Time and time again, Roann crashed his blade against that of his master, the song of the metal echoing off the stone walls. Isum, equally tired, tried to keep up. Both men dueled as if their lives depended on victory. Roann could feel the blood pumping through his veins, hear his heart thundering in his ears.

He would not lose.

Isum's strikes were precise and vicious, even in his exhaustion. With every blow rained down upon him, Roann's bones screamed for reprieve, his body begging him to surrender. He was slipping. They danced in a grand circle around the middle of the oval-shaped room, relentlessly deluging one another with hammering blows. It was only a matter of time before one of them gave up. Roann, feeling his grip loosen on his remaining blade, forced himself to outlast his teacher. It was times like this, when he was at his weakest point, that Isum had taught him to dip into energy reserves and make sure he wasn't taken down. Roann, however, wasn't sure his reserves even existed this evening. And, as if on cue, his moment of weakness finally came. His concentration faltered for a split second, allowing his opponent to strike.

92

Isum's blade nicked Roann's forearm, blood instantly trickling from the wound. Darkness suddenly cascaded over the emperor as the crimson liquid splattered on the floor, a seething fury bubbling up from the pit of his stomach. Like a rabid animal, Roann dropped his weapon and lunged for his trainer, grabbing him by the throat. Isum, in a surprised state, let go of his longsword as his student used the weight of his body to slam him against the wall. Roann held him there like a man possessed, his grip tightening with every ragged breath he took. The older man clawed at his hands as his face began to turn red.

Roann no longer inhabited his own body. Bristling rage took over and he continued to squeeze, watching Isum's eyes bulge. His expression hardened into a malicious smirk as the old man struggled to breathe.

"L-let go!" Isum slammed his closed fists against Roann's flanks, trying to get him to respond. Never in his life had he witnessed him act in such a way. His instinct to counterattack kicked in, and he reached down to his waistband. He grabbed the hilt of a small, concealed dagger, and had to make a split-second decision—defend himself with deadly force or just teach Roann a lesson. His thoughts were starting to fade as his oxygen supply was cut off.

Narrowing his eyes, Roann crushed his fingers tighter around Isum's throat.

Dran knew he had to react. He drew the dirk and flicked it against Roann's bare skin, slicing a short gash into the young emperor's flank. Roann immediately let go and recoiled away, bringing a hand across his abdomen to cradle the new wound.

The old man scrambled away and brought his hand up to massage the angry flesh of his throat. "You're a crazy son-of-a-bitch, you know that? You could have killed me!" He spluttered and coughed, trying to catch his breath. "And just because I marked you? You had fire in your eyes, boy!"

Roann looked down at his bleeding arm and abdomen, finally feeling the sting of the wounds as his adrenaline wore off. As—the power wore off. Nausea flowed over him and he sank down onto his rear end with a huff before hanging his head between his knees.

Dran moved to his side and sat down, his dagger still clutched in his hand, ready to strike back again if need be. "I'm chalking that asinine fighting tactic up to your grief-stricken state." The old man slapped him on the shoulder, leaving a reddened handprint on Roann's sweaty skin. "But if you think I'm going to let you get away with that garbage in the future, you're sorely mistaken. Never again."

Roann lifted his head as the old man rose next to him. Isum extended a hand, which he accepted. Heaving himself up off the ground, he looked his mentor in the eyes as he steadied himself. "Never again."

"Good. I think it's best if you take a break from training for a while. Give yourself some time. The arena will be here when you're ready."

Roann just nodded. It wasn't what he wanted to hear, but he knew the old man had a point. A distracted warrior makes mistakes. He was fairly certain Isum didn't want to be strangled again.

Dran leaned over to scrutinize Roann's abdominal gash, reaching out to lightly touch the bleeding wound. "You're lucky I didn't have it in my mind to kill you where you stood. It's not deep, just bandage it for a day or two. Get some rest. If you leave your blades, I'll give them a sharpen in the morning." Isum left the arena without another word.

Roann moved to retrieve his precious twin katanas from the floor, and placed them on Isum's worktable for service the next day. He ran his hand over the leather-wrapped hilt of one before drawing his thumb up and over the blade. Careful not to cut himself, he allowed his fingertips to linger over the shining metal for a moment before backing away. The young man grabbed a roll of gauze bandages from Isum's aid kit and wrapped his abdomen. He relished in the pain radiating from the tortured flesh as he pulled the gauze tight. As he slipped into his shirt, blood from his wounded arm immediately seeped through the thin fabric.

He buttoned up, and found himself missing the surge of power that had enveloped him. He was no stranger to the feeling, having been experiencing it since he was a child. It gave him confidence, strength, and determination.

Roann sighed deeply and blew out the oil lamps encircling the room. Standing in complete darkness, he waited. He knew it was just a matter of time. A few moments passed, the aroma of smoldering wicks lingering in the air.

Finally, the hair on the back of his neck stood on end and his skin prickled with goose bumps. He smiled in the pitch-black, welcoming the familiar feeling he craved. Inhaling deeply, the temperature of the room dropped as he filled his lungs with the chilled air. Once again, the thing he needed most had come.

Outside, fog enveloped the palace.

CHAPTER TEN

Aegis Mold: Thick blue- green mold that grows on cave walls high in the Screaming Peaks. Used in potions providing a temporary boost in defense, hence the name "aegis." Also known as 'slime mold.'

--Excerpt from 'An Alchemist's Primer', Sholden Witt, Professor of Alchemy, Whitehaven University

Ryris shifted uncomfortably on the wagon seat.

Ass of the East shuffled along, munching on a mouthful of hay. He had only been traveling for four days, and already cursed the route. The road—if you could even call it that—was bumpy and full of ruts, the wagon wheels bouncing violently over every pothole. At least the scenery was nice, he thought, as he rubbed his battered rear end.

The trail heading north out of the Crossroads Market wasn't considered a main thoroughfare, and therefore was relatively un-crowded. The trading hub had been his final stop—and chance to stock up on supplies—before he entered wilder country. As the Screaming Peaks loomed on the far horizon, he was reminded that his destination was a far cry from the city.

After restocking and enjoying a quick lunch at a meat pie stall—not as good as Keld, of course—Ryris meandered his wagon back onto the Snow Road, headed for Hewe. He had another two days in ever-increasing wilderness before he reached the village at the foot of the mountain.

The road was surrounded by old growth trees, towering a hundred feet or more in the air. A few lingering leaves of orange and red still clung tightly to the branches, but for the most part the canopy was barren. The fallen foliage took on a musky, wet smell on the forest floor. Birds called to their mates as they insulated their nests, small mammals stuffed their mouths full of acorns and berries to prepare for the approaching winter famine. He enjoyed the peacefulness of the trail.

Ryris adjusted his knit scarf, a parting gift from one of the doddering ladies in the neighborhood. He had assured her the weather was going to be just fine, not too cold, but she insisted he take it with. The memory made him smile, knowing the old woman was now looking after his shop. It wasn't that he thought she would slack in her duties, but now that he was a business owner, he was fiercely protective over his brand and property. The jeweler down the street even agreed to stock some potions in case the young alchemist's customers needed a quick fix. Ryris didn't anticipate being gone any longer than three weeks, and had left a sign in the window telling his patrons where to find his goods in his absence.

The Screaming Peaks loomed in the distance, his destination just at the bottom of the slopes. The towering pinnacles looked foreboding, their dark stone faces covered with snow almost to the ground. Trees dotted the sides, jagged, rocky precipices seemingly hanging on the sky itself. He had visited the area several times with Maxx, but had always approached from the east, giving him a very different view from what he was currently witnessing. Now, making his way from the south, he was awestruck at the height of the peaks. They soared into the sky, tickling the clouds that floated past.

The ingredient he was after—aegis mold—resided on the walls of dank mountain caves. It grew wildly in the summer, but was almost impossible to harvest until the winter gales dried it out. The window for extraction was small—too early and it stuck like glue to the cavern walls, too late and the winter winds would knock you off the slopes before you ever got close. There was a quaint village at the base of the mountain path that led to the summit of Mount Nevet, the tallest of the range. Ryris planned to stay at the inn, making a pseudo-base camp for his travels up to the caves. Remembering back to the days of hunting with his father, he recalled that every time they went back, the mold was more and more sparse. Deciding to take a risk, he set his sights on the opposite side of the mountain. The area he was scouting was uncharted as far as alchemical harvesting was concerned, and he hoped his hunch of an untouched bounty would pay off.

Ryris repositioned his rear end once more. He reminded himself that when he finally arrived in Hewe, he would be able to enjoy a hot beverage and hearty meal. Looking off to the horizon, he saw dark clouds billowing in the northwest. A cold wind picked up, assaulting his face with blowing leaves.

~~~

The Foolish Pig Tavern and Inn was warm and inviting despite the strange name.

When he arrived in the small hamlet of Hewe, Ryris had just enough time to cover his wagon before the snow fell. By the time he had gathered his belongings and headed toward the inn, the flakes were flying with such intensity they stung his face. Although it reminded him of home, he wasn't prepared to encounter snow so soon. Acclimated to the balmy weather of Keld, he found himself irritated to once again encounter winter's wrath. Sitting at a small table in the center of the room, he cradled the steaming cup of hot chocolate between his frozen fingers and inhaled the sweet aroma. Instantly, his hands began to thaw and, as he drank deeply, his body warmed.

A bard sat against the far wall, picking away on a lute as he sang a tune about giants. Two men laughed obnoxiously at the bar, obviously enjoying their mead. At the table next to Ryris, a father and his kids fought over who got the last roll in the basket. The older man settled the argument by grabbing the pastry and stuffing it into his mouth with a satisfied smirk. A steaming pot pie appeared in front of Ryris, the friendly waitress handing him a spoon with a smile. "House specialty. You won't find one better in all the empire."

He smiled his acknowledgement and dug in. Ravenous from his journey, he regretfully forgot to blow a cooling breath on his first bite. The roof of his mouth immediately felt like it was coated in lava. An emergency drink from his hot chocolate did nothing to squelch the fire of molten potatoes and cream sauce currently burning his tongue to a cinder.

A hand tapped his shoulder, and he turned to see the roll-stealing man, holding out a glass of water. Ryris greedily accepted the cup and drank until it was empty. Wiping his mouth with an embarrassed smile, he painfully mumbled to his savior. "Thank you for saving what's left of my mouth."

"Been there, done that." The man winked. "Where'd you wander in from? I can tell you're not from around here…your clothes are too nice."

"Keld. By way of Blackthorne, actually."

The man's expression fell somber. "Keld, eh? Sad business about the emperor. Real sad. He was a good man." The man took a long draught from a battered ale mug. "What brings you all the way up here?"

"Ingredients." Ryris extended his hand for the man to shake. "I'm an alchemist. Name's Ryris Bren."

The man accepted the gesture, squeezing Ryris' hand firmly. "Erold Lythe." He pointed to the pair of siblings accompanying him. "And these are my boys, Alix and Jord."

"Nice to meet you. Say, you wouldn't happen to know anything about the caves up on the mountain, would you?" Ryris pointed out the window at the peak, shrouded in snow flurries and darkness. "I'm looking for a very specific item."

Erold motioned to his sons. "These two can tell you, I reckon. Even though I tell them not to go up there—I know they do." He gave them an all-knowing eye. Embarrassed, the boys looked away, pretending to be distracted by the dancing bard.

"Have either of you heard of aegis mold?"

The two boys looked at each other, shrugging their shoulders. The older of the two siblings spoke for both of them. "Can't say that we have."

Ryris took a small book from his satchel, thumbing through the well-worn pages. He stopped at a picture of a greenish-yellow substance. Leaning over to set it on their table, he tapped the image. "Looks like this. In the summer it's wet and squishy, but right about now it'll get dried out. The green color will deepen and it'll start to flake off the sides of the cave walls."

Jord brought the book closer to him and his brother, scrutinizing it. After a moment, he finally replied. "Y'know…I have seen this stuff. There're a few caves above town that have it. It really stinks."

Ryris chuckled. "That it does. But it's essential in a lot of potions that enhance personal defense. It's a hot seller—and I'm almost out back at my shop."

The younger child chimed in, his eyes widened in awe of the mystery alchemist. "Do you cook the mold?"

"Sort of." Ryris accepted his book back from the older boy as he continued. "It's really dry and flaky, so I mix it with something called 'base fluid' before I boil it in a crucible with some other things. It's really thick and smelly at first, so it needs to bubble for a long time. It sticks to the side of the beaker like glue. After it's finally thinned out, I put the liquid into something called an alembic. It distills the potion, and increases the potency. It takes a while to get it just right, but it's worth it."

"Sounds gross." Alix wrinkled his nose in disgust.

"Got that right." Ryris winked. "But that's the fun part of alchemy. Sometimes you know what's going to happen…and sometimes no matter how prepared you are, it still blows up in your face." Both boys laughed as he gestured an explosion with his hands, before turning his attention back to Erold. "Is there a merchant in town that can restock me on some essentials before I head up the mountain?"

"If you need weapons, I'm your man. Otherwise, go see my brother-in-law at The Wolf's Wrath; he's got everything else you'll need—and then some."

"The Wolf's Wrath? Interesting name."

"The idiot got bit by one decades ago, before he ever opened the store. Lost a few fingers. My sister named the place to remind him of his stupidity." Erold smiled devilishly, obviously amused by his relative's misfortune. Then he flagged the waitress down so he could pay her. "When are you planning to go up the mountain? The path starts right outside of to—"

Jord interrupted. "I can show you where the caves are. You'll never make it up there by yourself."

"Now Jord…" Erold scolded. "It ain't right to assume this young man can't handle himself out in the wilderness."

Ryris raised a hopeful eyebrow. "Actually, a guide would be nice. If you'll allow it, that is. I don't want to put your son in unnecessary danger. I'll pay him, of course. It'll be an honest days' work."

Erold thought for a long moment before slapping Jord on the back. "My boys are tough. They'll get you to the caves."

Ryris held out his hand to Jord. "Deal?"

The teen shook the alchemist's hand firmly. "Deal. Alix and I can meet you at the trailhead tomorrow morning at dawn. Dress warm, it gets really cold up there. And bring water and some food, just in case we get stranded."

"Stranded?"

Alix took over the conversation. "It happens. You can just hide in a cave and wait out the storms. We'll bring a fire starter stone just in case. Don't worry, we won't let you die or anything."

Ryris had to laugh slightly as he replied. The thought of dying on the mountain wasn't something he had anticipated, so he brushed it off to save his sanity. He didn't want to give himself nightmares. Maybe the kids were just being dramatic to get more pay at the end of the day. "I appreciate it."

Erold stood, his boys following. "C'mon now, let's give Mr. Bren some peace so he can enjoy his dinner. Should be plenty cool by now." He offered Ryris a sly wink.

Ryris also stood, shaking the older man's hand one last time. "Thanks for lending me your sons."

"They're good boys, they won't lead you astray."

Jord and Alix shuffled past him, the younger boy looking up at the alchemist. "See you tomorrow, Mr. Bren."

"Tomorrow." He smiled at the boy before sitting once again. Ryris nervously poked at the still-steaming pie with his fork.

~~~

The morning was cold, Ryris' breath lingering on the crisp air as he exhaled. A few inches of snow had fallen overnight, coating the rooftops in white splendor. Looking out the door of the inn, he could imagine himself stepping out of his father's shop in Blackthorne, off to the bakery on a snowy morning to get a loaf of bread.

He walked toward the back of town, where the two Lythe boys waited at the start of the trail. Each had a large pack on their shoulders, the older brother tightening his sibling's straps as they stood in wait. Hewe still slept, the chimneys on the houses puffing gently. The stores were closed, the square empty. The only sounds permeating the hamlet this morning were the crunching of snow beneath the alchemist's feet and the armorer stoking his forge in anticipation of the days' work. As he approached, the younger boy waved excitedly.

"Hi, Mr. Bren!" Alix' face lit up like a lantern, while his brother stood back and observed. It was obvious to Ryris that Jord was very protective of his brother, and was watching them very closely. He knew the boys trusted him—as did their father—but, after all, he was still a stranger. The older sibling was well within his right to be cautious until he felt comfortable.

Ryris picked up his walking pace, meeting up with the youngest Lythe. The boy held out a small, condensed bar, studded with grains and berries. "I brought you something for breakfast."

Accepting the offering, he inhaled its delicate scent. "Home made?"

"Our mom picked the fruit herself. I'm sure she'd give you more if you wanted."

Jord came up behind his brother, punching him in the arm, like brothers do. Alix went to hit him back, but stopped himself, keeping eye contact with Ryris. The alchemist could tell he was trying to behave in his presence. Never having a brother to share his time with, Ryris envied the two. It was obvious Alix looked up to his older sibling—and now to him. The way the younger boy looked on him with awe, especially last night when he was talking about his craft, made him wonder if Alix might even have alchemical aspirations.

"Mornin', Mr. Bren." Jord looked up at the cloudy sky. "We better not dawdle, looks like it might snow again later."

"Please, call me Ryris." He turned his attention to the mountains looming before them. "You think we should wait another day?"

"Nah. If it does snow, I don't think it'll be much. Just enough to be annoying..." Jord tousled his brother's hair with a mischievous grin. "...like Alix."

"Shut up, Jord!" Alix kicked his brother's shin and turned to pout.

Ryris shook his head with a laugh. He motioned to the mountain trail. "Shall we, then?"

Both boys nodded in agreement, Alix staying well away from his brother. Ryris hoped their tiff wouldn't affect their journey. He knew the old adage, 'boys will be boys', but he really did have business to take care of, and his need for the ingredient was pressing. If he missed this small harvest window, he would have to wait until next winter. And that meant he would have to pay an arm and a leg for the mold from a specialty merchant.

Hours passed as they traversed the winding mountain path. The boys chattered away about their village, answering all of Ryris' questions regarding the surrounding area. According to the brothers, Hewe and the small province it resided in was quiet and kept to itself. They hadn't received a royal visit since before both boys were born. Their father was the town weapon smith, and their mother managed the small shop from which Erold sold his creations. Most of the men in the village worked in a crumbling silver mine in the valley to the east. The jewelry made from the spoils fetched a high price all over the kingdom.

Ryris learned that Alix enjoyed swimming in the cold mountain pools and climbing trees. It seemed he was definitely the more talkative of the two siblings, Jord only piping in when a query was directed at him—or when his brother answered incorrectly. Jord was very studious and precise when he spoke, reminding Ryris quite a bit of his younger self. When the alchemist had asked the older boy what he strived to be as an adult, he was very matter-of-fact in his answer. His father was a blacksmith and he would be a blacksmith. Both boys were being trained in the art of the smithy, although Alix wanted to attend Whitehaven University— for what, he didn't quite know yet. Jord had become quite talented at the craft, and fully intended to take over the family business when his father retired. There was a striking sense of pride in the young man when he spoke of his family talent, and Ryris suddenly felt himself missing Blackthorne. The young man snapped him out from his brief melancholy when he unsheathed a beautifully ornate short sword for him to inspect.

Ryris marveled at the craftsmanship. He accepted it with reverence; he could tell the weapon was lovingly made. The hilt was wrapped in red leather embossed with runes, the silver pommel shining brightly even on the cloudy morning. The blade shone with brilliance Ryris had never seen before, intricate swirls etched into the very metal it was struck from.

"This is incredible. Did your father make it?" Ryris handed the weapon back to its owner, the teen sheathing it at his side.

"I did." Jord's face beamed with pride.

Ryris was gob smacked. Jord couldn't have been more than seventeen years old, and yet he produced such incredible work that most seasoned blacksmiths couldn't even dream of. "This must have taken you forever."

"Six weeks." Jord sighed and shook his head at the memories. "I worked on it after school and when I wasn't helping my father. This is the third try, mind you. The others—well, they ain't as pretty."

"No one is good at something their first go-around. If you heard half the stories about my failed potions…"

Alix interjected. "It blows up in your face, right?"

"Exactly!" Ryris took his pack off and let it drop unceremoniously to the snowy path. He stretched his arms up above his head with a pained grunt. "What do you say we take a breather for a few minutes? My back is killing me."

The boys silently agreed with a shrug of their shoulders and also let their knapsacks tumble to the ground. Moments later, Jord produced a few strips of jerky, and offered one to his new companion. They ate in silence, enjoying the peacefulness of the mountain slope. The breeze was light, and the sun poked through the clouds every few minutes, casting momentary warmth on their chilled bodies. Ryris was definitely glad he wore gloves and a warm coat, because it became increasingly colder the higher they traveled. Alix' voice brought him out of his reverie.

"Hey Jord, are we going to tell him about the cave lady?" He immediately regretted his impulsive, unthinking decision to bring the subject up, and clapped his hands over his mouth. The older boy gasped and looked at him incredulously. Jord slapped the back of his brother's head sharply.

Ryris was suddenly very intrigued. "A lady? What lady?"

Jord shot his brother a stern warning glance. "N-nothing. He's making up stories."

The alchemist wasn't buying his answer. There was something—or someone—in the caverns, and he wanted to know more. "Alix doesn't seem to think it's a story."

"Way to go, dummy." Jord stared his brother down as he hesitated, then sighed deeply. He pursed his lips as he decided whether or not to explain. He tossed his jerky into the bushes with a huff and began speaking again. "It's not like you'll believe us anyway. You'll just think we're stupid kids."

Ryris leaned closer to the sitting boys, beckoning them to listen with his finger. "Let me tell you something you might not realize. I love mysteries. I love strange things, history, artifacts, you name it. And I most certainly believe you. Listen, you had me at 'lady in a cave'." He paused, watching the boys for their reaction. When they said nothing, he continued. "Tell me about her. Please?"

Alix looked to his brother for approval. Jord shrugged his shoulders and motioned for him to speak.

"We were playing up here one day, you know, exploring. We smelled something awful coming from one of the caves. It was dead oinox! So, we harvested the teeth to sell later." Jord loudly cleared his throat and nudged his brother. "Okay...*Jord* harvested the teeth while I watched. Then there were these brer-rats fighting over the oinox meat and one ran away into the corner. And then we decided to check out the cave more, and that's when we found her."

"She was just sitting there in the rear of a dark cave?" He imagined a withered old woman, mumbling some insane chants as she enticed the boys into her lair.

102

"Not exactly." Alix looked sheepishly down at his feet, kicking the pebbles of the path. "We…found this hole."

"Hole?"

"You see…we were sorta…"

Jord finished his brother's sentiment, exasperated. "We didn't *find* the hole, we made it. Alix kicked the wall when he was trying to get away from me."

The younger boy grumbled at his brother. "You were squeezing me too tight! See, there was this little rat, and Jord didn't want to save it…he said I'd get bone rot if it bit me. But I wanted to free it, and…"

"Shut up Alix, he doesn't care about the damn rat!"

Ryris held up a hand to stop the bickering. "Have you told anyone about the woman? Or the cave?"

"No. There's still some bones left to salvage from the oinox and we don't want anyone to take our treasure." Ryris nodded his acknowledgement and let Jord continue. "And no one in the village would believe us anyway. They'd probably just want to wreck everything in the room if we told them."

"Room? There's a room? What's in it? What does the lady look like? Is she alive? Dead? Did she talk to you?" Ryris couldn't contain his excitement, and knew he probably sounded like a raving lunatic with his excessive questioning. He and the boys just might be on the precipice of some significant historical discovery, or perhaps close to uncovering an ancient crime. Whatever it was, he was determined to get a glimpse of the mysterious cavern woman.

"It would be easier if we just showed you." Jord stood and put his pack back on. "C'mon Alix, get a move on. This is all your fault anyway—you and your big mouth." He began to walk, then stopped short and whirled around to face Ryris. "You promise you won't tell anyone? Or take any of our bones?"

Ryris put his hand over his heart. "I swear. I won't tell a soul, and your treasure is yours to keep."

Jord narrowed his eyes as he inhaled deeply through his nose. "I guess we can trust you."

Ryris silently followed the two boys as they continued up the mountain path. At seemingly no particular point, they veered off the trail and began to hike up the ragged, rocky slope. Soon, they reached a small clearing and just ahead, the mouth of a cave.

An old, rotten smell wafted out from the opening.

Ryris barely fit through the small hole the brothers had excavated in the brittle cavern wall.

His coat caught on a jagged rock edge, tearing a hole in the sleeve. He grumbled, knowing he wouldn't be able to fix it until he got back to Keld. As he pulled himself through the opening, he found the air to be stale, yet clean. A far cry from the horrible odor produced by the carcass near the maw of the cave. A faint lavender glow illuminated the chamber, the light producing an instant calming effect on him. He felt completely content, like he could stay here forever.

Alix tugged on his arm and pointed to the side. "She's over there."

Setting his knapsack down next to a bookshelf, he removed his gloves and took a moment to inspect his surroundings before moving further into the room. Weapons hung on racks, bottles and books lined multiple shelves. Everything looked old, yet perfectly preserved. He couldn't help but be extremely intrigued by the beautiful crystalline weapons displayed. Never in his life had he seen anything like it. Never had he...

...crystal.

Ryris suddenly found himself unable to breathe. He had to see the woman. To see if—it was *true*.

Slowly approaching the other side of the room, his eyes rested on the giant sarcophagus on the floor, made of opaque crystal. His feet crunched on the dried flower petals fallen to the floor. Licking his wind-chapped lips, he gingerly placed his hands on the object, the cool crystal smooth against his fingertips. It vibrated under his hands, and he knew he was standing in front of a machine. What the mechanism did, he had no idea. Ryris leaned forward and peered over the top.

And there she was.

His breath hitched in his chest. She was beautiful, laying there holding her bow, it was if she was suspended in time. Ryris had no idea how long she had been here, how long she had waited to be discovered. He ran his fingers over the smooth glass cover, tracing the outline of her face. The room closed in around him, and he could no longer hear the hum of the machinery or the movement of the boys.

Nothing else mattered but this woman.

His legs felt as if they were going to buckle beneath him at any moment. His childhood came flooding back, all the memories of Gran and her stories. But, they weren't just stories anymore. He was looking at the real thing, right in front of him.

The Crystal Guard was real.

She was real.

His eyes closed, hoping that when he opened them again, he would still be there, in the presence of history. His mind pulled him in, and for a moment, he could hear his grandmother's voice reverberating in his head. He saw his house, smelled the fireplace, and hung on her every word.

"...their armor glittered, crafted from unimaginably strong crystals harvested from ancient mines. Their weapons shone brightly, whether there was natural light or murky darkness, almost as if they gave off their own illumination. They fought valiantly against the evil armies of the damned, risking their lives to save the innocent. And risk their lives they did..."

Gran had been right all along, even when Maxx told her to stop telling him such silly stories. Here he was, looking history in the face. Ryris longed to reach out and touch her, to ensure that he wasn't hallucinating.

"You okay, Ryris?" Alix' voice was laced with concern. "You kind of went off into the clouds for a minute."

"Y-yeah. I just..." He stared at the warrior encased in her protective cocoon. "...I can't believe it's actually true."

"You can't believe what's true?" Alix peered over the top of the sarcophagus.

"Her. This." Ryris gestured wide with his arms. "When I was small, my grandmother used to tell me tales about people like this. Fantastic stories. I...I always hoped they were real, even when I knew it wasn't possible. And now..." He laid his hands reverently atop the glass lid. "...here she is. I wish Gran could be here to witness it."

"Are you saying you know who this woman is?" Jord questioned him with a skeptical tone and a quirked eyebrow as he approached, standing at the head of the coffin.

"Have either of you ever heard of the Crystal Guard?" Both boys shook their heads. Ryris slowly began to move to the foot of the sarcophagus. He fought the urge to touch the glowing gems recessed into the crystal. "I think she's one of them. They were elite soldiers. Sworn to protect the people of the world in times of distress, especially during the Old War."

"Old War?"

Ryris wasn't surprised that the boys had no clue. The tales were stuff of legend and had obviously been neglected through time.

"Centuries ago, there was a war fought between an evil force and the rest of the world. Magicians were hunted because of their powers, and the battle was deadly for both sides. To this day no one likes to admit they possess the power of magic. The old ways die hard." He could hear his father's voice intermingle with his own as he spoke. He resisted the urge to touch his amulet, tucked safely under several layers of clothing. "These warriors ended the conflict. Some of the stories were so terrible, so horrifying, it's no wonder people choose not to speak of it. People don't *want* to remember."

"One woman against the whole world?" Alix stared at the entombed soldier.

"Yeah, well…" Ryris scratched the back of his neck.

"You think we should let her out?" Alix' voice was hopeful and eager.

"Absolutely not. At least not until I research it more." He scanned the room, fixing his eyes on the numerous tomes on the shelves. "There must be books here that explain this mechanism."

"You really think she's alive?"

"Yes. I mean…probably. Why would whoever put her here go to all the trouble of this fancy coffin? If they wanted to preserve her after death, this would be over the top."

Jord stared at the crystal-clad woman. "Well, what do we do in the meantime?"

"We do nothing. She's not going anywh—"

A low, angry growl echoed from the outer cave and in through the secret chamber's entrance. Both boys simultaneously grabbed onto their alchemist friend, cowering behind him. Ryris immediately remembered the boys had left their knapsacks outside in the cavern, and hoped against hope their food hadn't attracted an unwanted visitor. Another growl, closer this time, confirmed his suspicions.

They were not alone.

CHAPTER ELEVEN

Concentration is key. Without concentration, magic fails. You may be able to bring flames to your fingertips or conjure ice beneath your enemy's feet, but without concentration your attempts will be futile and short-lived. Do not get ahead of yourself; take the time to think before you act. It may just save your life.

--Excerpt from pre-Old War magician's textbook, author unknown

"Stay back—and be quiet."

Ryris whispered harshly and pointed to the corner of the room, behind the mystery warrior's sarcophagus. The brothers immediately obeyed. The growling from outside their sanctuary continued, along with the telltale shuffling of large, clawed paws. Mustering all the courage he could find, he cautiously made his way toward the hole in the wall. He looked around for something—anything—he could use as a weapon. Fortunately, the room was filled with just that. Even though he abhorred the idea of having to arm himself, in times of peril, one couldn't be stubborn about his values. Quickly choosing a dagger from a shelf, he moved as silently as he could.

When he was a few feet from the hole, he knelt down to get a good look out into the cavern. His stomach churned as he got a whiff of an unpleasant aroma, one he knew meant trouble. Mixed with the scent of rotting oinox was the unmistakable musk of a saberstrike, a large feline with an extremely foul temperament. Ryris' heart sunk. The dagger in his hand had instantly become useless, and there was no way he could wield the axes and great swords behind him with any sort of expertise. He looked back at the two terrified brothers hiding in the dim light of the corner and knew they needed a savior.

He just wished it didn't have to be him.

Pressing his body closer to the stone floor, he tried to peer out into the cave to confirm his suspicions of the large predator—perhaps the same one that had killed the unfortunate oinox. He could hear the shuffling of giant feet, and smell the musty odor of wet, dirty fur. His body trembling, he poked his head through the hole just enough to see clearly.

The saberstrike must have caught wind of his scent, because in an instant it bounded over the oinox carcass and barreled toward him, mouth agape and fangs snarling. Ryris had a split second to react before a strong paw came crashing down on the entrance. Alix screamed from the corner, Jord trying desperately to shush him. The giant feline tore at the opening, its massive paws ripping apart the brittle stone. Chunks of rock fell away, the hole opening more and more with each passing second. The saberstrike roared with deafening ferocity as it tried to force its way into the chamber.

Looking back once more at the selection of weapons, Ryris darted to the rack and grabbed a longsword, only to have his wrist buckle under the massive weight. It fell to the floor as both terror and embarrassment consumed him. Within seconds, the creature would break through and kill them all.

Just as the thought crossed his mind, the saberstrike's head—massive fangs and all—pushed through. Time seemed to stand still as Ryris focused on the beast's yellow eyes. He was both awed and terrified at the cat's determination. It *would* kill them, and have an incredible feast.

In that instant, Ryris knew what he had to do. Glancing back once more at the terrified boys, he steeled his will and tried not to throw up.

As the saberstrike surged against the hole, flailing wildly, Ryris concentrated on his hands, his breath coming in ragged, terrified spurts. The amulet concealed under his clothing heated up, and he thought for a moment it would burn a hole right through his chest. His palms glowed with an intensity he had never experienced before. Flames danced on all ten of his fingertips before coalescing into two flickering balls of fire. He merged them by pressing his hands together and held the orb steady, hovering between his palms in shaky stasis. The bauble hanging around his neck flared with an incredible heat, Ryris grimacing as his flesh began to singe.

The saberstrike broke through even more, now almost entirely within the room. It gnashed at the air, drool dripping from its fangs, front paws digging into the floor to pull itself through.

It was now or never.

The cat broke free of the hole, and leapt at Ryris. He screamed, flinging the burning projectile at the beast. The flames hit it square in the mouth, sending the cat tumbling back through the hole with such force that it hit the far wall of the cave and fell into an unconscious heap. Its greasy fur catching fire, it quickly became consumed. The heat of its burning skin brought it out of its stupor, and it writhed in agony as the flames spread across its body. The smell was almost too much to bear, and the alchemist covered his mouth and nose. The glow of the flailing saberstrike flickered beyond the opening. Ryris slunk back into the soldier's chamber and watched the beast slam itself into the cavern wall in a frenzy. In a matter of moments, the creature was dead—burned to a crisp by forbidden magical flames. Smoke rose from the carcass, wafting up and out the skylight high above.

The alchemist's chest stung, the skin under the amulet burning with a pain he had never experienced before. Frantically grabbing at his clothes, he tore his jacket and shirt apart, buttons flying in every direction. He was certain the fabric was on fire, or at least smoldering. When he finally got to the inner layers and grabbed a hold of the talisman, he was astonished to find it completely cool. Confused, he moved it aside and felt his flesh. He winced as his fingertips brushed against the battered skin, already blistering from the searing heat. Drawing in a sharp, pained breath, he tried to determine how large the wound was. No bigger than the amulet itself, Ryris was certain it would leave a scar.

"You're…a wizard!" Alix' voice cut through the room and Ryris spun around to meet his excited gaze. Jord just stood there, mouth agape. Alix pointed at him as he ran forward. "Wait until Pops hears about this!"

"No!" Ryris' curt response boomed off of the smooth chamber walls, his voice more stern that he had intended it to be. He calmed himself before continuing. "Look, I'm not a wizard. But you can't tell anyone. Promise me!"

The alchemist began to panic. He had just committed the one cardinal sin his parents had always warned him against. Using his magic in Maxx' presence was stupid enough, but to send flames forth from his hands while being watched by strangers—he suddenly felt as if he would pass out. Scenarios raced through his head. Would the boys tell? Would the villagers be understanding—or malicious? He could very well be tried and jailed—or worse—for using his power. Steadying himself with a hand leaned against the cool stone walls, he rested his forehead on his forearm.

"Ryris…" Alix came up behind him, laying a comforting hand on his back.

"You saved our lives." Jord's voice was strong and honest. "I'll take your secret to my grave."

All doubt about the boys' loyalty melted away. Still, Ryris felt he needed to diffuse the situation, make them believe that he wasn't what they thought he was. Because, in all honesty—he didn't believe it either. 'Wizard' was a term used for someone who possessed incredible power with the magic arts—and that definitely wasn't him.

"Boys, I'm no wizard." He sighed heavily and stood straight once again, regaining his composure. The nausea was starting to abate, and he no longer felt faint.

Jord pointed to his hands with a mischievous grin. "Then how do you explain the fire?"

Ryris looked down at his fingers, covered with a layer of fine black soot. He honestly didn't have an answer that didn't involve the truth. "I, uhhh…"

The older boy approached him, holding his hand out to shake. He waited for the alchemist to accept the gesture. "Pops and the other villagers might not trust magic-users…but we do. Right, Alix?"

The child nodded excitedly and reached out to shake Ryris' other hand. "We thought wizards were fairytales, but you really are one! Even if they cut off my toes and shove a hot poker in my ears, I'll never talk."

"Well, let's hope it never comes to that." Ryris forced a hesitantly relieved smile. "I only did it because I felt that if I didn't, we would be killed."

"We were dead meat. What Pops doesn't know won't hurt him." Jord let go of Ryris' hand, and reached into one of his pants pockets. He pulled out several small, iridescent objects. Grabbing the alchemist's hand once more, he forced Ryris' fingers open and placed the oinox teeth on his palm. "We could never do enough to thank you, but I know these things are worth a fortune—and I don't just mean gamm. You can make stuff with them, right? Like, alchemy?"

Ryris stared down at the glittering teeth. His voice was quiet, a reverent whisper. "They're used to make life-restoring potions. Very rare." He sighed and tried to give them back. "I can't, these are too valuable. You don't have to pay me—I did it out of instinct."

Jord closed Ryris' fingers around the specimens and pushed his hand back toward him. "Please take them. I know you'll use them for something honorable."

Smiling thankfully, Ryris knew the boys wouldn't accept the teeth back. He pocketed them and turned toward the hole in the wall. "We should probably get going. We don't want to get caught up here when the sun goes down."

The boys agreed, and headed for the chamber opening. Ryris tossed one last glance at the woman in the crystal coffin, mentally promising he'd be back as soon as he could. He exited the room first; making sure the path out of the cave was free of any more intruders. When they were all clear, the trio carefully piled the rocks left by both the saberstrike and their previous excavations back into the clearing. Satisfied it was concealed, they made their way to the cave entrance. The alchemist took a moment to inspect the incinerated carcass of the predator that had stalked them, kicking it stubbornly for good measure. He hoped he'd never see another saberstrike for as long as he lived.

"Ryris?" Alix tugged on his jacket sleeve. "What about the lady?"

"I'm going to do some research." He peered out of the mouth of the cave, noting that large flakes of snow were beginning to fall from the sky. "This storm looks like it'll be pretty robust. It'll give me time to decide what to do. Just remember—don't tell anyone about anything. Not about the Crystal Guard, not about the woman—and certainly not about, well, you know…"

"To our graves." Jord hiked up his collar to protect his skin from the offending wind and led the way down the mountain. Alix gave a thumbs' up before following his brother.

Ryris tossed his knapsack onto his shoulders, wincing as the moving fabric of his shirt glanced over the burn on his chest. He would have to mix up some salve when he returned to the inn. As he began to follow the boys on their treacherous descent down the mountain path, Alix' voice chimed in from the front.

"Ummm, Ryris? You forgot your mold…"

~~~

Ryris soaked in the warm water.

He never expected such a small inn to give him a bathroom with a proper tub, but here he was, submerged up to his neck in suds. The burn on his chest stood up on his skin, a stark reminder of how close he and the boys actually came to death that afternoon. He ran his fingers over the raised, tortured flesh, wincing at the sensation. In all the times he had used his magic, the amulet had always warmed up—but never had it burned him. He let his eyes flutter shut as he watched the snow fall outside the bathroom window.

Awakened by the sudden coolness of the water around him, Ryris shivered and realized he had fallen asleep. The soapy bubbles had dissipated, the water taking on an icy chill. His teeth chattering, he climbed out of the tub and wrapped a towel around his waist. He stopped to scrutinize his burn in the mirror, moving his talisman aside before applying a small amount of salve. The ointment felt soothing on his battered skin, cooling the still angry wound almost instantly. Maxx would surely give him grief if he ever saw the inevitable scar.

The chill of the room air assaulting his exposed body, he hurriedly threw on a pair of woolen pajamas and thick socks. Wishing he had a mug of that delicious drinking chocolate he sampled the day before, he settled for a cup of tea. He pulled the only chair in the room close to the hearth and hung the kettle from a hook. As he waited for the water inside to boil, he decided to do some reading. Ryris rummaged through his luggage until he came across the book from his grandmother. He hadn't really given much thought as to why he brought it along. He just figured it might be fun reading material for long, lonely nights spent in foreign towns.

How wrong he was.

Setting the book on the bed, he carefully poured his now hot water into a mug and dropped in his tea ball. Taking the cup with him, he set it on the nightstand and waited for his drink to steep. He crawled into the cozy bed, layered with several blankets. The topmost quilt was down-filled, and he wrapped it around his body in an

111

attempt to rid himself of the bathwater's lingering chill. He leaned forward and grabbed his book. Leafing through the pages, he was determined to find out something—anything—about what he had witnessed today. It had been years since he looked through the tome, and even longer since he had seen or heard the ancient language contained inside. The better part of an hour passed, Ryris drinking his tea as he tried to make heads or tails of the foreign tongue.

Gradually, he began to remember what his grandmother had taught him, he could almost hear her voice speaking the lost language. His fingers drifted over the pages, tracing every line. Little by little, everything came back to him and before long; he was able to read without hesitation. He was amazed by his retention of the language, even after so many years of sitting idle in his mind.

He read aloud in a hushed whisper, the words of a bygone era tumbling from his lips with ever-growing ease.

"Ix partha madala su exparthis. Rylenta ai fracturno ex marchinata. Ello thia sarlokis pur aphlicanto…" He kept reading into the empty room, his words falling upon only the ears of the furniture and the fire.

"Never forget our faithful warriors. Revere them, for they have given us everything. In return, they asked for nothing. No payment, no spoils of war. Only to be remembered with dignity."

Remembered.

Ryris was disgusted by the ignorance of the world. They hadn't been remembered, they had been forgotten. Tossed to the winds of time. Disrespected by those who promised to keep their memory alive.

He flipped ahead through the book, coming to a stop when a colorful picture caught his eye. He instantly remembered it from his childhood. Chuckling softly when he noticed the crinkled page, he recalled a time where he would beg his grandmother to tell him this story, letting him sit on her lap so he could see the image better.

Dozens of warriors stood battle-ready. Their crystalline armor and weapons depicted in all their glory, even though the painting was old and weathered. Their story was one of bravery and honor, the battles they fought bloody and brutal. Not all survived, and the warriors who emerged from battle unscathed had the duty to inter their fallen comrades, so they might go on to the Gentle Reach.

Ryris marveled at the story, suddenly wanting to know much, much more. He remembered asking his grandmother about the Old War, but she would never tell him anything more. She said it would scare him. When he asked her why, she would just shake her head and let her shoulders slump.

"War is war—and this one was no different."

Now, as an adult, here he was with the book in his hands, the story of the war literally at his fingertips. No Gran to change the subject, no Maxx to pull him away and into the shop to learn the trade. Feeling like a naughty child, he turned several pages until he came to the telling of the Old War. The very first image he saw sent chills up his spine. An undead soldier, rotting flesh falling from exposed bones, the decaying, haunting eyes staring back at him from beyond. Ryris slammed the book shut, realizing exactly why his grandmother had refused to enlighten him about the conflict.

Taking a calming breath, he drank the last of his now-cold tea. The visage of the zombie warrior was horrifying. Not wanting to delve into history any more that night, he set the tome on the nightstand and extinguished the oil lamp. The flames in the fireplace had died down significantly, staying just warm enough to make him comfortable while he slept.

Laying there in the almost-darkness, his exhausted mind began to wander. His brain wasn't going to let him sleep—yet. He thought back to the cave, the secret chamber, and the mysterious woman. If he hadn't been so concerned for the boys' well-being, he probably would have stayed the night. It had been difficult to leave. He desperately wanted to know more about her. When he first laid eyes on her, on the treasures contained within her room, he knew he had stumbled onto something truly incredible. This was his chance to prove what his grandmother had so fervently believed in. Waking the warrior up, he mused, would satisfy his appetite for information. The knowledge stored within her memories must be immense. Wars, soldiers—history. The thought of everything he could learn from her made him borderline giddy.

But, then he relented to the more practical side of his psyche. He had no idea who or what he would unleash into the world if he woke her up. Perhaps she was sealed for a reason. Maybe no one talks about the myth because it *shouldn't* be talked about.

Sighing in the darkness, he refused to believe the latter idea. Not after what he had seen in the book, not after looking upon her with his own eyes. Ryris decided right then and there, lying in a bed that was not his own in a strange village far from home—that he would take history by the horns and rouse the crystal warrior. He didn't know if it was for his own interests or to prove—something—to whomever cared. But the winds of time had forgotten about this woman for far too long.

Ryris let sleep take him, drifting off as the image of the beautiful soldier danced on his dreams.

CHAPTER TWELVE

Am I really going to do this? This machine is basically screaming at me not to mess...but I just can't help it. If I read up enough on the mechanism, I can decipher the instructions...I think. I hope I'm not about to make a huge mistake...

--Journal entry, Ryris Bren, 96th Autumn, YG756

Being snowbound for nearly three days in the small hamlet of Hewe, Ryris couldn't contain his inquisitiveness any longer. He had spent the better part of his snowy incarceration poring over Gran's book, hoping there was something that would give him insight into how to wake the sleeping beauty. Coming up empty, Ryris convinced himself he needed to utilize the books within the mystery woman's chamber.

The trip up the mountain would be treacherous with the fresh blanket of snow. He knew there was a chance he could run into another saberstrike or be blown off the paths by the ferocious alpine winds. There was the very real possibility he wouldn't be successful in his endeavor, and she simply wouldn't come back. In the end, his curiosity won over sensibility and he packed up his belongings. Leaving in the pre-dawn hours, mostly to avoid the boys seeing him depart, he checked out of the inn. The owner had begged him to stay because of the weather. Ryris lied to her, telling her he needed another ingredient that was almost past its harvest point, and if he didn't leave now there would be no way to obtain it this season. She gave him a sandwich, wished him well, and reluctantly sent him on his way.

Bundling himself up against the cold, he hitched Ass of the East to the wagon and slowly made his way up to Mount Nevet. The wind screamed eerily, and he was reminded of how the mountain range had earned its name. The light of the lantern swinging from his cart barely shone through the blowing snow.

The sun had just risen as he entered the area he believed the cave to be. Ryris thought he recognized a rock formation, one Alix had commented looked like a turtle, and decided to stow his wagon there. Pushing it as far into the underbrush as he could, he took what belongings he could carry and covered the cart with the tarp. He was fairly certain there would be no foolhardy travelers on the mountain in these conditions, but he didn't want to take any chances.

The climb took longer than he remembered. Granted, last time he had guides, the snow wasn't a quarter as deep, and he wasn't dragging Ass of the East behind him. By the time he arrived at the cave mouth, he was frozen to the bone. He wanted so badly to rush into the secret chamber and begin working, but he knew if he didn't warm up, there was a real possibility he could die from exposure. He was shivering so violently he wasn't sure he could even crawl through the entry hole. Telling himself she wasn't going anywhere, he maneuvered his horse around what was left of the oinox carcass and found a suitable spot for a campsite. As he moved further in, he gagged slightly at the sight of the incinerated saberstrike. He hitched Ass of the East to a large log sitting on the floor and began to gather kindling. Knowing no one was around and with hands too cold to strike a flint; he quickly brought flames to his fingers and started a blazing fire.

After a quick snack huddled by the campfire, his shivering had subsided. Becoming antsy just sitting around, he made his way toward the back of the cavern, giddy with excitement. Ryris took a moment to remove the makeshift barrier from the entrance to the chamber. He easily scrambled through the much larger hole, the saberstrike having done all the hard work of excavating for him. Ryris found himself silently thanking the cat for its effort.

He hurried over to the sarcophagus. After removing the dried flower arrangement and setting it on the floor, he used his sleeve to wipe the dust from the lid. There she was, just as he left her. He studied her face, taking in every detail, every contour, every blemish. When he was in the company of the Lythe boys, he didn't really want to linger. But now, all alone, he could take his time.

Her skin looked like porcelain, her hair as gold as flax. Her beauty was unmatched, but she still had hero's look about her, represented by the scar bisecting her right eyebrow. Ryris surmised it to be a battle wound, but until he asked her personally, there was obviously no way to be sure. Her eyelashes were long, almost touching the skin of her cheeks below the closed lids. Her expression was one of peace; as if she were enjoying the most content sleep she had ever experienced. Ryris let his eyes wander down her body, noting how the crystalline armor hugged her physique. It was obviously handmade to fit only her. Sharp angles melded with soft curves to form a beautifully intricate pattern of crystal plates. It was impossible to tell how the suit of armor was held together, hinting to Ryris that the craftsmanship was unmatched. Although it looked to be very fragile, Ryris figured if they made armor from it, it must be extremely resistant to damage. The breastplate was scratched, a gouge directly over her sternum. Her left gauntlet bore a jagged slash mark, as if an enemy had attempted to sever her hand. The other gauntlet appeared charred, the fingers scorched and ashen. Pockmarks, possibly from arrow strikes, dotted the entire suit. Shining greaves covered her legs, a crystal cap resting over each knee. Her boots were dainty, yet hearty and war-worn. He couldn't wait to ask her about the action she had seen in wartime.

His interest turned to the weapon clutched in her hands. A bow, made of the same material as her armor, rested diagonally across her body. The bowstring seemed to also be made of crystal; something Ryris didn't think was even possible. Ornate swirls were etched into the material, the grip leather-wrapped and embossed with the same whirling pattern. Looking over his shoulder, the alchemist noted the other weapons in the room had similar markings.

Reminding himself he needed to get to work researching the apparatus in front of him, he ran his fingers along the seams, trying to find some sort of pivot point. Moving around the head of the coffin, he slipped his hands in-between the box and the cave wall, feeling for any hardware. He smiled when his fingertips came in contact with rigid hinges. At least now he knew how it opened. He moved back to the foot of the container and pulled his small journal from his jacket pocket. Quickly sketching a picture of what he believed to be the operating mechanism, he made sure to get every detail down. Ryris tapped his hands on the glass lid with a hopeful smile.

"Don't run off…"

Ryris grabbed as many books from the shelves as he could carry, hoping that at least one would have some semblance of instructions. Making his way back out into the cave and to a blazing fire, he got to work. Snacking with one hand and turning pages with the other, he sat for hours trying to make heads or tails of the ancient texts.

~~~

Ryris stood at the foot of the sarcophagus, his journal and one of the old books balanced on the lid.

After four hours of reading and note-taking, he believed he had decoded enough of the ancient instructions to safely open the apparatus. He stood there for a moment, contemplating the finality of his decision. Was he really ready to do this? Was she going to survive? If she survived, would she be kind—or cruel? He had never really stopped to think that she may have been interred as punishment. But after looking around the room—at the discarded floral bouquets from the lid, the treasures stored within—he figured no one would go to this much trouble for a convict.

Convinced he was doing the right thing, Ryris began the work he hoped would disarm the mechanism. He chewed his lower lip as he worked, pressing each colored crystal button in sequence. Taking quick moments to periodically check both his notes and the original text, he labored on. As each differently-hued button dimmed in order, the machinery got quieter and quieter. He scribbled notes as he observed. Ryris' hands began to shake as his finger hovered over the last glowing orb. This was the point of no return. If he pressed the button, the sequence would be complete and, in theory, the sarcophagus should open. Taking a deep breath and holding it, he lightly touched the button but did not press. He said a short prayer to Oleana and closed his eyes.

His finger depressed the button and the machinery went silent.

The lavender light dimmed and then snuffed out completely, leaving him in darkness. A momentary wave of panic swept over him as he began to run horrible scenarios in his head. Had he broken the entire mechanism? Would he be trapped in the room? Had he tripped a self-destruct contingency? Was he going to be killed? He began to breathe erratically, his nerves getting the better of him, as he contemplated making a blind dash for the exit.

Then, all in unison, the wall sconces lit themselves, an eerie illumination emanating from the crystal shards within the lamps. The room was immediately bathed in clear, white light. Ryris allowed himself a relieved sigh as his eyes adjusted to the new brilliance. Training his attention back to the sarcophagus, he placed his hands gently on the still-closed lid. He peered in, noting the sleeping woman did not stir. Unsure of what to do next, he just stood there, tapping his fingers impatiently on the glass.

Without warning, the seals on the lid popped, and a hiss of perfumed air rushed out as the sarcophagus began to open. Ryris jumped back, inhaling the aroma of flowers as fresh as if they had been picked that morning. The lid rose on its own, moving back and sliding down behind the coffin and out of sight. His journal and the book fell to the floor. The alchemist sidled back beside the sarcophagus, peered over the lip, and held his breath in anticipation. He watched her like a hawk, not wanting to miss any signs of life. She did not stir. Ryris told himself not to worry, this process probably took time. It was easier said than done, however, and he found himself nervously chewing on his thumbnail. He wanted so badly to touch her, to make sure she was truly real.

Suddenly, she took a gasping breath, mouth agape as she drew in air for the first time in centuries. Her fingers twitched around the magnificent bow clutched at her bosom, her eyes still fused shut. One breath became two, and before long her lungs had fallen into a normal rhythm.

Ryris contemplated reaching out to make physical contact, but stopped himself short when her eyes began to flutter. In an instant, they shot open, revealing ice-blue irises. They sparkled in the clear light of the room. She sat up with a start, her bow falling to the side. Her armor creaked as it moved, crystal-on-crystal joints grinding up against each other. Not seeming to notice him, she hung her head between her shoulders and moaned, letting out long, labored breaths. Ryris wondered if she was in pain. Not able to help himself any longer and concerned for her well-being, he gingerly extended his arm and wrapped it around her back. He knew she wouldn't feel the heat or gentleness of his touch through her mail, but he hoped the sentiment came through nonetheless.

"Easy now. Just breathe deep and take it slow. I think you've been asleep for a very long time."

The crystal-clad warrior didn't acknowledge him. Instead she bent her knees and turned on her bedding, in an attempt to exit the coffin. Her eyes were vacant, and she seemed to look straight past Ryris. Her hands shook, her body shivered. He tried

117

to assist her as she swung her legs up and over the side, sitting momentarily on the edge before sliding out. Unsteady on her feet, her leg muscles atrophied from centuries of disuse, she crumpled to the floor with a pained grunt. As the woman tried to get up, her legs buckled again and she slammed into the side of the sarcophagus. She leaned up against the crystal container, laying her cheek on the shimmering material. Ryris tried to ease her discomfort as best he could while she sat there, encouraging her with gentle, reassuring words.

"I know this must be confusing, but I'm here to help you. You don't have to be afr—"

The woman smashed her elbow into his side, knocking the breath from his lungs. She lunged at him, eyes frenzied. Baring her teeth, she grabbed him by the collar with strength Ryris didn't think she had and shoved him out of the room through the hole, banging his head on a low-hanging rock as he exited. Small loose stones and dust rained down on top of him. The alchemist saw stars as his head hit the stone floor of the cave. He shook the fog from his senses just in time to see her stumble toward the back of the room. Pressing her hand onto seemingly nothing at all, a glowing red seam appeared on the rock face. The stone wall disappeared, exposing a black void. She darted inside, the wall immediately rematerializing behind her. The seam disintegrated, leaving no trace it was ever there.

Rubbing his head at the impact site, Ryris cautiously made his way back into the chamber and headed toward the wall she had disappeared behind. He waved his hands over the area he thought she had used to activate the door, unable to find any sort of lock or secret touch pad. With a closed fist, he pounded on the rock face. Running his hands along where the seams should have been, he scowled when he found nothing. He couldn't believe eons-old stone could just disappear and reappear on cue. Grumbling, he slid his back down the wall and sat, his head pounding, his mind pondering.

What had he done? Why had she reacted in such a manner? Would she ever come back?

Ryris sat there, dumbfounded. Not knowing what else to do, he sighed heavily and decided to wait her out.

~~~

Searing pain.

Emperor Roann tumbled out of his chair, grabbing his temples as flashes of blinding light raced across his field of vision. His head hit the corner of his desk, gashing the soft flesh. Blood began to flow soon after.

Desperate to make the pain stop, he tried to call for Casmit, only to find his voice no longer functioned. He swallowed, the feeling of thousands of pins pricking as his throat constricted. The emperor writhed on the floor, his hair cascading over his face. Crimson blood trickled down from his wounded temple, leaving a thin red line to drip into his ear. He was only able to crack his eyes for a brief moment before succumbing to unconsciousness. Sunlight shined in through the grand windows of his office, glinting off his signet ring as his hand quaked.

Casmit arrived sometime later to deliver documents, and found Roann out cold, blood from his head wound staining the rug.

~ ~ ~

Ryris didn't know how long the mystery woman had been in there.

He couldn't see out into the cave from his vantage point, unable to tell how far the sun's light had moved at the mouth of the cavern. If he had to guess, it had been at least an hour, probably more—because his rear end was frozen and aching. Sitting on a cold stone floor wasn't the most ideal situation. Unsure of what to do, he continued to sit sentinel, hoping his new companion would eventually come out.

"I don't know if you can hear me. Hell, I don't even know if you're still in there. Maybe you went out some other secret door. But…" Ryris felt a bit stupid for talking to a stone wall, but at this point, he didn't know what else he could do. "…I want you to know I won't hurt you. I just want to get to know you. To hear your story."

He shivered and adjusted his jacket in an attempt to warm himself. He pulled his collar up and hunkered down, trying to conserve his body heat. Staring at where the false door should be, he sighed heavily. As he sat alone in the chamber, he started tumbling everything that had happened in his mind. What was he doing here? He had a job to do, a store to run, and ingredients that weren't going to harvest themselves. Ryris thought to his father, knowing that Maxx would surely have a fit if he knew what his son was doing—or wasn't doing.

"You don't have to be afraid of me. Yes, I might seem like a crazy person because I'm talking to a stone wall, but I'd appreciate it if you didn't hold that against me." He chuckled to himself, realizing how insane that sounded. "I've got a fire in the cavern, and some food. I'd be willing to bet you're pretty hungry."

"This is pointless," he thought. *"What the hell was I thinking?"*

He needed to get back to Keld. The store had been closed for close to two weeks now, and every day he was gone was money torn from his pockets. His food reserves would soon dwindle and the threat of another snowstorm was around every corner. Looking to the unassuming wall next to him, he was overcome with guilt. He

119

had woken this woman up, caused her to fly into a rage and disappear—and now he was contemplating leaving.

"You're such an idiot." He berated himself under his breath. Resting his head against the stone wall, thinking about the woman he hoped was still behind it, he let his eyes flutter shut. But not before pulling his chilled hands up inside his coat sleeves for extra warmth.

~~~

Ryris warmed his hands over the flickering flames before stirring the small pot of oats.

Ass of the East whinnied next to him, and he tossed her the last remaining apple to curb her hunger. They were quickly running out of food, and he was exhausted from keeping lookout for his still-unaccounted-for companion. An entire day had passed since he last saw her.

There had been no movement from within the chamber, no signs of life. Ryris spent that first day in the room while he waited, examining every shelf, every cabinet. What he found astounded him. The weapons were of a quality and material he had never encountered before. A crystal helmet matching the design of his missing friend's armor sat locked behind cabinet doors. The bolt was fastened tight, and even though he was dying to examine the accessory up close, he refrained from breaking the lock. He could have spent a week trying to figure out the chemical compositions of the potions. At least, he figured, he wouldn't die of boredom while the woman did— whatever she was doing in there. He sketched the armaments within the room, made detailed drawings of the sarcophagus. Ryris even attempted to duplicate the face of the warrior that had abandoned him. When he closed his eyes, her angelic face floated in his mind.

When the second dawn had risen that morning, he made the decision that tonight would be his last. Whether she came out or not, he had to leave the next day. The clouds on the horizon signaled a furious storm brewing to the west. He definitely didn't want to be stranded in the cave without food—which is exactly what would happen if he stayed. His decision had not come easy, and he was panged with guilt over the idea of leaving her to fend for herself. But, with the weapons contained within the chamber, he was fairly confident she could at least defend herself if the need arose. Ryris hoped, however, that Oleana would smile on him and bring the mystery woman out of hiding.

He was just about to pull the steaming pot from the fire when rustling near the entrance to the chamber caught his attention. Turning suddenly, his eyes fell upon his guest, clad in a lighter chain under-mail instead of her heavy armor. Her arms were behind her back. He smiled warmly, trying to contain his excitement. He most certainly didn't want to scare her off. Approaching cautiously, he wiped his sooty hands on his pants and extended one in an offer for her to shake.

"Well, hello there. I was beginning to think you'd never come ou—"

For the second time in as many days, she charged at him, knocking him to his knees. In a flurry of movements, she pinned him to the ground. His face smashed into the dust, getting in his mouth and up his nostrils. He instinctively tried to kick himself free, only to find her weight on the backs of his legs, effectively paralyzing him. The next thing he knew, Ryris found himself being flung into a sitting position, a shortsword pointed directly at his heart.

"Who are you?" Her voice was strong as she roared, no hint of the weakness she displayed in the past. "Where do your allegiances lie?"

Staring at her, watching her frenzied eyes, Ryris suddenly very much regretted waking her up. This was not what he expected when he gazed down at her beautiful sleeping face. He had forgiven her, in essence, for the first assault. She had just come out of stasis and was obviously very disoriented. But this time—he had been attacked for seemingly no reason. He didn't know what to say, or even if it would be believed. He tried to calm his shaking body, even as fear threatened to overtake him. "I...I don't have any allegiances! I'm just an alchemist! I don't underst—"

She pressed the tip of the sword harder, nicking Ryris' flesh. He hissed at the sensation, but didn't dare move. The blade moved to his neck. "You have five seconds before I slit your throat!"

It was then that he felt it. The burn. The tips of his fingers began to get hot. Once again, his life on the line, he had made the decision—unconsciously this time— to defend himself. The heat on his fingertips intensified and his breathing became ragged. He really didn't want to have to do this, but the warrior in front of him had left him little choice. Closing his eyes, he concentrated. Instantly, the sword left his throat and she grabbed his hands, twisting them to the point of almost snapping his wrists.

"Don't you dare do what you're thinking of doing."

Her stern voice broke his concentration. The feeling of heat left his fingertips, replaced by the jolting pain of his hands being bent awkwardly. He cried out, trying to wriggle away from her. She only twisted harder. Ryris felt like weeping. His breaking point had been reached, and he had no way of controlling the situation. He was certainly in way over his head. So, after a long moment, when the tone of her voice changed, he was taken completely off guard.

"If you calm down, I'll let go."

Ryris' head sunk between his shoulders. He really didn't have a choice but to trust her at this point. The alternative was death, of that he was certain. Not knowing how to even respond, he just whimpered.

"Do you promise to cooperate?"

"Do I have a choice?" His voice was hushed, his tone one of defeat.

"Yes. But I think we both know how this will end if you choose poorly."

Ryris sighed and nodded wearily. She let go of his wrists and knelt down, the fire illuminating her golden locks. The mystery warrior stared at him for ages, Ryris feeling more and more uncomfortable with each passing moment. Not exactly how he had envisioned this adventure would go.

"You and I are more similar than you realize." Her voice was calmer now. She extended her hand, Ryris instinctively flinching back, not knowing what her intentions were. He watched in awe as she produced a flame in the middle of her palm, then balanced it on the tip of her index finger. Letting it hover there for a moment, she finally guided the fire back to the center of her hand and snuffed it out by closing her fingers around it.

Ryris just stared at her, dumbfounded. The only other person he had ever seen use magic had been his mother. Sure, he knew there were others out there with similar abilities, but no one was stupid enough to broadcast their talents publicly. If she was willing to show him her powers, he hoped it meant she was a friend. He truly believed she would have killed him by now if she wasn't. His voice was meek as he finally spoke. "What's wrong with us?"

"It's a gift."

Ryris snorted. "If it's such a gift, why was I told never to use it? Why was I shamed?"

The woman's expression softened for a moment, her eyes showing pity for him before her demeanor returned to that of a hardened warrior. "Lyrax scared people into believing anyone who possessed the power of magic was a threat. Even if many of us had just given them salvation. Casualties at the hands of magic-users were unavoidable. Even after the war, the fear remained, however unwarranted. I had hoped time would heal that fear, but it would seem otherwise."

Ryris just stared at her vacantly as she continued.

"You are most certainly not alone." She smiled with encouragement. "If you learn to control yourself, you could be a very powerful wizard."

"I'm an alchemist. I don't want to be a wizard." Ryris' answer was quick and curt.

She extended her hand. "I am Kaia the Quick."

Surprised at her sudden friendliness, he accepted her handshake. Her grip was strong, but gentle. "It's an honor to meet you, Kaia the Quick. My name's Ryris. Ryris Bren."

She sucked in a short, surprised breath.

Ryris smiled, feeling more trusting of her with each passing moment. "I have so many questions."

She held up a hand. "We don't have time. We need to get out of here."

"What's the rush?"

She stood, giving his remaining supplies a once-over. "We need to find my fellow commanders. There are only three of us that survived the war. Now that I'm awake, the hunt will certainly begin."

"Who could possibly be hunting you after all these years?"

"There's a reason you woke me up."

"Please don't say destiny…"

Kaia stared at him blankly. "Why not? I've experienced destiny first-hand."

Ryris blew out a long breath. He hadn't known her very long, and he was already getting overwhelmed. "What does that even mean? Maybe destiny just decided it was time for you to have a normal life. It doesn't necessarily mean you're in danger."

"I don't have time to explain. Each minute that passes is one we can't afford to lose. We need to leave." She stood and made her way toward the front of the cavern. As she passed by the desiccated oinox carcass, she wrinkled her nose at the still-lingering odor of rotting flesh. A moment later, an ancient curse word escaped her lips, one Ryris had heard his grandmother utter more than once. He stood and joined her at the entrance of the cave, and immediately uttered a profanity of his own.

A full-blown blizzard raged outside.

CHAPTER THIRTEEN

Charred beyond recognition, he sobbed uncontrollably. Pleading with us as we threw him in. The intensity of his love for death was matched only by the fear of his own.

--Excerpt from the journal of Kaia the Quick, year unknown.

"...a resurgence..."

"...power..."

"...threatening..."

"...old..."

"...can't wait..."

"...death..."

The man listened to the spectral voice ramble, never hearing such frantic despair before. He watched intently as the blue flame in the font flickered, dimming every few seconds before trying to regain its strength. The air temperature in the chamber suddenly skyrocketed, and the azure light went out completely. The faithful servant believed he had lost his master. After several agonizing moments, the chill to the air returned, albeit very slowly.

"Something...strong..."

The voice was weak, laced with hesitation and slow to form words. Never had he heard it speak in such a manner. Unwilling to interrupt his master, he waited for the thought to finish, fearful it was the last time they would commune.

"...a long time...true power..."

The fire waned, almost disappearing into the recesses of the font's bowl. The man leaned forward, peering down into the abyss.

"...go...leave me..."

He was hesitant to obey; fearful he would no longer be able to speak to his master. Perhaps lingering a bit too long, the ghostly voice spoke again, harsh undertones cutting through the weakness.

"...leave!..."

Unwilling to disobey and face his master's wicked wrath, the protégé begrudgingly backed away from the font and disappeared into a cloud of red mist.

CHAPTER FOURTEEN

Lady Destiny—shall we tempt you? Lady Destiny—shall we tread in your hallowed halls?

--Poem by Rex Regalia, famed Dungannon bard.

Ryris watched Kaia intently as she arranged branches on the fire. He picked bits off the remaining granola bar from Mrs. Lythe, absentmindedly nibbling on them. The alchemist found himself captivated by this mysterious woman, even though she had attacked him less than twenty minutes ago. When she was finally satisfied the wood was precisely placed, she produced flames on her fingertips and gave the fire a little boost. He instinctively looked around to make sure no one had seen the display.

Kaia sat with a relieved grunt before looking to Ryris speculatively. She pointed at his chest. "You're bleeding."

Ryris' hand snaked across the fabric until he came across a wet spot. A red stain blossomed out from a hole—a hole suspiciously the same size as the tip of a sword. How could he not have noticed he was injured? He quickly undid the buttons, panic setting in. An irrational fear of dying took him over.

Kaia, sensing his impending meltdown, tried to calm him in her own unique way. "If it were a fatal strike, you would have been dead by now."

Not comforted by her words, he pulled the panels of his shirt open. There, just above his heart, was a small, oozing puncture wound. He thought back to the attack, and recalled the twinge of pain when the blade had pierced his skin. Ryris grumbled and reached for his knapsack, rooting around for some antiseptic. He didn't notice Kaia move on him until she was uncomfortably close.

Kaia knelt before him, scrutinizing his bare chest. If there was ever a time Ryris felt self-conscious, this was definitely it. He thought she was going to help him tend to his wound, but it was apparent something else had caught her attention. She extended her hand and gently grasped his amulet, bringing her face close to his body to inspect it.

No one besides him had touched the amulet in years—not since the last time he saw his grandmother alive. She had extended a frail, shaky hand to him, and wrapped her gnarled fingers around it. Warning him once more never to take it off, she had died peacefully in her sleep some hours later. Now, this mysterious woman was interested— not to mention she was touching his bare chest. Ryris nervously blew out a long breath as she turned it over and over in her hands. He noticed the skin on her right hand was scarred, perhaps the result of severe burns. But, he decided not to broach the subject and make her uncomfortable—he was uncomfortable enough for them both.

"Where did you get this?"

"My grandmother gave it to me when I was born. It's been in the family for generations." He pulled away from her, embarrassment from her touch sparking over his body.

"Do you know how powerful it is? Or what it does?" Her voice was awestruck and wispy.

"Of course, it protects me."

"Do you know from what…or whom?" She questioned him like she already knew the answer, and was trying to figure out if he was privy to the information.

"Magic-hunters? Gran said they can't sense my ability if I have it on." The alchemist absentmindedly rubbed his thumb over the inlaid gem. "Honestly, I think she was just trying to scare me."

"Your Gran spoke the truth. That talisman belonged to a very powerful man—and kept *him* safe. You wearing that amulet around your neck tells me you are of noble blood."

A chill ran down Ryris' spine. All these years he had secretly hoped that all the protection talk was just hooey, even though he dutifully did as he was told and never removed the amulet. He never wanted to believe he was in any real danger of being found out if it failed to be on his person.

"Noble? Me?" He tried not to laugh as he dabbed a bit of antiseptic on his cut. He hissed at the sensation before continuing. "I come from a long line of alchemists. There's nothing noble about us."

"That charm had a very important role in the war."

Ryris couldn't believe what he was hearing. His situation—their situation—just kept getting stranger by the minute. But, he was desperate to hear more. "Who was he? Why did he need the amulet?"

"He was the highest-ranking wizard of the empire. And…his name was Ryris."

The amulet on his chest warmed up for a split-second at the mention of his name, almost undetectable to the young alchemist.

"When you introduced yourself earlier, I thought it was just coincidence." Kaia sat back onto a log, across from him. "Your destiny was sealed the moment your grandmother put that chain around your neck."

Ryris thought back to what the old fortune teller had told him. That his name was old—and meaningful. At the time he had brushed it off as nonsense, the old woman likely trying to get more gamm out of him. But now, with Kaia's revelation, he was beginning to see an air of truth to this whole 'destiny' business. He poked the fire with a stick as he listened.

"During the war, each side had a battalion of battle-mages providing both offensive and defensive support. The Arch-battlemage kept watch and advised his warriors, as well as fought right on the front lines. When the enemy forces killed our ally's high wizard, it was decided that ours needed to be protected at all costs. An amulet was created—one that was imbued with special properties that would ensure his magical ability would never be sensed. He bravely fought until the end of the war, the enemy blind to who he truly was."

"And you think…"

"You're of his bloodline, there's no doubt."

Ryris sat in quiet reflection for a moment. He had just learned about an ancestor—one that had been forgotten across time. He felt sad for the man, his history left to the wind, his memory all but dust. But at the same time, he was excited to know that he shared a name with such a powerful and respected person. "So, what happened to him? After the war?"

"I don't know. He exiled himself shortly after it ended. He knew, just like we did, the danger would still be there for anyone who openly used magic." Kaia sighed. "When I saw the amulet around your neck, I was hopeful he was able to live a normal life. But the fact that you know nothing about him suggests that he probably spent the rest of his life in solitude."

"But then how did my Gran get the amulet?"

"That's a secret for the ages." Kaia smiled softly. "It's safe and that's all that matters."

"I guess…" Ryris mused, suddenly very curious about Kaia's war. He thought for a few seconds, before being struck by an idea. "Can I show you something? I mean, we've got time…" Ryris pointed toward the cave mouth, snow blowing in on raging wind.

"I suppose."

Ryris got up and fetched the book from his knapsack. When he returned, he took a chance and sat down next to her. He hoped she wouldn't be uncomfortable. "Gran and I spent hours looking at this. Maybe there's some clues about the other Ryris inside? Or about the amulet?"

"I thought you said you've read this countless times."

The alchemist looked down at the cover, an embarrassed smile crossing his lips. "She never let me go past a certain part. Said it would scare me."

"And now?" Kaia gave him a skeptical sideways glance.

"To be honest, the book got put away after she died. I just recently came across it." He set the book across his lap, bumping Kaia's leg. "Tell me about the Old War?"

"'Old War...'? Ryris, just how much time has passed?"

"It's been over seven-hundred years." He watched her closely for a reaction. Would she cry when she realized how much time had passed, understanding that everyone she ever knew and loved had been gone for centuries? Would she be furious for being kept secluded for all that time?

"I see." Her expression was thoughtful, her voice meek.

Definitely not the reaction Ryris was expecting, he tried to keep the conversation going. Opening the tome, he flipped to the page that showcased a garrison of soldiers clad in crystal. The paper was torn at the edge, grimy from years of being touched. "This was my favorite part."

Kaia stared at the image intently. Ryris could see the emotion in her eyes as her lips curled into a small, prideful smile. "That's the Crystal Guard. We were elite warriors, bonded by honor and entrusted to keep the world safe."

"I knew it..." Ryris' breath hitched in his chest as her admission tumbled around in his brain. Everything his grandmother had told him, and everything Maxx had tried so hard to make him forget, was true. To hear it come from her mouth was incredible. "You *really are* one of them. It wasn't just a fairytale."

"Far from it." Kaia turned the pages, flipping through until she got to the image Ryris detested. He looked away momentarily before forcing himself to gaze at the undead warrior. If the woman sitting beside him actually fought these things, he could muster looking at a painting on a page.

"What was it like?" Ryris posed the question; even though he wasn't sure he truly wanted to hear the answer.

"Terrible. We were fighting a madman, bent o—"

"...that Lyrax guy?"

Kaia huffed at Ryris' interruption. "Yes, '*that Lyrax guy*'. He was bent on destroying that which he had been shunned for."

"I'm going to go out on a limb and guess magic?"

"Partly. Before the war, magic was part of everyday life. Users and non-users alike co-mingled. Magic was utilized in abundance, with no shame or stigma attached—at least not for common magic."

"What do you mean?"

"As a teen, Lyrax fell into league with a band of necromancers. We may have embraced magical ability, but necromancy was a dark art and most certainly not accepted by honorable society. His parents begged him to leave the coven, but he refused and soon rose within their ranks. He was obsessed with death." Kaia sighed knowingly. "Left with no other choice, they went to their king, a magic user, for help. He sent agents to hunt down and arrest the young man. The soldiers destroyed the necromancers, leaving only Lyrax and a few others alive. When he was brought back to the kingdom, the royal advisors recommended execution, but his parents begged that mercy be shown for their only child—and the king banished him to the far reaches of their continent, Ashal. In hindsight, it was the greatest mistake he would ever make."

Ryris shuddered at the mention of the 'ghost country'. No one went there, for history said the land was poisoned and uninhabitable—the reason lost to time. "He came back?"

"With a vengeance. He spent the next thirty-odd years getting stronger, perfecting his bastard 'art'. Not only did he eventually raise his fellow necromancers from the grave, but methodically went through the sacred cemeteries of the people and raised an army. No one paid any attention because they ignorantly thought the threat had been dealt with." A small, disbelieving huff tumbled from her lips. "He was working right under their noses the entire time and no one even noticed. By the time he marched back to the heart of the kingdom, he had amassed legions of undead warriors armed with cursed weapons. They were unstoppable."

"Communication was very limited, and our people had no idea of the horrors that started far away. It wasn't until the armies of the undead came to our shores that we realized—almost too late. Envoys were sent from both Farnfoss and Zaiterra to Ashal, only to find the king and queen had been killed and that Lyrax had claimed the throne. He vowed to rid the world of all other magic-users and 'cleanse' the continents. For us, the war started the moment his zombie soldiers took their first victim on our land."

She kept turning pages until she stopped at one Ryris had never seen. The image sent chills up his spine. A peasant woman, begging for her life as an undead warrior pierced her heart. Further down the page, she reappeared—reanimated by unholy magic.

"He killed his own people…"

129

Kaia nodded solemnly. "All of them. Thousands of innocents, murdered for the sole purpose of invading and destroying. Men, women—even the children. All turned into rotting soldiers. Lyrax knew they'd never fight of their own free will. Most were killed quickly, with no idea of what their futures held. But those who openly opposed him were tortured and told what was to become of them. They knew their fate. The oblivious were lucky. They had no memory of what they once had. But the people who knew they would be turned? Lyrax corrupted their minds so they would remember their former lives while they mowed down their fellow countrymen.

"By the time my garrisons were called into action, the hordes had swept across the land. The soldiers of good—magicians and infantry alike—were of dwindling numbers. We had no choice but to fight. We enjoyed a short-lived period of victory, as the zombies weren't prepared for such formidable foes. But, they adapted quickly—and Lyrax made use of a secret weapon."

"Secret weapon?"

"The former king. Imbued with terrifying power, his reanimated corpse infiltrated the ranks, passing on incredible dominance as he swept toward the front lines. Magic the likes of which no one had ever seen. He razed villages with the flick of his wrist, slaughtered families with horrifying efficiency. Lyrax even gave him the ability to shift his shape, which he used with terrifying results."

"And all because he hated wizards?"

"He hated what he thought other wizards had done to him. Banishment. Shame. Dishonor. He promised vendetta on those who had wronged him—innocents in the way be damned. He wanted to be the one and only wizard left—so no one would ever threaten him again. By the end of his march across the world, he had lost sight of that initial reasoning, I think, and had his eyes on a bigger prize."

"Complete destruction?"

"He wanted the world for himself and his undead hordes. A new utopia—a horrifying utopia. His obsession with death reached a fever pitch, and his insanity overtook any last shred of his mind that might have remained."

"But you obviously beat him, right? I mean, I'm here aren't I? The world is peaceful."

Kaia sighed and closed the book. "We were victorious, but at a terrible price. Thousands perished before we could claim peace. Yes, we destroyed him, but the damage had been done. His vision of a world without magicians had been achieved. By the time the war ended, magic users were being blamed by proxy for something a madman had done. The magic that saved the people was now under scrutiny. Wizards went into hiding; parents shamed their progeny who were born 'cursed'."

Ryris' shoulders slumped. *Cursed.*

"We tried to make the citizens see the light. With Lyrax gone, our focus shifted on rebuilding—not just physical cities, but also morale. The moment we threw him in the volcano, we hoped people would come to their senses and stop blaming wizards. We were wrong."

"Wait, you threw him in a volcano?"

"Like I said, war is terrible. That's another story for another time." She shifted her weight, extending her legs out in front of her with a grunt. "In order to ensure there would be protectors should the need ever arise again, the remaining Crystal Guard commanders were secretly entombed to await destiny."

"There's that word again, 'destiny'."

"Don't be so quick to dismiss it, Ryris."

"It's just so far-fetched. I mean, I come from a scientific background. There's no 'wishing' a potion will turn out right, or hoping some mystical force will strengthen its potency. It either works, or it doesn't. You adjust recipes and techniques and try again until you're successful. I guess it's hard for me to put faith in some invisible force guiding my life path."

"Sometimes you have to let go of your critical thinking and act on instinct."

"Acting on instinct usually gets me into trouble." Ryris couldn't help but laugh quietly at himself.

"Oh? Should I be afraid to be in your company?"

"Well, I do have a knack for attracting predators." He motioned to the charred saberstrike carcass and burned wall.

"You did that?"

He nodded and looked down at his hands. "Two boys from the village told me about you, and offered to show me your chamber. While we were exploring, we got cornered by that saberstrike. I had to do something."

"You have incredible potential, Ryris. If you study diligently and are willing to learn, you can harness any type of magic you desire."

He looked at her, questioningly. "I can learn other powers?"

With a flick of her wrist, lightning crackled across the ceiling, causing Ryris to duck down to avoid being hit. When he realized the electricity was far enough away not to cause harm, he cautiously sat back up, embarrassed. As the charge dissipated, Kaia turned her attention to the fire. Pointing a finger at the flames, they instantly turned to solid ice, crackling as the heat was wicked from the surrounding area. The alchemist couldn't believe his eyes. He was mesmerized by her power. After a minute, she reignited the flames by tossing a sparkling fireball into the pit.

"That was incredible!"

"Magic has a very important role in everyday life…at least, it did. There were magically-created fires in every blacksmith's forge and ice in every summer cache to keep food from going bad. Warriors on the battlefield were supported by wizards talented in the defensive arts, their weapons charmed for superiority by battle-mages." She pointed to his hands. "Show me what you can do?"

Ryris stared at his fingers clenched in his lap, unsure if she should oblige her. His brain was screaming at him to refuse, that he'd already done enough damage by letting the Lythe boys see his powers. Even though he trusted Kaia even after such a short time, his stomach still churned at the thought of outing himself further. He glanced at his new friend, the woman waiting patiently for his display.

Finally taking a deep breath, he held out his palms, in much the same way she had done. Concentrating, he made a small flame appear on each one of his ten fingers, before melding them together a large ball. He tossed it into the fire, where it sizzled and joined its brethren.

"Not bad…"

"Until last week, I had only used it to start the hearth and annoy my father. Then all hell broke loose and I outed myself in front of those boys."

"Does anyone else in your family have the gift?"

A wave of sadness washed over him. "My mother…" He hesitated, not sure if he wanted to continue. "…she had magic too."

"*Had?*"

"Her name was Adriane. She could freeze things with her fingertips. I remember once when I was small; she stuck a stick into a cup of pellick juice and froze it." Ryris' lips curled into a small smile, sad and reminiscing. "When I was six…she died. Killed."

"War?"

Ryris shook his head, his voice low. "Cold-blooded murder. My father was convinced it was because of the magic, but never told anyone his suspicions to protect my mother's identity—and mine."

"May I ask what happened?"

He hesitated for a moment, unsure if he wanted to scratch open that old wound. Yes, he was beginning to trust Kaia, but he still hardly knew her, and didn't know how much he should be telling her. She looked at him with honest, caring eyes, no hint of malice or mistrust, and in the end he decided he would let her in. Maybe, he thought, it would actually do him some good to get this history off his chest.

The alchemist sighed heavily, his shoulders sagging. "It was nighttime. This man, a nameless traveler, broke in, knocked my father out and pulled her right out of their bed. I shared a room with my Gran, and she had been snoring—so I went to sleep in front of the fireplace in the kitchen. When he smashed the door from the shop open, I hid under the table." Ryris paused and willed himself not to get emotional. "He stabbed her. I don't know how many times. There was…blood…everywhere. She only had time to scream once."

Moisture welled in Ryris' eyes. It had been decades since he had relived that night. He wasn't sure he wanted to continue, but he knew if he didn't, it would keep haunting him. "Grildi, the town guard, came in while the guy was still there, I think he probably heard my mom scream or saw the broken-in shop door. He snapped the guy's neck, so the mayor never had a chance to interrogate him. Grildi always felt terrible for acting so hastily and not being able to protect us. I know it still hangs over him.

"My dad told me later that he 'just knew' it was because of the magic, that he must have seen her through a window making ice or something. He always told her not to use it, but she was stubborn. The mayor classified it as a random crime, and my father went along with it. He was fearful the villagers would find out about our family power, and wanted to protect me."

"The ignorance of people when it comes to magic is unbelievable. The war changed the very psyche of the citizens. I'm sorry you had to witness your mother's murder." Kaia's voice was stern, yet still had an air of caring.

"It's in the past. To be honest, this is the first time I've ever told anyone what happened. My father and I never speak of it. It felt…good. In a weird way." He smiled thankfully.

"I want you to promise me you'll learn to be proud of your power. Don't let the past hold you back, or let the fears of the masses prevent you from doing great things."

Ryris chuckled as he shook his head. "The masses are what caused this problem in the first place."

"Then take it upon yourself to change their views. Nothing will ever be different if there's no one to spearhead a movement. Be the one to make a difference."

The alchemist blew out a long breath and let her words echo in his mind.

CHAPTER FIFTEEN

The stones seemingly draw power from the ether itself. Never losing charge, never weakening. We believe it possible to harness this power for the purposes Your Majesty proposes.

--Notes from chief engineer of Farnfoss, year unknown.

Kaia sat across from Ryris, inspecting her bow. Her scrutiny was precise as she made sure it was still in working order after centuries of disuse. She snapped the crystal string a few times, testing the tension. Ryris had become quite accustomed to Kaia's company, even after only a short amount of time. He wondered how long they'd actually be together, or if they would eventually part ways at some point. The alchemist found himself hoping she would stick around.

"So, if you don't mind me asking—what were you doing in that little secret room of yours before you came out and attacked me?"

Kaia's face flushed with embarrassment. Her posture stiffened, and she turned her attention back to her weapon, her voice quiet. "Vomiting, mostly."

Definitely not the answer Ryris was expecting, he decided not to press the subject any further.

"I guess the side-effect of the stasis was nausea."

"Can I ask why you tackled me? Both times?"

The warrior set her bow down across her lap. "The first time I was disoriented and had no idea if you were friend or foe. Fight or flight kicked in, and I knew I needed to get to my safe room. And...I was on the verge of being sick."

"And the second time?"

"Again, I had no idea what your intentions were. You have to remember, I lived in a dangerous time. Yes, we won the war, but the reason I was interred in the first place was in case my skills were needed again. I had no way of telling when I woke up whether you roused me because you needed me, or if you were trying to hurt me. I'm a soldier, plain and simple—a soldier who can use magic."

Ryris absentmindedly rubbed the dwindling knot on the back of his head. "Fair enough. I forgive you." He winked.

"I didn't ask for your forgiveness. I was well within my right to subdue you."

134

The alchemist didn't know if she was joking or not. It hit him that he still wasn't that familiar with her, and was unsure of whether or not his humor would be appreciated.

"I, uhhhh…" He felt heat return to his face, and nervously tapped his fingers on his thighs. "…I was just joking. I'm sorry if I pissed you off."

"No harm done. I was just being honest."

Somehow, Ryris knew right then and there that things would be alright between them. He didn't know why, but he felt a very tight camaraderie with her—and they had known each other less than a day. He had told her two of his deepest secrets, something he would have never done even a week prior. Trusting her enough to let her into his life—to his emotions. No one other than his father and Grildi had ever seen him shed a tear, and yet, there he was not ten minutes before, showing raw emotion over his mother's death. She had truly cast a spell over him. And, she was stunning. Ryris caught himself staring at her from time to time, mesmerized by her beauty. His heart fluttered nervously whenever she smiled at him. He didn't want to admit that he was quickly becoming drawn in by her—and that his heart was being stolen. He wondered what his father would think.

His father.

The business.

What was he going to do now? He had to get back to the shop and resume his work. Would he take her with? Would she even come? His mouth suddenly felt dry as sand, his stomach boiling with nervous butterflies. Kaia, obviously taking note of the change in his demeanor, leaned forward, concern crossing her face.

"What's wrong?"

Ryris wrung his hands together. "I need to get back to Keld. My father will begin to worry that I haven't contacted him lately. The shop needs to open again, or…"

"You can't go back."

"What? Why not?"

"Don't you understand? Nothing else matters anymore. Not your shop, not Keld—nothing. I know you don't like to hear about destiny, but everything changed for you—and for me—the moment you woke me up." Kaia pointed to his chest, her finger boring a line straight through the amulet. "Isn't that enough to convince you? You've seen the book, I've told you the story of the war, and we've spoken of that talisman and your family history. It isn't just some bauble. You know what it does, and now you know who has worn it in the past. Did you think your parents just tried to scare you with it?"

135

He shook his head.

"Has it ever reacted to anything?"

"When I use my magic, it gets warm, and it burned me a few days ago when I killed the saberstrike." He moved the amulet out of the way, and Kaia moved forward to inspect the scar underneath. Her fingertips were soft against his skin, and once again, nervous heat cascaded over his body.

"Anything else?"

"No, not that I can think of..." He sat for a moment, wracking his brain. "Although...a few months back... never mind, it was nothing."

"What happened? Nothing is trifle now."

"The prince, well he's the emperor now, came to visit the shop after I first opened. He introduced himself, asked a few questions, and then I shook his hand. And...it was like a wave hit him. He got really pale and almost fainted. It took him a few minutes to regain enough composure to even speak, and he left in a hurry. He assured me in a letter the next day that his illness had nothing to do with me or my business and that was it. Weird thing is..." Ryris touched the talisman with a confused shake of his head. "...later on I noticed soot under my amulet. Nowhere else, just directly underneath. It never got warm, so I know it couldn't have been a burn. I figured I just rubbed my chest with dirty fingers or something."

"That's troubling." Kaia's brows furrowed.

"Why?"

"You say he was fine until you made physical contact with him?"

"Seemed to be. I figured he was overwhelmed by the smells in the store. Most of my ingredients are pretty pungent." He regarded Kaia cautiously. "You don't think that's it, do you?"

"I don't think the mark on your chest was related to touching the fireplace. Something isn't right." She tapped her fingers on her thigh. "Now can you understand that my fears aren't as unwarranted as you thought?"

"Why, because my amulet reacted strangely to the emperor?"

"What is it going to take to convince you that this isn't a game?" It was obvious Kaia was becoming irritated with his reluctance.

"Oh, I don't know...maybe more than just talk about destiny? This is a peaceful era, there's no war!" Ryris immediately regretted his sassy tone. But, before he could make amends, Kaia crossed her arms over her chest with a huff and stared directly at him.

136

"There's no war...*yet.*" Her words echoed in his head as he swallowed hard, suddenly very nervous. She continued before he could respond. "I don't think you understand the severity of the situation."

"You're right, I don't!" Ryris threw his hands in the air in exasperation, his raised voice echoing his sentiment. "A month ago, I was an alchemist running an extremely successful shop in Keld. Last week I was traveling to harvest aegis mold. Today, I'm being told by a mysterious warrior who has been sleeping in a cave for centuries that once again there's an evil power in the world and my amulet's reaction to a simple handshake is pretty much saying that I need to go and save the world." He blew out a long breath with the end of his rambling rant. He stood and started to pace. "You'll have to excuse me if I sound skeptical."

"History has a funny way of repeating itself, Ryris. Especially when the lessons of the past are forgotten. My people felt the same way—and they were slaughtered by armies of zombies who 'came out of nowhere'."

His voice rose again, and he had to try and keep himself from screaming at her. He didn't understand why she wouldn't just believe him. "But that happened so long ago! That's what I'm trying to say! Lyrax is gone. There's no evil!"

Kaia shook her head sadly. "We don't have much time, and I fear your inability to accept your new path will only lead to suffering—for you, for me, and for the world."

Her words stung. He felt as if he were back in the presence of his father, Maxx belittling him for this or that, blaming him for wrongs that weren't necessarily his fault. Although this time, it wasn't over some inventory mishap or incorrectly-mixed potion. There was a warrior standing directly in front of him—one of the very same that his grandmother had told him about in his youth—and she was reaching out to him for help. Yes, here claims were fantastical and hard to believe, with nothing to back up her premonition other than a gut feeling. But—that gut had fought in a terrible war, against an enemy that was hard to believe even existed. Kaia had been at the center of it all, surrounded by magic and intrigue, desperation and terror. Whether he wanted to be involved or not, he was now in deep. He suddenly felt very small—and stupid.

"I'm sorry if I offended you." Ryris sat down next to her with a defeated grunt. "This is just...a lot to take in. I'm not exactly the heroic type, you know?"

"Destiny does not choose her champions hastily, Ryris. One must allow her to take hold and not question what she asks of them." He nodded silently as she continued. "It's times like this when we must embrace what the stars hold for us. If we stop to question it, we lose precious time and end up making foolish decisions. Emotion can't get in the way."

She was right. He had been foolish—everyone had. Her words, though hard to take, bore elements of truth. He thought to the life he had led, to the lives all citizens

137

enjoyed. There was no war, no famine, nothing that made their lives miserable. Sure, he had to contend with the magical stifling, but he had always believed it to be the product of age-old fears, and obeyed his father because it was the only thing he knew. And now, this woman—a warrior who had fought in the very war that ushered in this peaceful time in which they lived—was telling him that all was not as it seemed. He had no reason to believe her—and yet, he did. In that moment, his heart decided he trusted her—even when his mind wasn't sure of what to make of it.

"I know it's difficult to hear, and I'll admit it unnerves me as well." The flickering flames illuminated Kaia's face. "But I truly believe that destiny has brought us together. This was not by chance."

Ryris could almost hear Maxx' voice in his head. *"Are you crazy? Trusting this strange woman? Why'd you even wake her up?"* All his life he had to endure his father's scrutiny, live with the older man always looking over his shoulder and trying to influence how he lived his life. When he had gone to Keld, it diminished somewhat, but Ryris still felt as if he were living in his father's shadow. The family businesses, after all, belonged to both of them. But now, sitting here in this freezing cave, he finally felt as if he were truly his own man. He alone needed to make the decision to follow Kaia.

"I can't promise I won't continue to question what's happening. But you lived through something horrible, and that has to count for something. And, if I've learned anything from my insatiable curiosity, it's that it gets me into trouble—and apparently makes me new friends in the process. I guess I'm trying to say that I trust you—even though we've only known each other a short time." Ryris billowed out a long breath. "Hopefully I won't regret my impulsiveness later, eh?"

Kaia's eyes crinkled at the corners as she offered a sincere smile. "I'm honored that you trust me. I know first-hand that trust isn't something that is given freely—it has to be earned. And I intend to earn it from you."

"That means a lot, Kaia. Thank you."

She smiled and got up to check the storm's progress. As she passed the saberstrike carcass, she paused to inspect it. She turned back to Ryris and motioned to the body. "There's a lot of good meat left. Come over here and help me."

"You want to *eat* it?" Ryris wrinkled his nose in disgust.

"You may enjoy living off of jerky and dried beans, but I need some real food." She held out her hand and shook it at him. "Bring me your dagger."

Ryris reluctantly got up and approached the soldier—and her newest interest. She accepted the blade from him and immediately began slicing into the burned skin of the beast to get to the meat underneath. The sound of the flesh ripping made Ryris shudder, and he couldn't help but notice the unpleasant aroma filling the surrounding area. "I think it's rotten…"

Kaia huffed and pointed at the oinox carcass with the bloody knife. "*That's* rotten. *This* just needs some careful carving." She pulled a hunk of meat from the body cavity and tossed it at him. Caught off guard, Ryris fumbled the bloody projectile and dropped it to the ground, immediately swallowing back a mouthful of impending vomit. He dashed back to the fire and glared at her from afar, feverishly wiping his hands on the side of a sack.

"Are you crazy? I'm not eating that!"

Kaia blew out a long, irritated breath and picked up the hastily discarded meat. "Suit yourself. More for me."

Ryris repositioned himself as far from the rancid meat and Kaia as possible when she returned to camp. The stench was definitely off-putting. She sliced the chunk into strips and laid them across a log in the fire. They immediately sizzled. She wiped the bloody dagger off on a cloth and handed it back to him.

"Our next step will be getting to Phia; she'll be able to tell us more, and give us the locations of my comrades."

"Phia?" Ryris begrudgingly accepted his weapon back, although he didn't know if he could ever look at it the same way again. He thought about conveniently forgetting it when they left.

"An old seer. Giants can live a thousand years or more. If she's still alive, she's our only hope of getting some answers."

"A giant?" Swallowing hard, Ryris tried to hide the tremble in his voice. The only ones he had ever seen were from a distance. People were taught to stay as far away from them as possible, that they were vicious killers who showed absolutely no mercy. Their settlements were hidden and cut off from civilization and anyone who wandered too close was sure to meet a grisly demise. And now Kaia was suggesting that there was not only one that was a thousand years old, but that she was kind and willing to help. "I'm not so sure we should be messing with giants."

"Phia is harmless. She's blind and wouldn't hurt a skellin." Kaia turned the saberstrike meat over with a long stick.

Ryris mulled over his options mentally before reluctantly agreeing to visit her. "Where does she live?"

"I assume it's still called the Heaving Marsh?"

Ryris detested the Heaving Marsh. Filled with every type of creepy, crawling inhabitant you could think of, its foul, humid atmosphere only welcomed the very brave—or foolish. Every time he had visited with his father, he ended up with leeches in extremely private places and a rash for weeks from the fetid water. "Great Goddess, that place is terrible! Why'd it have to be there?"

Kaia just stared at him. "You're awfully whiny."

"It's just that…" Ryris scowled. "…it stinks in there!"

"It stinks in *here*! How long has it been since you had a bath?" Before he could reply, she spoke again. It seemed she had made their decision for them. "We leave as soon as the storm stops. It'll be a long journey." Kaia pulled the meat from the fire and set it on the log beside her. She picked it up with her fingers, careful not to burn them. After a quick sniff, she shrugged her shoulders with acceptance and took a bite.

Ryris' stomach churned as he watched her eat the suspect meat. He couldn't believe she would take that risk. When she held out a chunk in offering, he shook his head very sternly. He had a feeling she'd be vomiting in a matter of hours. He just hoped she'd go outside to do it.

"Do you have a wagon?" She talked while she chewed.

"I have a cart hidden down the mountain."

"Is it large enough to stow my armor?" She spit some charred connective tissue into the fire with a grimace, then kept eating.

"Should be. But after all the vomiting you're going to do after eating that rotten meat, are you sure it'll still fit?" Ryris shot her a sassy glance. She just stared at him in defiance and took another slow, deliberate bite, narrowing her eyes as she chewed.

"Well, since we're stuck in here until at least tomorrow, can I ask you something else?" Ryris was hopeful she'd be receptive to his questions. Now that they obviously felt more comfortable with each other, he was looking forward to knowing more about her personal life. Kaia nodded her approval. "Do you miss your family? I mean, because you've outlived them?"

"I made my peace with leaving everyone a long time ago. My duty—and my safety—came first. They all understood that. And, I'm assuming my father's empire doesn't even exist anymore. After all, I was an only child, and the bloodline, it would seem, 'died with me'."

Ryris' eyes widened in surprise. "Your father's empire? You mean you're a princess?"

"Technically, yes."

"Royalty and a warrior. Strange, you don't strike me as the 'princess type.'"

140

"Sorry to disappoint," Kaia deadpanned. She picked up the last strip of meat. "I was born with exceptional magical ability. My parents wanted me to become a high wizardress. As I grew older, it became apparent that I was just as skilled with weapons and tactics. The Crystal Guard took an interest in me, and asked my parents if they would allow me to be trained. At first they were adamantly against it. I, on the other hand, instantly became attached to the idea. When I was nine, I even ran away for three days—and tried to sneak into their ranks. I was found rather quickly, and returned to my parents." Her eyes twinkled in the firelight, obviously proud of her childhood rebellion. "I think they realized that they couldn't keep me from being what I strived to be, so they reluctantly allowed me to join. As their only child and heir to the throne, it wasn't a decision they made lightly. I convinced my father that it was a good thing, and that military training that would make me a better queen in the future. He finally agreed. I think he honestly thought no harm would ever come to me—or the kingdom. When the war started, I know it weighed heavily on them."

Ryris sighed in understanding. "It must have been hard for your parents to seal you away."

"My father did what he had to do. My magical ability and high profile made me a prime target for the hunters. In order to keep me safe, and ensure the future citizens had a protector if the need arose again, he agreed to seal us away. Magic use wasn't the only prerequisite, though. Ealsig and Jaric were the only other two generals left. We had to ensure we were all safe. The technology was researched and created, and several months later we were put into stasis. We were honored." She held out her hand. "Give me your dirk, it needs to be sharpened."

"You weren't scared?" He handed his weapon over.

"Do I look like the type to be easily frightened?"

Ryris shook his head, fearful he had offended her. "That's not what I meant..."

Kaia laughed, drawing his knife across a flat stone she found at the campsite. "You're funny when you're nervous. Of course I was scared. There was a moment where I feared what would happen to me, what would be waiting 'on the other side'." She held her head high. "But I was bound to protect the innocent, just like I am now bound to you."

Ryris had never felt "bound" to anyone, not even his father. Yes, they loved each other and had a deep connection not only through family but their shared business, but Kaia's words had hit him in a way he wasn't prepared for. The tone of her voice, the sternness in her expression—she was now a part of his life whether he liked it or not. He suddenly realized that he would follow her anywhere, do whatever she asked of him. Never in his life had he felt this way, and he doubted he ever would again.

"Once we collect the others, we'll need to get to the armory. The headquarters of the Guard are more than likely in ruins or gone by now, but the armory…it was relocated during the war. If it's still intact, we'll need to begin raising an army. Recruitment will be priority."

And just like that, the feeling of following Kaia's every word was gone.

"An army? Recruitment? Listen, I know you think there's something looming, and I totally believe you. But amassing military forces? The people won't be so quick to join up. And I'm just an alchemist. I don't know the first thing about armies and war."

"Ryris, war is coming. Between good and evil. You need to choose a side." She blew some stone dust from the newly-sharpened blade and handed it back to him with determination.

"Are you calling me 'evil'?"

"Of course not. There will come a time where those who you thought were on the side of light expose their tainted souls. To ensure you stay pure of heart, you must never let yourself stray, or have dark thoughts."

Her words shook him. He had always considered himself a good person, with strong morals. The same went for his father and his friends, the people in the village. He had only been in contact with one "truly evil" person in his life—the man who killed his mother. To think that there were those out there, who he knew, that might stray and follow the course of darkness chilled him. So, he did what he always did best—decided not to think about it.

"Well then, we'd better get some rest. If we're leaving in the morning, we need to be ready." His voice was unusually chipper, and he hoped Kaia couldn't sense that he was trying to change the subject on purpose.

She eyed him under intense scrutiny for a moment, before turning her attention to the fire. A minute later, a loud, rattling puff of air broke the silence of the cavern. Ass of the East let out a satisfied sigh before nestling her head close to her body. Ryris chuckled nervously, completely embarrassed by his horse's lack of manners.

Kaia wrinkled her nose at the offending odor. "That explains the strange name…"

~~~

It seemed like he had been in the cave forever.

As Ryris followed Kaia into the chamber she had lay in for centuries, he couldn't think of one good reason keeping him there. It was cold, dark, and dangerous. The previous night he swore he heard growling outside the mouth of the cavern and

142

spent the rest of the evening huddled under his blankets, only his eyes poking out—keeping watch for any critters or beasts that may have wandered in, interested in their fire. He had been exhausted in the morning when Kaia finally stirred, but unwilling to admit he had enjoyed little sleep. Instead, he played the part of well-rested companion and dutifully did as he was told to prepare for their departure.

"Take anything you want, or feel we'll need." Kaia pointed toward the myriad of shelves and cabinets. "And choose a weapon. Your puny dagger won't fend off a skellin."

Ryris immediately took offense, fighting the urge to stick his tongue out at her behind her back. He had paid good money for that dagger, and was rather proud of his purchase. Yes, he knew it wasn't the heartiest of weapons, but he felt safe with it at his side. But, his mind suddenly thought to the incinerated saberstrike carcass out in the cave, and he realized there would be many beasts along their travel route—and a 'puny dagger' most certainly wouldn't cut it. He grumbled and made his abhorrence for weapons known, before choosing the smallest, lightest shortsword he could handle. He hoped he never had to make use of it.

Kaia returned to the chamber from her secret room, carrying the pieces of her heavy armor in her hands. "Do you have a crate on your wagon? I won't be able to wear this mail while we travel the road, it'll bring unwanted attention."

The alchemist shook his head. "Not one big enough for the cuirass, but we can conceal that well enough, I'm sure."

Kaia looked at her armor with reverence. "I guess that'll have to do for now. I'm going to need some civilian clothes. This under mail wasn't meant to be worn alone."

"We can get you something in the next town. I agree that you probably shouldn't be cavorting around in mystical armor."

"I don't cavort." She shot him a confused-yet-stern glance before she unceremoniously broke the cabinet door containing her helmet. Careful of the shards of glass dangling from the door frame, she unlocked it from the inside and removed the accessory.

"Lose your key?" Ryris quirked a suspicious eyebrow.

She didn't answer, setting the helmet down on top of her former coffin. Moving past him silently, she approached the bookshelves and curled her hands around either side. With a mighty heave, she slid the shelving to the side, exposing a hidden nook. Resting inside was a linen-wrapped parcel, no longer than ten inches. Kaia grabbed it and turned back, not bothering to move the shelves once more.

"What's that?"

Again, she didn't answer, and tucked the item into a backpack Ryris had given her. Taking a few moments to carry her armor and knapsack into the cave proper while her companion packed various items from around the room, she finally returned. Grabbing her bow, she tested the tension on the crystal string. "Did you get everything you needed?"

"I'm working on it!"

She stared at him for a moment and readied her weapon. Whispering a soft word, an arrow of pure flame appeared, ready to strike. Ryris instantly realized she was going to destroy the room, and scrambled to collect as much as he could before she unleashed her projectile. He grabbed books, potions, and anything else he could cram into his pack or balance in his arms. When he was unable to tote anything else, he reluctantly backed out into the cave. Kaia followed, standing at the exit hole he had excavated. With incredible efficiency, she shot several arrows into the chamber, engulfing it in flames. At her gesture, they moved to a safe distance and she unleashed one more arrow, this time causing a massive explosion that felt as if it rocked the entire mountain. The wall crumbled, sealing the room off behind a layer of quickly-cooling molten rock. Ryris knew there was no way anyone could ever enter that place again.

Waving his hand in front of his face to dissipate the sulfurous scent of melting rock, he looked at her questioningly. "Why'd you have to destroy it? We could have just piled rocks again and sealed everything up."

Kaia just turned and walked away from what had been her sanctuary for centuries, never to come back. "Let's move out."

Turning heel, Ryris quickly followed her, the heavy backpack pulling on his shoulders. On their way out of the cave, he hastily scraped some aegis mold from the walls.

INTERLUDE ONE

"Catch him!"

The boy ran like the wind, stumbling over his feet as he looked over his shoulder in panicked terror. The other children were gaining ground, one of the other boys swinging a large stick. He fell and scraped his knee, his pants ripping. Blood dripped down his leg. Scrambling back to his feet, he prayed he could escape them.

"You can't get away!"

Panting frantically, the boy continued to run, even though he was tiring. Exhaustion was setting in, his lungs burning from overexertion, his feet screaming at him to stop running. He ran blindly through the back alleys, trying desperately to evade his pursuers. The choices available to him were quickly coming to an end, and he knew soon he would be caught. Again.

Forced out in the open when his back-alley route suddenly ended, the young boy had only one option for salvation—the cemetery. He avoided the place like the plague, never wandering near for fear of ghosts. His fear of death was almost crippling. The creepy headstones were like a warning to him— stay away. But, he could either run into the graveyard, or face the bullies. And that meant a certain and swift attack. He barely escaped the last one, and left the encounter with broken fingers and a bloody nose.

He bolted through the iron gates and darted behind a large stone monument. Sitting on his haunches, he desperately tried to calm his heavy breathing, for fear of being heard. He hoped the other boys forgot about their pursuit.

They hadn't.

Following him into the graveyard, they quickly located him and dragged him to his feet. He kicked and screamed, the children paying no mind to his pleas. The boy was terrified of what they might do to him in this place. His hands instinctively heated up, and one of the attackers yelped in pain as his skin was slightly singed.

"Don't even think about burning us, jackass! We'll tell your dad!"

He immediately let the heat die from his hands, for the only thing he feared more than the boys' impending torture was his father's wrath.

They laughed at him, mocking his fear as they led him deeper into the cemetery. A grove of trees in the middle held the scariest place of all—the crypt.

Reserved for noble decedents, the door was always locked to deter potential grave robbers. Unfortunately, it did nothing to dissipate the stench emanating from within. Unluckily for him, one of the attacking children was the son of the mortician—and just so happened to have the key. He had a sudden realization that the whole chase—and ending location—had been planned.

"Hope you like skeletons, Mensu!" One of the boys pushed him in and slammed the door behind him. "Magic-using weirdo!"

The lock turned, and he was trapped. He banged on the door with every ounce of strength he had, begging the boys to release him. He pleaded with their decency, hoping against hope that they'd see their error and let him go.

Their laughter got quieter as they walked away from the crypt.

Mensu clawed at the door, claustrophobia setting in. His fingertips began to bleed, the rough metal tearing open his skin. Surrounded by total darkness, the sickly-sweet aroma of decay penetrating his nostrils, he screamed until his voice went hoarse. He begged the Goddess to help him.

He rattled the knob in the hopes that someone would hear his cries. As his hysteria grew, he began to hyperventilate. There was no escape, of that he was sure. He briefly thought he might die in this place, surrounded by the skeletons of the noble. His young mind did not afford him the luxury of rational thought in his panicked state. It wasn't long before his surroundings began to play tricks on him. Skeletal hands reaching for his collar, intertwining their bony fingers in his hair. Ghosts in the air, pulling him into the abyss. It felt as if a thousand eyes were watching him.

The boy didn't know how long he had been trying to escape, for minutes seemed like hours in the dark recesses of the crypt. He couldn't take the blackness any longer. Terrified of the dark, but also terrified of what lay within, he finally brought flames to his hands. Bloody streaks cascaded down the door where he had clawed at the metal. He looked to his fingertips, the blood slowly incinerating into smoky wisps from the heat of the fire. Mensu shook. His heart thundered in his ears.

The door mocked him. How was he going to escape? The barrier was locked tight. The mortician's son had the key, which was more than likely safely back in his father's lock-box already, with the undertaker none the wiser. Sweat dripped into his collar, and he felt as if he might vomit. A rat skittered past his leg, causing him to yelp in terror and do an abrupt about-face, turning around into the crypt proper. His flaming hands illuminated the interior of the chamber.

Mensu screamed.

The bloated, decomposing body of a noblewoman lay atop her ceremonial bier. Her satin dress, once pale lavender and pristine, was now stained with the fluids of decay. Her hair had begun to fall from her skull as her scalp detached, her eyes sunken in and rotten. Lips once colored with ruby-red pigment were now gray and withered. A hand, purple where the blood had coagulated under her skin, hung limply off the side. The stench was overpowering.

He collapsed to the floor, unconsciousness pulling him under before the flames disappeared from his fingers.

Floating in limbo, Mensu saw ghostly mist envelop him from all sides. The air was cold around him, chilling him to the bone. After a moment, he found himself back on the floor. Curled into a ball, he trembled as nausea overtook him. He lay there for several minutes until the quaking subsided

146

and the sick feeling left him. Finally forcing himself to stand, he shook the fog from his head and let his eyes rest once more on the noblewoman before him.

The corpse began to twitch, a rotten hand reaching up into the emptiness above her. A garbled moan bubbled from her lips. After a moment of convulsions, the woman slid off her bier, her putrid, ballooning legs squishing with each step she took toward him. Eyes devoid of life, she stared at him longingly, her arms outstretched, her crooked fingers beckoning to him. Mensu tried to run, but found his feet were somehow frozen to the floor. Wave after wave of terror washed over him, his lungs unable to produce any semblance of a scream. Hot tears streamed down his face. He screwed his eyes shut, only to find he could still see the horrible abomination through closed lids.

The dead woman lunged forward, wrapping her gangrenous arms around his body. Mensu desperately tried to escape her clutches, but her grip was inhuman. She ran her withered fingers through his hair, a fingernail catching within his locks and breaking off with a sickening pop. He felt her lips against his cheek, could smell the rotten breath wafting from her gaping, aggressive mouth. She kissed his face, pulling him close like a mother would her child. A strip of putrid flesh sloughed from her chin and stuck to his skin.

Her touch sent jolts of electricity coursing through his veins, made goose bumps appear on his skin. Every time he tried to pull away, she just hugged him tighter, her disgusting hands digging into his back. She kept kissing his face, coagulated blood adhering to his flesh. He begged her to let go, but was met with malicious laughter. Her phantasmal voice echoed off the walls.

He knew he needed to get away, or he risked being dragged into the underworld with the hideous woman. Mensu pushed back with all his might, clawed at the tattered sleeves of her dress until he scratched through to rotten flesh. Nothing he could do caused her strength to wane.

"Mensu!"

He shrieked at the sound of his name, horrified that the dead woman knew who he was. Banging on her bloated chest, he flailed wildly in one last attempt to get away.

"Mensu, stop!"

His eyes snapped open and he saw his mother, panicked tears running down her face. Her eyes were wide with concern for her only child. Soft hands replaced that of the corpse-woman, strong-yet-gentle arms lovingly held him close. He fought to get away, scrambling from his mother's embrace in confusion.

Lying on the cold stone floor of the crypt, feeling his mother's soothing hand rub circles on the small of his back, all emotion left him. His thoughts, once filled with magical fantasies and hopes of being left alone by his bullies—were now inhabited by flashes of death, power, and rebirth. Malice. Decay. Ecstasy.

"Come, let's get you home." His mother tried to ease him up from the floor. He slapped her hand away, his body stiffening at her touch. She looked at him in saddened shock at his refusal of her help. Mensu pushed himself standing on his own, brushed off his clothes, and composed himself.

147

"Mensu? Baby?" His mother tried to get in his field of vision. "You're going to be alright…"

He stared past her, not seeing her caring face any longer. His gaze settled on that of the dead noblewoman. She lay exactly where she had been when he first set eyes on her. He was entranced by her decaying corpse, no longer afraid. No longer weak.

As his mother led him away, he noticed the name engraved into the stone below her body.

Lyta Farthrax.

CHAPTER SIXTEEN

"A man is not what he makes readily known. In truth, he is the sum of all that he hides."

--Excerpt from church homily, Father Oswin Morigar, 77th Winter, YG740

"How did you sleep, Your Highness?"

Emperor Roann squinted as Dr. Thal directed sunlight through a small lens at his eyes. He really wished he'd just quit already. His head was pounding, he was exhausted, and was moments away from throwing his physician out of the room out of sheer irritation.

"How do you think I slept? Between you and my mother waking me up every hour to make sure I was alright, I didn't really have a chance for quality rest. This has been going on for days; I think you can leave me be." Roann swatted his hand away.

The doctor recoiled at the young man's biting remarks. "I'm sorry, Your Grace. I didn't mean to offend. I am merely attempting to make a physical examination. You suffered a concussion, and it's my duty to make sure you're recovering normally."

"Just make it quick. I'd like to be left alone."

Thal pursed his lips into a scowl as he finished his exam. Roann huffed as he checked his pulse, changed the dressing on his head wound, and listened to his heart. The emperor saw it as a complete waste of time, and didn't feel much like cooperating any longer.

"Are you finished?" Roann was on the verge of losing his patience. He wanted them all to leave so he could suffer from his unrelenting headache in peace.

"For now." The doctor put his instruments back in his medical bag and bowed. "I'll be back this evening to check on you."

"No, you won't."

Eilith gasped from across the room, Roann shooting her an irritated look seconds later. Thal scurried away silently as the former empress rose from her seat, her face flushed, her eyes piercing.

"I can't believe how you just treated the man who brought you into this world!" Eilith rarely raised her voice, but Roann didn't really care that she was upset.

"He's annoying me—you both are. I'm not a child. I think I know my own body well enough to realize when something is wrong, and this isn't one of those times."

149

Eilith fumed. "Roann Vrelin, you've been irritable and moody since your father's death. I know we all deal with grief in our own way, but I don't think it's fair that you take it out on poor Dr. Thal—or me."

"I'm very stressed. You'll have to forgive me if I've been snippy." He tried to make his voice seem at least a little sincere.

Eilith sat down next to her son, patting his thigh. "It's not like you to act this way. I know that you're trying to deal with your father's passing the best you can, but I'd like you to stop and think before you speak. You've got an image to uphold, and mistreating your physician or other members of the offices isn't going to help you. They can only chalk it up to grief so many times."

Roann rolled his eyes, well aware that his mother could see his reaction. She immediately furrowed her brows in disappointment.

"Don't roll your eyes at me! I don't know what has come over you, but for your own sake and for the sake of your reputation, I suggest you nip whatever it is in the bud and move on. We're all grieving—don't make it harder by being an ass."

The young emperor laughed, his mother slapping his cheek seconds later. He rubbed his stinging face with a smirk.

"You haven't heard a word I've said. I'm leaving. You had better take this time alone to adjust your attitude." Eilith stood with a huff, and stalked away from her son, not even bothering to kiss him goodbye. Tears streamed down her cheeks.

Roann sat alone in his den, thankful he had finally been left alone.

~~~

"Oswin, I'm not bothering you, am I?"

Father Morigar turned to face the empress. Setting his holy book on the altar, he walked toward her with open arms. "Of course not, Your Highness. It's always a pleasure to see you."

Eilith extended her hands, which the priest took in his own and kissed. "The chapel is looking lovely. I'm amazed the flowers from Artol's service are still so fragrant." She leaned over to sniff a blossom.

"It's my honor to keep them fresh as long as possible." He motioned to a pew, and invited the empress to sit. "What brings you by today?"

"It's Roann…" She sighed as she sat, adjusting her flowing skirt underneath her. "I fear for him…he's not dealing with his grief, and I believe it's tearing him apart."

The old cleric nodded solemnly. "We each have our own ways of coping with the passing of a loved one. Granted, not all are conducive to healing, but we need to let

150

him grieve on his own terms, and in his own timeframe—however long or short that may be."

"But, he's so distant. And when he *is* present, he's downright mean-spirited. Today he snapped at Dr. Thal, all but banishing him. He got horribly mouthy with me and I...I slapped him. I've never in my life raised a hand to Roann; I don't know what came over me. His disrespect just made me so...*angry*." She began to weep softly, dabbing her eyes with her worn lace handkerchief. "I fear that I'm losing my son."

Morigar took her tiny hand in his and squeezed gently. "Eilith, that young man has just lost his father. He's trying to rule this country, take care of you, and make sure that Artol's memory lives on. He's stressed, and has never faced a demon such as this before. Now, I don't want it to seem like I'm making excuses for his behavior, but I want you to remember that he's human—we all are. Roann is kind-hearted and intelligent, but that doesn't mean he's not without flaws. I think we've come to expect perfection from him—especially since he demands it of himself—and we lose sight of the fact that, at the end of the day, he's just a man. A man who has devoted his life to his country and family. A man who needs to let off a little steam every now and then."

"Yes, but he's never acted this way—ever. I'm worried that he's...I don't know..." She held the handkerchief over her mouth and cried.

"Roann has lived so long in his father's shadow. It's now time for him to make a name for himself." The old man smiled warmly. "We're bound to see changes in him. We have to nurture and encourage him so he makes the right decisions."

"I know. It's just so difficult to watch him suffer—and I know he's suffering. Call it mother's intuition, but there's something troubling him, and its much deeper than his father's death. He's changed, Oswin."

"We all change, grow. Artol's stroke put him in a position of power that, even though he handled with grace unheard of in a young man his age, he more than likely wasn't ready for emotionally. He was only twenty-two years old, a time in most men's lives where they're just beginning to decide what they want to do with their life. But Roann—he was suddenly an emperor. Yes, he had been groomed to take his father's place one day—but he was thrust into it way sooner than anyone could have ever imagined. He was never given a chance to explore who he really was."

"I know your words are meant to be comforting, but I still can't help but feel like something is amiss. Will you talk to him, please? I trust your judgment, and if you think there's nothing strange, that it truly is just terrible grief, then I'll take your word for it and move on."

"I promise you he'll be just fine." Morigar smiled and leaned forward to embrace Eilith. There were few people she allowed such an honor, and he felt blessed that he was one of them. She rested her head on his shoulder and cried.

151

~~~

Morigar knocked on the heavy wooden door for the third time. The vase of flowers in his other hand was getting heavier by the moment. He knew Roann was in his private apartments, Casmit had told him as such. Looking to the antique clock hanging at the end of the hall, he contemplated returning later. He had an evening mass in a few hours' time, and still needed to finalize his sermon. Just as he was about to leave, the door swung open, producing a stern-faced emperor.

"Father Morigar, to what do I owe the honor?"

The cleric regarded him closely. He seemed to be physically fine, aside from the small bandage secured to his temple. But the sarcastic greeting the emperor had bestowed on him was very out of the ordinary. Roann's eyes didn't sparkle like they once did, and his posture was stiff and uninviting. He decided to proceed with caution.

"A friendly visit. We haven't really had the chance to speak since your father's memorial." Roann's eyebrows furrowed at the mention of Artol. "May I come in?"

The young sovereign hesitated for a long moment, silently watching the priest, before allowing him entry. "Let's talk in the den."

"If that is where you feel the most comfortable, Your Grace."

Roann turned without saying a word and walked deeper into the residence, expecting the priest to follow. Morigar looked around the apartment, noting the absence of light. Roann had always enjoyed his abode to be bright and cheery, with either the drapes thrown open to allow natural light in, or dozens of lamps to bathe the rooms in their soft glow. Yet here they were, just after two o'clock, and the rooms were dim and claustrophobic—very atypical of the young man's former preferences. The curtains were drawn, the lamps left unlit.

"Does your head hurt, Your Highness?"

"Of course it hurts. I hit it on my desk and bled all over my rug." The tone in his voice was condescending, something Morigar had never heard from him before. He crossed into the den, not bothering to hold the door for the cleric.

"I'm sorry to hear that. I only ask because you've extinguished all the lamps, and the curtains are drawn. I thought perhaps light is giving you a headache."

Roann huffed and plopped down onto a plush chair. "Can't a man sit in darkness without being questioned about it?"

"Your preferences are your own, Grace." Morigar followed Roann's actions and sat on a small sofa, facing the former prince. Placing the vase of blossoms on the table, he smoothed out his white robes before speaking. "I thought you might like some of your father's flow—"

152

"My mother sent you, didn't she?" Roann stared directly into his soul.

Morigar instantly felt very uncomfortable. The young man had never looked at him in such a manner, and certainly would never interrupt. The old cleric was beginning to think Eilith wasn't imagining things. He sighed and decided to be honest. It was apparent that Roann was in no mood to be trifled with. "Yes, she did. She's worried about you."

"Why? Because I was sick of Thal quite literally being in my face?" Roann threw his leg over the arm of the chair, lazily draping his arm around the back.

"She says you've been very distant since your father's death, and irritable."

Roann rolled his eyes. "I'm assuming you're going to give me a lecture about how everyone grieves differently and that I should try and be nicer to those around me, right?"

Morigar couldn't believe what he was hearing. The kind, sweet prince he once knew had been replaced by a sarcastic bully. He wanted to believe the young emperor was just overtaken by grief in the wake of his father's death, and didn't properly know how to deal with it. Folding his hands in his lap, he inhaled deeply, considering his words carefully before he responded.

"Hear me out—please. I understand that losing someone dear to you is very unsettling. I lost my father when I was not much older than you, and to the same affliction. It's something no one ever wants to experience, even though we know it is inevitable. But you must remember that you are the sovereign of the most powerful nation on the planet. You can't just go belittling your physician—or your mother."

"Are you going to slap me, too?"

The old priest huffed in annoyance, trying to keep his composure. He was quickly growing tired of the young man's antics. "It worries me that you're obviously not seeing the bigger picture. If you get too comfortable being so harsh with those you love, even in a time of grief, it may bubble over into your official duties—and I know for a fact that your father would be very ashamed of you."

"My father is dead."

The coldness in Roann's voice sent a chill down the cleric's spine. In that moment, he came to the terrifying realization that Eilith was more right then she knew. A mother's intuition, it would seem, was never wrong. The young emperor was slipping from them. Morigar sensed that this went beyond grief, but he couldn't for the life of him figure out how—or why. He suddenly wanted to be very far from the young man. But, his duty to the people included ensuring that the members of the royal family were taken care of—and he intended to help Roann come to terms with whatever was causing him to behave in such a disrespectful and ill-fitting manner. Sighing deeply, he finally found the words he was looking for.

"Your Highness, I know you don't want to hear it right now, but you're in need of guidance. If you won't accept it from me, I urge you to seek it from Oleana. She can help in ways that I cannot."

Roann laughed, his voice echoing off the high ceilings. "Oleana? Since when has she been of any use?"

"She helps us live our lives to their fullest, guides us in times of need."

"I don't need anyone's guidance!" Roann's eyes bulged with fury and he leapt out of his seat, roaring at the surprised cleric. "I don't need some moldy goddess to tell me how to live my life. She can't help me—because I've never believed in her!"

Morigar sat, utterly stunned. Roann's words cut through his heart. The young man that had dutifully attended services with his parents, who prayed along with him at his own coronation, who never once spoke ill of the Goddess—had just renounced his faith. Whether or not he never believed in the first place, or if it was a new occurrence, the priest did not know. He understood that in times of great grief, people had been known to abandon their religion, believing their deity had somehow wronged them by taking their loved one or bestowing tragedy on a family. But the way Roann spoke— the cleric suddenly realized the former prince had been living a sly charade his entire life.

In that moment, the priest knew no more of his words—if any were before— would be accepted by the emperor. He finally stood, hands shaking, face flushed. With Roann's revelation, his entire world had just crumbled before him and he didn't know what to do. He tried to diffuse the situation, still holding onto the small kernel of hope that the emperor's enormous grief over the death of Artol was wreaking havoc on his mind.

"I...I can see that you're upset, Your Grace. And that you're obviously not thinking clearly." Morigar began to back away. "I'm going to leave now, and I hope that you can get some rest."

Refusing to acknowledge the cleric any further, he waved his hand dismissively and slumped back in the chair. He turned to face the wall with an irritated huff.

As Morigar hurried from the emperor's apartments, the air temperature dropped, forcing the priest to pull his robes tightly around his body for warmth.

~~~

The deep snow of the mountains was a distant memory. Alchemist and warrior bounced on the wagon seat, the late-autumn sunshine warming their bodies. The central plains spread out around them, tall grasses swaying in the light breeze. A small forest of trees grew in the distance, dotting the grassland with greenery directly in their path. Where arctic winds had taken hold on the north, the central portion of the empire enjoyed a temperate climate suited for comfortable travel year-round.

"You look really nice."

Ryris admired Kaia in her new clothes. She sat beside him on the wagon seat, dressed casually in riding pants and a cropped jacket, looking every bit the part of a civilian. Gone were her armored boots, replaced by simple leather ones. Her shirt was light yellow, the color of her hair, her pants a deep chocolate brown. The coat was leather, adorned with a few metal buckles. She had pulled her hair back into a loose ponytail, securing it with a simple cotton ribbon. Her crystal suit of armor and under mail was safely stowed beneath the wagon tarp, away from prying eyes and greedy hands.

He had to admit, she was radiant. Ryris stifled the butterflies when she turned with a smile to acknowledge him.

"Thank you." Kaia pushed a stray lock of hair behind her ear. "I'll admit I was weary of the fashion choices of your time, but I'm pleasantly surprised." She adjusted her jacket, pulling it down to cover her hips.

"Must be nice, after wearing that armor for centuries."

"I miss it, actually. The weight." She sighed.

"I've never worn armor. I guess it would be interesting to experience it just once. Then again, I'd probably trip and make a fool of myself." Ryris chuckled. "On second thought, I think I'll be happy without it."

"It's definitely not something you can just 'throw on' and resume like normal. It takes training to be able to move in it. You might benefit from light armor at some point; most of the battlemages wore some form or another."

Ryris' mind wandered. A battlemage? Could he ever be such a thing? Would he even *want* to? The closest thing to war he had ever experienced was playing 'storm the castle' when he was a child. He and Grildi would take turns building forts from barrels, crates, tarps, and various other materials and then the other would try and knock it down. Grildi always won—but Ryris still enjoyed playing for hours on end.

Once again, their true situation hit him as he realized she had only suggested armor because they would be going to war at some point. Ryris swallowed hard and focused his attention back to the road, his companion gazing out at the thick forest suddenly surrounding the path. He maneuvered the wagon through the grove.

After several long moments, Kaia called out, breaking the silence. She pointed through the trees to a glade of glowing buds in the distance. Putting her hand on the

155

hilt of her shortsword laying on the seat out of instinct, she readied herself for impending danger. "What is that?"

Ryris brought Ass of the East to a stop and squinted, peering off into the thick underbrush. It took him a moment to locate what she had seen, but when he did, his eyes glittered with delight and a huge smile spread across his face. He jumped down from the seat and dug under the wagon's tarp, finally finding a small bucket and a set of clippers. "Dragon's talon!"

"What are you doing?" Kaia seemed irritated that they had stopped. "We can't waste time picking flowers."

"I'll only be a few minutes. And they're not flowers, they're rare seed pods. I can't pass up the opportunity." He trotted off into the woods, leaving Kaia to mind the wagon before she could object further.

Trudging through the dense foliage, the sunlight waned as the canopy above him became thicker and thicker. The light from the curved pods atop the stalks lit his way, beckoning him toward the patch. This ingredient was almost as rare as oinox teeth, and equally as valuable. Contained inside the glowing green pods were seeds that, when crushed and mixed properly with a few choice ingredients, could stop a man's heart in seconds. The thick stalks only grew in acidic soil left behind by rotting Kenaf trees and even then the probability of finding any was slim to none. That wasn't necessarily a bad thing, when one looked at what the ingredients were used for. Most people had no idea they could be harvested to make a deadly poison.

Ryris made quick work snipping the stems with his clippers, grumbling as the thorns snagged on his clothes and hair. One particularly aggressive stem dug into his collar, and as he leaned forward to clip the last bunch, tugged at the chain of his amulet—pulling it from his neck. It hung on the thick, reedy stem, swinging in the wind.

It took Ryris a full minute to notice.

~ ~ ~

He was finally alone.

Roann had managed to sneak out of the palace soon after the annoying priest took his leave. Making use of access tunnels and delivery alcoves in the basement, the emperor had stealthily exited the citadel—and the city—and soon found himself in the forests surrounding Keld.

The presumptuous cleric had irritated him to the point of anger, and he knew he needed to let off some steam. There had been a moment, when the priest had been close enough to strike, that Roann had briefly contemplated lashing out physically. But he knew that there'd be no talking his way out of the consequences. A few months ago,

Roann would have felt horrible for acting so horribly—or wouldn't have behaved in such a way at all. But he was at a new juncture in his life, and had new power in which to utilize. His destiny changed the moment his father passed, even if those around him didn't understand how.

Tightening his grip on the bow in his hand, he stalked his prey. Hunting always relaxed him, allowed him to become one with nature. In his youth, Artol had taught him the value of all living things, and that they only killed an animal to eat it and utilize every part possible. Now, with his father gone and his morals dwindling, Roann was enjoying the hunt for the sheer thrill. He hoped whatever he killed would bleed profusely.

Locating his target—a grand buck with a majestic and sturdy rack—he quietly skulked around a tree, making sure his footfalls went unheard. Pressing his body flat against the massive, rough trunk, he peered around to make sure the deer was still in range. It stood just over fifty feet away, head close to the ground as it munched on a berry bush. Roann had a clear shot of its left flank, and readied his bow. Cocking an arrow and pulling back on the string, he held his breath.

Pain tore through his chest seconds later, causing him to drop the bow and fall against the tree, trying desperately to remain standing. The buck, sensing the commotion, turned and galloped off in the opposite direction. The emperor struggled to breathe as all his nerve endings jolted with unseen electricity. The pain was more unbearable than he had ever encountered before, much more so than what he had experienced earlier in the week. He couldn't see. He couldn't hear. His body felt as if it were on fire. The pain was so intense; Roann began to wish for death. It seemed like the only way to achieve salvation from the agony.

His eyes screwed shut, and blood seeped from underneath the lids. The crimson liquid also dripped from his ears and nose. He was still alone, screaming in agony in the dense forest. His body shook as if chilled to the bone, even though his skin was flushed red with wave upon wave of unrelenting heat. Vomiting near the base of the tree, he finally collapsed, his knees sinking into the muddy ground, his hands clutching at the bark to steady himself. Finally unable to hold on any longer, he curled himself into the fetal position and writhed on the forest floor.

As his body lay on the mossy ground, his hands clenched into rigid claws, his knees locked. Saliva dripped from the corner of his mouth as a seizure wracked his entire body. His eyes rolled back into their sockets, images swirling in his brain, sending him deeper into confusion.

Warriors, battles, shimmering weapons…magic.

Roann laid seizing on the forest floor for several moments, the wildlife casting a curious glance at the man in their presence. Gurgling sounds emanated from his throat as he choked in the throes of his violent quaking.

After what seemed like an eternity, he was granted reprieve from the episode. His body still trembled, his mind was exhausted. His bones ached in their marrow, his nose trickled with warm blood. Utterly spent of energy, he ultimately lost consciousness. Moments later, a skellin sniffed at his hair and decided to move on.

When Roann awoke, it was dusk. His clothes were dirty, his hair matted and full of burrs. Mud caked his knees, and trails of dried blood snaked their way across his face and disappeared down into his collar. He was slow to rise, sitting first to allow his senses to recuperate. Pinching the bridge of his nose, he swayed slightly as a sharp pain erupted from behind his left eye. Taking a few deep breaths, the feeling finally subsided, and Roann was left to his thoughts in the middle of the forest.

He had no idea how much time had passed, or what had happened. The last thing the emperor remembered was tracking the buck—and then losing consciousness. He looked down to his side to find his ornate bow, covered with dried leaves from the canopy above. Knowing he needed to get out of the forest before he caught his death, he grabbed the weapon and used it as leverage to hoist his aching body from the ground. He would try and figure out what had happened to him when he got back to the palace. Using his bow as a makeshift walking stick, Roann slowly made his way back to Keld— the lights of the city just beginning to flicker on in the distance.

~~~

"..."

The hair on Roann's arms stood on end and his back stiffened as he drew in a deep, surprised breath. He knew this feeling—and welcomed it, especially after the event he'd just encountered. Perhaps he would finally get some answers. Emerging from the dank access tunnel leading into the palace, he took a quick look to make sure no one was watching. The basement was empty this time of night, and he knew he was alone. Deftly moving down the hallway, he ducked into a familiar room, a menacing smile creeping over his lips.

He moved to stand directly in the middle of the arena, his footsteps clicking on the cobblestones. Racks of weapons glittered in the warm light of the lamps. With a flick of his hand, the bolt on the door locked on its own.

"...come...now..."

The prince's eyes fluttered shut for a moment. He stood motionless in his place, taking even breaths in preparation. When his eyes snapped open once again, the emerald green hue had been replaced by a jet black iris and white. Iridescent swirls floated through the abyss of his blackened eyes, like an oil slick. One stern glance at the lamps flickering on the wall, and the flames dissipated, leaving thin wisps of smoke trailing upwards into the air.

A surge of power coursed through Roann's body as he sunk to one knee. His eyes rolled back into his head as he concentrated his mental energy. A low hum reverberated from deep within his chest as he reached out his consciousness in search of his destination. When he made contact, he threw his arms wide, arched his back, and craned his neck backwards, his face pointed upwards toward the buttressed ceiling. The young emperor's mouth hung open in anticipation as his entire body was enveloped in a red light. A split second later, he disappeared. The faint acrid smell of burnt ozone lingered for a long moment before the oil lamps re-lit themselves.

~~~

Roann flashed into existence within the chamber, the volcanic heat instantly assaulting him. Undeterred by the familiar oppressiveness, he wasted no time in approaching the stone font in the middle of the room. He wanted answers. After a long moment, the pedestal flickered with a familiar blue flame and he smiled maliciously, the azure fire reflecting in the black pools of his eyes. The glow illuminated the dried blood streaks on his face, imparting a ghostly visage on the young man.

"Did you...feel it?"

"Yes, Master. But I don't know what it was." Roann tapped his signet ring on the font, the gold clinking against the stone with precise rhythm.

"It was...brief." The voice paused. *"What...did you experience...in the forest?"*

"Unrelenting pain." The emperor stood tall, unwilling to waver at the memory of the agony he had felt. "It hit me with no warning. One moment I was about to kill a deer and the next thing I knew, I couldn't breathe. My body felt like it was on fire."

"Did you have...a vision?"

"I saw a shimmering warrior. But the image was gone in a split second, replaced by more agony." Roann inhaled deeply, the sulfuric stench of molten rock surrounding the chamber ceasing to bother him years ago. "What do we do?"

"We cannot afford...to wait. The wheel...is in motion. We...no longer have...any obstacles. We cannot...ignore the signs. It is...time for me to...return."

Roann smirked maliciously in the the eerily-lit chamber. Decades of training, planning, and waiting had all led up to this moment. He could hardly contain his excitement.

"Yes, Master Lyrax."

159

CHAPTER SEVENTEEN

Giants, while interesting specimens to observe from a distance, will nevertheless not hesitate to viciously attack if they feel provoked. With subpar intellect, poor eyesight, and aggressive tendencies, they are best left alone.

--Excerpt from 'Compendium on Giants', Trina Xanderfal, Anthropology Professor, Whitehaven University

After three days of travel, the companions had left the snowy Screaming Peaks and crossed into the central plains. Eight days later, they had entered the Lake Browal basin, and after a brief stop in Dungannon, only four days remained before the Heaving Marsh welcomed them with muddy, musty arms...

"Do you know why it's called the 'Heaving Marsh'?"

Ryris shrugged. He had honestly never thought about it. All of his time there was spent daydreaming about the moment when he could leave. "Because the stench makes you want to heave your guts out?"

"An amusing guess, but nonetheless incorrect." Kaia's eyes crinkled at the sides as she smiled at his response. "Tens of thousands of years ago, the area had been a deep valley. A great geologic upheaval—literally—occurred and pushed what is now the swampland hundreds of feet above where it once lay. Natural springs and rainwater over generations eventually filled in, creating the murky land there today. When the spring rains arrive, the swamp 'breathes', the moisture causing the land to undulate on its own."

Astounded at the information that seemed to drip out of Kaia's brain at every turn, Ryris sighed and smiled. "You're really smart, you know that? I've learned so much history the last three-odd weeks."

"Think about how much more you'll know by nightfall."

She was speaking of Phia, of course, and everything she hoped to glean from her centuries of knowledge since the war. Kaia was convinced that their only hope lay in what the ancient giant knew—or remembered. Ryris was still very skeptical that this enigmatic Phia would be able to help them.

The edge of the marsh loomed in the distance, and Ryris knew he would soon be enjoying all the *wonderful* aromas and scenery it had to offer. He shuddered and wished Oleana would just pluck him from the wagon seat and rapture him.

160

As they crossed the boundary, Ryris was immediately assaulted with the moldy, stagnant stench of the marsh. He briefly considered asking Kaia if she could go on ahead, prepared to volunteer to watch the wagon. Kaia never even flinched at the offending odor. Holding his hand over his nose and mouth, he encouraged Ass of the East to move forward into the darkness of the Heaving Marsh.

Three hours of slogging through the mire had rendered them exhausted, filthy, and irritable. The path, if you could call it that, was unforgiving and not always present. The wagon had been stuck in the mud no less than five times—Ryris stopped counting after the last incident. Though he was fairly certain he felt swamp worms wriggling within his pants, he was not about to put his hands in and check. Just as he was about to give up and force Kaia back to respectable land, she pointed into the distance, at a thin column of rising smoke.

"Phia's house."

Ryris squinted in the dim light, barely able to discern flora from fauna, let alone make out a building. Every bit of scenery blended together, forming a gray, dingy landscape. He reminded himself again just how much he hated the swamps as he swatted a giant insect from in front of his face.

"I don't see anything. Just mud."

Kaia forcibly turned his head in the direction she had been pointing. "Right. There."

Again, the young man narrowed his eyes and tried to find this mystery hut. After a moment of searching, he finally spotted it. A single, dome-roofed structure made of mud bricks. There was no way, he thought, that a giant could live there without hitting her head on the ceiling. A faint light flickered in the hollowed-out window, devoid of glass or a proper shutter. As they continued forward, Ryris noticed a piece of fabric strung across the doorway, fluttering on the humid swamp breeze. A barrel sat against the side wall, overflowing with murky water. An animal carcass, half dissected, hung from a post a few feet from the hovel, flies swarming around in a dark cloud. Wrinkling his nose in disgust, he really hoped Phia wasn't at home.

"Stop the cart. We walk the rest of the way."

"I'm not walking in any more muck!" Ryris scoffed, pointing to the soggy ground. "Besides, something will eat East if we just leave her here." As if on cue, a mysterious growl floated through the air, allowing the alchemist to look at Kaia incredulously. "See? You hear that?"

"You're imagining things." The warrior hopped down from the wagon seat and began digging through the bed of the trailer. After a quick search, Kaia pulled her armored boots from a crate and slipped them on before grabbing her knapsack. "Phia can be skittish, and if she hears a wagon coming, she's liable to get spooked. If she runs, we won't see her again for weeks. She'll recognize the sound of my armor, trust me."

Scowling, Ryris realized that once again, he needed to rely on his companion's judgment. Everything about this adventure was new, and he was at her mercy. Huffing, he jumped down from his seat, immediately sinking into the spongy ground. He took a moment to gather some supplies into his knapsack before tying Ass of the East to the nearest tree. Setting two buckets down on the ground, he filled one with clean water from their waterskin and the other with oats. He petted her mane as she drank from the bucket. "Be good, girl. Watch out for beasties."

"We're wasting time." Kaia had already trudged on ahead of him, using a fallen branch as a walking stick. It sunk into the mud with each step, but she didn't pay it any mind.

Ryris followed, grumbling as his boots flooded with murky water. Every step sucked them down, and the companions had to work twice as hard to pull themselves out. In hindsight, even if they had taken the wagon, it would have never made it to the other side of the swill they were attempting to cross. When they finally made it to relatively solid land again, they were tired and sore, and more than ready to sit down and rest.

Kaia kicked her booted feet against the trunk of a giant old-growth tree to remove the sediment. Ryris did the same, instantly regretting it, as his simple leather footwear didn't protect him against jarring blows. He yelped in pain as his foot smashed against the tree, Kaia shushing him with a finger over her lips. Her voice was a harsh whisper.

"Quiet!"

Walking in a slow, deliberate manner, Kaia made her way toward the hut. The crystal joints of her boots creaked softly with a very unique sound. Ryris now understood how Phia would distinguish her footfalls from that of any other visitor. As she neared the structure, a low gravelly voice floated out from inside the building.

"I can hear your squeaky boots a mile away, Kaia the Quick."

Ryris couldn't believe his ears. She had been right. As they approached, an old and pained grunt bellowed from within the hut, followed soon after by heavy-footed shuffling. The fabric floating across the door pulled back, courtesy of a humongous hand. Seconds later, ducking to exit, Phia appeared. Ryris gasped in awe.

Towering several feet taller than Grildi even with her old-age stoop, Phia was an impressive sight. Her dark gray skin was emblazoned with centuries-worth of ornate tattoos, though faded with time, her head shiny and bald. Her pants were ragged, the sleeveless shirt she wore much the same. Heavy black boots, worn and crusty, adorned

162

her gargantuan feet. She moved slowly, her age obviously a factor. The butt-end of a large whittled tree branch rested under the palm of her massive hand, helping her to walk and feel out her surroundings. Her face was saggy and pocked, both eyes clouded over milky-white. She approached them with purpose, no hint of fear or hesitation in her movements.

"Well what are you waiting for?" Her face erupted into a large grin seconds later, her yellow teeth gleaming against her dark skin. Kaia smiled and hastened her steps, inviting Ryris to do the same. A moment later, she was directly in front of Phia, the giantess reaching out a hand to lovingly stroke her hair, much like a mother to her child.

"I've missed you, young lady. I knew you'd come back to me—some day." She turned in Ryris' direction. "Who's your friend? He smells nice."

Covertly lifting his arm, he sniffed, grimacing at the powerful aroma of sweat and swamp infiltrating his nostrils. He didn't know how he'd classify his scent, but it definitely wasn't 'nice'. Ryris realized her lack of vision more than likely tripled the potency of her other senses. She probably heard him stomping ungracefully through the mud, and had obviously smelled him. Looking to Kaia for silent instructions, he was unsure if she would introduce him or he should take the helm. His companion gestured to Phia with an open hand, imploring him to stop being rude.

"I'm Ryris Bren. It's nice to m—"

"Ryris?" Phia gripped her giant cane tightly and as quickly as she was able, moved to his side. Reaching out her other hand, she ran her fingers across his face and through his hair without invitation, finally trailing them down his arms before grabbing one of his hands. "You resemble him. Hair's different, though." The alchemist inhaled sharply in surprise, and before he could reply, she spoke again, seemingly answering the unasked question on the tip of his tongue. She squeezed his hand. "Yes, I knew him. A good man. Brave and powerful."

"You really are as old as Kaia says…" Ryris' voice was wispy with awe.

"That's no way to talk to a lady, young man." She straightened her posture as much as she could, her impressive height obscuring what little sunlight filtered down through the heavy swamp canopy. Ryris had to crane his neck up to look her in the face. Her mouth had curled into a stern scowl.

"S-sorry. I didn't mean to offend you…" He nervously wrung his hands together. This was the second strange woman in a month that he had successfully insulted—and his track record was looking mighty bleak.

Phia bellowed out a mighty laugh and clapped him on the shoulder, nearly knocking him down. "You're funny! Let me tell you something—I'm too old to get

163

offended." Grabbing him a little too hard by the hand, she led them toward her house. Ryris allowed himself to be dragged—he really had no choice in the matter—for her grip was strong and unrelenting. He just hoped she knew where she was going.

Seconds later, he found himself inside the hovel, the stench of mildew and stagnant water assaulting his senses. Phia let go and blindly found her way to a huge rocking chair. It creaked under her massive frame as she sat. With a great sigh she set her walking stick against the wall at her side.

"Sit. Rest. Are you hungry?"

Ryris shrugged as he looked to Kaia, a bewildered expression crossing his face. There wasn't any more furniture to sit on. Kaia just rolled her eyes with annoyance at him and plopped down onto the floor, motioning for him to do the same. It was apparent both women weren't big on formalities.

"We'd be honored to share a meal with you, Phia. It's been a long time." Kaia smiled, even though Phia could not see it.

The giantess nodded. "Yes. A long time. But…" she leaned forward slightly, her voice taking on a knowing tone. "…I knew you were coming. There's been a foreboding presence in the world for ages now, but it was always weak, faint. I didn't pay it much attention because frankly, what could I do? Just in the last thirty-or-so years, it's grown ever stronger and more powerful. And now…you're here. It's not a coincidence. I fear terrible times are upon us." She shifted her weight on the poor, creaking chair. "Tell me, Ryris…how did you come to find the lovely Kaia?"

Ryris blushed at the mention of Kaia's beauty, thankful that the hut was dim and Phia was blind. "Chance, really. Some kids found her chamber and then let it slip to me that she was there."

Phia rocked in her chair, a great sigh escaping her lungs. "No. Not chance. You may not have known exactly who was in that cave, but you knew of her nonetheless."

The young alchemist was filled with wonder. It was like she could see into his thoughts. "My Gran told me stories as a child about the Crystal Guard, and always alluded to the fact that there was something to do with our family history."

"As does that amulet."

Again, the giant had astounded him. Here she was, blind as a bat, and knew the talisman was in her presence. All this destiny business was getting more and more real every moment more he spent with Kaia—and now Phia.

"Phia," Kaia's voice was soft, but strong and determined. "We need guidance. It's essential that we fin—"

164

The giantess held her hand up, and Kaia immediately stopped talking. "I'll tell you where your comrades are later. First, the amulet. You've had it since infancy, yes? Do you know why?"

"To protect me. Kaia explained it in greater detail, told me about the war and the other Ryris."

"Yes, I'm sure she has. Come closer." Phia beckoned with her finger and the alchemist obliged, kneeling before her chair. The giantess leaned forward and reached out, blindly finding the amulet before taking it in her massive hand. On her finger, a shiny metal ring with a tiny shard of crystal caught Ryris' eye. She ran her rough fingertips over the smooth cabochon. "This stone is unique. It's called 'Shimmerbane'. It belonged to Kaia's family, and was said to have strange properties. It once rested atop a beautiful scepter, kept locked in the coffers and away from prying eyes. The seers claimed they could view the future within it; the wizards thought it would enhance their powers. Whether those legends were true, no one ever really knew. What was known was that it did possess *something*. When you held it in your hands, surges of power ran through your veins, the feeling of invincibility coursed over you. That's why it was kept hidden. If it fell into the wrong hands, the consequences could be dire. What those consequences were exactly—well, no one knows. No one wanted to find out." She let go of the bauble and sat back once more.

Ryris moved back to his spot, resting his weight on his arms behind him. He listened intently as Phia continued.

"When the time came to protect your ancestor, Shimmerbane was the natural choice for the amulet. Its inherent power made it the perfect vessel to imbue with more potential."

"How was it enchanted?"

"There are some things even I do not know, child." Phia smiled wryly. "Tell me, has it ever reacted to anything? Or anyone?"

This was the second time in as many weeks that someone had asked him the very same question. "It gets warm when I…" he hesitated.

"Use your magic?"

No longer shocked by any of her revelations, Ryris replied honestly. "Yes. Usually it just heats up my skin, but a few months back—"

"…And people? Has it ever reacted to a person?"

"One. I think." He tried to remember back to the incident, recalling every detail for Phia. "The prince, before he became emperor, came to pay his respects after I opened my shop. He asked me questions about my inventory and alchemy in general.

Really nice man, seemed genuinely interested in what I was saying. I even showed him some ingredients he had been admiring. After a few moments, I realized I hadn't introduced myself properly, and we shook hands. That's when..."

"He was overcome."

"How did you know?" Ryris stared blankly at his hostess.

"Please, go on."

Ryris sighed as he brought the memories back to himself. "I immediately helped him sit, and broke contact. After a few minutes, he was well enough to stand on his own and left. Later I got a letter from him, apologizing for falling ill."

"And the amulet? How did it react?"

Ryris shrugged. "That's the thing—it didn't. Later that morning, I rubbed my hand on my chest and noticed soot on my fingertips. I checked in the mirror and there was a smudge directly under the amulet—but nowhere else. I figured I had touched the hearth sometime during the day and had marked myself. Kaia seems to think there's more to it."

Phia shook her head somberly. "The amulet protects you. That bauble sees in men what the naked eye cannot."

"So what? You're saying that Roann is the source of this 'evil' you two sense? I think you're mistaken."

"Your talisman may not always react in ways you can feel or sense, but in ways that affect others as well. I don't believe Roann's sickness was due to anything in your shop. Your amulet—and the power that it exudes—protected you that day. *It* was what caused him to fall ill—and the soot was just a byproduct. You said so yourself, it heats up when you use your *magic*. Unless I'm mistaken and you were setting fires in the presence of the prince, it would not have reacted like usual. Just because you only know it to have one effect, does not mean there aren't more you haven't discovered yet. I fear Roann's physical reaction to touching you is an omen—a sign. A sign we cannot ignore in good conscience."

Ryris scowled, his frustration mounting. "I don't see how this one instance can be damning in your eyes. It doesn't make any sense, he seems like a good guy. I'm beginning to think all this 'evil' nonsense is being blown way out of proportion, or you're looking for an easy scapegoat." He stood and shook his head, his face feeling flushed, before heading for the door. "I need some air..."

Kaia moved to go after him, but Phia grabbed her arm and pulled her to sit once again. "Let him go. He'll see the truth eventually." She sat back in her great chair and rocked. "Tell me what you know of the emperor. I'm quite out of the loop when

166

it comes to politics, and no one ever visits me." The giantess shot Kaia a mock-dejected look, trying to guilt her for staying away so long.

"I only knew what Ryris had told me, and Roann seemed too perfect. No one is that wonderful." Kaia shook her head and continued. "As we were traveling, I began gleaning more from small talk in pubs and inns…"

Kaia told Phia everything she had learned about the newly-independent emperor. The giantess listened intently, nodding with an acknowledging hum when something particularly interesting came up.

"…and something's not right. Where others might see a grief stricken man, I see too abrupt a change to be normal wallowing. It's almost like someone—or something—finally saw their way in and took over completely. I think there's something more sinister at work. I wouldn't be here if there wasn't."

"You have a good head on your shoulders, Kaia. I've known you far longer than our young alchemist friend, and I trust you. In time, Ryris will come to trust you as well."

"I just hope we're right—that I'm right. We've crossed the threshold, and once we find my comrades, there'll be no turning back. Am I doing the right thing? I've dragged Ryris into this without giving him a choice and on what, a hunch?"

The giantess reached out for Kaia's cheek, the warrior leaning forward so Phia could touch her. Phia lovingly rubbed her rough fingertip over the porcelain skin. "Child, you always do the right thing. You're not capable of any wrong-doing, that I know for a fact. Your heart is pure, and your will is strong. And as for Ryris, he'd follow you no matter what, of that you can be certain. You know what is on the horizon, yes? You can feel it?"

"Yes, but…"

"Then don't doubt yourself. The time has come, whether we're ready or not." Phia rubbed her stomach. "Now, help me gather vegetables so we can get a meal prepared. The lad will be back soon, don't you worry."

Kaia did as she was told without any doubt left in her mind.

CHAPTER EIGHTEEN

"...the arc blasted across the land...incineration for many...victory for us all..."

--Final words of Meridian Velken, last known Farnfoss casualty of the Old War.

The aroma of stewed vegetables tickled Ryris' nostrils. The scent was so intoxicatingly delicious that he had to remind himself he was in a swamp—and not back in Keld. As he pushed the cloth door aside and re-entered Phia's hut, the herbed air assaulted his senses and he was suddenly extremely hungry.

"Ah, you've come back to us. We were starting to think you ran off for good." Phia rocked in her chair as Kaia stirred the bubbling cauldron over the hearth. The young heroine looked over her shoulder at Ryris, saying nothing.

"Yeah, I..." Ryris nervously scratched the back of his neck, forcing himself to make eye contact with the two women. He moved to Kaia's side, peered into the churning pot, and spoke sincerely. "I overreacted, and I'm sorry."

Kaia stirred the stew for a moment before responding. "You're forgiven." She pointed to a chair she had uncovered, and invited him to sit.

"I did a lot of thinking while I was out there. I didn't want to believe what you two were saying, because if I did, it would mean that everything I thought to be true would change. I didn't want to face the reality that Roann could behind whatever you fear is on the horizon."

Phia raised a finger. "Now remember, I haven't said he's behind everything...just that it's a very good possibility that our impending situation has something to do with him. There's a big difference."

Ryris responded as Kaia handed him a steaming bowl of stew. "I understand. Whatever is going on, the world is a much darker place than I've ever known it to be. I'm willing to admit that I'm very afraid."

"As you should be, young Mr. Bren." Phia's expression hardened. "Lives will be lost, cities destroyed. The lurking forces will once again wash over our shores."

Ryris sat forward, his mouth overflowing with food. "Lyrax."

Phia jumped at the mention of his name, nearly dropping her bowl.

Kaia sighed and put her own bowl down on the floor in front of her. "Who else could produce such a terrible aura, such a cloud over the fate of the entire world? Ryris and I talked earlier about destiny—and who else but Lyrax could alter it? He almost destroyed us once..."

"That's a mighty big assumption, dear. But not totally unfounded. I had my doubts, even after his fiery demise. Magic is a powerful mistress, and she has her ways of surviving."

"You said you killed him, right?" Ryris looked at the two women questioningly.

"One would think plummeting into a lake of lava would end a man's life, and I'm sure it did. But who are we to say that his spirit—as black and tainted as it may have been—didn't find a way to linger? A man is only as strong as the body he inhabits, but his soul..." Phia rocked slowly, contemplating. "He would need human pawns to do his bidding. Then when he was ready, he would regain form again, if that is what he seeks."

"Roann." Ryris set his bowl down on a box beside himself, no longer hungry. "But how? He's so—"

"Perfect?" Kaia raised an eyebrow at him, and the young alchemist could only nod his acknowledgement. "Now you see. If we're correct, Lyrax needed someone strong and intelligent. A man who already had power—a common peasant just wouldn't do. I'm sure no one in Keld knows."

And there it was. His two companions had laid it all out—and it suddenly made sense to Ryris. Roann was the perfect puppet.

"But how could Lyrax have taken control of him without anyone knowing? Surely his parents would know if someone was molding their son behind their backs."

Phia tapped her giant fingertips on the arm of her chair as she thought. "First contact must have happened when he was very young, maybe even as an infant. If it truly is Lyrax, he would have had immense pull on a young mind. But I would think he'd want to work in private, at least until Roann was old enough to be able to keep a secret—and somehow get away from Keld without being noticed. That way, no one would be any the wiser in the royal court."

"But what about Roann's loyalty to his parents? His country?"

"Even the most powerful of men can harbor weak will. If he was told from a young age that there was more to his life than service, that he could be rewarded with unlimited power if he cooperated and did as he was told—it's entirely possible that whomever is behind this surge convinced him to bide his time like a good boy and 'play nice'."

Kaia sat up straighter, her brow furrowed. "And that's what makes him so dangerous."

169

"Exactly." Phia nodded knowingly. "We must proceed cautiously, but with haste."

"So now what?" Ryris looked to his two companions.

Phia thought for a moment. "You must wake Ealsig and Jaric"

Kaia sat forward, her eyes pleading. "Phia, *please* tell me my father told you where they are. You're the only one he would have trusted with the information."

An honored smile covered the giantess' face. "I'm flattered you think so highly of me, child. And it just so happens that you're correct. King Galroy was truly wise...for a human." She winked with a chuckle. "Jaric was entombed in the southern deserts, hidden amongst the sandstone bluffs. The superstitious nomads there don't wander into the canyons; they believe them to be haunted. And Ealsig is interred near Blackthorne Village."

"Blackthorne?" Ryris' eyes widened as he tried to contain his emotions. On one hand, he was eager to see his father and Grildi, for he missed them both terribly. But, he also knew he would face Maxx' wrath upon returning—for abandoning the Keld shop, for not keeping in contact. He was sure the older man would yell. His palms began to sweat as he hesitantly offered, "I'm from Blackthorne."

"Then you should be able to navigate the forest due east with ease. You know what I'm talking about..."

Of course Ryris knew what she was hinting at. The forests surrounding Blackthorne were filled with prized tandlewood trees, coveted for their beautiful dark and hardy wood. But wander further into the woods and one would quickly find himself surrounded by old stone temples, said to have been left behind long ago—even before the Old War. Ghostly lights flickered from inside their walls, even though they were long known to have been uninhabited. Sometimes, screams echoed out from the depths of the underbrush, the din of wars fought long ago. Whatever inhabited the lost settlement never strayed far from their ghostly home, and the residents of Blackthorne were eternally grateful for that. No one from the area was foolhardy enough to seek their fortune in the spectral fortresses, but every once and a while a foreign adventurer would gain the courage—never to be seen again. And, of course, it was exactly where they needed to go. Ryris suddenly felt sick to his stomach.

"The ruins," Ryris weakly whispered, his mouth dry as cotton. He tried to appear brave, and was failing miserably. Phia nodded knowingly.

"I've only seen one fool in my lifetime make that trek. Said he was going to find treasure. No one ever saw him again. The villagers warned him not to go." He leaned forward in his chair, resting his elbows on his knees and lacing his fingers together in front of his body. "If I were going to hide something, those creepy castles would be the perfect place."

Phia nodded again.

Kaia chided him, a wicked smile crossing her lips. "And you didn't want to take a better weapon…"

"We're going to need a lot more than your bow and my sword that I can't use properly. If what everyone says is true, those ghouls in the forest are out for blood."

"Speaking of weapons…" Phia turned her attention to Kaia. "Do you still have them?"

Kaia grabbed her backpack. Undoing the buckle, she flipped the leather top over and removed the parcel she had retrieved from behind the bookcase in her chamber. She knelt in front of Phia, setting it in the giantess' lap, before loosening the silken string holding the fabric together.

"Hey, that's that thing you wouldn't tell me about!" Ryris scrambled from his chair and also knelt beside the two women, eagerly anticipating the unveiling of whatever was concealed beneath the wrappings.

Phia laid her hands on the package with reverence. "Thank the Goddess they're safe. If they were to fall into the wrong hands…"

"What *are* they?" Ryris leaned forward to get a better glimpse.

Kaia untied the string completely and let the fabric fall to the side, revealing a shining silver sword hilt and a shard of crystal, one edge razor sharp. The items glittered even in the low light of the hut. Ryris was mesmerized by the artifacts, watching Phia run her rough fingertips over the smooth material.

"I have been blind since birth. But when I touch these pieces, as I once touched the original weapon, I imagine it to be spectacular." She smiled in the darkness, her solemn eyes betraying her feelings. She picked up the hilt, turning it over in her hands. "These items saved mankind—with the help of a brave warrior."

"I did what I needed to do."

Ryris stared at Kaia, watching her steely expression in the flickering light of the fireplace. Her voice was laced with hardened determination.

Phia handed the hilt to Ryris. It was lighter than he expected it to be, the metal cool on his skin. The opal adorning the butt of the pommel glittered, despite harboring a thick crack. Turning it over in his hands, he noted the ornate scrollwork on the guard, several tendrils converging into one line before disappearing under the leather-wrapped grip. The craftsmanship was exquisite and Ryris understood that he was in the presence of history. What exactly that history was, he had no idea. "Looks broken."

"This is the weapon that finally defeated Lyrax." Kaia took it back from him and held it reverently. "It had been enchanted by our Arch-battlemage—the other Ryris. Meant for one use—to cleanse the land of the undead and ensure that their master could never again acquire the power he once commanded."

"How?"

"When activated, the sword unleashed a terrific shockwave, sweeping across the battlefield and incinerating everything with holy magic. It was our last resort. The power it discharged did not differentiate between friend and foe." Kaia's tone was solemn.

"How did you activate it? A magic word, or something? Like, 'abracadabra'?"

Kaia stared at him, his attempt at humor lost in her seriousness. She rubbed her thumb over the opal on the pommel. "This stone was the 'switch', so to speak. Our Ryris enchanted it so that my thumb alone would start the reaction. All I had to do was take off my gauntlet and make skin contact with it—and it would release the holy fire. The attack could only be used once, and would destroy the sword in the process." Kaia held out her right hand, Ryris finally getting an explanation for her burned skin. "A permanent reminder of that day."

"What happened after the blast? To Lyrax?"

"He was near death, a charred shell of a man. His skin had been singed beyond recognition, his bones visible where flesh was burned off. We knew the only way to destroy him once and for all was to render him to ash." Kaia furrowed her brows as she inhaled deeply. "He cursed us...all while pleading for his own life. The perfect testament to how truly insane he was. We threw him into Mount Vorik in Ashal. Cruel, perhaps, but deserved. After what he did to our people, to the innocent victims on all the continents—we hoped Oleana would forgive us."

Ryris shuddered at the thought. He couldn't even imagine being punished in such a manner, even if he had been the most evil man in the world. Again, it hit him just how horrible war could be. He looked to the shimmering crystal shard on Phia's lap. "And that's a piece of the blade?"

"One of ten," Phia responded, handing the delicate package back to Kaia. "The sword shattered when it was activated. Many insignificant flecks were lost, but the main pieces were safely held by the royal quartermaster of Farnfoss until King Galroy could decide what should happen to them."

"When the decision was made to seal us away, we were each given a piece to protect. Father felt it was my honor and responsibility to also carry the hilt." Kaia took the parcel from Phia's lap and re-tied the string while she spoke. "Alone, the shards and hilt are useless, nothing more than shimmering spoils of war. But put back together once again…"

"I thought you said it was a one-time use?"

"If a master sword smith working with a talented magician were able to cobble it back together and place another enchantment on it, in theory, it could work again. That's why they all needed to be protected—and couldn't possibly be housed together. If they fell into the wrong hands, the consequences, however unlikely, could be dire."

"So where are the other pieces? You said there are only two other generals left, right?" Ryris, noticing the fire was beginning to die down, added another log to the hearth.

"Each of my comrades was entrusted with one shard. The other seven were given to faithful servants of my father and hidden in the far reaches of the realm. It was the ultimate goal that no one person knew where they all were…except for a certain giantess?" Kaia winked at Phia. "I'm assuming my father told you their locations?"

Phia sighed tiredly. "Unfortunately, no. But…" She slowly lifted her heavy frame from the chair with a grunt, and shuffled past her two visitors toward the other room in the cottage. "Come with me, young man."

Ryris obeyed, following her into to her bedroom. A chest of drawers sat under the only window in the room, listing to one side, a leg having rotted away years prior. Her gargantuan bed rested along the far wall, a scraggly, thin blanket tossed on top. Using her walking stick as a pointer, Phia motioned under the bed.

"Be a dear and pull out that chest for me? My knees are old and stiff."

Ryris busied himself with retrieval as Phia rummaged around in her drawers. Tugging with all his might, the cumbersome box refused to budge. His face turning red and his muscles bulging as he pulled, he could hear his heartbeat thundering in his ears as his blood pressure rose. After a long moment of struggle, he finally freed the chest from beneath the bed, pulling it into the center of the room with a loud grunt. A cloud of dust came along with it. Ryris sneezed, wiping his nose on his sleeve. Phia turned at the noise, an old, dull bronze key in her hand. She held it out to the young alchemist.

"The lock is old, and it sticks."

Ryris inserted the key into the ancient lock, attempting to turn it. Phia was right, it definitely stuck. Jiggling it, the latch began to slip and within a few seconds had popped open. Setting the key on the floor, Ryris lifted the latch and opened the lid. His nostrils were tickled by the sweet scent of perfume, an aroma he didn't expect to smell in a swamp. Peering inside, he saw colorful silk scarves, a gold goblet encrusted with jewels, sparkling brooches, and an entire pot of gold gamm. It seemed Phia had her very own treasure chest.

"There should be a box, about ye big," the giantess added, holding her hands in front of her body to show a size comparison.

"Where did you get all this loot?" Ryris carefully moved objects aside to find what he was looking for.

"Gifts, mostly. From Kaia's father and the nobles. Call it pre-payment for services rendered. I have no use for any of it, but it was a nice gesture. I would have aided them anyway."

"Nice folks." Ryris' hand brushed against a hard object. Pushing a fur stole to the side, he brought out a wooden box, beautiful scrollwork intricately etched into the material. Silver covers had been tacked onto each corner, a latch and lock of the same metal adorning the front. "This what you're looking for?"

Phia held her hands out as Ryris placed the box in her palms. She ran her fingers over the object. "Yes. Would you close the trunk and push it back under the bed? I don't want to trip over it tonight."

Ryris grumbled as he struggled to place the chest back where he found it. When he was finished, he followed Phia out of the room, returning just in time to see her sit back in her massive chair and present the box to Kaia.

"Open."

Kaia obeyed, flicking the latch up with her thumb. The tiny hinges on the lid creaked with age. As the interior was revealed, a small smile crossed the warrior's lips. "My tiara..."

"Your father gave it to me. It may be able to help you find the hidden shards."

Kaia lifted the delicate accessory from the box and placed it on her head, resting atop her golden locks. Almost instantly, the blue stone embedded in the ornate metalwork began to glow.

"It remembers you, that's good." Phia leaned forward, reaching for the box. She blindly foraged under the layers of silk until she found what she was searching for. "And these will help me communicate with you."

Kaia eyed each token with suspicion, accepting one of the pink jewels from her hostess. It flared in unison with the one nestled in Phia's hand. "I've never seen these before."

"Your father went to Fallswood after you went to sleep and personally picked them out. He hoped that if the time ever came where your skills were needed again, I

174

could contact you. Mind you, they only work in our dreams, but they should be effective nonetheless." Phia took the gem back. "They're called Witching Stones, and despite the sinister sound to their name, I assure you they have nothing to do with evil. They were highly sought-after for their ability to assist in telepathy, especially on the new moon when the filaments inside glow. The mines they came from were very dangerous. Many workers died trying to excavate them. Their price was astronomical."

"How does it work?" Kaia turned the gem over in her hand. It glittered.

Phia leaned forward, and beckoned for Kaia to meet her halfway. She wrapped her fingers tightly around the stone. "Hold it tight. Press your forehead against mine, dear."

Kaia obeyed. Instantly, they were both enveloped in a misty, pink cloud. It shined from the inside-out. The gems hidden by their closed hands glowed brightly. After just a few seconds, it was over. The mist dissipated, the brightness from the stones subsided. Phia leaned back with a satisfied smile.

"Now we are connected."

"This is crazy…" Ryris breathed, awestruck. "Tiaras that can divine the locations of sword shards? A magic gem that can send you messages in your dreams? Am I hallucinating?"

Without hesitation, Kaia drew her arm back and unleashed a mighty whack across Ryris' shoulders. "There, you're not hallucinating."

"That was mean, you know that?" Ryris scowled at her with a humph and reached around to rub his aching shoulder.

She smirked and turned away from him. "Phia, do you think the shards are safe?"

"There's no way to tell until you get to them."

"Then we can't waste any more time." Kaia began to stand, but Phia grabbed her hand and pulled back down.

"First, you finish your dinner and spend the night. There are many miles between here and your next destination. I can't in good conscience let you leave with an empty stomach and tired feet. One more day won't matter after seven hundred years."

Kaia sighed with a tired smile. That night, on the dirt floor of a swamp shack, she and Ryris slept sounder than they had in weeks.

CHAPTER NINETEEN

The southern deserts pose serious threat to life and limb. Not only are they parched and without sufficient vegetation to sustain life, they are home to a motley band of nomads who do not take kindly to trespassers on their lands.

--Excerpt from 'A Child's Gazette of Geography', Alerius Pram, noted author and scholar

"Maxx! Maaaaaaaxx!"

The old man grumbled, fumbling the decanter of base fluid in his hands as he was interrupted. He turned just in time to see Grildi burst through the door of the shop.

"Did you get a letter?" Grildi beamed hopefully, his smile crossing his entire face. He nearly knocked an entire dish of moon gems to the floor in his exuberant tizzy.

"Not today." He set the bottle down and pointed accusingly at his visitor. "And watch where you're swinging your arms! You nearly destroyed a thousand gamm worth of inventory!"

"Sorry, Boss. It's just I saw the carrier bird come this morning. I hoped it had something for you. It's..." Grildi cast his eyes downward, nervously fiddling with his belt buckle. "...been too long."

Sighing, Maxx hated to admit he agreed with the town guard. Seven weeks was way too long to go without hearing from his son. He knew Grildi was worrying, and he knew that Ryris being so quiet couldn't mean anything good. Maxx' mind would race at times like this—or when he was eating alone in the quiet house, or laying in bed at night—and he'd come up with all sorts of horrible scenarios to justify why his son hadn't written. Perhaps the shop had burned down, taking Ryris with it. *"No,"* Maxx thought, *"someone in Keld surely would have contacted me. After all, my name is on the deed."* Maybe his son had gone missing on a harvest expedition, stranded in the mountains or stuck in a swamp. *"What if he's pinned under his wagon? He could be laying there dying."* He always had to stop himself, reminding his conscience that his son was a smart man, and wouldn't put himself in harm's way or do anything stupid on purpose. He motioned for Grildi to approach the counter, and fished a small hard candy from his apron pocket.

"I know. We have to remember that he's busy in the big city. He's got a new life now."

Grildi accepted the treat. "You want to go check on him?"

"Can't leave the shop for that long." Maxx took back the paper wrapping from Grildi's sweet and tossed it into the fireplace. "I'm sure he's just fine." He tried to hide his worry from his guest. Grildi was very emotionally sensitive, and if he caught wind that Maxx was more worried than he let on, he'd be a blubbering mess.

"Well, you just give the word and I'll find him. I'll keep him safe." Grildi puffed out his chest with pride.

"I don't doubt that one bit."

Grildi smacked his lips around the candy like a child. "You think he has a wife?"

"He better not. I told him to meet new people, not get hitched."

"Aye. No time for that, huh?" Grildi raised a hopeful eyebrow at Maxx. "Would you help me write to him? Like last time?"

"Why not? I can't concentrate today anyway. Oleana only knows the potions would be garbage if I tried to force it. Let me grab some paper and a quill—you're writing this time."

"But..."

"No 'buts'. You need the practice."

Grildi pouted and began to nervously tap his fingers on the countertop. He wasn't confident in his penmanship skills, but he knew Ryris wouldn't mind—and would be proud of him for the effort. Maxx returned quickly, tan parchment and a short quill in tow. He grabbed a pot of ink from underneath the counter.

"Get crackin'. I'll help you when you need it."

Sticking his tongue out in concentration, Grildi dipped the end of the quill in the ink and applied it to the paper. A sloppy blob fell in the margin.

Deer Ryris,

I miss you something feerce. I hope you are alrite. Maxx says my writeing is getting better all the time...

~~~

"I've never felt heat like this. I think I'm going to pass out." Ryris wiped the back of his hand across his forehead, noticing the ever growing absence of moisture. Feeling dehydration beginning to take hold, he reached for his waterskin, only to find it bone dry. "Kaia, if we don't find some water soon, we'll die."

"Don't you think I know that?" Her voice was raspy from lack of hydration. Ryris hadn't heard her snap so harshly in quite some time. It was obvious they were both affected by thirst. "If we can just make it over this next dune, there's bound to be an oasis."

"You said that three dunes ago. I think we should turn back."

"Turning back would mean certain death." She pulled at her thin shirt, fanning it to get some air circulation over her torso. "We're close, I know it."

Ryris looked back over the wagon, the horizon rippling in the scorching midday heat. She was right—she always was. They had travelled too far into the desert to go back. Canyons loomed ahead of them, and he hoped against hope that some water lay within. The wind whipped up, blowing sand into his face.

They plodded on for another two hours, Ass of the East's speed waning with every step. Ryris knew she would die soon if she didn't get water—they all would. The last hill had been steep to descend, but they were rewarded with solid ground at the base. Giant sand dunes were replaced by towering red canyon walls, natural stone arches carved out by eons of wind erosion. The desert began to give way to arid scrubland— sure sign water was near. Subtle hints of moisture on the air currents tickled their nostrils and they both looked to each other with excitement. Moving on, they entered an outcropping, the rock walls on either side soaring into the sky, mercifully blocking out the unrelenting sun. The wind blew with ferocity around them, echoing a haunting "scream" through the surrounding area. If the nomads Phia spoke of were truly superstitious, there was a good reason to believe this was the culprit.

Ass of the East whinnied, shaking flies from her mane with a flick of her head. Emerging from the shady corridor, the companions found themselves presented with the most beautiful sight they had ever seen.

A clear blue pond shimmered at the end of the path, partly shaded by the high canyon walls. Scrubby trees encircled its shores, brown birds fluttering from one perch to the next as they shrieked their social calls. Ryris jumped from the wagon, causing Kaia to lunge for the reins to hastily steer in his absence. "It's magical!"

She called after him with a curt, forceful tone, causing him to skid to a halt mere inches from the water's edge. "Don't you dare!"

Ryris turned and balked. "Why not? It's practically calling for us!"

"Get back here!" Her voice was commanding as she dismounted the cart. She scanned the tops of the canyons, keeping a keen eye on their surroundings.

Ryris looked around and shrugged his shoulders. "There's no one here. We've got the place completely to ourselves."

"Until we know if we're truly alone, we need to be on our guard—even though you've most likely blown any element of surprise we may have had on our side." She scowled at him, her face turning red. He hadn't seen her this mad since she tackled him the first time.

Ryris felt like an ass. Here she was, a warrior with years of strategic and tactical training, and she was forced to babysit an incompetent alchemist who had acted a fool on more than one occasion. He returned from the edge of the pool, his head hanging low. Kaia pointed to the cart. "Stay over there, let me do the reconnoiter."

He did as he was told, and took his position beside the wagon. She removed her sword from storage and attached it to her belt. Kaia slowly circled the oasis, peeking into alcoves and peering up into the tallest reaches to make sure they were safe. She stopped once, hand at her side, ready to draw her weapon. Seconds later, a group of pygmy deer scrambled from a small cave in the outcropping wall and out into the surrounding desert. When she was finished with her reconnaissance, she returned to Ryris and stowed her weapon once more.

"Let's make camp."

"It's safe?"

"I wouldn't suggest we stay if it wasn't." She grabbed a supply backpack and the shabby tent they had purchased and walked toward the water, untying Ass of the East to lead her to a refreshing drink.

"I'd love to jump in first…" Ryris raised a hopeful eyebrow at his companion and motioned with his head in the direction of the pool.

"Not until we hydrate, pitch the tent, and get some training in."

"Training?" Ryris didn't try and hide the whine in his voice.

Kaia grabbed the waterskins from their supplies and shoved one in his hand. She knelt at the side of the pool and dipped it in, bubbles popping to the surface as the canteen filled. "We're safe for the moment, but you're nowhere ready for battle should it arise. You need practice, and I can't think of a better time than now."

"But I'm hot, tired, and sore!" Ryris lifted his own waterskin from the refreshing water and drank deeply. He hoped she'd be sympathetic.

"So am I, but the enemy doesn't care. Whether you're full of energy or nearly dropping from exhaustion, when the time comes to defend yourself, you need to be ready."

Ryris faked a cough. "But…I'm sick…"

"Quit being a baby." She pointed to the wagon. "Grab the other bags and get the fire going."

"Fire? It's a thousand degrees out here!" Ryris balked with exaggeration as he hoisted a pack onto his shoulders.

"…and the oasis has a fly swarm…" Kaia pointed to an undulating black cloud hovering over the far side of the pond. "If we don't start a fire, they'll be eating us alive before sundown."

Looking at the mass of hungry insects in the near-distance, Ryris instantly agreed with the idea of a smoky fire. He got to work collecting dried wood and reeds to use as kindling. Striking a flint on his dagger, he quickly became discouraged as the sparks refused to ignite the fuel. He blew out an irritated breath and stomped his foot. Ryris tried and tried again, failing miserably as the fire starter wouldn't cooperate.

"…just use your damn magic." Kaia's exasperated voice floated from behind him as she pitched the tent.

He almost yelled to her that she'd lost her mind, but then remembered there wasn't a living soul for miles—probably. Even so, Ryris took a quick look around on his own before bringing flames to his fingertips. He tossed the fire from his palm onto the dry kindling and the campfire immediately blazed strong. Ryris added a few larger logs and stood back to marvel at his accomplishment. He had to admit, it felt slightly liberating to use his powers without fear of being murdered for it. At least—not at the moment.

Kaia came up behind him and slapped him on the back, knocking him forward slightly. "Nice fire, Bren. Now grab your sword and let's get to it."

Ryris pouted, hoping that she had forgotten about her previous orders. He really didn't feel like practicing with a weapon. The cool, shimmering water of the oasis called to him, taunting him with the slight ripples on the surface. They had been traveling so long, and all he wanted was a bath. He knew he probably stunk something awful.

"Let's go!" Kaia drew her sword from its scabbard, the crystal glimmering in the fading sunlight. "You need to at least learn the basics if you want any chance at survival."

The alchemist sighed and resigned himself to his fate. The enticing water of the oasis would have to wait. He removed his shortsword from the wagon, his own crystalline choice from Kaia's chamber, and approached her at the oasis' edge. She stood at the ready, sword held out in front of her. As soon as he took a tentative stance, she abruptly charged at him. Ryris only had seconds to react, and brought his weapon up just in time to block her volley.

"Dammit, Kaia! Watch it!" Ryris swung his weapon wildly, barely missing his sparring opponent's arm. "How about a little warning next time?"

She swung again, forcing him to defend himself. Her blade crashed down on his, knocking him to the ground. He tried to scuttle away, but Kaia was on him like lightning, pointing the tip of her sword at his face. "You're dead!"

Ryris sat, red-faced and panting. He glared at her. "If you think this will help me learn, you're wrong!"

"I disagree." She retracted her blade and extended her hand to help him up. "You need to expect the unexpected."

"Well, almost killing me doesn't seem to be the best way to go about it." He went to sheathe his sword, a mixture of embarrassment and anger sweeping over him. She stopped him with a forceful slap to the calf with the broad side of her weapon. He sighed and rolled his eyes when he realized she wanted to go at it again.

"I wouldn't have killed you…"

"Could've fooled me."

Kaia readied her sword in front of her. Ryris instinctively flinched. "We'll start simpler, if it'll make you feel better." He nodded, sweat pouring down his face. He reluctantly brought his sword up. Kaia shook her head and clicked her tongue in a scolding manner. She sighed as she sheathed her weapon and moved behind him. She placed her hands on his hips. Ryris' cheeks flushed. "Your posture is all wrong. Straighten up, but relax your back. If you're stiff-muscled, your movements won't be fluid."

Ryris swallowed hard as she ran her hand up his spine, forcing him to straighten his posture. Her fingers ended up on his shoulders, where she squeezed firmly. His entire body began to tingle. "Relax…the sword isn't *that* heavy."

"I'm not tensing because of the damn sword," he thought.

Kaia laid both her palms on his shoulders and pressed down. "The trick is to have control of your weapon without white-knuckling it. If you tense your upper body, you're more liable to grip your sword incorrectly. Let your arms do the work, not your hands."

Ryris allowed her to manipulate him into a proper fighting stance. He fought the urge to move away when she pushed her knee between his legs to give him a more stable footing. Once again, he could feel heat taking over his face, and butterflies fluttered in his stomach. He hoped she couldn't sense his nervousness.

"If you stand wide-footed, it's harder for your opponent to knock you on your ass. Once you're down, you lose the advantage…so make sure it never happens." She backed up to take note of his positioning. "Much better."

Ryris stood there, feeling very awkward. The weight of the sword was starting to make his arms dip. He definitely wasn't used to this kind of physical activity. And being hormonally flushed wasn't helping his situation. Kaia unsheathed her weapon and stood beside him, mirroring his posture.

"Now, take four steps forward—watch me. Make sure you keep the sword pommel in line with your navel." She moved, Ryris following her. "Not bad. Let's try again, eight steps this time."

They practiced the walking drill over and over again, Kaia adding more steps each time. As he moved, Ryris became more comfortable with the weight of the sword. By the end of the exercise, they had walked around the entire oasis, and she had added simple sword positions into the mix.

"Posture's better. Time to get swinging." She stood in front of him, weapon raised defensively. "Attack me."

"Are you sure?" All of Ryris' confidence seeped out in an instant. Walking around was one thing, but actually using his weapon was a totally different animal. He wasn't sure he was ready.

"It's not like I'd let you hurt me." She beckoned him with a crooked finger and a cocked eyebrow. "Let's see what you got."

Ryris took a deep breath and swung. The sword's weight changed his center of mass and he stumbled awkwardly. He never even made contact with Kaia's weapon. He expected her to laugh, but she never did. Instead, she grabbed him by the arm, readjusted his stance, and told him to give it another try. Ryris moved again, this time ready for the change in his balance from the sword. His movements were more fluid as he clashed his sword against Kaia's. He actually felt proud of himself. Again and again, he attacked, his blows becoming stronger with each passing minute. His confidence rose. Before long, he was sweating and his muscles felt as if they were on fire. Adrenaline coursed through his veins and he welcomed the new sensation of success. Kaia cheered him on as she defended herself with ease, encouraging him to strike harder and with more precision. Even though he still had strong reservations about actually using a weapon in battle—against real enemies—he was inspired by his budding skills. Perhaps he was stronger than he had originally thought.

Kaia finally held up a hand to stop him. "And you thought you couldn't do it..."

Ryris smiled his thanks for the compliment as he panted, stooping over as the euphoric rush of extreme physical activity waned. He wiped his brow with his arm before resting his sword against his leg. His shoulders slumped when he heard Kaia's next words.

"You're not off the hook yet." She raised her weapon with a determined look on her face.

"Kaia, I'm beat and starving. Haven't we trained enough for one day?"

"No." She charged at him again, just like their first encounter. Now armed with a new set of skills and some extra confidence, Ryris jumped back and properly defended himself, parrying her blow with a swipe of his sword.

He surprised himself, the counterattack coming more naturally that he had expected it to. The alchemist-turned-warrior kept up his defense, even getting a few jabs in at his opponent's expense. But, Kaia's attacks were precise, and Ryris soon grew tired. She was relentless, darting around him while swinging her sword. Kaia challenged him to tap into his reserves and channel all his strength to keep her at bay. Ryris knew she wasn't going easy on him. They sparred for several minutes, Kaia showing no signs of tiring. Ryris, on the other hand, began to lose steam. His grip faltered on his sword, and his legs felt like jelly. Ryris let his mind go off-track for just a moment—and that's all it took. A stinging pain erupted from his forearm, and he looked down to see blood seeping through a newly-cut gash in his shirt.

"You hit me!" Ryris dropped his sword to the ground and cradled his injured arm.

Kaia dashed to his side, ready to inspect his wound. He tried to pull away, but she held on tight and forced him to allow her to look. "You lost focus. Be thankful it was me and not a real foe." She rolled up his sleeve and scrutinized his arm. "You'll be fine, it's not deep."

"That's easy for you to say. You're not the one oozing blood." He began to feel lightheaded at the sight of the crimson liquid.

"You think I don't have scars?" Her expression was stern.

"You're not even going to apologize?" Ryris' feelings were bruised, and he wasn't going to let her make him feel bad for her. She could at least pretend to be a little sorry.

"What for? Soldiers spar—and soldiers hurt each other while sparring."

"I'm not a soldier…" Ryris' voice was hushed as he pulled his arm away and walked toward the wagon. He found his alchemist's satchel and dug for a vial of ointment. Kaia approached and stopped him, forcibly turning him to face her.

"I know you're not a soldier." Her voice was uncharacteristically quiet. "I'm sorry, alright?"

He turned away, unconvinced, and dabbed a piece of cloth on his weeping arm laceration. The fabric immediately became stained red.

She leaned around him and looked him in the eyes. *"I'm sorry."*

He had never heard Kaia be remorseful like that. Her eyes were sincere, her apologetic smile warm, and he couldn't remember a time where she had looked more radiant. She gripped his arm firmly, but with a gentle touch, soft fingers against his wounded flesh. He found that his mouth had gone dry, and he didn't know if he could reply. Her touch—and her apology—had left him speechless.

"I, uhhh..." He swallowed hard. "...thank you. I...didn't mean to bite your head off." He unconsciously moved his hand to cover her own—and he was surprised when she didn't pull away. They stared at each other for a long moment, not speaking. Ryris' chest bubbled with a feeling he hadn't felt in a long time, and before he knew it, they were moving closer together. He knew he should stop, that it wasn't right to do this, but his brain wouldn't listen. Just as their lips were about to connect, Kaia pulled away.

"If you want to go swimming, now's the time. It'll wash the cut before I clean and bandage it." It was obvious she was trying to change the subject—or perhaps felt uncomfortable.

Ryris snapped himself from his lusty haze. He stood there, dumbfounded. Had he really been that close to kissing her? Had she almost let him? He didn't know what to do—what to say. So, he did what he always did in awkward situations—he stumbled over his words.

"Kaia...I...didn't mean to..." He nervously tapped his foot in the sand and tried to make some sort of eye contact so he didn't seem like a total dolt. He scratched the back of his neck.

"What I meant to say is..."

She stared at him blankly. Did she really not realize what had just *almost* happened? Didn't she care? A wave of unexpected melancholy momentarily swept over him. It's not like they were an item—but would he be upset if she were to reject him? Ryris had to tell himself to snap out of it, to push those thoughts from his mind. They were on an important mission. They had monumental tasks at hand. They had no time—for whatever had just transpired.

What *had* almost transpired?

Ever since he laid eyes on her, there had been that feeling of attraction. First physical—her beauty was nothing like he had ever seen in his life. Then, as he got to know her, he found himself attracted to her wit, her intelligence, and her bravery. She inhabited his dreams, only to be there again in the flesh every day. Ryris now realized he had spent a great deal of time trying to talk himself out of developing feelings for her. And yet, here they were—his hormones raging as he realized he was falling hard.

What was he going to do? He didn't want to ruin a good thing; their friendship meant so much to him. But, after all, he was a man—and he hadn't felt this way about a woman in a long, long time. Was he really ready to take this step? What if she rejected him? This was happening so fast, and he didn't know how to react.

"You worry too much, Bren." She slapped his cheek playfully, once again snapping him from his rambling thoughts. "Now either get in the water or start dinner."

Her eyes twinkled in the dimming sunset light and he instantly knew he at least hadn't caused any damage to their relationship. He figured at some point, there would probably be a discussion about—*something*—but for now, he felt at ease. Kaia always did that to him.

Ryris gazed longingly at the water. It did look refreshing. But, his arm also smarted something fierce and he wasn't sure if he wanted to anger it by dunking it in water. Taking a moment to weigh his options, he finally decided—and ran toward the pond like a giddy child, his romantic worries no longer at the forefront of his mind. He jumped in, fully clothed, and swam underneath the surface. When he finally emerged, he saw Kaia at the water's edge, arms crossed over her body, laughing at his spontaneity.

"You do realize most normal people undress before they swim?"

"And you should know that I'm far from normal." Ryris swam closer to the beach. The cool water washed over his injury, calming the angry flesh. "Why don't you join me? I don't think there's any water snakes…"

Kaia eyed him speculatively for a moment, before slipping off her boots and socks. She dipped a toe into the water and smiled in satisfaction. "Not too cold…"

"It's perfect." Ryris floated away on his back. "I could stay here forever."

"No you couldn't. You'd complain about the heat after a few days and beg to leave." She unbuttoned her shirt and dropped it to the ground.

Ryris averted his eyes and immediately turned around. His stomach tightened into a nervous knot, and he was instantly whooshed back in time mere minutes, to when they had almost kissed. Once again, Ryris found himself experiencing feelings he didn't want to deal with at present. He tried to calm the nervousness in his voice. "You're undressing?"

"Grow up, Ryris. It's just a bra and underwear. I'm sure you've seen them before." She walked into the water and immediately submerged herself. When she surfaced, she smoothed her hair down over the back of her head and exhaled deeply.

Ryris had never felt more uncomfortable in his life. Well, maybe the time in the cave where she had touched his bare chest, but at least then she had been clothed. Here she was, next to naked, in the water beside him. His hormones took over and he tried not to spiral out of control. This was definitely not the place he wanted to be caught lusting after her.

Kaia smacked her hand on the water, peppering his face with droplets. A mischievous smirk crossed her lips. "Get your mind out of the gutter, Ryris."

He stared blankly at her for a moment, unsure if dying of embarrassment right then and there would save him. He moved away from her slowly, trying to come up with a clever, in-no-way-incriminating response. Of course, his mind was drawing a complete blank. He was dumbfounded as to how his mouth could go so dry when he was chest-deep in an oasis.

Kaia wiped the water out of her eyes. "If I'm making you uncomfortable, I can get dressed."

"You don't have to…if you don't want to." Ryris instantly cringed at his reply. *"Real smooth, Bren,"* he thought.

"You're cute when you're nervous."

What was she doing? Was she…flirting with him? He had never been so confused in his life, and finally decided that it was the heat of the desert and lack of food that was making them both uncharacteristically forward.

"I'm not nervous…"

"Sure…" Kaia laughed, her voice echoing off the canyon wall. She swam away, kicking water at him as she departed.

Ryris watched as she dipped below and resurfaced several times, ending up on the opposite side of the pool. She turned and focused her attention on the surrounding canyon, staring out at the environment for what seemed like an eternity. While her back was turned, he quickly scrubbed under his arms to try and dissipate some of the travel aroma he knew he carried. He finished just in time, for she turned and dove under again, like a mermaid. Within seconds she was back at his side.

"It's getting dark. Time to get out, or we'll catch our death."

She was at the water's edge and up onto the beach in a flash, picking up her dry clothes and heading toward the wagon. Ryris remained in the water a moment longer; until he was confident he could get out without embarrassment. He soon followed, and joined her at the cart. In the low light of the campfire, Ryris thought he caught a glimpse of several scars on her torso. He squinted, trying to get a view.

Kaia, dry undergarments in hand, shot him a stern look. "Turn around!"

"Oh, so now you're shy?" Ryris was utterly confused. One moment she was seemingly flirting with him, the next moment she was back to her commanding self. He resigned himself to the fact that there was a good possibility he would never understand women.

She threw an apple from the supplies at him, the first thing she could grab quickly. "Just do it."

"I could make the same demand of you, you know." Ryris internally hoped she'd take him up on his offer. In his current state, he really didn't want to be caught— quite literally—with his pants down in front of her. He grabbed his own dry clothing from their luggage.

"That's fair." She went to the other side of the wagon. "Let me know when you're decent, and I'll do the same."

They both turned, and Ryris began the arduous task of peeling wet, clammy clothes from his shivering body. He cursed himself for impulsively plunging into the water fully-dressed. A quick swipe of a scratchy, poor excuse for a towel and he was sufficiently dry to dress again. He fought the urge to sneak a peek at Kaia. Only to make sure she was keeping up her end of the bargain, he reminded himself.

"Are you ready yet?"

Ryris grumbled as he pulled dry undergarments up around his hips. "You had less to do, gimme a minute!" He quickly stepped into his pants and fastened them. As he slid his arms into his shirt, he rolled up the sleeve on his injured arm and gave her the all-clear. His amulet sparkled on his exposed chest.

They both faced each other across the cart, an awkward silence falling over the oasis. Of course, she looked beautiful, even with her hair starting to frizz as it dried. She pulled it back and tied it with a string before grabbing the sack filled with their foodstuffs. He followed close behind her, toting his alchemist's satchel. His arm was beginning to ache, and blood had started to ooze again. The grumbling in his stomach was becoming uncomfortable.

Ryris laid out a blanket beside the tent and began to work on his arm. The firelight didn't give him much illumination, but it was better than nothing. Kaia had been right, the wound wasn't that deep. He had been lucky, for he knew had she been fighting at full potential; she could have killed him where he stood. He held a piece of cloth over his laceration, soaking up the waning blood flow.

Kaia dipped a pot into the water and set it directly on the logs. As she waited for it to boil, she parceled out a small serving of dried legumes for them both, along with some jerky and dried berries. After her prep was completed, she joined Ryris at his side, taking over his wound care. "Let me help."

He obliged with a sincere smile. It felt nice to have someone take care of him.

187

"Do you have any antiseptic left?" She lifted the gauze from the cut and leaned in to inspect it.

"No, but I made this ointment before I left on my trip to Hewe." He handed her a small glass jar.

She twisted off the lid and sniffed the contents. "It'll have to do. Lay your arm on my lap."

Ryris obeyed, hissing as she applied the salve with her fingers. It stung as the mixture seeped into the wound.

"Almost done..."

Kaia replaced the cap and wiped the excess balm on a thin strip of bandage from the kit. She expertly wrapped it around Ryris' injury and pinned it in place. "Give it a few days to form a scab, then you can let it breathe."

"Thanks, Kaia." Ryris rubbed his hand over the bandage. He didn't have the heart to tell her that he had a potion in his satchel that would close small wounds. She had been so gentle and caring in her treatment that he decided to let this cut heal on its own.

"Don't mention it." She smiled sincerely and got up, heading back to the fire. After she dumped the beans into the water, she put her hands on her hips and looked up to the starry sky. "It sure is beautiful here."

Ryris kept his attention trained on her, watching as she took in the night's majesty. In that moment, standing underneath the vastness of the night sky, she looked very unlike the warrior that she was. In that moment—she was just a woman. A beautiful woman. Ryris' voice was hushed as he replied.

"It sure is..."

High above, nestled in hidden alcoves of the oasis canyon, dozens of eyes looked down on them.

CHAPTER TWENTY

Bees in spring, a harvest bring. Bees in fall, a pox upon all.

--Ka'liik children's proverb.

"Wake up!"

Ryris jolted up so abruptly he nearly collapsed the tent with his flailing. His stomach immediately lurched, a hated side-effect of a hasty awakening. It took him a moment to get his bearings before he realized Kaia was hunched in front of him, thrusting his shortsword and scabbard into his hands. Her bow was already slung over her back. "Whatever you do, don't draw that thing unless I say. Let me do the talking."

The alchemist swatted the weapon away, still trying to wake up properly. "What's going on?"

"We're being watched." Her voice was hushed, even though they were in the confines of their tent.

Ryris' mind immediately began to race. The thought of unknowns peering down at them, knowing their every move made his spine tingle. His mouth suddenly became very dry as his brain fully woke up. "Who do you think is out there?"

"Most likely the nomads Phia mentioned."

"Have you seen them?" Ryris awkwardly buckled his weapon belt around his waist, no easy task when confined to a cramped tent.

She turned, still on her haunches, and peered out the tent flap. "I'm assuming those big canyons are the same ones she said they won't go near. If my hunch is correct, that's exactly where Jaric is. If we want to get there safely, we'll have to let our peaceful intentions be known."

Ryris tapped the sword at his side. "This isn't exactly my idea of 'peaceful'."

"Being cautious is one thing, being stupid is another." She ducked out of the tent.

Ryris reluctantly trailed her, the bright morning sun immediately blinding him. He squinted and shielded his eyes from the assault. It took a moment for his vision to clear. Once able to see properly, he sidled up to Kaia and they moved.

The pair stuck close to the outcropping's walls and out of the open, quickly moving to the other side of the oasis. It was then that they finally spotted them—the battle-ready nomads perched high above on the rock face. Ryris surmised they only saw

189

them because they had allowed themselves to be seen. Their clothing blended in with the sandstone they sat upon, their faces covered by material to keep the sand out of their mouths and eyes. Their weapons—clubs, maces, and pole arms—were the only items to stand out, made from a dull silver metal. Kaia immediately put her hands up as a show of good faith, and urged Ryris to do the same.

"Follow my lead—and stay quiet." Kaia slowly approached the edge of the pool and began to speak, her voice strong and clear. "My name is Kaia. We mean no disrespect to your lands and implore you to let us pass. I assure you we have no nefarious intentions."

Ryris could feel dozens of pairs of eyes on them, far more than could belong to the smattering of figures he saw above. He knew there had to be more hiding just out of sight. A long, tense moment passed, with no response from the nomads. Kaia stood firm, not moving from her sentinel position. Never once did she make a move for her weapon.

"If you wish us to leave, we will do so. But please allow us to break camp and give our horse refreshment before we go." Kaia kept her hands raised high. "We have many items to trade, and my friend is an alchemist. He would be happy to mix solutions for you."

Ryris fought the urge to yell out at her. Here she was, supposedly this smart warrior, and she was spilling all their private information. What would she do next, tell them exactly how much gamm they carried? He stood there silently and stewed. A male voice, low and booming, finally echoed out from the other side of the pool, effectively snapping him from his angry thoughts.

"An alchemist, you say?"

Kaia motioned with a flick of her head for Ryris to step forward. She muttered under her breath, "Introduce yourself. You said you were talented, here's your chance to prove it."

Ryris wasn't sure his voice would work at all. "Y-yes, I'm an alchemist. My name is Ryris."

"Can you cure blindness?" The phantom voice filtered down around them.

Ryris swallowed hard, reluctant to answer. No one could cure blindness, at least not with a simple potion. He suddenly feared for his life, and thought about his poor father getting the news of his grisly demise in the desert.

Kaia nudged him with her elbow, questioning him with a hushed voice. "Well, can you? If not, you had better come up with something good in response."

190

"I'm s-sorry, but I can't. There's no potion to my knowledge that can do such a thing. But…" He flinched and took a step back as a figure jumped down from its perch, gracefully landing on two feet even from such a long fall. Ryris knew he had only moments to salvage the situation, his last words rushed and urgent. "…I have a potion in the cart that can allow you to see in the dark!"

The figure ran full-force at the pond and leapt, his boots skipping effortlessly across the surface. Within seconds he was directly before them, his razor-sharp shortsword hanging at his side. His loose tan robes billowed in the breeze, exposing form-fitting leather armor underneath. A partial mask obscured most of his face, exposing only his mouth—full of gleaming white teeth. He smiled devilishly, crossing his arms over his chest as he leaned his weight onto one leg.

Ryris' fumbled words tumbled from his lips before he had a chance to stop them. "H-how did you…"

"Walk across the water?" The man smirked, lifting one of his boots to expose the bottom. The sole of his shoe was covered with tiny, glittering, golden spikes. "To help us across quicksand. The water-walking was an unexpected benefit. Now, night vision, eh? That would come in handy around these parts." He extended his hand. "You can put your hands down."

The pair lowered their arms and Kaia accepted his gesture, shaking his hand. "Thank you for not attacking. We're honored to receive your trust."

The man laughed, the sound echoing off the walls of the outcropping. "Don't thank me, thank that crystal bow on your back. Stories of those weapons have been passed down for generations. I am very intrigued as to where you found it."

"It's mine. Always has been." Kaia smiled, a small hint of pride gracing her lips.

"Well then, you should consider yourself lucky. I've never seen one in person, only in pictures."

All his life, Ryris thought he was the only one who had heard the legend. No one ever talked about it otherwise, so he figured no one even remembered. And now, this strange desert man admitted it was part of their legend as well. He couldn't help but feel happy the story of the Crystal Guard had managed to live on, even if it was through the stories of desert nomads with almost no contact with the world outside their lands.

The man smiled again, his teeth shining in the sun. He unclipped one side of the cloth mask from his face and slid it under his head wrappings. His skin was deeply tanned, his eyes dark and seductive. A shock of black hair peeked out from underneath his hood. Tall and handsome, Ryris suddenly felt uncharacteristically inferior. "The name's Nar. I'm the leader of my people, the Ka'liik." He spread his arms wide in greeting. "Welcome to our oasis."

Behind him, more people jumped down from their perches and approached. Others came out from small corridors and alcoves within the canyon walls, children hot on the heels of their parents. Some did as Nar had done, and gracefully skipped across the water, while the others went around the pool. A few milled around their camp, snooping inside their tent and sifting through their wagon. Ryris immediately tensed, protective of their belongings—and the several-hundred gamm they had hidden within.

Soon, the two companions were surrounded by nomads. Several youngsters immediately went to Ryris and Kaia's side, examining their clothes, touching the scabbard at the alchemist's belt.

"You'll have to excuse our little ones." Nar suddenly snapped in their native language, sending the children scattering. "It's not every day they get to meet strangers that aren't bound and gagged."

Ryris' eyes bulged in surprise at Nar's comment, suddenly unsure if he was joking. His palms began to sweat.

Nar, sensing his anxiety, put his mind at ease with a hearty laugh. "Don't worry, if we had perceived you as a threat, you would have never made it into the oasis. Follow me and we'll see about getting you two something better to eat than just beans and jerky."

"We're honored that you'd accept us into your lands, and would share your precious resources." Kaia followed Nar, beckoning Ryris to join. The children scuttled in the sands behind them, jabbering in their nomad language. They rounded the pool once more, both companions relieved to be back in the shade.

"We might be nomads, but we're not savages. We help those in need." Nar looked back over his shoulder. "And from the looks of your dusty clothes and gaunt faces, you most certainly fit that bill."

A group of natives had set up a temporary camp alongside the canyon wall while their leader greeted their guests, and a fire was just beginning to blaze. A few Ka'liik had laid out several large blankets on the sand, and even erected four medium-sized tents. They worked hard in the sweltering heat, never once shedding their layers of clothing. A stooped old woman took Ryris' hand and led him to an awaiting blanket. He and Kaia both sat and were immediately greeted with full waterskins and a bowl of fruit.

"Please, eat. Fresh food is a luxury I feel you probably haven't had in quite a while." Nar removed his billowy outer-robe and sat across from the pair, crossing his long legs under his body. He grabbed a knobby orange fruit from the bowl and bit into it, juice immediately running down his chin. "Messy, but worth every drippy bite. It's a cactus fruit, harvested from the far wastes."

Kaia and Ryris exchanged glances before helping themselves. Nar was right—it was definitely worth the sticky face. Ryris had never tasted anything so delicious in his life, but he wasn't sure if it was because he was so sick of dehydrated fare or it truly was that utterly divine. "This…this is incredible! I wish I could take some with us."

"Ryris, don't be rude." Kaia scowled, unaware of the black seeds stuck to her lower lip. Ryris tried to stifle his laughter as she questioned him. "What's so funny?"

The alchemist rubbed his thumb across his own lip, clearing his throat knowingly. "You've got a little something…"

"Where?" Kaia stuck her tongue out, attempting to rid herself of the seeds.

"You're missing the mark, my dear." Nar butted in, leaning forward to run his finger delicately across her mouth. "Those seeds can be pesky. And not to worry, young Ryris, there's plenty to go around and we don't mind sharing with friends."

Ryris couldn't help but notice the dreamy look in Nar's eyes when he gazed at Kaia. He had the mark of a man who was instantly smitten. And the tone of his voice—especially when he referred to him as 'young Ryris'—the alchemist was quickly becoming defensive. Nar couldn't have been much older than himself, and yet his tone implied he had many years on Ryris. He suddenly found himself feeling very protective of Kaia. Scooting closer to his companion, he fought the urge to wrap his arm around her, to show Nar that he needed to keep his hands off. Not that Kaia was in any way 'his', but, after the previous night, he didn't really know what to think anymore. As he sat and watched Nar move in and seductively wipe seeds from her lips, Ryris' feelings bubbled up once again. Just as he was about to say something, even though his jaw was clenched tight, Kaia moved away from Nar's touch.

She shifted uncomfortably at the contact with the Ka'liik leader, pushing back a good few inches. The soldier immediately put her fruit down and rested her hands on her lap with a sigh. "Nar, I…"

"I have offended you. Please forgive me. It's just…" Nar's brow furrowed as he ruminated on his next words. "…your beauty is otherworldly. I didn't mean to be so forward. And in front of your lover, as well." He looked to Ryris. "As one man to another, I beg you to overlook my foolish behavior and continue on as friends."

Ryris knew he had a split second in which to respond. He surely wasn't Kaia's lover, but her body language a moment before indicated to him that perhaps their best course of action was to play along with the charade Nar had inadvertently imposed on them. He sat up confidently put his arm around Kaia. "You are forgiven. Her beauty *is* unmatched. Who could help but be captivated by her?" He immediately hoped he hadn't made Kaia uncomfortable—because it was the honest truth.

"Thank you, Ryris—and Kaia. I feel I have made a fool of myself nonetheless."

"Water under the bridge." Kaia smiled warmly and took another bite of her desert fruit.

"If I may ask, what brings you to our land? The Ka'liik rarely get visitors on purpose, but something tells me you're not lost." Nar grabbed for a waterskin and drank deeply.

"We're searching for a friend." Kaia's words were precise and clear, and hinted that she was not about to divulge any more of their mission parameters.

"A friend, eh? I'm afraid we haven't seen anyone in quite a long time. Are you sure they came this way?"

"The story is long and boring, I assure you. But, he *is* here—somewhere."

Nar nodded knowingly. "Well then, if I were a certain someone with a crystal weapon and I was looking for a friend…" He gazed off at the horizon, in the direction of the looming rocks in the distance. "…I would check the canyons."

Kaia didn't reply, and instead just exchanged a knowing glance with the nomad.

"The Ka'liik have been in this desert since before history was written. We don't forget when strangers enter our land—especially ones bearing crystal accoutrements. It may have been over seven-hundred years ago, but the stories live on. And…" He reached forward and took Kaia's hand. "…I can most certainly assure you that your friend is safe."

Ryris' spine tingled at the sight of Nar holding Kaia's hand. She didn't seem to mind, or was just being polite, for she didn't retract. He had to snap himself from this constant—and uncharacteristic—jealousy. Nar had just admitted that the secret Phia had hoped would have been kept for eternity—was not so secret after all, living on in Ka'liik lore.

"And furthermore," Nar added. "I can take you to him, if you wish."

Kaia responded quickly, but politely. "There's no need to accompany us, but we would be grateful for directions."

"Of course. He's atop the Devil's Canopy. Two days' travel should get you there."

"Devil's Canopy?" Ryris licked his dry lips, and tried to keep his voice from trembling. He really didn't like the ominous sound of their destination. Maybe Kaia would reconsider and allow Nar to travel with them.

"The area is rocky, the trails up the canyon wall steep and craggy. You'd be wise to prepare yourself before you attempt the climb."

"I was under the impression your people never went near there. You seem to know an awful lot about the area for being superstitious." Kaia quirked an eyebrow at their host.

"Superstitious? My grandparents, maybe." Nar sighed. "The oases are slowly drying up. We realized the only way we were going to survive was to trade for the supplies we needed. The caves in the canyons are rich in minerals that fetch a high price from the traders brave enough to come to our lands. Besides, the legends that kept my ancestors out of those hills are nothing more than wild fairytales. I mean, who would honestly believe there were demons in the canyons?"

"Demons?" Ryris swallowed hard.

"The people who inhabited these lands eons ago were wiped from the earth for their sins, leaving behind ghostly apparitions bent on vengeance. The souls of their victims glow red at night, trapped in the rocks for eternity." Nar eyed Ryris as he talked, taking note of the alchemist's apprehension. "A fate worse than death…"

Ryris tried to hide his nervousness. He knew Nar was messing with him, but it didn't make the story any less spooky.

Nar erupted in a great bellow of laughter. "Children's tales! Ryris, my boy, you need to relax!"

Ryris balled up his fist, hidden in his lap. He knew he needed to be calm, or he could jeopardize their whole mission in the desert. He forced a fake smile and chuckled. "Good one, Nar. You…really had me going."

Nar's teeth gleamed, even in the shade, as he smiled broadly. "My pleasure."

Ryris eyed him, hoping the man got the message that deep down, he had not been amused.

Nar continued, "When I was a boy, my father decided to test old myths and went into the canyons. When he returned unscathed a week later, the people realized they had been spooked over nothing. Now, that's not to say there aren't Ka'liik who still believe the old tales, but their numbers are dwindling. We respect their right to keep old traditions alive. The only inhabitants of those canyons are rock goats and buzzards. And the occasional scorpion." Nar smiled broadly and grabbed his canteen. "I'd be more worried about falling to my death scaling those walls. You friend's tomb is practically touching the sky."

"Thank you for your concern, Nar." Kaia drained the last of the water from her canteen. "I assume it's safer to travel at night?"

"Sometimes. If you're not used to the heat, a nighttime journey might be a better choice. However..." He rose, plucking a pair of well-worn binoculars from a pouch at his side. After a quick moment of searching through the opening in the oasis walls, he found what he was looking for. Motioning for Kaia and Ryris to rise, he handed her the looking glasses and pointed her in the right direction. "...those are called telek. Highly territorial—and nocturnal. They're sleeping in the daytime heat, that's why they were easy to spot. If you come too close to their pack, they're likely to attack—especially since they have young this time of year. Those horns are poisonous."

Kaia peered through the binoculars, locating a pack of horned beasts in the distance. Their fur was short and tan in color, blending almost perfectly with the terrain. Long, feline tails whipped sand flies from their bodies, sharp teeth shined in the glaring sun. Standing on muscular, powerful legs, it was easy to understand that if they gave chase, they would most certainly emerge victorious. She handed the binoculars to Ryris. "Any tips on avoiding them? Or, if worse comes to worse—engagement?"

"Stay downwind, and leave your horse and wagon here in the oasis. She'll be safe, don't worry. You'll have to backtrack through here on your way out anyway. As for defending yourselves—how good are you with that bow?" Nar eyed her.

"Good enough." Kaia smirked right back at him.

"Then you should be fine. If you can poison your weapons, it'll help as well. You can handle that, can't you, alchemist?"

"Of course I can." Ryris didn't appreciate Nar's condescending tone. He was quickly getting the impression that, even though he was nice when he wanted to be, the Ka'liik leader was very much an arrogant son-of-a-bitch. Ryris was ready to be done with him.

"If you're leaving tonight, I suggest you rest up and eat your fill now." Nar sat again, beckoning behind him with a flicked wrist. Within moments, several Ka'liik approached with platters laden with grilled meat, flatbreads, and more fruit. "Leaving an hour-or-so before dusk will ensure you still have plenty of sunlight before dark. There's a small rock plateau halfway between here and your destination. It will be a safe place to camp. You can even make a fire, if you'd like. Ryris has quite the technique..." Nar's eyes twinkled mischievously.

Ryris immediately felt the cactus fruit heave in his stomach. Everything he had ever been taught—about keeping his magic a secret—just came back to haunt him.

196

They had seen him the night before—and he suddenly feared for his life. The alchemist felt his face flush.

Nar, sensing his sudden mood shift, quickly reassured him. "You're safe here. We Ka'liik have no qualms about magic use."

Ryris blew out a relieved sigh and silently nodded his appreciation.

"Now, as I was saying, the fire will keep the telek away. They don't like the smoke. My lookouts will be watching as well."

"Thank you for your generosity." Kaia accepted a plate from a Ka'liik woman, and began to fill it with food. Ryris did the same, still keeping a close eye on Nar.

"I hope you find your friend. That you're looking for him, *Kaia the Quick*...tells me there is change on the horizon."

Kaia and Ryris exchanged dumbfounded glances.

"Yes...I know who you are. I know of the battle you fought. Our elders passed those stories down so no one would forget. Know that when the time comes—the Ka'liik will take up arms to fight by your side."

"I'm going to hold you to that, Nar." Kaia's eyes crinkled in thanks.

"I sincerely hope you do."

~~~

Kaia's tiara glittered in the sunlight filtering through a sandstone arch in the chasm.

She walked down the canyon floor, her arms spread wide to catch the desert breeze. Early that morning they had left their rocky base camp and made the trek into the canyons. The walls soared higher than those surrounding the oasis, and Ryris dreaded having to climb to the top to find Jaric. Kaia had taken the tiara out some hours earlier, hoping it would allow her to divine the exact location of her comrade by sensing the sword shard he possessed.

She had spent most of the time since entering the canyons deep in thought, trying to acclimate herself to the sensations her tiara was giving her. Ryris could tell she was sensing—something—but what it was, neither had any clue. And now, here they were, sweltering in the early morning heat, hoping they could find Jaric's tomb before they burned to a crisp.

"Anything yet?" Ryris called after her, taking a small sip from his waterskin. His feet ached, his leg muscles burned with fatigue, and he suddenly missed his wagon very much.

Kaia stopped, putting her fingertips to her temples. After a long moment, she finally responded, pointing up the side of the cliff. "I think we're getting close. The jewels on the side are getting warm."

Ryris mumbled under his breath as he tugged on his sweat-soaked collar, "How can you tell anything is warm? It's too blasted hot…"

She stood still as Ryris approached. Her voice was hushed as she pointed. "Looks like there's a carved landing up there."

Ryris peered up at the canyon wall, shading his eyes with his hand. "All the way up there?"

"I'm sure of it. Now," Kaia moved toward the side of the chasm. "We just need to find the trailhead. Nar said there were concealed paths."

The pair searched for several moments, before Ryris stumbled upon what looked like a set of wind-worn steps. The alchemist tested the strength of the crumbling stone with one foot, scowling when it broke apart under his feet. He turned to his companion. "Well the good news is, I think I found the beginning of the trail. The bad news is—I doubt it'll hold our weight."

Kaia pushed him aside and began her ascent. "Let's go."

Ryris shook his head at her perseverance. She wasn't the least bit worried about risking life and limb in order to get to Jaric. At least, he didn't think she was. Had she any doubts, she disguised them incredibly well. Realizing she was leaving him— literally—in her dust, he meandered up the virtually nonexistent trail behind her.

~~~

Ryris had never been so happy to see a flat rock surface in his life.

After over an hour of climbing the most treacherous path he had ever traversed, he and Kaia finally reached the Devil's Canopy. He certainly understood why the area had been given its ominous moniker. On their ascent, they had both lost their footing more times than they could eventually count, with the alchemist almost falling down the rock face twice.

"You need to let me rest for a minute, Kaia." Ryris stooped over—well away from the edge—hands planted firmly on his thighs. He tried desperately to catch his breath. "I'm gonna collapse if you don't."

Kaia slumped against the rock wall, also obviously feeling the fatigue of their impressive climb setting in. "Two minutes."

Ryris nodded, his body exhausted. He felt as if he barely had enough energy to accept a waterskin from his partner. After a few moments of silent rest, Kaia stood up straight again, repositioning her bow across her back. "Time's up."

"Can't we wait just a little longer? My calves feel like they're on fire."

"No." Kaia's tone was curt.

"Oh, fine. Kill me, why don't you?" He slowly stood, arching his back in order to get it to pop. "Just make sure to bury me deep enough so the buzzards don't pick at my eyes."

"I'd much rather just push you off the side and be done with you. It's too hot to be digging a grave." Ryris just stared at Kaia incredulously. He sincerely hoped she was joking. "The door is close, I can feel it. We need to move."

Blowing out an exhausted breath, Ryris followed his companion. They inched their way along the canyon wall, the path narrowing uncomfortably in some places, until they reached a dead end. Kaia approached the wall blocking their way, running her fingers over the smooth sandstone. Ryris wondered how they would open the chamber—if it was even there. Back above Hewe, careless fighting amongst brothers had accidentally cracked Kaia's room open. Standing here, hundreds of feet above the desert canyon floor, he wondered just how they were going to manage to break through solid sandstone.

"Do you see anything?" Ryris moved closer to his friend, and began to inspect the wall along with her. Kaia knelt and a small chuckle soon escaped her lips. "What's so funny?"

She hovered her palm over a small indentation in the rock's surface, near the ground. "I guess they thought if anyone was foolhardy enough to make the trek up the rock face, then they might as well be rewarded with an obvious marker." Kaia lifted her palm and pointed to a small symbol, no bigger than a baby's hand, etched into the stone. Years of sandblasting from the winds of the desert had eaten away at the rune, but it was still visible if one looked hard enough.

"It can't be as simple as pushing a button, can it?"

Kaia shrugged. "Would you like the honor?"

Ryris shook his head with apprehension. "You do it..."

Kaia took a deep breath and pressed her hand against the emblem. Within a second, the sigil began to glow blue and the rock face suddenly recessed, letting out a puff of stale, dusty air. Moments later, the door swung open, revealing a soft lavender light beckoning them to enter.

CHAPTER TWENTY-ONE

For bravery unmatched by any soldier in the Guard, I bestow a commendation of honor onto Jaric the Bold. For saving the life of an endangered child and risking his own in the process, he is hereby awarded the Diamond Medal of Valor.

--Heroic commendation, Harald Mrazen, Crystal Guard Elder Council

Ryris had the uncanny feeling he had been in this room before.

The layout was exactly the same as Kaia's chamber, right down to the placement of the sarcophagus. Weapons racks lined the walls, books adorned the shelves. Even the glass case housing an ornate crystal helmet sat waiting to be opened. Kaia immediately set her weapon against the wall and moved to the side of the coffin.

"Jaric the Bold...it's been a long time." She brushed the dust from the lid and leaned over to peer inside.

Ryris joined her after shedding his knapsack, the back of his shirt sticky with sweat. The feeling of déjà vu was incredible. He closed his eyes momentarily and imagined himself back above Hewe, gazing upon Kaia for the very first time. "*If I only knew then what I know now,*" he mused inwardly.

"Can you open it?"

Kaia's voice snapped him from his thoughts. Clearing his throat, he moved around to the foot of the container and examined the mechanism. It was exactly like the panel that had controlled his partner's stasis. "I don't see why not. Everything seems to be the same."

"Then get going." She laid her hands on the lid.

Ryris nodded and ran back to his backpack, pulling out his journal. Even though he had successfully opened Kaia's coffin, he wasn't confident that he could reproduce the same results from memory. He would definitely need his notes. Returning to his position at the foot of the sarcophagus, he set his journal on the glass lid and got to work.

"How long will it take?"

"Ten minutes? Each time I power a circuit down, there's a small delay until I can do it again. I'm assuming it's some sort of failsafe mechanism to keep the machine from releasing stasis too quickly." He depressed the first glowing button. "When everything is done, the room should go black. Those lights on the wall will flare within a couple seconds."

Kaia inhaled deeply, keeping her hands firmly planted above Jaric's still form. Ryris wondered what could possibly be going though her mind. He made the split second decision to ask.

"Gamm for your thoughts?" He depressed another button, and it dimmed beneath his fingertip.

"Pardon?" She looked at him, surprised.

"I just...I'm wondering what you're thinking. I mean, we're really to the point of no return, aren't we?"

"Indeed." Kaia kept her hands on the lid, tracing her finger down the smooth glass. "Jaric is my most trusted general. Yes, he and Ealsig are both well trained soldiers, but I always felt a different sort of camaraderie with him."

Ryris swore he saw Kaia's cheeks blush in the low light. Before he could stop himself, more words tumbled from his mouth. "Was he your boyfriend?"

Kaia turned and shot him a stern glance, the young alchemist instantly regretting saying anything.

"Sorry, I didn't mean to pry."

Kaia didn't acknowledge his apology. He worked the rest of the time in silence, covertly watching Kaia for any reaction. But she just kept staring at Jaric through the clear lid, never giving any indication that she wanted more conversation. Ryris swore he saw a tear roll down her cheek, but in the dim light of the chamber, it was quite possible his eyes had deceived him. As he pressed the last button on the panel, he warned Kaia that the room would soon go dark. Seconds later, the lights blinked out, leaving them in pitch-black. Within moments, the crystal lamps on the walls blazed, bathing the room in clear, white light. Kaia kept her palms planted on the lid, waiting.

"How long?" Her voice was strong, no hint of the emotion she may have been showing in the moments leading up to the blackout.

"The lid should open on its own any minute now." Ryris left the foot of the sarcophagus and joined Kaia at the side. "He's going to be really out of it. I don't know how much you recall."

"I remember enough."

The lid cracked open, air hissing out of the broken seal. Kaia flinched at the sound. Sliding back exactly as the cover on Kaia's coffin had done, the lid was soon out of sight, exposing Jaric to the environment for the first time in seven-hundred years.

His dark brown hair ruffled on the artificial breeze created by the movement of the lid. He laid there peacefully, his chest still and his eyes unmoving beneath their lids. A goatee surrounded his mouth, a thick scar protruding from the whiskers on his chin. Another blemish crossed just underneath his right eye running from his ear to the bridge of his nose. It was obvious to Ryris that Jaric had seen his fair share of battlefield action. His armor was covered with scratches and dents, several patches adorning various plates of crystal. A longsword lay at his side, his left hand bent slightly to cover the hilt. Attached to the scabbard were red leather straps, tucked neatly under the weapon. Kaia reached forward, as if to touch her slumbering friend, but was startled when he took in a giant, gasping breath.

Jaric jolted upright and lurched forward, pained gasps billowing from his lips. His legs twitched in front of him, one hand reaching up to clutch at his throat. A thin stream of saliva dripped from the corner of his mouth as he struggled to fill his lungs. Disorientation overtook him.

Kaia laid her hand on his back and leaned close, her voice more soothing and quiet than Ryris had ever heard. "Jaric...stay calm." Her movements were gentle as she eased him into a more comfortable position. Even when he flinched away from her touch, much like she had done with Ryris, she held firm and tried her best to assist him through his discomfort.

Jaric trembled, his breaths still coming in ragged spurts.

"I went through the same sensations. You'll feel sick for a day or two, but your strength will return in time." She snaked her arm around his body, trying to steady him as he dry heaved. "Jaric? Can you hear me?"

The warrior groaned painfully as he brought his knees to his chest, his armor creaking from centuries of disuse. He hung his head, laying his cheek on the cool crystal kneecap of his mail. "K-kaia...?"

"Yes." She smiled softly, Ryris just able to make out a relieved expression on her turned face. "You've been asleep a long time."

Jaric turned to face her, his eyes squinting in the bright light. Licking his dry lips, he spoke once again, his voice gravelly and unused. "What happened? Why...?" He coughed, holding back a gag.

"Don't try to speak."

He nodded wearily, turning his attention to Ryris with a confused look. Kaia, sensing his impending question, answered before he could ask.

"This is my traveling companion—and friend. You can trust him."

Jaric eyed Ryris suspiciously for a moment before his face took on a sudden green hue. He tossed his gauntlets off hurriedly as he tried to scramble from his bed. "Out...I need to...get out..."

Kaia motioned for Ryris to help her, and they both guided Jaric from his sarcophagus. Barely out for a few seconds, Jaric fell on his hands and knees, and threw up all over Ryris' boots. The young alchemist nearly vomited himself. He resisted the urge to scoff when Kaia shot him a stern glare.

"Can you stand?" Kaia wrapped her arm around Jaric's waist and urged him to his feet. "You'll feel better once you get that armor off."

The weakened warrior followed her lead, and gingerly tried to stand. His legs held his weight for a few seconds, before letting his body collapse once more. Jaric grumbled, his brows furrowing in exhausted frustration. "Why can't..."

"Your strength will return, I promise. Come on, we'll get you something to drink." She noticed Ryris, suddenly obsessed with removing Jaric's vomit from his shoes by wiping them against the side wall. His nose wrinkled as he gagged. Her voice rose, an irritated command tumbling out. "You can get new boots in the next town, get over here and help me!"

Ryris abandoned his cleaning regimen and knelt beside them. Mirroring Kaia, he grabbed Jaric under one of his arms and guided him upwards. Jaric's legs wobbled, his body heavy from the fatigue of hundreds of years of stasis. They led him to the side of the chamber, where their packs lay against the wall. A warm breeze blew in from the open door. Letting go of her friend for just a moment, Kaia lifted a blanket from her knapsack and laid it on the ground as a makeshift cushion. Ryris struggled to keep him from falling. Moving back to Jaric's side, she and Ryris eased him down so he could lean back against the cool stone wall. Ryris reached for his waterskin and offered the exhausted warrior a drink.

Jaric winced as the liquid touched his parched throat. After only a small sip, he pushed the flask away and hung his head between his shoulders. "I can't."

"You must drink." Kaia's voice was laced with concern. "We're in the middle of the desert. Dehydration is a real threat."

"What good is the water if I can't keep it down?" He looked at her with exhausted, pained eyes.

"I might be able to help..." Ryris raised a hopeful eyebrow at the pair. Rummaging through his pack, he finally produced a small red vial. He held it out, hoping Jaric would accept. "This will settle your stomach."

The warrior looked at him suspiciously, refusing the bottle. "I don't need any magic potions."

"Jaric..." Kaia rested her hand on this knee. "Trust him."

His face still tinted green with sickness, Jaric relented and accepted the vial. Twisting the cap off, he hesitantly sniffed the tincture before downing it on one gulp. He sat quietly, patiently waiting for any and all effects to take hold. After a few moments, he sighed deeply, his color returning to normal.

"*You* made this?"

Ryris smiled with pride as he nodded.

Jaric reached for the waterskin. "May I? I feel like I can keep it down now."

"By all means, drink up. You'll need your strength to get down from here."

Jaric took a long draught from the canteen. "Don't remind me. That ascent nearly did me in."

"You and me both." Ryris drank from another flask, savoring the cool water.

The trio sat silently for several minutes, Jaric eventually draining his canteen. The potion Ryris had given him had eased his stomach somewhat, but his muscles still ached and his head pounded. Kaia kept close watch on him as he sat; head leaned back against the chamber wall, eyes closed. Deep, even breaths billowed from his lips.

When nearly ten minutes had passed without any conversation, Ryris decided to break the ice. "So, are we going to stay the night here, or...?"

"I don't think I can make it down the canyon. Not tonight." Jaric's voice was feeble, exhaustion taking hold. "Why do I feel so spent? I've been asleep for...how long?"

"Over seven-hundred years." Kaia regarded him closely, looking for any hint of despair. She obviously knew better than anyone what it felt like to be given the news that you had outlived countless generations. "And stasis isn't sleep. It will take a few days for your vigor to return."

"Seven-hundred, eh?" Jaric exhaled deeply through his nostrils, tapping his fingers on the crystal knee caps of his armor. After a moment, he slapped his hands on his thighs and turned his attention to his partner. "No sense in dwelling on it, right? Dust and bones, eh, Kaia?"

"Dust and bones..."

Ryris looked intently at the pair. Something in their tone, they way they looked at each other in solidarity—he wondered if he would ever share in that feeling of camaraderie with the warriors.

"We'll spend the night up here, protected from the heat and predators. I think we can make do without a fire, the wall sconces will give us plenty of light." Kaia leaned in toward her friend. "Let me help you with that armor. You'll feel much better once it's off."

"Undressing me now? You minx…" Jaric smirked devilishly before removing his boots.

Kaia rolled her eyes. "I see your personality has remained undamaged by stasis…" She removed his greaves while he unbuckled his breastplate from the pauldrons. Within moments, Jaric's outer armor was shed, leaving him clad in the thin crystal chain mail he wore underneath. After rubbing his neck with a strong hand, the warrior let out a relieved sigh and turned his attention to Ryris.

"So, just how is it that you came to be in Kaia's company? You don't seem like her type." Jaric eyed him suspiciously. It seemed to Ryris that his thankfulness for the potion—along with his politeness—had waned.

Ryris regaled him with the tale of the boys, saberstrike, and the time he and Kaia spent together snowbound above Hewe. The warrior showed no emotion when Lyrax' name was mentioned, only nodding solemnly as they told him about their suspicions with the newly crowned emperor. Jaric watched him closely as he recalled the events of their travels, ending with Nar and the Ka'liik, and their climb to his tomb. Hoping he had quelled the soldier's assumptions about him, Ryris was discouraged when Jaric shook his head with a huff.

"But what's so special about *you*, alchemist? You just happened to stumble upon her. Do you even realize who we are?"

Ryris was immediately offended, and felt the urge to lash out and slap the bastard across the face. He knew his type—bold, brave, and arrogant. Always looking down at the lowly tradesmen, the weirdo intellectuals who spent their time with their noses in books rather than at a sword's edge. "What's that supposed to mean? Of course I know who you are. My Gran used to tell me stories about the Crystal Guard."

"Stories?" Jaric snorted incredulously before raising his voice. "Do you even understand what kind of danger we faced—that we'll surely face again?"

Ryris' cheeks flushed with anger, and he found himself very relieved when Kaia intervened.

"Jaric, watch your tongue!" Her eyes were seething with fury. "How dare you belittle the man who risked his life to find you?" She pointed to Ryris' chest. "Show him what an ass he's just made of himself."

Obeying his friend, Ryris unbuttoned the top of his shirt and fished out the silver chain hanging on his chest. When the amulet emerged into the bright lights of the chamber, it sparkled brilliantly. Jaric's expression immediately sobered, his mouth hanging open in awe.

"It can't be…" He scrambled forward, grasping the bauble between his thumb and forefinger. Pulling a bit too hard, Jaric yanked Ryris' body forward as he inspected the talisman. "This…this is…"

"I think you owe Ryris an apology." Kaia glared at her fellow general.

"*Ryris?*" Jaric let the amulet go and immediately hung his head in shame. "I'm a fool."

"Yes. You are." Kaia slapped him forcefully on the back of the head.

Jaric looked up to the alchemist with an expression of humility. "Forgive me. My remarks were uncalled for. You're his ancestor, aren't you?"

"So I've been told."

"I'm the unworthy one, then. To be in your presence, to be in the presence of that amulet once more." Jaric nodded to no one in particular. "It's…good to know that it's safe."

Ryris, willing to forget Jaric's prior disrespect, wanted to know more about his bauble—and his ancestor. "Did you know him well? The other Ryris, I mean."

"Know him? I'm the one they sent to get the amulet created." Jaric smiled, mentally reminiscing. "It was his expertise that ended up saving us in the end. Kaia may have activated the sword, but he enchanted it. It was an honor to have served alongside him."

"If I may ask, who made my amulet? Where did it come from? I've had it my whole life—but know nothing about it." Ryris unconsciously touched the talisman around his neck, rubbing his thumb over the smooth stone.

"The thing nearly got me killed. Ran across a pack of undead ghouls on my way. They gave me this." He moved his thin under mail aside as he turned his back toward Ryris, exposing a long, jagged scar down his shoulder blade. "Damn things overran me; one jumped on my back and tried to jam its stinking sword down my armor. But I would have faced a thousand of them to get our Arch-battlemage the protection he needed. As for the craftsman, his name was Laren Foyt. He lived in the central forests, I think the village was Shadewick."

Ryris was unfamiliar with the family name or the village. He knew the area, but couldn't recall any such town. "Shadewick…doesn't ring a bell."

"That doesn't surprise me." Jaric's expression sobered. "It was razed near the end of the war. All of the inhabitants were…" He looked to Kaia, as if to ask her permission to continue. He wasn't sure just how much Ryris knew. At her nod, he continued. "…*turned*. The only way to save them was to destroy them. Believe me, it was the humane thing to do."

Ryris shuddered, thinking back to the terrible image in his book. The face of the woman begging for her life—and then her haunting, lifeless eyes and rotten, putrid skin after the deed had been done—had been forever burned into his brain.

"Jaric's bravery is unmatched." Kaia's proud voice cut through the sudden silence of the chamber. "He was the perfect candidate to send on such an important mission."

"Don't flatter me, Kaia." Jaric's eyes glimmered mischievously. "We both know if it wasn't for me, we would have never defeated that necromancing bastard. Because, well, I'm just that great."

"You're an ass." She shoved him, causing him to push back in childish response.

"Seriously though, do you realize just how incredible she is?" Jaric motioned to Kaia. "Youngest general the Guard had ever seen. And she'll kick your ass into next week without so much as a bat of her eyelashes."

Kaia's voice became humble. "I trained intensely, just like everyone else."

"Don't sell yourself short, Quick. No one even comes close to your warrior's will." He leaned over and punched her in the arm, which she immediately returned with double the force.

Watching the two old friends exchange boasts suddenly made Ryris feel uncomfortable. Pangs of jealousy began to rise within him, even though he had only known Jaric for a very short time. *Had* they been involved? The way he looked at her, the way they interacted—Ryris just didn't know. He had to remind himself that Kaia wasn't *his*, and that he needed to keep his budding feelings in check if he wanted to continue on. This was definitely not the time or place for soul-searching. Ryris smiled sincerely and hoped his impending compliment would seem genuine—even though his mind was aflutter.

"You two seem to have a great relationship. It must be nice to be with an old friend again." Ryris' voice was wistful as he thought back to the friendships he really never had.

"Old friend—and a new one." Jaric grabbed Ryris' hand and shook it firmly. "You're one of us now, whether you like it or not."

"I've really never had close friends. Well, there's Grildi, but he's—different. It feels nice to belong."

Kaia smiled warmly at Ryris' admission before digging in her knapsack, finding a small pouch of dried berries. She offered a handful to Jaric. "Eat. You need to regain your strength. We need to move as soon as possible."

"You really do think it's Lyrax, don't you?"

Kaia looked straight into his eyes with determination. "Have I ever given you any reason to doubt me?"

"No." Jaric sighed deeply, with a shake of his head. "I just didn't want to believe it could be true. After all we endured—to be faced with the horrible reality that he has once again, by all the mysteries, come back..."

"...it just means we were meant to protect again, just like my father and all the citizens had hoped for us." Kaia looked to Ryris. "Remember when we talked of destiny? This is it. Destiny has awakened. You can't explain it, but it can't be ignored."

"You're right about that." Jaric blew out a long, purposeful breath and stared down the young alchemist. "So, if we're going to go to war, can we count on you? Do you have any battle skills?"

Ryris swallowed nervously. He wasn't a soldier. Hell, he was hardly a wizard. But, he didn't want to seem totally incompetent in front of the hardened warrior. Anxiously tapping his fingers together, he meekly responded, "I...I have magic."

"Well that'll definitely do! C'mon, show it off!"

Meeting Kaia's encouraging gaze, Ryris decided to go for it. What was there to lose? Only his pride, he figured. But, with practice comes results—and better to practice in the safe company of friends rather than in the frenetic chaos of the battlefield. He cracked his knuckles, stood, and moved toward the open door. He took a deep breath and concentrated, feeling the tips of his fingers begin to heat up with a familiar tingle. Looking down to his hands, the flames flickering on his palms exploded with brightness, and he morphed them into the largest fireball he had ever produced. The heat on his face was immense as he manipulated the sphere of plasma in the air, levitating it above his hands. The sight of his creation brought a proud, albeit surprised, smile to his lips. He didn't even mind the uncomfortable warmth emanating from his amulet. With a push of his hands and a hearty scream, he unleashed a fireball through the door, out into the hot, dusty desert air. It struck the far canyon wall, shattering the sandstone and sending rocky shrapnel showering down onto the sandy ground below. A flock of goats atop the canyon rim scattered.

Jaric stood and flew to Ryris' side, clapping him on the back with gusto. "By the Goddess! You really are of his bloodline!"

Ryris stared at his hands in awe, thin wisps of smoke rising from his sooty fingertips. He couldn't believe he had just created something so powerful. It felt really rewarding to have someone react so incredibly to the thing he had always been told to hide. To finally have someone acknowledge his powers in a positive light. Turning to face Jaric with a hopeful expression, he brushed his hands together to rid himself of the ash. Feeling the warrior embrace his shoulders, he couldn't help but start to feel the camaraderie that he knew Kaia and Jaric shared. "You think it'll do on the battlefield? I've never made one that big before."

"Are you kidding?" Jaric ushered him back into the chamber out of the glaring sunlight and motioned to Kaia to join them near the entrance. When she moved into the small circle, Jaric extended his arm around her shoulder as well, Ryris mirroring his actions. "We're a team now. With our strength and your magic, we'll make sure we rid the world of evil again. Adding Ealsig will only strengthen our power further."

The trio stood there for a long moment, thinking on what was to come. Ryris finally broke the silence. "Are you two scared?"

Kaia pulled back from the embrace, but left her hand on the alchemist's shoulder reassuringly. "I wouldn't be a good warrior if I wasn't. Courage isn't something that defines you as a soldier. This isn't a war game. This is real life. There's a possibility that we'll perish, and we need to accept that before we ever get onto the battlefield."

Hearing Kaia speak with such bravado in her voice, even when she talked about fear, eased Ryris' apprehension somewhat. But he knew better than to think his courage was going to be bolstered just because of a pep talk. To think his life might end on some strange plain, surrounded by enemies that would do who-knows-what with him afterwards made him shudder. But he knew it had to be done, even if he didn't want to admit he needed to be a part of it. It would take him a long time, maybe even never, to achieve the level of bravery that his companions possessed. He couldn't help but try and hide the meekness in his voice as he responded. "I just hope I'm enough. You both have years of training, countless hours on actual battlefields. I'm…I'm just an alchemist. I might be a liability."

"Maybe." Kaia's response was unexpected, but not untrue. "But, you're integral to making sure we defeat Lyrax for good this time. You'll get better as time goes on, you'll see. Remember what I told you—if you concentrate and study efficiently, you can be as powerful, or even more so, than your predecessor."

"She's right. And besides, Kaia's magic can only get us so far, and mine is nonexistent."

"You mean?"

"Can't even make a damn spark. Never could. Born without the gift." He pointed to his sword, leaned up against the wall. "That's why I have my crystal beauty over there. She's saved my life more times than I'd care to admit."

Kaia moved to sit once again at their makeshift camp. As her two companions took their seats, she continued the conversation. "One's merit on the battlefield isn't measured by prowess with a sword or the ability to set one's enemy on fire in a timely manner. Everyone does what they can, they best they can do it. All help is welcomed. We need alchemists. We need weapon masters. We need people to cook meals, wrangle horses, and survey land. If you decide that you'd rather stay off the front lines, then so be it. Bravery isn't measured by the amount of your enemy's blood on your boots."

Kaia's words made Ryris feel much better. And knowing that his two warrior friends wouldn't think any less of him if he made the decision to make potions instead of run combatants through with a sword, eased a lot of worry.

"I'll tell you what *would* help us, though." Jaric slowly eased himself to his feet, the fatigue of stasis still holding him tight. He looked to Ryris and pointed toward the bookcase. "Give me a hand."

The two men shoved the shelving aside, exposing a small niche. Jaric retrieved a familiar-looking, albeit smaller package. He tossed it at Kaia. "I'm assuming you still have yours?"

"Of course. And once we awaken Ealsig and retrieve her shard, we'll have made real headway." She sighed. "You don't, by any chance, know of the locations of the other pieces? Perhaps you overheard something, or were told information I wasn't?"

"I wish. All they said was, 'lie down in this crystal coffin and relax'."

"Then we'll just have to double down on our progress. Search out-of-the-way locations, dig deep with our reconnaissance. We can't afford to let Roann or Lyrax, if that's who is truly behind the surge we've all felt, get their hands on any of the pieces."

"But they can't use them without the hilt right? And not if there's any shards missing?" Ryris nibbled on a piece of jerky, his stomach beginning to growl from lack of food. He offered his friends both a portion.

"In theory, no. But the fact is we just don't know with absolute certainty. That's why we can't allow even one of the shards to fall into the wrong hands."

Jaric belched loudly after consuming his serving of jerky, completely wrecking the serious mood Kaia had just set. "Well then, it's settled. We leave in the morning. We head toward Ealsig's location, and hopefully find some little glittering sword pieces on the way."

Ryris tossed Kaia a hopeful glance. He wanted to believe they'd find what they were looking for, and defeat whatever was conspiring against them sooner than later.

Jaric reached for Ryris' knapsack without permission and began to rifle through. "So, what else you got in here? I'm starving…"

CHAPTER TWENTY-TWO

...are as follows: All buildings razed. Spoils confiscated and relegated to quartermaster. Necromantic paraphernalia destroyed. Twenty-seven dead, three in custody, including the aforementioned Lyrax, slated for execution after questioning.

--Scrap of Ashal army general's field report, year unknown. Found in ruined royal library.

"...are you sure you weren't followed?"

Roann scowled in the darkness of the volcanic cavern, offended by the remark. He fought the urge to bite back as Lyrax' disembodied voice continued.

"...You are the emperor. Surely they would send a security detail with you...for your protection..."

"I'm not a child. I know what I'm doing." He dropped the heavy satchel from his back, bottles clinking inside as it hit the pumice floor. "I've properly threatened and that's all they need. No one would dare go against my orders."

"...ahh, yes. The last one to do so..."

"...is long silenced. Have I ever given you reason to doubt me?"

The chamber was silent for a long moment.

"...not yet..."

Again, the young emperor found the condescending tone of his master's spectral voice offensive. He had done everything Lyrax had asked of him and more his entire life, but sometimes still felt like a child being watched by a parent—just waiting for him to make a mistake. He wasn't an idiot—he was the leader of the most powerful nation in the world, and commanded the respect that went along with it. However, Roann decided not to press the issue any further. They had important matters to take care of, and he couldn't waste time or energy being angry.

"I brought everything you asked for. I sent a page to retrieve the supplies from the old alchemist in town." Roann opened the knapsack and began to remove containers and vials, setting them on a natural rocky shelf jutting out from the volcano's wall.

"Aren't you concerned it...raised suspicions? What could the emperor possibly want...with alchemical ingredients?"

211

Roann clenched his jaw and internally stewed at Lyrax' tone. "I've developed a new hobby…"

"Well then…we can't wait any longer. I have one last task before we begin…and a special gift…"

Roann's interest was piqued. Approaching the font in the middle of the room, he peered into the blue flames. "A gift?"

"Change forms…"

Roann backed away from the pedestal and concentrated, channeling his energy. His body twisted and morphed, his clothing disappearing into nothingness. Blonde hair was replaced by horns, smooth skin consumed by darkness. Within moments, the handsome emperor had been replaced by a grotesquely beautiful beast, black scales shimmering over its muscular body. Roann stood tall and proud, clicking his sharp toenails on the stone floor.

"Kneel…"

Roann obeyed, maneuvering his large body into the required position. Seconds later, a hot crimson fog bubbled from the font and enveloped him, seeping under the scales on his back. He cringed at the sensation, the feeling of thousands of red-hot pins being jammed into his shoulder blades. Fighting the urge to wince and move away, he stayed strong, knowing that whatever Lyrax was bestowing upon him would be well worth the pain. After a long moment, he felt a new heaviness tugging on his neck muscles. He released a relieved breath as he stood and was greeted by two massive, leathery wings protruding from his back.

"Take flight…"

Roann instinctively flapped his new appendages and rose gracefully into the air. After a moment of flight corrections, he circled the chamber, flying higher with each pass. As he reached the top of the cavernous room, he hovered before diving with incredible speed, stopping himself mere inches from the floor. Landing with ease, he approached the font.

"I don't know what to say…" His monstrous voice was low and menacing.

"Say nothing. Use your new 'toys' to…carry out your final task for the day…"

"Yes, Master." Roann's wings flapped languidly behind him, creating a soft breeze and giving him relief from the oppressive heat of the room.

"Go southwest. Cross the Blood River…and travel over the Fields of the Damned. There you will find…the remains of the necromancer's coven. The buildings are gone…but a reinforced cellar remains. Inside is an object—a blade. It is essential for the ceremony…"

212

"Anything you require of me, I will dutifully accomplish." Taking off once more, Roann barreled his way upwards, crashing through the thin cooled-lava ceiling that entombed the chamber. Shards of obsidian rained down onto the floor below, and sunlight filtered in through the dusty remains of the ceiling for the first time in centuries. They no longer had to hide.

~~~

The wind blew across Roann's scaly skin as he glided through the wispy clouds above Ashal. Having flown from the volcano in the north, he skirted over the barren landscape below. Burned-out villages marred the surface beneath him. Thousands of skeletons littered the ground. Their abominable flesh rotted away centuries ago, leaving only bones weathered by the howling winds. Weapons rusted where they fell. When Lyrax had been defeated, the hordes of undead stopped in their tracks and crumpled— no longer under the control of their master.

The continent was wholly abandoned. Only trees had made their claim on the once-prosperous land, ruling over the earth as the branches danced on the wind. No flowering blossoms, no succulent fruits—just craggy trees, even their leaves dull and devoid of bright colors.

Floating over the once grand castle of the former king, Roann circled briefly as he took in the sights. Broken towers crumbled from the structure, caved-in roofs fell into the rooms they once enclosed. The marble walls were stained and moldy from years of abuse by the elements, the remaining windows were cracked, letting the rain in to ruin the interiors. The chapel stood at the far end of the complex, the hallway connecting it to the castle proper having long since collapsed. Impressively beautiful in its heyday, the citadel now sat abandoned—left to die on a forgotten continent that no longer welcomed the living. Roann swooped down, landing gracefully on the sloped roof of the former meeting hall.

The remnants of tapestries fluttered in the warm volcanic breeze, their vibrant colors faded over time. Chairs sat unoccupied, surrounding tables that would never again host extravagant state dinners. Jumping down onto the dusty ground, Roann walked the perimeter of the castle, his claws digging into the gravel paths. Shattered windows allowed a glimpse into the moldering halls, once ushering guests and royalty alike from one opulent room to the next. Gilded lanterns still hung on some of the walls, their metallic coatings flecking off as moisture attacked from all sides.

Coming up on the cathedral, Roann shoved his massive scaled frame against the heavy wooden door, forcing it open. A cloud of dust rose from the hinges, unused for centuries. The marble floors heaved up in places, the once-smooth surface no longer traversable without considerable difficulty. No matter to the emperor, however, as he flapped his new wings and floated over the rubble of wrecked pews and fallen chandeliers. Approaching the altar, he circled it, knocking over a lone candelabrum as

213

he moved. Paying the fallen accoutrement no mind, he moved behind into the apse to take in the grandeur of the forgotten place of worship. Before turning to gaze upon the remnants of Ashal's royal sanctuary, he made note of the statue of the goddess keeping watch behind the altar, a silver baptismal font clasped in her stone hands. Tipping to one side from years of being ignored, the material it was sculpted from still shone brightly, its pristine stonework seemingly untouched by the wrath of neglect. A pink stone shimmered within a carved tiara upon Oleana's head, and he recognized it immediately. He now realized why Lyrax was insistent on performing his ritual in this place.

Roann laughed out loud, his monstrous voice echoing off the buttressed ceilings. He couldn't wait for the ceremony to begin. Taking one last look around the place that would soon bear witness to a rebirth; he took to the air once more and ascended through a giant hole in the roof.

~~~

Nothing remained of the necromancer's village. Centuries-worth of scraggly forest had reclaimed the land. If Roann hadn't been airborne, he wouldn't have seen the former spot at all. Only when he noticed a small clearing in the trees, a scorched foundation emerging from the undergrowth, did he realize he had found his destination. Swooping down to land, his wing caught on a gnarled branch, gouging the black leathery flesh. Tiny droplets of blood beaded on his wing, and he winced audibly, hot air puffing from his monstrous nostrils. Slamming his clawed feet down to the ground, he huffed in annoyance at his injury.

Now earth-bound, he was able to discern more remnants of the hamlet. A crumbling brick wall here, dilapidated forges there. The woods had all but obliterated the once powerful coven, but hadn't stamped it out completely. Striding purposefully through the thicket, Roann used his massive legs to push aside piles of rocks and debris, searching for the fortified bunker Lyrax knew to be there. A charred skull popped beneath his monstrous feet, shards of bone scattering in all directions. Looking down, he found the rest of the skeletal body, arms and legs splayed wide in his or her death throes.

After a few moments of searching, he came upon a mass of thick bushes, growing out of what was once the foundation of a house. The wood long since rotted away, Roann could just barely make out the stained outlines of the building material left on the stone floor. Pushing the dried-out foliage away, he allowed himself a satisfied smirk as he uncovered a heavy iron trap door. He wondered how the king's garrison could have missed it, for it was still padlocked and secure. They must have been too busy cleansing the hamlet to pay it any mind, or the building may well have been on fire, the soldiers unwilling to risk their lives to check for anything out of the ordinary.

Using one of his long claws to pry at the lock, he grumbled when it wouldn't budge. Steadfast, he smashed his monstrous hand into the rusty metal with unimaginable force. His talons stuck in the trapdoor, and with a mighty tug, he tore the entire barrier from its hinges. Dusty, rank air billowed out from underneath the hatch, finally free of its confines after centuries. Peering inside, Roann was undeterred by the pitch-blackness of the cellar. He tossed the door aside and jumped down into the abyss, his beastly eyes adjusting almost instantly. The whole area glowed green in his field of vision, the ability to see in the dark one of the many wonderful attributes awarded by his horrible form.

Crumbling crates and barrels sat covered in dust. A moldy smell wafted through the space, years of rotten food and ingredients creating a sickening stench. Roann searched for anything that looked like it might contain a precious artifact. Most of the containers were simple, once housing supplies or various other items. Nothing out of the ordinary. He was becoming irritated when a glint of silver caught his eye, illuminated by his night vision. The corner of a box, covered by a tattered quilt, stuck out from beneath a pile of crates. Smashing the cartons above it with a mighty heave of his arm, he picked through the remaining shrapnel to unearth what he hoped contained his prize.

The box was sturdy, not made like the rest in the basement. An ornate lock adorned the front, which Roann pried off with ease. The tandlewood splintered as the latch was forcibly removed. He grasped the hilt of the dirk within carefully, mindful not to damage it with his grotesquely strong hands. A jewel studded the pommel, ancient symbols etched into the blade. Roann dashed up the stairs and out into the forest light to get a better look at the weapon. His eyes adjusting to normal, he inspected the dagger in higher definition.

It was made of silver, centuries of tarnish coating the once-luxurious metal. The blade was nicked and scratched, but the tip was still pointed and sharp, more than likely still able to inflict major damage if needed. The stone in the pommel was ruby-red, small inclusions of black peppering the gem. Once exposed to the light of day, it was obvious it had been faceted by a master jeweler, for it shimmered brilliantly. Roann didn't know just what Lyrax' intended use for the blade was, but he would honorably return it to him without question.

Looking to the sky, he noticed rain clouds moving in. He tucked the blade close to his body, his clawed fingers making sure it stayed with him on the journey back to the volcanic lair. With nothing more in the destroyed hamlet that needed his attention, he leapt into the air, his mighty wings carrying him onto the currents.

~~~

"...do you have it?"

Roann landed in the stifling chamber, his wings flapping behind him. He approached the font and reverted to his human form, protectively clutching the blade to his chest. Once his transformation was complete, he set the dirk on the edge of the font, and obediently waited for his master to praise him.

"...at last..."

Roann lingered on Lyrax' every word, waiting for the appreciation that did not come. Trying to hide his disappointment, the emperor brushed it off and moved on. "When do we begin?"

"...you must bring my remains to the cathedral of the king..."

Roann looked over his shoulder at a cloth parcel on the floor. Contained within were the bones of Lyrax, obtained at great peril to the young man. He had almost fallen to his fiery death within the volcano. Finally changing into his monstrous form to not only escape the heat, but aid his climb into the cauldron of heaving lava, he had managed to grab the skeleton and remove it to safety. Lyrax hadn't, as the old warriors had hoped, fallen into the molten lake. Instead, he had landed on an obsidian shelf just above the undulating liquid rock, finally succumbing to the intense heat and splashing lava. His flesh burnt from his bones, they lay undisturbed for centuries, safe from the magma as it retreated down into the caldera over time. They baked in the furious heat of the volcano, awaiting the time when they would be needed again. The emperor quickly packed away the ceremonial materials before kneeling beside the linen-wrapped bones. He picked them up with reverence, carefully nestling the parcel within a simple box.

Roann smiled maliciously in the chamber, his black eyes a haunting reminder that who he once was no longer existed. A moment later, he was gone, flashing from the room in a hail of red sparks.

CHAPTER TWENTY-THREE

8 fluid ounces Base fluid, 5 Viper's Cress buds, 1 clove Emperor's Garlic (crushed), 10 Fire Wasp wings, 8 fluid ounces sugar solution. Boil constantly for 2-4 hours, until oil released from buds goes from red to yellow. Remove wings before bottling.

--Recipe for muscle pain relief potion, Maxxald Bren

The salty wind blew through Ryris' hair.

He stood barefoot, staring out at the endless blue stretching clear to the horizon. His toes dug into the sand, the waves crashing over his feet in icy torrents. The water soaked the cuffs of his rolled-up trousers, and the sun baked his bare shoulders. His amulet gleamed in the morning light. Shielding his eyes from the blazing sunlight, he took a deep breath, the crisp ocean air tickling his nostrils. With a great sigh, he turned from the coast and meandered back toward the small camp they had erected on the beach. Ass of the East nibbled on some dried berries, her tail flicking sand flies away from her backside.

Kaia tended the fire, poking at the meat of a lizard she had trapped at dawn. The scent wafting up from their prospective breakfast was tantalizing. Jaric lounged lazily under the makeshift tent constructed with the assistance of Ryris' cart, the fabric billowing in the sea breeze. An arm thrown over his face, it was hard to discern whether or not he was awake. Ryris plopped down on the sand, leaning back to let the sunlight kiss his cheeks. After a serene moment, he slipped on his shirt, not bothering to button it, and focused his attention on his companion.

"I'm glad we decided to come up from the desert along the coast. I'd never seen the ocean up close like this before our journey." He accepted a small portion of charred lizard, gnawing on the meat as he continued. "I mean, Keld has a harbor, but I never got close enough to enjoy it. And I certainly couldn't see out over the sea wall from my vantage point."

"It's definitely beautiful." Kaia helped herself to the last of Nar's gifted cactus fruits, leaving the rest of the meat for Jaric. "If you think the ocean is spectacular here, you should see it from Zaiterra's southern coast. The waves crash against the break wall at the base of the Everbright Lighthouse with unimaginable force."

"What's it like? Zaiterra?"

"Windy." Jaric's voice grumbled, gravelly from a night of disuse. He sat up, clearing his throat before reaching for his waterskin. "Filled with forests, and the wind whips through the trees like no one's business. Sounds like spooks. Always cold, too."

"I wonder how much it's changed since you've been there? I mean, we learn about them in studies as children, but you really can't know a people until you walk amongst them, right?"

"True." Kaia wiped pink fruit juice from her chin with the back of her hand. "The citizens were industrious and kind. The continent isn't very big, and their culture relied heavily on their trades, namely weapons, armor, and gems. Their martial arts school was legendary."

"Now *that* I know. There was a man that came through Blackthorne when I was a kid, and did a demonstration in the village square. He swung these incredibly thin swords around, slicing fruits and leather like they were butter." He tossed the inedible lizard skin into the fire, watching it curl up and turn to ash as the heat overtook it. "I was only ten, but I was so mesmerized by his talents that I actually wanted to become a fighter for a while. Then one day Grildi accidentally hit me too hard 'practicing', and that was the end of that. I ran back to alchemy so fast—and my dad had a great 'I told you so' moment for sure."

"Fighting isn't for everyone. You fall into the place in life that suits you best." Kaia smiled at him. "Alchemy is definitely your calling."

"Thank you. I've worked hard to get to where I am. I just hope..." Ryris stared off to the west, knowing that Keld was hundreds of miles away. "...I can return soon and pick up where I left off. I feel like I've abandoned my life's work—and my father's trust. I hope he understands when we get to Blackthorne."

"He will."

Ryris snorted. "You don't know Maxx. It isn't going to go over well."

"Well then, we'll just *make* it go over well." Jaric smirked, patting his loyal crystal sword stowed in its scabbard.

"Ha ha. He may be old, but he'd scold you into submission, trust me. Your weapons are useless against his stubbornness. And besides, when his money's involved, he can be very tenacious. I don't blame him, but he's...well..." Ryris honestly didn't know how to prepare his two cohorts for Maxx and his antics. They may have been seasoned soldiers, having fought wave after wave of rotting garrisons, but his father was a completely different animal. He chuckled inwardly at the notion that they had no idea what they were in store for.

"I can take him." Jaric puffed out his chest with pride, a wry smile crossing his lips.

"Okay then, you'll see." Ryris quirked an eyebrow before turning his attention to Kaia with a longing sigh. "I suppose you won't let me stay in this tropical paradise forever, huh?"

"We'll leave in the afternoon, when the sun gets lower on the horizon. If we make good time, we'll be able to camp in that forest where the beach ends by nightfall." Kaia pointed down the coast. "A ten-or-so-day walk and we'll be in Blackthorne."

Ryris swallowed hard, his throat suddenly as dry as the desert they had left earlier in the week. He was admittedly nervous about returning to his hometown. Maxx' wrath would be at legendary levels, of that he was sure. But, with his two companions at his side, he was confident they could make the headstrong old man understand just what they were up against—and why the shop in Keld didn't matter at the moment.

"Dad can't stay mad at me forever, right?"

Jaric shrugged and reached for the slice of lizard Kaia had set aside for him. "Couldn't tell you. My parents died when I was a baby. I got sent to an orphanage and when I started fighting with the kids, they asked the Guard if they'd take me. As soon as they saw how I swung a club, they stuck a sword in my hands and trained me."

"Was it hard growing up without them?"

"My father was a drunk and my mother sold drugs. Not exactly a quaint family life. They got killed after a deal went sour. I was asleep in my cradle, the guys never even saw me. I'd like to think that I was better off without them." Jaric tore into the charred lizard, ripping a giant piece of meat from the exposed bone. It was obvious he was done reminiscing about his lost childhood. "Listen, I suggest we all get a nap in after we've filled our bellies. It's a long walk up the coast, and I don't want to have to drag your heavy ass when you get tired."

~~~

Kaia followed her companion through the thick underbrush. She watched as he tried to navigate around a burr-covered bush, grumbling when dozens of prickers became lodged in the fabric of his pants anyway. Ryris tried in vain to brush them aside, only to find himself on the receiving end of their wrath. They embedded themselves in his shirt, and before long had even ended up in his hair. Unable to control her laughter at the pathetic sight, she jogged forward and offered her assistance.

"You know, if you swat at them, it just makes it worse." She tried to pick the brambles from his brown locks.

Ryris glowered at her, pushing her helping hands away in frustration. It was obvious to her that he was trying to hide his embarrassment. "I think I know how to remove burrs."

"Obviously not." She smirked, picking at the offending pods.

He huffed and reluctantly allowed her to assist him. Kaia couldn't help but chuckle at his flushed cheeks. He was so adorable when he was frustrated and embarrassed.

She noticed the way he chewed on his lower lip—perhaps unconsciously—as she brushed her fingers over his ear in an attempt to remove a burr from his hair. Admittedly, she found herself uncharacteristically nervous making contact with him. It perplexed her to a degree, having never been this unsure about her feelings ever before.

Their hands touched the same bramble on the alchemist's shirt, both attempting to pluck it from the fabric. A brief moment of awkward eye contact followed, quickly ended when Ryris hurriedly looked the other way. Kaia removed the burr and tossed it to the ground.

In that moment, her stomach fluttered in a way she hadn't felt in centuries. Swallowing hard, she forced herself to concentrate on the task at hand—and not her confused heart. When the last of the burrs were discarded to the forest floor, she finally received a word of gratitude.

"Thanks." Ryris rubbed the back of his neck nervously. "Sorry I snapped at you."

"No worries. Those little bastards are unrelenting." Kaia winked at him before putting her hands on her hips and looking up into the forest canopy. She hoped taking a moment to focus on something else other than Ryris would give her some emotional clarity. Thin beams of sunlight filtered down through the leaves. "It's so peaceful here."

Ryris mirrored her actions by craning his neck backwards. She glanced over just in time to see him close his eyes, a shaft of light illuminating his face from high above. She marveled at how innocent—how young—he looked in that instance, even though she was fairly sure they were close in age...or they *had* been, before she was interred. They stood there quietly for a long moment before Ryris finally spoke.

"Reminds me of home. Although it's warmer here."

Kaia regarded him closely, noting the yearning tone in his voice. She felt for him, knowing that he left his comfortable life with his father for new adventure in the big city—only to have his world turned upside-down. He wouldn't be returning home with tales of fortune in Keld, but rather news of an uprising on the horizon, toting two ancient warriors alongside him. Kaia knew all the emotions he was experiencing must be weighing heavily on him.

Ryris suddenly gasped and grabbed Kaia's hand, dragging her before she had time to object. He led them to a small adjacent patch of thin stalks swaying in the forest breeze. They looked simple enough to her, but she had learned long before that with

Ryris, things were not always what they seemed. He knelt, pulling her down with him. Picking one of the stems, he broke it in half and rubbed the pieces between his fingers. A sweet aroma wafted up from the greenery.

"What is it?" Kaia accepted a stem from him, gently touching the small pink bud perched on the top.

"Viper's cress. It's used to make pain relieving tinctures, mainly for muscle aches. You boil it for hours in a sugar solution to bring out the oils. You can also eat it raw." He motioned for her to pluck the bud from the top. "Go ahead."

As the seed hit her tongue and she began to chew, a bitter, acrid taste filled her mouth and she spat the material onto the forest floor with a gag. Grimacing at the horrid aftertaste, she turned to Ryris, irate. "I thought you said it was edible!"

"It *is* edible, but I didn't say it tasted any good." The alchemist laughed, his eyes glinting with mischief.

"You're such a child." She threw the plant stalk at him with a huff.

"Come on, it's not that bad." Ryris tried to pacify her with a charismatic smile.

"Why don't you try some, then?"

Ryris shook his head. "I've already had the pleasure."

Kaia glared at him, eyes narrowed.

"C'mon…" Ryris rose with an apologetic smile, extending his hand to her. She sighed and accepted, her anger melting as his hand closed around her fingers. Smiling in thanks, she quickly withdrew her palm and picked up her basket. She followed him off into the forest once more. They walked in relative silence, Ryris occasionally pointing out a specific flower or tree. Kaia was enjoying her impromptu alchemy lesson, and was in awe at the vast knowledge that resided in her friend's mind. He was a walking alchemy textbook for sure.

After an hour or so, they had ventured fairly far from their camp, where Jaric had stayed to tend to the fire and keep an eye on the horse and their belongings. The sun was getting lower on the horizon, the forest animals beginning their dusk routines in preparation for the night. They had made small talk about Ryris' hometown, the alchemist regaling her with tales of his childhood with Grildi. He had asked about her tenure with the Crystal Guard, but Kaia was having such a wonderful time listening to his stories that she didn't want him to stop. She promised him she'd return the favor and tell him all about her life at another time. He accepted the deal, and happily went on describing everything from the shop he and his father owned, to the beautiful scenery that made up his small hamlet.

"…and if you get too close to the river, Grildi is liable to throw you in, so be careful." He enjoyed reminiscing about his friend. "The water is miserably cold, even in the summer."

"Sounds lovely."

Ryris nodded with a nostalgic smile. He stopped and arched his back, stretching out the tired muscles. When he had sufficiently adjusted his spine, he rolled his neck and sighed contentedly. "You want to see something neat?"

Kaia was intrigued, albeit cautious. After all, the last time he had shown her something interesting, it had left an awful taste in her mouth. "Depends…"

"Come on, I spotted it just ahead. You'll like it, I promise."

She followed him through the underbrush until they came upon a large fallen tree trunk, covered in tiny silver spheres. They glistened in the mottled light of the forest, like little jewels on a crown.

"Those are called moat pearls. If you eat it, you can 'blow smoke' from your mouth."

"Smoke?"

"Well…not really. They're little spore pods. If you break it open on your tongue, you can blow them out and it looks like wisps of smoke." He plucked one off the bark and placed it on his tongue. His voice was garbled as he tried not to bite down on the object. "Shee? Washh…" He moved it around, nestling it in the side of his cheek. His face bulged outward as he maneuvered the sphere carefully, mindful not to pierce the thin membrane containing the spores until he was ready to do so. He finally bit down, forming his lips into an 'o' before expelling the cloud of spores into the air. It indeed looked like silvery smoke. Kaia had to admit, it was mesmerizing. The alchemist tracked his head from side-to-side, blowing a stream of 'smoke' onto the currents, even making a ring. Kaia laughed at his antics. When he was out of spores, he spat the empty pod onto the forest floor, wiping his mouth on his sleeve. "Give it a try."

"No way!"

"I promise it doesn't taste bad. In fact…it tastes kind of like chocolate."

"I don't believe you." Kaia crossed her arms over her chest defiantly.

"It does!" He held one out, narrowing his eyes as he scrutinized her. "Oh, I get it. Don't want to be childish…"

"You don't know what you're talking about."

"But I think I do." He smirked tauntingly, waving a palmful of spheres in front of her face. "Live a little. These things don't grow all over, you know. This might be your only chance."

She huffed and grabbed the item from his hand, ripping it a little more forcefully than she had planned. Ryris smiled as she placed it on her tongue, rolling the sphere into position in her mouth before biting it. He did the same with another pod, and began to blow the spore 'smoke' along with her. Within a moment they were both giggling like children, their laughter echoing off the trees surrounding them.

"You know, those spores make a potion that can paralyze a man in ten seconds." Ryris' tone was nonchalant as waited for her to run out of "smoke."

Kaia immediately spit out the material and feverishly wiped her tongue on her shirt sleeve. "Paralyze? And it's in my mouth?"

Ryris laughed heartily, trying desperately to fend off her striking blows. She slapped his arms, wailing on him from all directions. "Hey, stop it!"

"You're trying to poison me! I can hit all I want!"

"Don't worry; it's perfectly harmless by itself!" He grabbed her hand in an attempt to stop her assault. She finally relented and he continued. "That's the beauty and magic, if you will, about alchemy. Something that seems harmless can kill, and something that looks dangerous, like needle weed, is actually used to soothe."

Kaia scowled at him.

"Trust me."

"Maybe…" She finally smiled and cast her attention back the way they came. "We should get back to camp; it's going to be dark before we know it."

Ryris nodded in agreement and scooped a few handfuls of the silvery spheres into a small wooden bowl he had in his basket, careful not to rupture the thin skin keeping the spores contained. "I can dry these out on the back of the wagon and harvest the spores for later. Should be a good haul."

"Let's stop on the way back and gather some of those other plants. I think Jaric deserves a taste…"

Ryris narrowed his eyes devilishly. "I like your style."

~~~

"Are you sure there's something over there? It just looks like underbrush." Jaric tapped the tip of his sword against his heavy leather boots. His crystal ones rested in the wagon, having been replaced when they stopped to resupply after their desert

223

adventure. A soft rain fell from the sky, filtering through the canopy of the surrounding forest. Not enough to soak, but definitely enough to be annoying.

"Don't doubt me. My tiara is making my skin tingle." Kaia trudged ahead, cutting through thick, spindly saplings with a razor-sharp shortsword. Grunting purposefully with each whack, she forged on, quickly leaving her two male counterparts in her dust. Her voice floated out from the brambles as she disappeared into the foliage. "There's a shard here, I know it. What else could it be?"

"Monsters." Ryris mumbled under his breath.

"I heard that!" Kaia's voice was strong as she chopped a particularly thick vine blocking her path. "Now get up here and help me scout. There's an overhang up ahead, jutting from that rock formation." She pointed with her sword.

Peering into the forest in front of them, Ryris and Jaric followed their leader into the clearing she had made, knowing better than to argue with her. If she thought there was something there, then there was something there.

Kaia sheathed her blade as she approached the rock face, the overhang blocking the falling precipitation. The wind blew ferociously for a moment, moving a great clump of swaying vines. As they floated on the air currents, the trio caught a glimpse of white marble, weathered and spotted black with lichen from years of being ignored. Jaric pushed the greenery out of the way and exposed a forgotten statue, cracked from centuries of neglect. Nestled in the hidden alcove was a nearly life-size body form of Oleana, her face smoothed to almost nothing from years of exposure to the elements. The arms had broken off, falling to the ground where they had crumbled to nothing more than pebbles. The stench of mildew wafted around the team, the spots of mold peppering the stone statue and the surrounding alcove giving off a pungent aroma.

"Well? Is this where your fancy crown thinks something is hidden?" Jaric eyed Kaia skeptically.

Ryris still wasn't used to Jaric's brash way of speaking, and had to remind himself that the only reason Kaia allowed such disrespect was that he was practically her brother—a brother-in-arms. He had no doubt that if any other person dared address her in such a manner, they'd be eating their boots or find themselves on the receiving end of a sword pommel to the back of the head.

"It's here. I'm sure of it." She moved around the side of the effigy, pushing her body flush with the back of the alcove. Running her fingers along the stone, she moved her hands down the length of the statue, kneeling as she got closer to the ground. She began to knock on the pedestal, searching for any evidence of a hidden chamber. She finally smiled with satisfaction and held her hand out to Ryris. "Give me your dagger."

Obeying without question, he handed her his knife and she pried open the back of the platform on which the fading Goddess stood. A panel popped off and Kaia reached in, producing a small velvet pouch. She beamed with excitement as she waved the parcel above her head. "And you said I was crazy!"

"I never said you were crazy." Jaric knelt next to her, and held the package while Kaia undid the ties. "I may have thought it…but I'm tactful enough not to say it to your face."

She rolled her eyes and busied herself unwrapping the precious artifact contained within the pouch. Even in the low, gloomy light of the forest, the shard shone with crystalline brilliance. Ryris moved closer to the pair, sitting on his haunches as he inspected the item in Kaia's hand. It was smaller than the two belonging to his friends, but equally as beautiful. The edges were jagged, and Ryris couldn't tell from which part of the original blade it had emanated from. He gingerly accepted it when Kaia handed it to him, careful not to knick his fingers on the razor edges.

"Three down, seven to go."

Ryris stared at the glassy shard in his hands, thinking how it seemed almost impossible that they were going to locate the other pieces. Yes, they were guaranteed another shard when they got to Ealsig, but that still left six—and they had no clue as to where they might lay. Handing the blade fragment back to Kaia, Ryris couldn't help but think out loud.

"I don't want to be a downer or anything, but the empire is huge…and we have so many left to recover. What if we never do it?"

"Failure isn't an option." Kaia's answer was determined, her expression steely. "Let's not waste time dwelling on something we can't control. Blackthorne is still more than a week away, and we need to make headway before it gets too dark to travel tonight."

Jaric and Kaia slipped from the alcove and headed back toward the cart. Ryris lingered for a moment more, reaching out to wipe the dirt from the Goddess' withering face. By the time the next century would turn, the visage would be unrecognizable. A sudden sadness washed over him at the sight of the forgotten effigy, wasting away alone in the woods. There was a good chance that no one would ever gaze upon the statue again, and it would be left to fade into oblivion without a second thought. Saying a small prayer to Oleana, he inhaled the musty aroma of the dank alcove before taking his leave. The vines returned to their original position, obscuring the niche and leaving the Goddess in dark solitude.

CHAPTER TWENTY-FOUR

I often imagine what it will be like the next time I set foot in Blackthorne. No doubt, I'll be laden with gifts for Grildi. A warm reception would be nice, especially if there's another chocolate tart. Who knows, Maxx might even smile.

--Journal Entry, Ryris Bren, 9th Autumn, YG756

Blackthorne's gate caught his eye in the distance, and Ryris' stomach immediately fluttered with equal parts happiness and terror.

He knew Maxx was behind that gate, and would express his opinions on why his son was home in a way that only he could. He'd more than likely yell, his face turning red as he clenched his jaw. Ryris really wasn't looking forward to it.

The morning was crisp, the sun peeking out every so often from behind increasingly growing clouds. By nightfall there would be large snowflakes falling from the skies, adding to the already large piles of the white stuff on nearly every exposed surface. The chilled air froze Ryris' nostrils from the inside out, and he relished in the feeling of having to pull his jacket snugly around his body to keep warm. He had missed Blackthorne more than he realized.

As the trio ascended the gradual hill leading toward the village, the cart rattled on the path, laden with armor, weapons, supplies, and belongings. The trees around the village began to clear, and Ryris caught a glimpse of a very familiar figure perched in the lookout tower. Hulking and massive, the man had a small paddleball in his hand, counting the strokes as he kept vigil on the peaceful surroundings. The noise of the wagon on the trail getting his attention, it took Grildi Amzod less than ten seconds to bound down the stairs of his keep and rush out the gate at full force. Ryris braced for impact.

"Boss!" Grildi embraced him with all his might, crushing Ryris against his barrel chest with exuberance. "You came back! I just knew you would!"

Ryris' voice was muffled by Grildi's heavy fur vest. He allowed the big man to squeeze him, knowing full well he was well on his way to asphyxiation. But he didn't care. He had missed his giant friend, and, well…he was cold. The pelts lining the outside of Grildi's vest were very warming to the skin.

When the village guard had his fill of affection, he plopped Ryris back down onto his feet, smoothing out the young alchemist's coat. A giant grin crossed his face, tears flecking the corners of his eyes. He grabbed him by the hand and dragged him into the village, Kaia and Jaric following close behind. As they entered the town proper, the eyes of all the residents were on them—Grildi's excited yelling having brought them out of their homes. Ryris scanned the crowd for the most familiar of faces, blowing out a long breath when he didn't see Maxx. He didn't know if he was disappointed—or relieved.

The mayor ran from his house, immediately grabbing Ryris' hand in an exuberant handshake. Villagers crowded around the small group, giving them barely enough room to move. The baker's wife pushed her way into the crowd and threw her arms around Ryris' neck, planting a wet kiss on his cheek. He was immediately reminded of the last time he stood in this very square, surrounded by Blackthorne's residents. Although last time—he wasn't afraid of what his father might do or say. Once again, he scanned over the tops of the citizens' heads, trying to see the storefront. He swore he saw Maxx' face quickly appear in one of the frosty windows before disappearing again.

"The prodigal son returns! And you brought friends!" The mayor reached out to shake their hands, Jaric eyeing the man suspiciously as he reluctantly accepted the gesture. "Tonight we feast in celebration!"

Ryris' cheeks flushed with embarrassment as he dismissively waved his hands in front of his body to get the mayor's attention. "That's really not necessary."

"Pish! You'll stay longer than a night, and you'll eat your fill in the meantime! We won't take 'no' for an answer!"

The crowd bellowed their cheers, all scattering off to prepare what would be, no doubt in Ryris' mind, a grand spectacle. He knew better than to try and stop them, and accepted their fate. At least they'd be fed into next month.

Grildi stayed after the townsfolk had all gone back to their morning business. Wrapping an arm around his friend, he smiled hopefully. "Did you bring me anything?"

"Does a pair of new friends count?"

"And how!" Grildi looked to the strangers. "Are they nice?"

"She is…"

Jaric snorted and glared at Ryris.

"This is Kaia," Ryris said, taking her hand and pulling her forward to meet his lumbering companion. "…and he's Jaric."

"You're awful pretty, lady." Grildi's cheeks blushed. Kaia's eyes crinkled in delight as the giant man took her tiny hand in his own and kissed it. He then turned his attention to Jaric, pointing to the scabbard on his back. "That's the most beautiful sword hilt I've ever seen!"

227

Jaric nodded with pride. "You like weapons?"

Grildi replied with excitement. "Always! I've got my own special club; do you want to see it?"

Ryris patted him on the arm. "We've got plenty of time for that later. But right now…" He glanced cautiously toward his father's shop.

"Aye. You best go see your dad." Grildi patted the alchemist on the back. "And I better get back to my post. Can I come by later, though? I want to hear all about Keld!"

"Of course you can. I've…" He looked to his companions hesitantly. "…got a lot to tell you."

Grildi beamed and jogged off, clambering back up the rickety wooden stairs that led to his lookout tower. He waved excitedly from his perch as he sat, resuming his sentry activities.

Ryris heard the familiar creak of a heavy old door, and turned just in time to see Maxx emerge from the store. He leaned against the jamb, arms crossed over his chest. Never speaking, it was obvious that Ryris would have to make the first move—something he really didn't want to do.

"He looks friendly." Jaric clapped Ryris on the back. "You sure you don't want me to dispatch him? I promise it'll be quick and relatively painless."

"Not funny." Ryris sighed and willed the butterflies in his stomach to go away. He clenched his fists, the leather of his gloves squeaking, and swallowed the lump in his throat. He knew this wasn't going to be pleasant and briefly contemplated turning tail. A reassuring push on his lower back comforted him, as Kaia gently nudged him to go. Finally mustering the courage to move forward, his friends followed in tow behind him.

"You'd better have a damn good reason for leaving the shop." Maxx stared his son down with piercing eyes.

"Nice to see you too, Dad." Ryris could feel sweat rolling down his neck and into his collar, even though the outside temperature was beginning to dip into freezing territory. His entire body tensed and he tried to hide his shaking hands. He hadn't been this nervous to confront his father since he had accidentally destroyed a very expensive piece of equipment in his youth.

Maxx looked around behind his son, taking note of his unlikely companions, never moving from his sentinel spot. Acknowledging them with a curt nod, he puffed a burst of air out from his flaring nostrils. He pushed forward off of the door frame with a grunt, motioning them inside. "Get in here before you catch your death. I'm sure you'll want to get right at your explanations."

Ryris silently walked past his father, avoiding eye contact. As he crossed into the store, he was immediately hit with a wave of nostalgia. A fire roared in the fireplace, Maxx' alembic churning away on the worktable. The scent of thousands of ingredients melded into one familiar aroma. Jaric and Kaia shuffled in behind him, with his father bringing up the rear. He pulled the mighty door shut, the bitter cold wind sealed off from the toasty interior.

"Wipe your boots." Maxx grumbled as he forced his way past the trio. "And flip the sign. I don't think I'm going to have time for any customers today."

Ryris did as he was told. After a long moment, all three had sufficiently dried their shoes and milled about in awkward silence. Maxx puttered behind the counter, extinguishing oil burners and emptying beakers. Setting his rucksack down with a heavy sigh, the younger Bren finally couldn't take his father's ignoring any more.

"Look, Dad…"

Maxx flew around, squeezing the glass vial in his clenched hand to the point of explosion. His eyes were seething, his face red with anger. "Do you have any idea what you've put me through?"

Ryris flinched at his father's harsh tone.

"I thought you were dead!" He winced as he noticed his finger had been cut by a shard of glass. Maxx stuck his finger in his mouth to soothe his wound. "You had no right to stay out of contact that long! No right!"

"I know. And I'm…"

"Sorry isn't going to cut it this time."

Ryris swallowed hard. Never in his life had he seen Maxx this upset. The look on his face when he spoke of his son's pseudo-'death' was enough to break his heart. He knew it must have been eating away at Maxx. He submissively held his hands up in front of his chest to try and pacify his father's wrath.

"Dad…everything's changed. I…don't even know where to begin." His voice warbled with uncertainty.

"Then you'd better think long and hard about where you take this conversation. And don't think I have all day. You see that stack of orders?" Maxx pointed to a pile of parchment scraps, a river stone acting as a paperweight. "I've been bogged down since you ran off to the capital to do who-knows-what."

Kaia moved next to Ryris, ready to step in. He figured she could tell he was floundering fast, and beginning to crack under the harsh words of his father. But, he knew it was his duty to explain to his only living relative what was to become of him—of everyone. Ryris glanced her way for just a moment, reassuring her that he had the

229

situation under control with a meek, hopeful smile. She nodded knowingly and stepped back.

"Please believe me when I say there's a very good reason for me to be here today. It's important."

"More important than running your business?"

"Yes." Ryris' reply came quickly, and with purpose, surprising him. "Remember those stories Gran used to tell me?"

Maxx rolled his eyes. "Ha! Don't use that nonsense as an excuse for abandoning your business. That's pretty pathetic, even for you."

"Listen to me!" Ryris' voice echoed off the walls, startling not only himself, but his father and companions as well. It took him a few seconds to regain his composure. "This isn't some fairytale I'm lost in, and I didn't just leave the shop willy-nilly. This is real, Dad—and dangerous."

Maxx' nostrils flared. "The only thing that's dangerous is you coming back here with stupid stories!"

"What will it take to get you to listen to me?"

"Try actin' like a man. You can't use the mumbo-jumbo that old woman filled your head with to weasel your way out of whatever you did in Keld."

Ryris clenched his fists. "I didn't 'do anything' in Keld!"

"Obviously. I suppose we'll have to go back and empty the storefront now?"

"This has nothing to do with the store! It doesn't matter anymore!" Ryris couldn't believe his bravado and willingness to stand up to Maxx. He heard his own voice continue to rise with anger. "Gran's stories were true, Dad. And you need to realize the world is about to change because of them."

Maxx stood there silent and defiant. Ryris knew this was the turning point. He was growing tired of his father's antics. Ryris turned to Jaric, motioning to his back. Nodding his understanding, the warrior untied the straps holding his weapon and brought it around in front of his body, the scabbard still obscuring the telltale blade. Jaric reverently handed over his prized sword, knowing that his friend would never allow any disgrace to come to it. Taking it in his still-shaking hands, Ryris approached the counter, and laid the weapon down. He unsheathed the blade, the crystalline material instantly shimmering in the light of the shop.

Maxx' eyes widened, his jaw falling slack as awe overtook him. Staring at it for a moment, he finally reached out and gingerly ran a finger down the smooth side of the blade. Ryris watched the older man try and process what had been set before him, and wondered what must have been going through his mind. Needless to say, his response was not what he was expecting. Maxx' face soured.

"Just who'd you steal this from, lad?" He looked to Jaric, accusingly. "No one as rough-looking as you has the gamm to possess such a weapon."

Jaric lunged forward, Ryris having only seconds to stop him before he assaulted Maxx for his accusation. "Watch your tongue, old man."

"I'll do no such thing. Friend of my son or not, you don't threaten me in my own store." Maxx stood his ground and Ryris became more and more frustrated with each passing second. His father's stubbornness was embarrassing, and costing them precious time.

"Stop it, both of you!" Ryris' voice peaked, anger and frustration taking hold. "Jaric, stand down. And Dad...you need to listen to me, and listen good." Maxx just stood there, an eyebrow quirked, his skeptical expression boring right through Ryris as he continued. "I didn't come back here to be scolded, or for you to offend my friends. I came back because there's something more important than you or me or this village on the horizon. This isn't about you and your disappointment about what you think I have or have not been doing."

Maxx just stared at his son before inhaling deeply and blowing it out as he spoke. "I never thought I'd see you grow a pair like you just did. My boy, giving his old man a stern earful. What a day indeed."

Ryris snarled and began to turn, motioning to his companions to follow him out the door. "This is pointless. Coming here was a mistake."

Maxx grabbed for his son's arm across the counter in an attempt to stop him, the young man evading his grasp. "Wait. I'm...willing to listen to whatever silly story you've concocted."

"Don't patronize me. I'm not a kid anymore. I've experienced something life-changing recently, and you think it's some kind of fantasy. Well I can tell you that it isn't. After all that I've seen in just the last few months alone—I don't have time to waste with you. If you're not going to take me seriously, then I have nothing more to say."

This was it. Was Ryris ready to walk out the door, never to return? His father's remarks had pushed him over the edge, yes, but was his only alternative really to abandon his kin and focus on what lay ahead? He stared his father down, mentally trying to decide when to turn and leave for good. Maxx finally replied, uncharacteristic pleading in his eyes.

"Ryris..." The old man shook his head solemnly. "I'm sorry. You know I tend to lash out when I'm hit with something I wasn't prepared for."

"You got that right."

The old alchemist regarded his son sincerely. "You've grown. Changed. If it means that much to you, I'll listen."

"I want you to *want* to listen. Not just because you think it'll make me happy."

"All a father ever wants is for his son to be happy—and perhaps not be a horse's arse. But I'll hear you out—because I want to."

Ryris accepted his father's proposal with a curt, silent nod.

"Now, why don't the lot of you c'mon back and I'll give you a proper breakfast. You're looking awful scrawny."

The young alchemist returned Jaric's sword and motioned for his friends to follow Maxx, taking one last look at the shop before he closed the house door behind them. His companions stood near the side wall, unsure of what do to or where to go. It occurred to Ryris that they hadn't even been properly introduced to his father yet. Maxx threw another log on the fire, turning to face them as he brushed the soot from his palms. It was obvious he was thinking the same thing.

"Don't be rude, boy. I'm assuming your mates have names?"

Ryris motioned to his companions. "Dad, I'd like you to meet Kaia and Jaric. They're...*old* friends."

"Maxxald Bren's the name. Maxx for short." He shook each warrior's hand in sequence, stoic face accompanying the action. "Old, huh? Don't look that old to me."

"Looks can be deceiving, Mr. Bren." Kaia smiled warmly, trying to diffuse the thick tension that still lingered in the room.

"I'll be the judge of that." He pointed to the table. "Sit down. Seat on the far side is mine, though, so don't even think about it."

The three companions shed their outerwear and sat, Maxx taking a moment to put a kettle of water over the fire. He grabbed a basket of biscuits from the shelving, along with a small pot of jam, and set it on the table. When he finally took *his* seat, he stared the three visitors down. "Get on with it, then. Why the hell aren't you in Keld?"

Ryris nervously tapped his fingers on the tabletop, unsure of where to begin. "I left on a routine ingredient harvest, and was only planning on being gone three weeks. I had fellow merchants watching the home front, and one stocked my goods so I could make money even while gone." He waited, hoping his father would at least praise him for the shrewd business move. When Maxx stayed silent, he continued. "I was up on the Peaks, in Hewe."

232

"That tiny town? Why'd you go up there? There's nothing of value anywhere near it."

Ryris sighed with irritation, trying to resist the urge to tell his father off for not having faith in his methods. He was unsuccessful. "For your information, I decided to act on a hunch—and it paid off more than I ever expected." He looked to his companions knowingly. "If you remember, the aegis mold harvest had been dwindling for at least a decade. I took a risk and went to the other side of the mountains, and found a bounty."

"The other side, eh? Never thought of that..." Maxx' voice was almost undetectable with his last muttering. Ryris smirked ever so slightly at his father's 'not-so-admission' of his good idea. "But what has that got to do with you ending up back at my doorstep, prattling on about your granny's stupid stories?"

Ryris glared at Maxx for his accusation before continuing. "Things...didn't go as planned."

Maxx eyed his son's two friends.

"I hired two local boys to lead me up the mountain, and they accidentally told me about a woman they found sealed in a cave. Not having any intentions other than just seeing her, I persuaded them to show me. And that's how I found Kaia. Dad...she's..."

"She's one of them? Those shining soldiers?"

"I thought you said the stories were stupid..."

"That sword on his back," Maxx pointed to Jaric. "There's only one kind of man that has a piece of that caliber. And I can guarantee no one in ages has seen one."

"Now do you believe Gran?"

"Do I have a choice?"

"Yes, you do. You can continue to believe that what she tried to teach me was nonsense and look like a fool when everything goes to pot, or you can accept the fact that Kaia and Jaric still exist and listen to what we need to tell you."

Maxx eyed the trio before relenting. "Alright, you've got my attention."

"Jaric and Kaia fought in the Old War. They were sealed away after their victory to wait for the time when they might be needed again. I won't go into too much detail on the technical parts—I really don't understand it myself, to be honest. But what's important is that they *are* needed again."

"Why? I don't know if you've been paying attention or not, but I don't see any soldiers marching across the plains. There's no war fires burning in the forests.

233

And last time I checked, Emperor Roann wasn't amassing armies and hoarding weapons."

The three friends looked to each other, concern crossing their collective expression. Maxx immediately took notice.

"What did I say? You all look like death just tapped you on the shoulder."

"The emperor may not be amassing armies yet..." Kaia's tone was serious.

"I think you've slept a little too long, young lady."

Ryris' eyes were pleading. "Dad, darkness is looming. And Roann is at the heart of it."

"Listen to you—*'darkness is looming'*. You sound like one of those damned fortune tellers!" He stood and moved to a small cupboard, retrieving enough tea cups for them. Setting them on the table, he walked to the fireplace and grabbed the boiling kettle. "I said I'd listen to your story, I didn't say I'd believe you. Besides, what proof do you have that it's Roann? You can't just go accusing the emperor of being in league with the devil without something solid. He'd have your head—and I can't protect you from that."

"Hasn't there been any strange news from Keld? Nothing about his behavior?" Ryris questioned his father.

Maxx shrugged his shoulders. "We don't get much information from the capital."

Ryris looked to Kaia for guidance, desperate to find some way for Maxx to pay more attention. He was relieved when she took over the conversation. "An old giant with long standing ties to my family agrees with us, Sir."

"A giant!" Maxx laughed heartily, pouring scalding water into the cups. His body quaked as he guffawed, splashing searing drops all over the tabletop. "Have you three been eating crazy mushrooms?"

"Just listen to her, Dad."

Maxx sat again, prying the top off of a small wooden box. He offered each guest a tea bag before choosing one for himself. Plopping it in his cup, he sat back with crossed arms and waited for Kaia to begin again.

"My father was the ruler of this land before Roann's family took over. His name was King Galroy Farnfoss. He..."

"Princess, eh? Not bad."

"Dad, stop interrupting." Ryris glared at his father. Maxx held up an apologetic hand.

Kaia continued. "He had a confidant—a blind giant named Phia. She was trusted more than anyone in his royal court and was the only one who knew where Jaric, myself, and our other companion, Ealsig were interred."

"I don't see anyone else with you, Lass."

"She's hidden in the forests surrounding your village. And yes, we know it's dangerous."

"Better you than me." He lifted the tea bag, checking the potency of his beverage. "Go on."

"Phia still lives, thanks to the longevity associated with her heritage. We had a day to sit and talk with her about what the future holds, and unfortunately—it's not good." Kaia removed the tea bag from her mug, setting it on a saucer. Maxx offered her a small bowl of sugar, which she politely refused with a smile. "During the war I fought in, we were up against a terrible foe named Lyrax. We finally defeated him, but at great cost of life and land. Phia—and we—think that somehow his soul lingered and laid in wait until he could find the perfect protégé to help him."

"Help him do what?"

"Return. I know it sounds too simple, but hear me out. This world is peaceful, submissive. It's the perfect target for a power-hungry maniac bent on revenge."

"And you think Roann is this protégé?"

Kaia nodded, sipping her tea. "We know it sounds completely unbelievable, but there's no other explanation for the events of the last few months."

"What do you mean, 'events'?"

Kaia looked to Ryris, silently imploring him to tell his father about what happened in Keld. The young alchemist sat up straighter, squared his shoulders, and told him about Roann's visit to the shop. Maxx listened intently, dipping a biscuit in his tea. When his son finished, he offered his opinion.

"I'm skeptical this one instance has any bearing on an impending world war."

Ryris shifted his weight in his chair. "Sometimes people aren't what they seem, no matter how hard you want to believe they're doing right by you."

Maxx sat silently for a long moment. His gaze flitted between the three friends, watching as they anticipated his response. He finally nodded with a great sigh. "You might be impulsive, but you're no dummy. I've got no reason not to believe you, even if it is a bit far-fetched." He looked to the two stern warriors. "Your friends here don't seem like the type that would waste their time on some ninny-chase. So…" he paused, carefully contemplating his next words. "…what do we do now?"

Ryris was relieved to hear his father finally accept his tale. True, he was obviously still a bit skeptical about certain aspects of the story, but Ryris knew Maxx was now committed to them. It felt good to have the old man on their side.

"You don't do anything. You stay right here and keep on running the business like nothing is amiss. We can't afford to let on to Roann and whoever else is watching or listening that Kaia and Jaric—and soon Ealsig—have returned. They're already afraid Lyrax may know they're awake, we can't afford to bring more attention to ourselves." Ryris rubbed his chin. "Our goal right now is to get to Ealsig and find…" He stopped himself at Jaric's deliberate throat clearing. It was obvious the warrior didn't want Ryris to reveal their whole hand quite yet. But Maxx, being quite the observer, wasn't going to let his son's verbal misstep go unnoticed.

"Find what?" He raised an eyebrow.

Ryris knew Maxx was a man of his word. He'd stay silent even if the hounds of hell were chewing his feet off. The alchemist glanced knowingly at Jaric, assuring him it was safe to let Maxx in completely. Jaric just sat there, silent.

Kaia rose, grabbed her knapsack, and returned to the table. A moment later, she had produced the cloth pouch containing the sacred shards and hilt. "These are the remnants of a sword. This weapon ended the war. When I deployed its power, it shattered, and the shards were collected and taken from the battlefield. My father decided they needed to be hidden—to ensure they never fell into the hands of evil. We're trying to locate them all, in the hopes that we can somehow put them back together and use the weapon again—if so needed."

"Why not just make a brand-new one? There's plenty of sword smiths in the world."

She sighed deeply. "I wish it were that simple, Mr. Bren. The material came from a well-protected mine in Zaiterra, and the master weapon-makers with the technique are long gone. Plus, we'd need an extremely talented wizard to enchant the weapon."

"Don't know where you'd find one of those nowadays…" Maxx eyed Ryris mockingly, causing the young man to roll his eyes and huff. An uncomfortable silence fell over the group. Maxx pushed a biscuit crumb around on the table with his thumb. After a few awkward, quiet moments, he finally spoke again.

"Well, seeing as that you fools have a long road ahead, you'd better shack up here tonight. I won't have anyone in the village sayin' you died in that forest because I didn't feed you properly."

~~~

"You're not using enough force. They'll never turn to dust with such a weak hand."

Ryris scoffed at his father, mouth hanging agape in offense.

"Sorry...you know what you're doing." Maxx went back to his own work.

Ryris returned to his mortar and pestle, pulverizing some troll teeth. The two Brens worked in silence for most of the afternoon, only talking now and then to go over a recipe or ask one another for an out of reach ingredient. Ryris was enjoying his time back with his father, doing what they both did best, making quick work of Maxx' impressive order pile. His companions were hunkered down in the house behind the shop, cleaning and polishing weapons and armor.

"So Dad...did Mom or Gran ever tell you more about their family history?"

Maxx carefully measured a beaker full of thick, blue willywort syrup. "Not much. Only that they were from far away and they weren't alchemists. Her old dad was furious when she married me." A satisfied smirk crossed his lips at his wife's rebellion.

"They never talked about ancestors or anything like that? Or where they got my amulet?"

"I've told you, boy, they didn't tell me a damn thing. But, I was so smitten with your Mum that it didn't matter. Love is strange that way, I suppose."

Ryris smiled as the old man spoke of love—and his life with his mother before he came along. It was in rare times like this, when Maxx was relaxed and loose-lipped, that it was hard to imagine him as the hard-nosed bull he really was. He hoped what he was about to reveal to his dad would interest him.

"Well...I have information now."

Maxx kept working, using a small pipette to fill vials, never looking up to his son.

"The man my amulet was made for was the highest-ranking battlemage in Kaia's army. *He* enchanted her sword." Ryris lit a burner underneath a crucible. "Guess what his name was."

"Maxxald."

"Come on, Dad. Be serious."

"It's an old, honorable name!"

Ryris sighed and poured base fluid into the rapidly-warming bowl. "It was Ryris..."

Maxx set his pipette down, and laid his hands on the worktable. "That wily old bat..."

Ryris looked to his father with confusion.

"Your Gran. She chose your name. Said we didn't have a say in the matter. I would have smacked her for being so forward, but there was something in your mother's eyes that melted me—and I agreed. She put that amulet around your neck the minute you were born. Looks like she knew something we didn't, eh?"

"Destiny isn't just some cliché—it's real."

Maxx stared at the flame under the crucible. Ryris knew Maxx to be a man of few words, so when he was quiet like this, he knew better than to interrupt his train of thought and just let him continue at his own pace.

"I know you think I was always trying to keep your Gran from filling your head with all her gobbledygook. Truth is, I knew deep down there was something about your ma's family that was bigger than just some story. I...was selfish—and afraid. Afraid that if I let you get too enthralled by her stories, that you'd forget all about me and want to run off to who-knows-where and try and prove what she said was true. That's why I tried my damndest to teach you the craft..." Maxx covertly rubbed moisture from his eye. "... to make you see that alchemy was the way—not those tall tales."

Hearing his father speak so candidly made Ryris proud of him. He knew it had to have been hard to admit it all—to himself and his son. "I'm still an alchemist, Dad. I would have been one regardless of the history she taught me. I wouldn't want to be anything else, it's in my blood."

"But so is destiny, it would seem." Maxx grabbed his son's arm, squeezing firmly. "I'm sorry I kept you from learning about family. I suppose your mother would be awful ashamed of me right now."

"Don't say that. You raised me, taught me everything I know. You've ensured that I had a happy life, a good head on my shoulders, and the know-how to make a name for myself outside our gates. I couldn't have done anything I've accomplished in my life without you."

"And now you're off to save the world..."

Ryris realized how absurd it sounded coming from someone other than his companions. "You could say that, I guess."

"You'll do the family name proud. And not just 'Bren', either." Maxx' hand lingered on Ryris' arm for a second more before his demeanor changed back and he pursed his lips. "Now back to work. If I've only got you for a day, I'm damn well going to work you to the bone."

<center>~~~</center>

The house was quiet, Maxx dozing in a chair beside the fire after a satisfying dinner. Kaia and Jaric had been dragged off by Grildi on a tour of the village, leaving Ryris alone—and bored.

He knew he could have gone with the trio on their walkabout, but truth be told, he really didn't want to mingle with the townsfolk. Answering questions about the business in Keld seemed so futile at this point, and he didn't feel like feigning interest when his mind was occupied with much more important matters. He needed a distraction. Looking around the empty house, he decided there was only one thing he could do.

A little alchemy.

Grabbing his personal alchemist's satchel filled with various ingredients procured on his adventure, he quietly made his way into the shop, mindful not to wake Maxx. Back in the familiar confines of his father's store, he got to work. Yes, he had spent most of the day working with Maxx, but that was business. What he had in mind was for fun.

He dug into his knapsack and retrieved the rare dragon's talon seed pods. Ryris wasted no time in cutting through the leathery skin of the pods with shears. He dumped the kernels out onto the workbench and sorted through them, picking out the withered or discolored pieces. Knowing he had to work quickly to ensure the room air wouldn't spoil the seeds, he began to concoct his deadly poison. It was a recipe he knew by heart, even though the ingredients were rare. Maxx had always told him he needed to commit one poison recipe to memory, just in case he ever needed to whip one up in a hurry. Ryris had always laughed at the prospect of having to concoct something so lethal on the fly, and purposely mesmerized an obscure reference. But now as he stood there making the very poison he had locked away in his mind, he had to marvel at his father's wisdom.

Gathering the other components of the poison, he cooked with dazzling efficiency, preparing the tincture in record time. As it cooled on the countertop, he readied a small vial and label. Marking it "**DRAGON TALON POISON**" in large, bold letters, it would ensure that no one would accidently imbibe the deadly mixture.

His father snored loudly in the other room.

<center>~~~</center>

That night, Ryris slept sounder than he had in months. Snuggled in his childhood bed, under his old, warm blanket, he cuddled the bear Grildi had brought back for him that evening. Professing he had indeed kept him safe, the town guard gave the toy one last hug before relinquishing him back to his previous owner.

239

And, even if it was just for one night, Ryris ceased to be destiny's apprentice—and enjoyed being a simple alchemist from Blackthorne.

CHAPTER TWENTY-FIVE

Do not fear the dead, for they are the catalyst of a new beginning.

--Necromancer's mantra, origin unknown.

Roann soared high over the once-proud nation of Ashal.

Having left the searing heat of the volcanic lair for the last time, he swooped in and amongst the clouds. He clutched a wooden box close to his scaled breast, his long claws careful not to let the precious cargo tumble to the earth below. Contained within was the last piece of the puzzle—the final 'ingredient' to make Lyrax whole again.

Diving down toward the ruined cathedral of the dead king, he landed on the crumbling steeple, half the size of its former glory. The statue of the goddess that once adorned it had long since crashed to the ground, taking the bulk of the spire with it. He dove through the hole in the roof, landing gracefully on the marble floor below. Setting the crate down in front of the altar, he quickly regained his human form before approaching the holy table.

Roann hadn't been in contact with Lyrax for days. The font had gone dark for the last time, instructions having been given.

… "The king's shrine to his whore goddess will be of greatest use. Taint that which is holy to one man—and make it holy to another…"

Roann had questioned his master—albeit carefully—about his plan to use a religious relic. He didn't believe in its power, nor did Lyrax. So what was the point?

"It is not the inherent believed power of such a piece we seek—we know that to be fraudulent. The witching stone adorning it…it is the power of the gem that will herald my rebirth. We shall poison the font—an ultimate insult to the bastard king and his false goddess—and use it for ourselves."…

He was to wait until this day—when the moon would be new—to start the ceremony. Their combined fates were riding on everything going smoothly. And now, circling the altar in front of him, the emperor knew destiny was close at hand.

Lyrax' bones lay on a silken sheet, exposed to the dry air of the chapel. They were blackened and burnt, centuries of baking heat and splashing lava rendering them nearly destroyed. Staring at the skeleton, Roann's gaze lingered on the haunting skull, the eye sockets devoid of any life. He knew that soon they would once again harbor the ability to see. Lyrax' limbs would move, his heart would beat. Breaths would fill his lungs and give him a proper voice. The blade Roann had retrieved from the necromancer's coven lay beside the skull, ready for use. A human heart sat in a bowl,

241

still warm from that morning's procurement. Roann rearranged the pilfered alchemical ingredients: solutions shimmering in their bottles, small pouches of various dusts protected from any breezes that might blow through the forgotten church.

The disciple looked up to the heavens, taking note that the sun was beginning to set. Knowing he needed to work quickly, but efficiently, Roann lit the candles surrounding the altar with a wisp of his mind. Carefully cupping the heart in his hands, he reverently laid it within the charred ribcage before him. His hands sticky with coagulated blood, he made sure it was precisely placed before moving on. He took a moment to clean his palms on a linen handkerchief, knowing he mustn't sully his next step in any way.

The ornate wooden box sat at the young emperor's feet, waiting to be utilized. It contained the final piece of what would become Lyrax' new body, and it had been obtained through messy means.

Perched in the trees, the leaves obscuring his scaled form, Roann had waited, peering down at the man hunched in the underbrush, aiming his bow at an unsuspecting doe. Just as the hunter waited for the perfect moment to strike, so did the beast.

Before the man could take his shot, the winged creature was on him like lightning, pinning him to the ground. The woodsman struggled, his bones shattering under the monster's feet. He screamed in agony, writhing as his captor readied the death blow. Hesitating for just a moment, it seemed to the man that his attacker may have had a change of heart, for it suddenly released the vise-like hold on his body and retreated, disappearing into the darkness of the surrounding woods. Lying helpless on the forest floor, the hunter prayed the beast had changed its mind. How he would get home with broken limbs, he didn't know, but he was sure a villager would find him in the morning—if he survived that long. He could smell his own blood soaking into the ground; feel the chill of death creeping up on him. Turning his head while searing pain coursed down his spine, he tried to locate the being that had attacked him. Unable to see clearly in the dark, he tentatively breathed a sigh of relief, believing the monster to be gone.

After a long moment, he saw a figure approaching—that of a man. Relieved to the point of tears, the hunter called out to the mysterious person for help. When he received no response, he called out again—but was met only with the sound of foliage crunching under boots. Squinting in the darkness, the man saw long blonde hair cascading over the person's shoulders.

"Please help me!"

The person came to his side, kneeling on the cold ground. The hunter was taken by surprise as he realized he was in the presence of his emperor. Blood loss clouding his ability to think rationally, he never once questioned what the sovereign was doing so far away from Keld.

"Your Grace…I've been attacked…"

"Yes, I know."

"You...know?"

"Don't worry. Everything will be over soon." Roann's voice was soothing and calm. He brushed his hand over the top of the hunter's head.

"Over...soo—?"

A knife pierced the man's heart, ending his life within seconds. Roann wasn't concerned with the woodsman knowing his identity; there was no one around for him to tell. Truth was, he always found pleasure in revealing himself to his victims right at life's end, so they had just enough time to process their fate at the hands of someone they revered. He also had a practical reason this time—his task was not easily accomplished with the hands of a beast. No, what he needed to do required dexterity and steady fingers, something only human hands were capable of.

Setting a wooden box down on the grass beside him, he drew his blade and cut through the man's clothing, removing them to be burned along with the remains after he finished.

Now, that very box in his hands, Roann opened it, revealing the thin, peach skin of his victim. Carefully removed from his body, the pieces brought forth had no rips, no blemishes; save for the small puncture wound that ended the hunter's life. Divided into several flaps, it wasn't enough to completely cover Lyrax' bones—the huntsman had been more difficult to skin than originally thought—but it would complete the ceremony nonetheless. Roann took his time positioning the flesh atop the charred remains before him, draping it over the skeleton like bed sheets. When he was finished, he took a step back and marveled at what lay on the altar. Soon it would be so much more than old bones and stolen skin.

With the days' light almost completely gone, he continued to work. With no moon present, encroaching darkness was fast taking hold. Gathering the alchemical ingredients in a small basket, he approached the shrine, Oleana's feminine form still beautiful even after centuries of neglect. The jewel embedded in her stone tiara shimmered, the inclusions within beginning to react to the arrival of the new moon. Soon they would shine brightly, giving the goddess a haunting crown. He took a moment to push the tilting statue back completely upright, ensuring none of the precious solution he was about to concoct would spill over the sides of the bowl.

His measurements were precise, each ingredient commanded by Lyrax himself. Most were common, found in any alchemy shop in the empire. Roann snickered as he poured in dusts, oils, and pastes, amused by the fact these everyday items could be used in something so out-of-the-ordinary. Nothing seemed amiss, and it would look to anyone gazing in from afar that the young man was simply creating a potion for something as simple as insomnia—not necromancy.

But it wouldn't be until he added the final ingredient that the tincture would show its true nature. He removed a beaker, filled with black, sludgy liquid. He grimaced as he remembered how he came to have it in his possession. Changed into his beast form, Lyrax had instructed him to pierce his own flesh, allowing his life blood to trickle into the font within the volcano. As soon as it had come in contact with the sinister vessel, it smoked, changing from deep red to jet black—boiling until it resembled sooty syrup. The blood loss had been significant, but Roann was honored to become part of his master.

Now, standing in front of a statue of a goddess he did not believe in, Roann was moments away from changing the course of history. The emperor looked up through the hole in the cathedral roof, the heavens dotted with hundreds of stars. The dark, moonless night had finally arrived. He turned around to once again face Lyrax' body. Spreading his arms wide, he chanted the mantras his master had instructed him to commit to memory, the words foreign to him. The gem in Oleana's crown flared with incredible brilliance as the incantation continued. A veil of snow white fog enveloped the statue and the young man at the altar, as the witching stone fought to keep peace. Once finished chanting, he laid out a series of talismans and scrolls around the body. The lettering on the parchment immediately began to glow, the paper charms fluttering on the stone bier.

Knowing the next step needed to be completed in a timely manner, Roann turned and poured his blackened blood into the bowl. It swirled within the mixture. The ground trembled as the potion bubbled, and Roann found himself needing to grasp the statue in order to remain standing. The gem flared once again, a small crack racing down one of the facets. The mist surrounding Roann turned ice-cold as it ebbed and flowed, taking on a red hue. He hoped it meant the stone was losing the battle to purify the tainted tincture. The freezing fog assaulted him, blasting against his face with frightening intensity. The color of the mist kept changing as it fought with the sinister aura quickly overtaking the chapel. From red to white and back again, it held on. The mist tried to seep into his nostrils, icy knives of wind pricking his skin and making his hair stand on end. He would not allow it to win, however, and stood his ground. Hands tightly gripping the smooth marble goddess, he rode out the bitter-cold storm. The quaking continued, threatening to spill the mixture from the bowl before him. Finally, the witching stone shattered, sending glittering shards in all directions. Roann had only a split-second to shield his eyes from the crystalline shrapnel. The red fog coalesced into a roiling mass and hovered over the font before plunging in and mixing with the liquid. It churned on its own, producing a thin film on the surface, which immediately caught fire. The dancing flames illuminating his face, Roann watched as they burned themselves out, leaving a clear blue solution in its wake. He was amazed that something so beautifully colored could have such a sinister use.

Dipping a bottle into the well, the liquid bubbled inside, filling within seconds. Turning to face the altar, he wasted no time in dousing the skeleton and flesh with the potion. It seeped into the dried bones, beaded on the fresh skin. The heart drank it greedily, the tincture pouring into the open end of the severed aorta, filling it to the brim. Making sure he coated every last possible surface, he let the empty bottle fall from his fingers, shattering on the ground.

And then he waited.

~~~

Hours passed.

Roann sat vigil as the skin draped over the skeletal remains began to glow a deep blue. Little by little, the pieces had knit themselves together, pulling taut over open holes, covering the bones until no recesses could be found. A face formed, eyelids sealing over the hauntingly empty sockets. No hair adorned the bald head.

And finally, long after the stroke of midnight had passed, the recombination was complete.

He stared at the naked body before him, the flesh wrinkled and desiccated. It resembled a man, true, but one that had been mummified and left to disintegrate in the hot desert sands. It definitely was not what he had expected. But then again, he had never witnessed necromantic rituals.

He knelt before the altar, paying his respects to the man whom he had resurrected. A chill breeze blew through the open door of the cathedral, and Roann whirled around just in time to witness a ghostly blue fog whip in from the night. It flew over his head, the force of the wind nearly knocking him down. An eerie spectral scream accompanied the disturbance, so loud it hurt Roann's ears and pierced into his very soul. He jumped to his feet, hands covering his ears, and watched in awe as the apparition circled the body on the holy table. The mist hovered before seeping in through the corpse's nostrils. Over in a matter of moments, the chamber fell still and silent.

Cautiously approaching, Roann licked his dry lips. A frail, shaky breath echoed off the walls, and Roann was finally able to look upon his living master. Fingers twitched, limbs jerked as the nerve endings in Lyrax' new body jump-started. He began to shiver, as the chill wind of the moonless night assaulted him. Roann just stared, unsure whether or not his master required help—or would even accept it.

Several quiet moments passed, all while Lyrax' soul reacquainted itself with a living vessel. A pained groan escaped the necromancer's lips as his new muscles constricted. He arched his back on the stone altar in an attempt to straighten his spine. The new joints popped and cracked as he feebly raised his arm above his body. His eyes still closed, he called out to his protégé.

"My child…"

"Master, what do you require of me?"

245

The hand rose, reaching blindly for the young man. "…help…me…to sit…up…"

Roann leaned down, his loose hair falling around his face. Without warning, Lyrax' hand shot up and grabbed the golden locks, tugging with might the emperor didn't think he possessed. His first instinct was to pull back from the threat. But before he could react, Lyrax' other hand grabbed the ceremonial dagger his protégé had retrieved. The etched runes on the weapon glowed red. Lyrax' eyes were jet-black and bottomless.

The blade pierced Roann's throat, quickly severing the main artery.

The emperor's eyes widened in both surprise and agony, shocked that his master had lashed out. He instinctively reached for the hilt of the knife jammed in his throat to wrench it away, only to find Lyrax suddenly possessed the strength of two men. There was no way Roann could force the newly-strong hand away. As the blade dug deeper into his neck, his vision blacked out, and he barely noticed his own lifeblood spilling down over Lyrax' face. The pain was unimaginable. Lyrax opened his mouth, allowing the crimson liquid to flow down his throat. Roann gagged as the knife slipped and punctured his windpipe.

Still tightly grasping Roann's hair, Lyrax flew into the air, hovering over the altar. Roann hung limply in his mighty grip, weakly kicking his legs as he grabbed for the knife in his throat. Lyrax removed and dropped the blade, the young man's blood splattering on the floor as the dagger tumbled out of the air.

"M-mas…ter…" Roann struggled to form words as his ability to breathe waned. "Wh-why…?"

Lyrax repositioned his pawn in his arms to allow him better access to his slashed throat. Forcing the young man's head back, he used his free arm to hold him steady against his own body while keeping the other planted firmly in Roann's hair, the flaxen locks becoming damp and stained with his own blood. Wrapping his lips tightly around the wound on the emperor's neck, he imbibed until he required no more. The color drained from Roann's face, his skin turning a ghostly gray. His limbs no longer had strength, and hung loosely at his sides. One of his boots slipped from his foot and fell to the floor.

Lyrax hung in the air, feeling incredible power seep into every inch of his body. The nerve endings jolted, sending electricity coursing through his veins—along with the healthy blood of his obedient disciple. His skin flushed and his veins plumped. A red aura enveloped them both as Lyrax took advantage of the young emperor's life force.

He hadn't lied when he told Roann the dagger would be integral to the ceremony. Without it, Lyrax wouldn't be able to drain the emperor of his life essence, which he so desperately needed to complete his transformation. The blood had to be

246

strong and viable, and certainly not from some lowly peasant. Time and time again, Roann had accomplished his tasks for his master, and this one was the crowning achievement. Without knowing it, the young man had not only fulfilled Lyrax' destiny, but his own as well. Everyone would remember their names.

Lyrax released his mouth from Roann's neck with a satisfied, ecstatic groan, bringing his own head close to stare into the young man's lifeless eyes. The green irises had taken on a dull hue, losing their once vibrant color. Roann's eyes were pleading and confused as he gagged, trying desperately to breathe.

"You have been a faithful servant, Roann. Your sacrifices will ensure a new dawn for our people." Lyrax' voice was virile, echoing off the walls of the crumbling cathedral. He smoothed the emperor's hair down with a soothing hand. "Do not fear. Your loyalty will not go unrewarded."

Roann whimpered, his eyes fluttering as he struggled to remain conscious. A moment later, he fell from Lyrax' hands, the necromancer letting him drop like a rag doll. His body crashed onto the altar, both legs snapping upon impact.

Lyrax remained hovering in the chill night air of the chapel, a red glow surrounding his body. The final transformation was complete. His body was strong, his mind sharp. No longer would he have to rely on others to communicate, to do his bidding. He was ready to reclaim that which had been stolen from him centuries before.

He floated down to the ground. Steam rose from his head, electricity crackled over his skin. As he moved, a set of clothing took form on his body from seemingly nowhere. Regal attire, befitting of a king. Supple leathers and satiny silks, ornately cobbled boots. He had no need to make himself a royal robe, for he would feel the weight of Roann's vestments soon enough. When he was fully dressed, he turned from the altar and faced the statue of Oleana. With a satisfied sigh, her head exploded with only a flutter from his mind.

Behind him on the stone altar, Roann's gasping weakened as he entered his final death throes. His body convulsed, what was left of his blood trickled from the gaping wound on his throat. Eyes that had once been a vibrant emerald were once again deep ebony pools. His last breath came with a feeble whimper, his body falling still seconds later.

The cathedral was eerily quiet and consumed by utter darkness. Lyrax laid his hands on Roann's chest and uttered a few mantras. One of the scrolls on the altar burst into flames as the words exited his lips. A shudder ripped through the young man's body before falling still once again. When Lyrax removed his hand, a sigil appeared underneath on Roann's skin. It flared once, the geometric pattern etching itself into his body above his heart. Tiny wisps of smoke rose from the new mark, permanent black lines adorning the dead emperor's chest.

Lyrax disappeared into a cloud of red fog, leaving Roann's body behind. His protégé's lifeless, black eyes stared out into the empty church. Wind blew in from the far door, blowing his blood-matted locks around in a frenzy. After several minutes, the gash on the young emperor's throat began to knit itself back together.

Hours later, as the sun rose, a single, gasping breath broke the silence as Roann returned to the realm of the living.

The emperor writhed on the altar, his heart thumping back to life. New blood flowed through his veins and his brain flashed back into consciousness. All his nerve endings erupted with sizzling feeling, sending painful jolts cascading through his muscles. He screamed out in agony, every inch of his flesh feeling as though it was on fire. Roann sat bolt upright, clutching at his chest, his hand lingering over the rune on his skin. His again-green eyes sparkled in the dawn light. Confusion overtook him, and he was unable to remember what had happened. His mind cried out for some semblance of recollection, only to be met with blackness. He sat there for what seemed like an eternity, listening to his heartbeat whoosh in his ears, trying to recall how he came to be on the altar.

Roann brought his knees to his chest, his legs no longer shattered beyond repair. Fleeting images began filtering into his mind.

A blade.

Pain.

Blood...

...his blood.

All at once, the shocking memory came flooding back and he brought a tentative hand to his neck, expecting to find a gaping wound. Surprised when he found no such laceration, he tried to come to terms with what had happened. Lyrax had killed him...and yet here he was. Alive. He tried to reason with his conflicting emotions. He had been betrayed—and yet he felt the need to return to the necromancer. The unyielding yearning to follow his master, to make him proud. After all, Lyrax had assured him he would be rewarded, and they were now bonded by his life essence.

Roann brought his hands out in front of his body and stared at them, his skin no longer deathly gray. His signet ring glittered in the light of the rising sun. He had been reborn, just as Lyrax had. A wave of peace washed over the young emperor and he smiled to himself in the silent cathedral. The sigil on his skin pulsed once, sending a jolt through his heart. He looked down just in time to see the red glow fade. He was neither confused nor afraid, and never questioned the new addition to his body. It was as if it had been a part of him since birth.

He scrambled from the altar onto wobbly legs. After regaining his balance, Roann flashed out of the chapel in search of his master.

CHAPTER TWENTY-SIX

STOP! TRAVELING FURTHER INTO THE WOODS MAY RESULT IN YOUR DEATH. STAY CLEAR OF THE TEMPLE COMPLEX AT ALL COSTS.

--Warning placard placed at the boundary of the Tandlewood Grove, east of Blackthorne

"Grildi Amzod, you put me down right now!"

The burly man trotted out of the Brens' shop, Ryris thrown over his shoulder like a sack of potatoes. The alchemist kicked and screamed, pounding his fists into his friend's muscular back.

"No can do, Boss! If you won't let me come with, I'll just have to punish you!" Grildi laughed like a naughty child, mischief gleaming across his face.

"I mean it! Don't you dare!" Ryris tried in vain to wriggle free, his raucous behavior attracting the attention of a good portion of the village's residents. They emerged from their houses; some still in their nightclothes, dazed and confused at the unwelcomed interruption of their early morning routines.

"What's that, Ryris? I can't hear you over the sound of all this cold, rushing water!" The town guard came to a stop a couple feet from the banks of the river bisecting the hamlet. He turned to allow his captive one quick look at his icy fate before tossing him in.

Ryris spluttered and splashed in the water, his clothes immediately soaked, his mood irrevocably altered. He had been thrown in the river more times than he cared to admit, but this morning he wasn't in the mood for a soaking. His ire was stoked even more by his companions—and his father—laughing hysterically at his frozen misfortune.

"You look like a drowned skellin!" Maxx pointed at his son, not trying for one minute to hide his jubilation. It was obvious he was enjoying his son's discomfort way too much.

Ryris waded to the shore, the water coming up to his waist. Steam rose from his body as the cold morning air interacted with the waning heat of his drenched skin. He glared at his massive friend with fury in his eyes. "You're definitely not getting any presents from me for a very long time!"

Grildi stood on the bank, wiping his hands together with a determined look on his face. "Doesn't bother me, Lad. Because I'm going with you—end of discussion. I can buy myself as many presents as I want on our adventures. I have a whole pouch of gamm saved up."

Ryris hobbled out of the stream, his clothes dripping with the frigid water of the Whispering River. His teeth chattered as the cold air wicked what little heat was left from his body. He rubbed his hands furiously over his arms, his chattering teeth making him quite hard to understand at times. "It's too dangerous. I can't in good conscience ask you to risk your life. You need to listen to me."

"Protectin' you means more than my life." Grildi's voice was determined.

Ryris couldn't help but feel loved in that moment. The sincerity in Grildi's voice, the yearning in his eyes as he spoke of protection—Ryris knew it was a lost cause trying to convince him to stay in Blackthorne.

"There's nothing I can say that will talk you out of it, is there?"

"Not in a million years. Now, can I come with, or am I going to have to push you in again?" Grildi approached Ryris, hands out, ready to dunk the young man if the need arose.

"Now wait just a minute." Jaric stepped forward, arms crossed over his chest. "Don't we get a say? This isn't a picnic excursion in the park, you know."

"I promise I won't get in the way." Grildi's eyes were hopeful, then turned mischievous. He cracked his knuckles and approached Jaric, hands in prime dunking form. "Besides…"

"Not another step!" Jaric reached around and put his hand on the hilt of his sword. "Ryris, do something about your over-eager friend, here."

Kaia interjected, coming between the giant man and the warrior. She took Grildi's hand in her own and stared up at him. "It's going to be very dangerous. There's a chance we could be killed."

"All the more reason to protect Ryris…and you, Lass."

Kaia offered a warm smile and released Grildi's hand. She turned to Jaric. "Not another word."

Shivering, Ryris finally spoke again. "I guess it's settled then."

Grildi lunged forward, Ryris flinching in expectation of another dunk, and embraced the alchemist in a giant bear hug. He didn't care one bit that his own clothes were beginning to dampen. Grildi finally released him, trying to smooth the wrinkled, wet fabric hanging limply on Ryris' shivering body.

"Looks like our departure will be delayed…I need to change clothes before we head out or I'll die of pneumonia before we even get out of the province."

~~~

The forests outside Blackthorne were dark and foreboding, even when the sun blazed above in the clear winter sky. Snow piled on every surface, covering the underbrush in a blanket of white. No one could deny why the legends surrounding the area persisted as long and as strong as they did. Anyone walking this deep into the woods would be hard pressed to linger any longer than needed. The logging trails ended miles ago, the companions leaving the relative safety of the prized tandlewood groves and emerging into the eerie unknown. The birds stopped their calls, the wind ceased blowing. Grildi noticed the abrupt change and immediately began to panic.

"I don't want to go no further, Boss." The hulking man anxiously wrapped his hands around his club, his knuckles turning white as he squeezed.

"Grildi, you have to. We can't turn back."

"But Ryris, there's spooks in there." He pointed into the dark emptiness of the forests before them, the black trunks blending in with the darkened background. Even the snow seemed to turn gray. Jaric grumbled under his breath behind them, Ryris immediately shooting him a stern glare. The warrior rolled his eyes and quieted, leaning against the remnants of a rotten tree with an irritated sigh.

Ryris put his hands on Grildi's biceps, squeezing firmly. "Yes, there *are* spooks in there. But you have to be brave. You wanted to come with us, to protect me and help find Ealsig."

The large man shook his head, tears threatening to spill from his frightened eyes. "But…"

"Remember what you would tell me when I was scared as a boy? *'You have to stomp away all your fear and find your inner lion'.*"

Grildi took a moment to process his friend's words. He finally steeled himself, wiping his eyes with the back of his hand. "Aye. My inner lion." He pounded his chest with closed fists. "My inner lion! I'm brave!"

Jaric cleared his throat. "Can we go now? I'd like to get there before it gets dark." He looked up to the canopy with a scowl. "Although you can't much make out the difference around here."

"Yes, we can go." Ryris looked deep into Grildi's eyes. "Right?"

"We can go. We're brave!" Grildi forced a smile, still keeping his hands tightly clasped around the handle of his tandlewood club. He followed his companions deeper into the forest.

Hours passed, the increasingly-tired party delving deeper into the unknown. No sunlight penetrated the thick canopy, and they had to resort to torches to light their way. Ryris was beginning to think the stories of the ghosts were myth—because they hadn't encountered anything but the occasional lost skellin.

Jaric, obviously sharing the alchemist's skepticism, chimed in with his irritation. "Who exactly said there were ghosts out here? Because all I see is dead trees."

"Oh, they're here. The ghoulies are watchin', that's for sure." Grildi stuck close to Ryris, partly to protect his friend—partly for his own protection.

"Well they certainly aren't as menacing as we've been led to believe, now are they?"

All Grildi could muster was a soft, stern, *"You'll see..."*

And see they did.

Another hour passed and soon they spied the crumbling ruins of a great temple complex. The first thing the companions noticed was a ghostly aura hanging over the entire area, a thick yellow fog clinging to the air currents. It ebbed and flowed, leaving one to believe either their eyes were playing tricks on them—or there were indeed ghosts parading within the mist. The buildings were old—older than Ryris had ever seen. The architecture wasn't that of the Vrelins, or of any style he had ever witnessed in his travels throughout the Empire. Short, squat walls of quarried stone with flat roofs made what appeared to be a ring of buildings sprawling out from a central core. The complex was quite massive, with several outbuildings surrounding the main fortress. Forges, storehouses, and barracks dotted the landscape—all long abandoned. Hard to discern in the dim light of the deep woods, the walls were covered with intricate carvings of beasts, some recognizable to the friends, some lost to history. Who built them and what they were for, no one knew. The only thing that *was* known was that suddenly, they felt as if they were not alone. A low rumble, like a spectral voice that spoke no words, reverberated from somewhere within the complex, prompting Grildi to seek cover behind his friend. A chill ran up Ryris' spine and he suddenly wanted to be very far away from this place.

"R-r-ryris!" The large man trembled. "It's the spooks!"

The young alchemist's gut told him to run. Anyone would be insane not to want to turn tail. The groaning from all around them intensified, the yellow fog thickening every second. He sidled up to his friend and scanned the horizon for any threats. Jaric and Kaia followed suit, weapons drawn. Their crystalline armor—donned at the forest's edge—shimmered even in the low light and dense mist. They all stood at the ready, waiting as the moaning intensified, then suddenly ceased.

"Why'd it stop?" Grildi's voice was a hushed whisper.

"Don't know…" Ryris unconsciously tightened his hand around the hilt of his shortsword. Jaric's feet crunching in the snow caused him to snap his head with a startle. He shot Jaric a stern glance, silently scolding him for the fright.

"There's only one way to find out…" Kaia's voice broke the silence as she purposefully moved forward, her bow at her side. She trudged ahead toward the half-lowered portcullis of the main building, a shimmering relic catching her eye. The three men followed right on her heels, not wanting to be left behind. Whether it was chivalry or cowardice, no one would ever know.

The fortress was covered in moss, the stones remarkably intact after countless centuries of neglect. The iron portcullis was rusted, the mechanism appearing to still be in working order. Something was stuck to one of the great spikes of the barrier. As the companions approached the main wall, they were greeted by the most macabre of sights.

A glittering crystal helmet, untouched by the elements, hung from the tip of the iron spike. Just visible inside were the skeletal remains of a skull and severed spine. The rest of the body lay in a heap underneath, frozen in time. Several more bodies littered the ground, most covered by overgrown underbrush and snow, their shimmering armor a testament to their identities.

Kaia silently held up a hand, halting any further progress. She jerked her head to the side, motioning for Jaric to follow her lead. Looking back to Ryris and Grildi, she put a finger to her lips before urging them to stay put with a gesture of her palm. The two warriors separated, each approaching the temple from different angles. The alchemist and town guard just stood there dumbly, Grildi squeezing Ryris' bicep just a little too hard for his liking.

The soldiers cautiously approached the bodies, weapons at the ready. Kaia knelt down to inspect a cadaver, moving the snow-covered overgrown brush aside to get a better look. The armor was most definitely that of the Crystal Guard, the rivets and hinges crusted with eons of calcified deposits. His or her sword lay beside the body, a skeletal gauntleted hand still grasping the hilt. Jaric crouched before the portcullis, reverently removing the helmet from the gate's spikes. The crystal material made an awful creaking noise as he guided the helmet down over the rusted metal. Finally free of impalement, he gently set the head next to the body it once topped. Jaric knelt, head bowed with respect. Whether Kaia or Jaric recognized any of the fallen warriors, they never said. Locking eyes with one another, the two soldiers stood and beckoned for Grildi and Ryris to join them.

"They were running for their lives." Kaia pointed to the bodies, fallen to the ground in the throes of panic. "Whatever attacked them waited until they were on their way out to strike."

"Is Ealsig is with them?"

Kaia scanned across the bodies. "No." She took a deep, cleansing breath. "We need to press on. I don't want to be here any longer than we have to."

Ryris' hands began to shake and he suddenly wished Ealsig to be interred somewhere else—somewhere much safer. A feeling of dread washed over him, so strong that he felt faint. Grildi noticed and immediately caught him by the arm, steadying him. The large man leaned in close, whispering, "*Like a lion...*"

Ryris patted Grildi's hand, silently letting him know it was alright to relinquish his hold. Bravery needed to prevail right now, or none of them would get out of the forest alive. He just wished he didn't have to participate in courageous activities right this second.

With each companion holding their torch high into the air, they pushed on into the fortress. The flickering lights bounced off the stone walls, the dank, musty air permeating their every pore. Ryris was quite certain he would never get the moldering smell out of his clothing. Chilled to the bone, both from fear and winter's wrath, Ryris was hyper-aware that the temple felt ever-increasingly "off" with every step they proceeded within.

Just inside the main foyer of the complex, they stumbled upon a skeleton, unlike that of the soldiers outside. A leather knapsack, worn from the passage of time, lay beside it, filled with gems and treasure. The contents were completely untouched.

"I guess whatever's in here isn't interested in anything precious—except maybe souls." Jaric poked at the backpack with the tip of his sword. Ryris shuddered as the skeletal hand resting atop the pack slipped and fell to the side, several fingers breaking off. Jaric moved again without another word, leaving the party and the skeleton behind.

They came to a crossroads in the complex hallways, a dingy, cracked skylight soaring high above in a cupola, letting in an insufficient amount of light. Suddenly, all four torches snuffed out with no wind present, thin wisps of smoke rising from the burnt ends of the wood.

Never in his life had Ryris heard silence as deafening as this.

Scraping sounds soon began to close in on them from all directions, the hallways surrounding the foursome seemingly coming alive with the shuffling sounds of the unknown. Metal scratching on stone echoed down the corridors, a ghostly white light illuminating the entire area.

"We aren't alone." Kaia's voice was low. "Arm yourselves."

Ryris shakily removed his shortsword from its sheath, only to have it clatter to the ground, slipping from his sweaty palms. Horrified, he quickly bent down and collected his fallen weapon from the dusty floor, as his fellow fighters looked on incredulously. He hoped against hope that whatever it was that was closing in on them hadn't heard the commotion.

He was wrong.

Without warning, a garrison of ghostly soldiers appeared out of the opaque illuminated fog, coalescing into ghoulish renditions of their former living selves. Weapons drawn, their lifeless eyes stared ahead at their quite alive targets. Misty legs strode effortlessly down the corridors, the sword blades dragging across the cobblestones the source of the terrifying scraping sounds. Spectral armor hung on their bodies, glimmering just like the soldiers that wore it. Whether or not it was solid, the companions did not know. An eerie whisper accompanied the troops, like the breath of the dead.

"What do we do?" Ryris' voice was borderline panicky. His fingertips instinctively began to heat up, his amulet warming his chest.

Scanning the corridors, Kaia realized they only had one option. They had been surrounded, with no escape route. The young alchemist dreaded her response, knowing it would mean he needed to act like a warrior.

"We fight."

Ryris' heart jumped into his throat. He knew this would happen eventually—that he would need to assist his friends in battle. But here? Now? Surrounded by ghost warriors? He just wanted to run away. Looking to Grildi, he could tell by the expression on his friend's face that he felt the same way. Before he could mentally prepare himself, Jaric charged forward with a mighty battle cry. Sword out and pointed toward his foes, he rammed the soldiers, only to find his weapon completely useless. Running full force through the ranks, their gaseous bodies split in half to let him pass. He slammed into the wall as he lost his balance. Shaking the stars from his head, he turned around and charged again. Once more, his weapon did nothing to the ghosts. They floated toward him, swords and axes swinging. The ghosts may not have had mass—but their weapons did. A shortsword struck the wall, sending sparks falling to the floor.

Their faces contorting, their ghastly voices echoing off the corridor, the ghouls encroached. Grildi wildly swung his club. The misty bodies of the ghosts parted as the tandlewood bludgeon cut through them, re-forming seconds later as if nothing had disturbed their forms. A haunted axe caught his club, chipping a small piece off the tip.

"Our weapons are useless!" Jaric screamed, taking a defensive stance.

"Theirs aren't!" Grildi backed up against a wall, pulling Ryris along with him. The hulking man put himself in front of his smaller friend, protecting him with his own body. "We can't win!"

256

Kaia readied her bow, her face soon illuminated by a red glowing light. A flaming arrow materialized on the crystal string. She let the projectile loose, hitting the front-most warrior. The misty body of the ghoul sizzled, exploding into a giant fireball. His hand axe clattered to the ground. The acrid stench of burning miasma infiltrated the group's nostrils as the specter faded into oblivion.

Grildi's eyes bulged with shock as he pointed at Kaia and screamed. "Y-you...magic?"

Ryris grabbed him by the arm and pleaded for him to listen, over the frenetic and ghastly sounds of the oncoming spectral warriors. He tried to keep his growing terror from spilling over while comforting his friend. "Trust us, alright?"

"But, Ryris! Magic is forbidden!"

Jaric's voice cut through the frenzy. "Fight now, discuss morality later!"

Ryris forced Grildi to look at him. "Trust *me*." Grildi reluctantly nodded and turned just in time to dodge a jagged, rusty axe blade.

Chaos ensued, Kaia getting off shot after shot of magical ordinance, Jaric and Grildi swinging their useless weapons in a last-ditch effort to defend themselves. Ryris just stood there, sword hanging limply at his side, frozen with fear. Two of the undead soldiers pinned Grildi against the wall, one of their hand axes piercing the soft flesh of his forearm. He cried out in pain. It was obvious they were quickly being overrun.

Turning to her wizard friend, Kaia screamed, her voice cracking with force. She unleashed another flare as she commanded, "Ryris! Flames! Now!"

"I...I don't know if I can!" Ryris' mouth felt as if it were full of cotton, his tongue stumbling over every word he tried to force from his lips. He wasn't a battlemage. He was an alchemist—a terrified alchemist. His hands quaked as crippling uncertainty washed over him.

"If you don't, we die!" Kaia grunted audibly as she let loose her shot, obviously beginning to feel the fatigue of battle. "Help me!"

Ryris looked to his other friends, Jaric and Grildi hopelessly whipping their weapons at an unyielding target. They were faltering, just like Kaia. Soon, none of them would have any strength left. The image of their lifeless bodies at his feet flashed before his eyes, before he envisioned himself being run through by an ancient, ghostly sword. The thought of rotting away with ghouls hovering over his corpse made him shudder. Ryris didn't know how they had been transformed into their malicious forms, but he wanted to avoid joining their ranks.

Summoning resolve he didn't think he had, the alchemist no longer thought—he just *did*. With angry ghouls charging from all directions and his friends in danger,

Ryris unleashed a torrent of fire. Like a flamethrower, streams of searing hot plasma shot from his fingertips, impacting the frontline demons attacking Grildi. Not paying any attention to the searing feeling assaulting his fingertips, he continued to attack, spraying flames in a grand arc at the specters. He was amazed by the new form his magic had taken.

"That's it!" Kaia encouraged him as she shot her own flaming projectiles. She frantically motioned with her bow. "There's more coming down that hall! You push them back; I'll finish these bastards off!"

Hands no longer shaking, Ryris' new-found courage surged through his body. One by one, he picked off the spectral assailants with flames and fury, his palms illuminated by the raw power of his magic. After several minutes, through his and Kaia's precise attacks, the malicious apparitions faded into oblivion, their discarded weapons lying smoking on the stone floor.

"By the goddess!" Jaric hoisted his sword high into the air with a battle whoop. He twirled it above his head before pointing the tip at Ryris. "You did it, you damn fool! I didn't think you had it in you!"

Grildi's hands shook as he turned to face his friend. His voice trembled, his lips quivering in sad surprise. "Ryris?"

Unable to catch his breath, Ryris couldn't answer him, but he hoped what Grildi had just witnessed hadn't broken his heart. The hurt in his eyes, the disbelief at what he had just seen. Before he could say anything, Kaia hesitantly let her bow down.

"They're gone."

The corridors were eerily silent. A charged aura still lingered in the air, leaving the companions with the distinct impression that their battles were far from over.

"For now…" Jaric kicked a leftover claymore, his crystal boot scraping against its jagged blade. "I don't think we should linger."

Kaia sidled up next to Ryris, laying a hand on his heaving back. "Breathe deep and even. The adrenaline will subside in a minute."

Surges of energy shot down his nerve endings. He knew his cheeks were flushed red, feeling the heat radiate over his face. Sweat rolled down his neck. A moment later, the waves of adrenaline indeed began to wane and he could see and breathe clearly again. Staring down at his palms, he saw the telltale signs of magic use. Rubbing his sooty thumb and forefinger together, he was suddenly hit with the notion that his chest didn't feel as if it had been burned to a cinder—like the last time he used his ability in such a powerful way. In fact, he hadn't felt anything more than a soft warmth as the first ghastly solider was spotted. No searing heat, no painful singe. Taking calming breaths as Kaia had suggested, he snaked his hand in-between the buttons of his shirt, feeling the bare skin of his chest under the amulet. Shocked, he felt no new blemish, only the puckered scar left behind from the burn above Hewe.

"Did you hear me?" Jaric shook Ryris by the shoulders to get his attention.

"Huh? I…" He ran his fingertip over his chest one last time before removing his hand from his shirt.

"Ryris! We need to move. We don't know if there's more."

Nodding silently, he patted Grildi on the arm, reassuring the brute that he was alright. Grildi said nothing as he shouldered his club with a sigh. As they made their way down the corridor of original choosing, not exactly knowing if it was even the right direction, Ryris gave one last look to the abandoned weaponry at their feet.

~~~

Ryris stopped counting how many spectral soldiers they had encountered after he passed fifty.

They had wound through the maze of corridors, sometimes circling back around to a point he knew they had passed before. One hour turned into several, the companions exhausted and battle-worn. Blood had been spilled on all fronts as they had all faced the blade. The wounds were minor, nicks and cuts and certainly nothing deep, but it was nonetheless a reminder that their assailants didn't differentiate between the living and the dead.

They were no closer to finding Ealsig's chamber or any further evidence of the Crystal Guard. Nearing the point of total exhaustion, they had finally holed up in a small concealed chamber, hopeful the heavy wooden door would keep out any would-be ghostly visitors.

Kaia held out a waterskin to her alchemist friend. "You need to drink. Your body is going to give out if you don't replenish."

Ryris accepted the canteen and drank greedily. His muscles ached, his hands sooty from magical flames. He peered over the flask as he gulped, seeing Grildi slumped against the wall with his club cradled across his chest. The massive man was tapping his fingers nervously on the wooden handle of the bludgeon. Grildi hadn't said a word since their first battle. Ryris resolved to just let it be for the moment. Their survival was of the utmost importance. At some point he would have to discuss what had happened. Ryris just hoped Grildi would understand—and forgive him.

Jaric stood guard at the door, peering out of a tiny crack in the wood. His sword rested against his leg, tip scratching the stone floor. He kept his hand tightly gripped around the hilt, at the ready for an attack.

When he had drunk his fill, Ryris handed the canteen back to Kaia, the warrior finishing off the rest of the water. He sighed heavily, sliding his back down the wall, coming to rest on his haunches. "This is never-ending. It feels like we're traipsing around in circles. And those *things*...they just keep coming. It's like a whole army after us."

"It probably is." Jaric never turned from his sentry position. "Whatever war they saw, whatever 'side' they were on, I believe they still think they're fighting. It doesn't matter that the enemy has changed. They might not even know the difference at this point."

"Who do you think they are?"

"Beats me. Their armor is unlike anything I've ever seen."

"How can all these ghosts just be bent on killing anything that comes into their territory? That doesn't make any sense." Ryris snorted, shaking his head. "I can't believe that just came out of my mouth. I sound like a crazy person. I mean, killer ghosts?"

Kaia offered a curt laugh. "Then we're all crazy—because we've all witnessed it first-hand."

"So what now?" Ryris looked at her with tired eyes. "We're trapped in this temple."

"We keep moving. We delve deeper. We..." She sighed. "...find Ealsig and get the hell out of here."

Jaric nodded his agreement and turned back to watch their exit. His posture suddenly stiffened and his hand tightened around his sword's hilt. "Looks like we decided just in time. There's light coming from down the corridor."

"How many?" Kaia removed her bow from its sling and brought it to the ready.

"Can't tell. What do you want to do?"

"If we stay here, there's a chance they'll skirt right by us. On the other hand, if we stay put they could float right through the door and we'd be sitting in our own tomb." Kaia thought for a moment. "Let's move. We know their weakness and can push through their ranks. Ryris, are you rested enough?"

"No," he thought.

All he wanted to do was run far away from this haunted place. He had seen enough supernatural phenomena for one day, and really wasn't keen on pushing forward to find more. He focused on his friends, though, and saw the same fatigue on their

260

faces, the same fear in their eyes. They had all experienced exactly what he had. All three bore the scars of battle: trickles of blood dripping from noses, scrapes and cuts oozing on battered flesh. Glancing down at his own body, he took inventory of the bloodspots spattering his shirt and pants. Granted, some of it was not his own, but he could definitely feel the telltale stings of cuts rubbing against fabric. Knowing that his companions shared in his discomfort and exhaustion, he knew he had to press on. They were in this together, and if one faltered—they could all be in jeopardy. Taking a deep breath, he finally replied to his friend.

"I'm ready." His voice was strong and sure as he rose to his feet. "Grildi?"

"Aye, Boss." His tone was quiet, yet determined as he hefted his club onto his shoulder. Grildi never made eye contact with the alchemist.

"Jaric, open the door." Kaia stood battle-ready, her fingers barely ghosting across her crystal bowstring.

Jaric did as he was commanded, the door creaking open with a loud squeak. He hesitantly stepped out, his sword locked firmly in his hands in front of his body. Peering around the door, he momentarily stepped back in and silently gestured to his left down the hall. His voice was almost inaudible as he whispered. "Light's getting brighter, but there's no way to tell how many. They're down a side corridor, I think."

"Quiet—and stay behind us." Kaia's voice was a hushed whisper as she beckoned to the alchemist and giant.

They crept out the door, following each other in a single-file line. The ghostly illumination got brighter and brighter as they approached another crossroads in the halls. Jaric held up a hand, halting their progress. Pushing himself flush with the craggy fortress wall, he tentatively poked his head around the corner to do his reconnaissance. He sucked in a surprised breath and quickly returned to his original position.

"What is it?" Kaia moved in close, Jaric blocking her way to see around the corner. His expression was one of surprise and sorrow. When he didn't answer, her voice became sterner. "I *said*, 'what is it'?"

The light grew closer, the haunting glow illuminating the entire area. Jaric looked away from his friend with saddened eyes. "It's…"

Mist floated in from all directions, the hairs on Ryris' neck standing on end. A foreboding presence crept in on the group and the temperature dropped so low they could suddenly see their breath. A glittering crystal sword appeared from around the corner, a spectral hand tightly grasping the hilt.

"…the Guard."

The soldiers, six in all, marched in a macabre pattern, backed by their headless commander. Ryris thought back to the bodies at the entrance of the complex and shuddered. It seemed the temple truly didn't care who its victims were. Like all the other ghostly combatants they had encountered, their bodies were misty, covered in spectral forms of their once-incredible armor. Ryris couldn't be sure, but it seemed as if they knew who they were going to be fighting. The front-most soldiers smirked when they saw their opponents.

Jaric tightened his grip on his sword's hilt and pushed on ahead, coming face-to-face with the spectral garrison. Kaia motioned for Ryris and Grildi to bring up the rear. Without warning, the dead warriors attacked.

Crystal clashed with crystal, Jaric's prized sword barely holding them back. The ghostly soldiers quickly surrounded the companions, closing in on them from all directions. With a grand swoop of his sword, Jaric managed to push two of them back, their phantasmal bodies ebbing and flowing as they made contact with the walls. It gave the party enough time to dash down the corridor and out of the dead-end alcove they had been pushed into. With the ghostly soldiers hot on their heels, they had little time to prepare.

"Ryris, you and Grildi get to one side and hold them back! Incinerate them!" Kaia's instructions were stern. "We'll take care of the other flank."

They got into formation and waited for the onslaught to reach them. The demonic soldiers soon rounded the corner and immediately charged. Ryris unleashed a volley of pure fire, illuminating the dim corridor with a haunting orange light. His attack hit the first soldier square in the chest. His form fizzled for a moment, but did not dissipate. Shocked, Ryris attacked again, only to find his magic either wasn't as strong as it had been—or these soldiers were resistant.

"I'm not hurting them!" Ryris' voice was panicked. Here they were, used to having the upper edge with magic, and these new foes weren't affected. Grildi lunged out in front of them, wildly swinging his club. Like before, his weapon passed right through its body. The soldier raised his own sword and whipped it around, narrowly missing the giant man's head. It clashed against the wall, sending sparks flying.

"I have an idea!" Kaia shot an arrow of pure electricity at the guardsman, the energy arcing across his phantasmal armor. It shocked his ghostly system, and he dropped his sword. "Ryris, now!"

Ryris unleashed a torrent of flames. The already compromised ghost warrior crackled as the new attack struck, and he finally fizzled from existence. His crystal sword clattered to the floor.

"I'll attack first, you finish!" Kaia charged forward, dragging a surprised Ryris along. "You two keep the others at bay until we can get to them! One at a time!"

Ryris found himself pulled into the fray once more, frantic yelling and the sound of clashing weapons echoing through the corridor. He noticed that, while the ancient warriors seemed more sluggish and untrained, these ghostly guard soldiers did not waver in the slightest. Even in their spectral forms, they were formidable opponents, highly trained and deadly.

One-by-one, Kaia expertly hit each soldier with a bolt of pure lightning, giving Ryris just enough time to strike with his flames. The magical combination overloaded their spectral power and each one fell where they stood. With Jaric and Grildi keeping the others occupied until Kaia and Ryris could get to them, they made quick work of the former Crystal Guard.

The last warrior standing was the headless commander. They didn't know how he did it, but it had been obvious he was controlling his soldiers, telling them where and how to attack. They had all seemed to wait for instructions, even though there was no audible sound to be heard over the clashing of swords. They had moved in perfect sequence, dodging physical attacks on their way to eliminate the magical opposition. Adapting to the fighting style of their opponents, the ghost soldiers had forced the party to their breaking point, exhausting them in an attempt to gain the upper hand. But, Grildi and Jaric held them back, giving the wizards the time—and room—to deal with the garrison.

Now, faced with their final foe, Kaia and Ryris unleashed their volleys once again. The bolt of electricity bounced off of the commander's ghostly armor and ricocheted off a wall. The entire party ducked to avoid the errant projectile. Undeterred, Kaia tried again, this time aiming for the junction of his chest armor and where his head once sat. She hoped that one "soft spot" would allow her the power she needed to pacify him enough for Ryris to attack.

With a hearty battle scream, she unleashed her magical arrow, crackling and bright. It flew at the soldier with incredible speed, hitting his severed neck and sizzling down his armor. In an instant, his spectral "skin" flashed and bubbled and Ryris knew it was his cue to finish the job. Seconds later, a ball of plasma shot from his hands and impacted the dying ghostly soldier. A horrid scream erupted from the walls and made a chill run down Ryris' spine. His crystal sword clattered to the ground, wisps of smoke rising from the hilt.

The party stood there and stared at the discarded blade, chests heaving with adrenaline-laced breaths. Jaric picked up the weapon and inspected it closely. His face became drawn, his eyes sad. After a minute, he reverently laid it back down on the ground with a bowed head.

"Goddess bless your souls..."

"Aye." Grildi looked down at the smoking weapons with pity.

"We can't stay and mourn them." Kaia moved past the two men and down the corridor. "We have to keep moving. Ealsig is here—somewhere…"

CHAPTER TWENTY-SEVEN

...someday I will make you my wife, I promise you that. After the war, after
everything goes back to normal, we...

--Scrap of a letter, found in the ruins of the Guard barracks

Ryris slumped against the stone wall of the corridor, seconds away from total collapse. He had been using his magic almost constantly for hours. The battle with the spectral Guard members had not been their last. They spent the last hour dodging rusty phantasmal swords as they dashed up and down increasingly confusing hallways. Soot covered his palms, his fingernails caked with the grime of magic. He couldn't remember the last time he actually saw bare skin. Grildi dashed to his side, his strong hand grabbing him under the arm to steady him. Ryris was relieved to feel his touch, hopeful that he was on his way to earning the giant man's forgiveness.

"I can't go on. I need a minute, please."

Kaia and Jaric skidded to a halt. "We can't stop. The longer we stay, the more vulnerable we are." She moved to Ryris' position and laid a hand on his shoulder. "I know you're exhausted, but we have to keep going. We're close, I can feel it."

"That's just it...we've been 'close' for hours now. How long do we keep doing this? Those things won't let us win. For all we know, it's been them forcing us in circles this whole time." His tired eyes pleaded with her as his voice softened. "We need to admit defeat. I don't want to die here."

She stared at him in silence for a moment before her jaw tightened and she narrowed her eyes in defiance. "I will not leave without her shard. I will not leave without *her*."

"She could be anywhere in this complex."

"And that's why we have to keep going."

The determined longing in her voice was unmistakable, the loyalty to a friend pressing through. There was no way she was going to leave, even if it meant their lives. Maybe that was something he didn't quite understand about unwavering loyalty. Yes, he *said* he would give his life for his friends, but when push came to shove—would he really? This was the first time he was faced with the fact that he really, truly might not leave alive, and that he had no choice in the matter. He could leave on his own, looking like a coward and probably be killed by evil's minions before he even got out of the complex—or he could stay and help his friends. He knew the decision should be easy, and yet—it wasn't. He felt like an ass.

"Are you coming or not?"

Ryris took a deep breath and decided. He wasn't a coward. He wasn't disloyal. He was trustworthy and had no intention of letting his friends down. Facing his own potential death, he finally realized what loyalty meant. With Grildi at his side and Jaric and Kaia surging forward with him, the option to run simply wasn't available.

"I won't let you down." The alchemist stood and stretched his neck out until it popped. He tried to put bravado into his voice.

Jaric hoisted his sword onto his shoulder to rest and offered Ryris a proud wink. "Good man."

Ryris exhaled deeply, totally at peace with his decision. He then realized he had something that might aid them in battle. He shrugged off his backpack and rooted around until he found what he sought. Ryris pulled out four small glass vials and handed them to his friends.

Jaric eyed the bottle in his palm. "What's this then?"

"Agility-boosting potion. It'll also help your stamina." Ryris pried the cork from his own vial and downed the tincture in one gulp. He had forgotten how bitter it was, and winced at the horrid taste. "Drink it fast, trust me."

The others followed suit and drank the mixture. They sat for a moment and waited for the effects to take hold. Suddenly, Jaric let out a satisfied sigh and pounded his chest. "Well I'll be damned! I feel like I have pure energy flowing through my veins!"

Ryris smiled proudly. He was relieved his concoction had worked.

Kaia threw a small, thankful smile in Ryris' direction. "It looks like there's a larger chamber ahead." She pointed at a set of heavy, wooden double doors, a haunting red illumination filling the hallway in front of them.

The group hurried toward the oaken doors. As they approached, it appeared the surface was covered with intricate etched runes, all glowing red. They pulsated both light and pressure waves. Ryris could actually feel the 'beat' of the carvings as they oscillated. Several heavy chains ran through the handles of the doors, clearly unbreakable by weapons. Four giant padlocks hung from the links at various junctions. Whatever was in this room, it most certainly garnered protection. Jaric yanked on the chains, rattling them loudly.

"You'll wake the dead, Lad!" Grildi covered his ears at the racket.

"I don't think that'll be an issue, seeing as they're already chasing us." Jaric slammed the chains back down against the door with an irritated huff. He looked to

Kaia and Ryris. "Well, one of you needs to do the honors." He made an exploding gesture with his hands.

Kaia readied her bow. "I don't think flames will do the trick. But, if we freeze the chains, we can shatter them with a blade."

"What about those glowing symbols? Do you really think we should be throwing magic at them?" Ryris didn't try to hide the worry in his voice.

"Unless you know the incantation to release the runes, this is our only option. Look at the locks; they're glowing just like the carvings. If we destroy one, the others should fail along with it."

Ryris knew better than to distrust her, although he would be the first to admit that his knowledge of all things magical started and ended at how to start fires with his hands. He hadn't studied wizardry one bit—ever. If she thought it would work, then who was he to contradict her?

With everyone in agreement, she conjured a shimmering arrow of pure ice, the projectile freezing solid as it formed. Firing it at one of the junctions on the chains, it struck and immediately froze the metal. Icy tendrils of magic swept up and down the strand of links, overtaking the enchanted locks. They crackled and popped as the bewitched metal froze. Satisfied the chilled spell had taken hold, Kaia instructed Jaric to deliver the breaking blow. As his sword crashed down, the links shattered into hundreds of tiny shards, littering the ground with quickly thawing metal fragments. The locks dropped to the floor, their red glow fading. The runes on the door flared momentarily before also going dark. A great howl echoed through the entire complex, accompanied by a blasting wind from all directions. It swirled around the group like a small tornado. The building shook for several seconds before falling silent. The companions all looked at one another, unsure of how to proceed.

"I don't think the beasties want us in that room." Grildi's voice trembled.

A mischievous smirk befell Jaric's lips. "All the more reason to go in then, wouldn't you agree?"

"No…" Grildi nervously scratched the back of his neck.

"A lion, remember?" Jaric punched Grildi in the arm, encouraging him with a warrior's bravado.

Grildi mustered a weak smile. "If you say so."

Kaia paid the men no mind, and instead eased the door open with a cautious push. The hinges were rusty and took a great deal of force to budge. As the aperture swung open, the moaning from behind them intensified and a great rush of wind once again overtook their position. They all turned, terrified to see an entire garrison of undead soldiers floating up from the floors and through solid stone walls. Forsaken weapons clutched in their ghostly hands, they pressed forward in attack formation, eager to claim their living prize. The companions had only seconds to push through the door and slam it shut before the first spectral warrior made it to the barrier. A wooden bar fell into place on the back of the doors by itself, tumbling into a cradle on the jamb. Jaric tried to budge it, but found it to be stuck tight. The runes glowed once again, re-activating themselves. The ghost warriors outside scraped their blades against the door. Hideous moans wafted under the crack at the bottom as they pushed their abominable bodies against it. But the door held steady.

"We're safe…or trapped, depending on how you look at it. I don't think those bastards can get past the enchantment." Jaric gave the door a strong pound with his fist for good measure.

Suddenly, the air temperature dropped, the companions able to see their breath in front of their faces. A ghostly beat enveloped them, as if the room was alive. Sound waves pulsed from the back of the chamber, their source unknown. They cautiously turned around, scanning the area for threats. The center of the room was dark, and the party was unable to see just how large it was with no light. From the sounds of their footsteps echoing, Ryris figured it was quite expansive. The air temperature continued to drop, forcing Ryris to shove his shaking hands in his pockets for warmth.

Without warning, the same reverberation that heralded their arrival to the complex hours earlier tore through the chamber, rattling the walls and rumbling the ground beneath their feet. Ryris instinctively grabbed onto Grildi to keep his balance. A figure emerged from the darkness at the rear of the room, a haunting blue glow enveloping their body.

Jaric's voice was wrought with surprise sadness. "…Ealsig."

The apparition floated toward them, coming to a halt mere feet from the party. Her shimmering spectral boots hovered just off the floor. Phantasmal crystalline armor hung on her ghostly frame, a gaping slice in the breastplate. A shining crystal battleaxe rested in a scabbard across her back. She was silent, the breathy sound of the dead warrior whispering throughout the room. She cocked her head slightly at the party, but did not make any move to strike.

Ryris was immediately taken aback by her appearance. Where the others had been ghoulish, their ghostly skin rotting from beyond the grave, their empty eyes boring directly into your soul—Ealsig was hauntingly beautiful. Her skin was intact, her eyes clear. Her flesh took on a milky sheen, yet transparently opaque. Shocking red locks floated around her head, dancing on currents of air produced by her supernatural aura. Emitting her own radiance, she literally glowed—a faint blue halo surrounding her entire phantasmal body. The foul stench of death accompanying the garrison of soldiers did not linger in her presence.

Kaia's mouth hung agape, her eyes disbelieving what she saw. Jaric moved to stand behind her, placing a comforting hand on her shoulder. His jaw trembled.

"She's been turned, too." Grildi cautiously moved forward, bumping Ryris in the process. "I can see right through her."

"No…it's got to be some sort of trick." A single tear dripped down Kaia's cheek. Ryris was stunned. He had never seen her weep. She was usually stoic and calm—except for when she was yelling at him. Now, looking upon the ghostly visage of her former general and friend, she was stricken with emotion.

The torches on the walls suddenly blazed alive on their own, illuminating the chamber in bright light. It was then that they noticed dozens of skeletons scattered around the room, weapons and armor discarded where they fell. A pedestal became visible on the back wall, a large, jet-black stone obelisk sitting on top. Visible shifts in the air surrounding it pulsed outward in all directions. The object gave off an unnerving, demonic aura. Ryris couldn't help but stare at the stone, as if it were drawing him in with unwavering power. His stomach tied itself in knots, and his strength drained from his body as a pressure wave overtook them. He leaned forward with a groan, resting his hands on his thighs to steady himself. A wave of nausea swept over him. It was apparent his comrades were feeling the same effects, for Jaric's shoulders slumped, causing the tip of his sword to tap against the ground. Grildi brought a hand to his head and massaged his temples with a wince. Kaia let out a shaky breath—due to both the shock of seeing her fellow general and the fatigue that now consumed them. None of them noticed the sly, knowing smirk cross Ealsig's lips.

Without warning, Ealsig drew her axe and lunged forward, the blade slicing into Kaia's forearm at the junction between her gauntlet and upper body armor. Blood spilled from underneath the crystal plates as she howled in pain. Jaric grabbed his injured companion and threw her to the side, just as Ealsig struck again. With his waning strength affecting him, he was slower than usual to move and just barely missed being sliced in half. A blast of energy flew out from her weapon's arc, knocking all the companions to the ground. Ryris tumbled backwards, his head smashing to the floor with a thud. It took him a few seconds to regain his senses, stars blinking in front of his eyes. He gingerly crawled back to his feet, with Grildi's assistance. The amulet on his chest started to heat up. He didn't know what to do, so he just stood there dumbfounded. He knew he should be helping, but his body was hopelessly fatigued, his mind sluggish and disoriented. His attention fell to the stone on the pedestal for just a moment before being yanked back into the fracas.

Kaia scrambled to her feet and drew her bow with shaking hands. Blood from her wounded arm splattered onto the ground. She backed away from the ghoul as best she could. Ealsig charged at her, her axe cutting through the air with incredible precision. It nicked a shard of crystal from Kaia's shoulder pauldron. "Ealsig, stop!"

Ealsig ceased her onslaught for a split-second, a surprised jolt shaking her body. It seemed Kaia's command had struck a nerve. It only lasted an instant, and the spectral soldier's eyes flared red and she swung again. Kaia brought her bow up to defend herself just in time. The shaft of the weapon clashed against the upper limb of the bow, the sheer force of the blow threatening to shatter the crystalline material. The bow bent under the impact, but did not yield. Ealsig pushed Kaia backwards, using her axe as a ram, until she slammed her into the side wall. Kaia's bow fell from her hands, allowing Ealsig to jam the shaft of her axe against Kaia's throat, cutting off her air supply. Kaia clawed at the obstruction with frantic hands. Ealsig leaned in close, nose-to-nose with her captive, and snarled.

Grildi, club swinging, ran at the pair, only to be forced back by an unexpected blast of energy. It seemed to come directly from Ealsig's body. He somersaulted backwards and came to a stop in a sprawl of limbs, his head smashing against the wall. Dazed.

Jaric, watching this unfold in seemingly slow-motion, stumbled forward under the fatigue of the menacing obelisk and tried to attack his former comrade. He raised his sword high above his head and brought it down, slicing through her back with a pained, sorrowful yell. Ealsig's body parted, allowing the blade to pass right through. Jaric narrowly missed hitting Kaia. Ealsig's momentary fading gave Kaia enough time to slide down the wall and out of her grip, gasping for air. She rolled to the side just in time to avoid Ealsig's blade once more. Her ghostly opponent turned and went after Jaric, an orb of ice materializing in her outstretched hand. She flung it at him, the icy projectile hitting him in the legs and bowling him over. She seemed to pay no mind to Ryris.

Once again, Ryris' attention was drawn to the stone in the back of the room. His foggy brain struggled to decide whether or not to fight, or figure out what was going on with the object. He tried to get Jaric's attention, but found his mouth had gone dry and unable to produce words.

Jaric, still disoriented, crawled on the ground, the remnants of Ealsig's icy ball melting on the floor. Ealsig approached him, kicking his legs out from underneath him before he could stand. Without touching him, she pointed and he rose into the air, high above their heads. A flick of her wrist sent him crashing to the ground. Jaric screamed out in pain as his body slammed against the stone floor. Blood trickled from a new cut to his scalp.

The amulet on Ryris' chest was burning him now, and he knew there was only one thing he could do. They were in great peril, and he didn't know how much longer they would survive. He knew he had the skills...he just had to muster the courage to use them. After all, this wasn't some nameless ancient ghoul—this was Kaia and Jaric's friend, their comrade. But if he didn't do something, they'd be killed. There was no doubt in his mind about that. He summoned all the strength he had and conjured a ball of flames, flinging it at Ealsig's back with a hefty battle cry. To his shock, it hit her—and immediately disappeared into a cloud of smoke. He stared in disbelief as he remnants of his volley wafted around her ghostly body.

Kaia, watching Ealsig's reaction to the attack, noticed a slight wavering in her concentration. The assault had definitely rattled her. Whether it had any effect on her strength or accuracy would remain to be seen. Ealsig turned and focused her attention on her new opponent.

"Again! Do it again!"

Kaia's desperate plea shook him from his reverie. He concentrated again, all the while watching his comrades form up behind their spectral friend. Ryris knew what they were doing. He was being used as a distraction. He steeled his nerves and quickly flung another fireball at the spectral warrior.

This time, Ealsig actually laughed at his attempt. A mocking, ghoulish chuckle that made Ryris' hair stand on end. She stared him down, all while forming a glittering spike of ice in her hand. She held her axe high with one hand and readied a giant icicle with the other. It hovered just above her head as it took shape. The icy weapon crackled and popped as the heat from the room began to melt it.

Just as Ealsig was about to deliver the fatal blow to the alchemist, Jaric leapt at her and knocked the frozen projectile out of the air. It crashed to the floor and shattered. Ealsig immediately roared with anger and whirled around to face him. Her eyes flared and her hair billowed around her head on furious currents. An animalistic growl reverberated from both her lips and the room itself as the obelisk against the wall pulsed again, sending out a crimson-tinted wave of energy. It surrounded Ealsig, seeping into her misty body. In a matter of seconds, her feet touched down to the ground and she stood once more—this time on solid appendages. With a flick of her wrist, she sent Jaric hurtling backwards on a wave of energy.

She was no longer a specter. Her armor took on mass along with her body, and she was suddenly much more dangerous. Phantasmal fire wicked up around her as power surged through her newly-formed body. The ground beneath their feet shook. Grildi grabbed Ryris under his arms and dragged him back, away from Ealsig.

Kaia, wasting no time, brought up her bow and conjured an arrow of pure light. She fired it at her former partner as the spectral wind knit her body back together. The projectile hit her in the abdomen, her ghostly armor absorbing the energy with ease. Undeterred, Kaia attacked again, even though her injured arm struggled to hold her bow. As soon as the holy arrow struck, Jaric followed up with an attack of his own, hopeful he could take advantage before Ealsig's transformation was complete. He swung his mighty sword at her, only to have Ealsig grab the blade between her hands and wrench it aside, throwing Jaric and his weapon to the ground.

Grildi ran at her, whipping his club around in a graceful arc. It connected with Ealsig's shoulders, knocking her forward. She needed a second to regain her footing. When she stood straight again, she turned toward the lumbering man and blasted him with a frosty wind, rendering him unconscious before his body ever hit the floor.

"Grildi!" Ryris bolted to his friend's side, slapping his cheeks in an attempt to get him to come to. Grildi laid motionless, blood oozing from his nostrils. A thin sheen of ice covered his entire body. Ryris wiped the frosty coating from his eyes and mouth, completely unaware that Ealsig was ready to pounce on him. It was only when Jaric's booming battle cry ripped through the air did he turn to see he was about to be cleft in two. He barely dodged the attack, Ealsig's axe smashing into the ground right beside Grildi's head. Jaric soon followed, jumping on her back and attempting to hold her in a bear hug. She desperately tried to hang onto her weapon.

Ealsig roared in fury, her eyes burning red as she fought off her friend. Kaia readied another holy arrow and let loose, hitting Ealsig in the chest. The ghostly warrior, angered by the attack, screamed and forced Jaric's arms from her body. He fell onto his backside and rolled away. Ealsig drew her axe and charged at Kaia.

"Ealsig, what are you doing?" Kaia held her bow, cocked and ready with another magical projectile. "Don't you recognize us?"

Ealsig stopped momentarily, confusion crossing her face. Her eyes darted to the side, resting on the stone in the back of the room. Within seconds, she snapped out of her haze and continued her onslaught. She swung at Kaia, her axe blade narrowly missing the junction of her armor between her cuirass and thigh plates. Kaia doubled over from the ferocity of the attack and dropped her bow. Not bothering to pick up speed, Ealsig leisurely strolled toward her, knocking the rest of the companions back with a blast of energy from her hand. She knelt down and grabbed Kaia by the collar of her breastplate, lifting her high in the air. Blood gushed from her arm, staining the dusty floor below.

Ryris watched through hazed-over eyes as Ealsig shook Kaia before tossing her aside like a rag doll. She laughed, her head thrown back, her red hair cascading down over her glittering armor. Kaia groaned as she desperately tried to pull herself to her knees. She spat a mouthful of blood onto the cobblestones.

The sight of her struggling filled Ryris with rage. He suddenly had the driving urge to defend her. Before he knew it, he shot a ball of plasma at Ealsig. She knocked it out of the air with her hand like she was batting away a gnat. Before he could react, she grabbed him in the same manner she had Kaia. With absolutely no effort, she tossed him aside and moved on to her next victim.

272

Jaric scrambled out of the way and made a bee-line for his sword. Grabbing it, he swung wildly with none of the precision that his training had awarded him. Surprisingly, he made contact, crashing into Ealsig's gauntlet. With new determination burning in his eyes, he kept up his assault, his sword smashing into her armor with a ferocity Ryris had never seen from him. Time after time, his weapon sliced into Ealsig's defenses, his blade cutting into her spectral flesh on more than one occasion. Thick black blood dripped from her wounds, coagulating on the floor. Rage burned in Ealsig's eyes, but she did not attack him back.

There was something else in her expression, something that Ryris almost missed. For just a moment, her face showed remorse—and fear. Once again, her eyes shifted toward the obelisk at the back of the room before a great arc of energy shot out from its surface. It enveloped Ealsig and she roared in defiance, finally returning Jaric's assaults with vicious accuracy. She charged at him, her axe blows precise and vengeful. The loving, pitiful look in her eyes had been replaced by sheer malice. Her blade tore into Jaric's breastplate, slicing a hole over his heart, mirroring the one her armor bore. His under mail had thankfully stopped the otherwise-fatal blow. The force of the strike knocked him backwards. Kaia tried to crawl to him, but was stopped by Ealsig's boot on her back.

"…pitiful…"

Ealsig's ghostly voice reverberated through the room, seemingly coming from her mouth and the stone in the back at the same time.

Something in Ryris snapped when he heard her insult. They had tried their best to defeat her, knowing it was the only way to bring peace to her soul and to get out of there alive. And here she was calling them pitiful. Whatever had corrupted her, whatever was making her act in this uncharacteristic way—Ryris knew it needed to be stopped. If he didn't do something, they would soon join Ealsig as undead warriors. His hands clenched at the sight of Jaric and Kaia laying helpless and bleeding under Ealsig's malicious stare. She twirled the axe arrogantly in the air above her head, staring Ryris down. Daring him to be the hero.

His amulet began to burn his skin, and he looked down to see it glowing brightly, even under his shirt. Suddenly, electricity crackled over his body, as if it were erupting from his very soul. He was afraid in that moment, for he had never experienced anything like this before. His head began to swim, a thousand voices calling out to him from across time and space. They melded into one voice, although Ryris had no idea what it was saying. He heard it, yet didn't understand it. All he knew was it seemed to be encouraging him.

Ealsig bared her teeth, kicked Kaia in the stomach, and raised her axe above her head, ready to take Kaia's as a trophy.

Time suddenly stopped. Ryris saw the axe, saw Kaia's terrified face. The screams of his friends stretched out, the words unintelligible. He felt as if he were floating, his consciousness seeping out from every pore. It was as if he was leaving his body and being sucked deeper into it at the same time.

The amulet flared, and his hands erupted with grand arcs of lightning. He had no control as powerful bolts of electricity erupted from his fingertips and flew at Ealsig. The energy crackled across her armor, tendrils of lightning flashing out in all directions. Ealsig screamed—a bloodcurdling, horrific scream—and fell to the ground. Her axe clattered down next to her. She held her head in her hands, the inhuman cry continuing to erupt from her lips. The obelisk in the back of the room bellowed out a grand pulse of energy and Ealsig ceased to scream. Black fog poured from underneath it, and rolled across the floor toward them. The acrid stench was unbearable.

Ryris was suddenly sucked back into his body and fell to the ground. His hands were smoking and shaky, his stomach threatening to empty itself from stress. He couldn't breathe. Kaia clambered to her feet and stared at him in awe as she covered her mouth against the putrid fog. Ealsig curled into a ball on the ground, electricity still arcing across her spectral armor. Her body began to flicker. Jaric grabbed her axe, so she was unable to re-arm herself again.

His mind once again his own, Ryris finally realized just what Ealsig had been trying to tell them in her fleeting moments of clarity. He pointed to the pedestal and yelled out to Jaric.

"The stone!"

Jaric tightened his grip on his comrade's axe and ran toward the obelisk, leaping over the rolls of poisonous fog as he moved. With one grand swing, he raised Ealsig's awesome weapon above his head and brought it down with a mighty strike, shattering the dark artifact. A spectral wind blasted out from the remnants of the object, blowing the barred door wide open regardless of the lock. Out in the corridors, the clattering of weapons dropping to the ground rattled through the complex, as their owners were sucked into the void.

The room became freezing cold once more, and Ealsig's misty body rose up and hovered a few feet above the floor. She no longer had an air of malice about her, and didn't move to attack. Her expression was one of peace—and relief.

"...I'm sorry..."

Kaia scrambled to her feet and ran to Ealsig, reaching out a hesitant hand to touch her. She stopped short, her fingers barely penetrating the spectral body of her friend. "Ealsig...I..."

The ghost soldier offered a sincere, loving smile. *"Don't...cry over me. I'm...at peace."* She pointed to the remnants of the dastardly obelisk. *"That thing...held us here...made us kill. We couldn't...destroy it."*

Kaia fought her tears. "I couldn't save you..."

"You're wrong... You saved us all..." She floated around to face Jaric. He stared at her longingly, holding her axe at his side with a shaky hand. Her phantasm began to fade as she spoke. *"Jaric...we never had the chance...to..."*

He reached out for her, his fingers passing directly through her outstretched spectral hand. She lifted her other hand and traced her fingers down the side of his face. His shoulders slumped and he hung his head sadly. Kaia moved beside him, and together they stood in solemn solidarity. They finally looked up to their fallen comrade just in time to witness her final words.

"Dust and bones..."

Ealsig smiled, finally at peace, and faded from the room in a cloud of mist, leaving no trace of her existence. Kaia and Jaric stood next to one another in silence for a long moment before turning to Grildi and Ryris. The giant man had regained consciousness moments before. Kaia's arm oozed, blood dripping out of the junction in her armor. Ryris tried to get a look, but she pulled away.

"Kaia, let me see. You're bleeding really badly." He tugged on her arm, and she hissed in pain. "I have something that can help."

"I'm fine." She pulled the injured limb back, and cradled it across her body.

Jaric holstered Ealsig's axe without a single word, wedging it in-between the straps for his own sword, before moving away from the group, head hung between his shoulders. Kaia watched him go, a pity crossing her face.

Even though he hadn't known Ealsig, Ryris felt sad that she was gone. She would have been a great asset to the party—and it was obvious her death deeply affected his friends. But he knew she was in a better place now, at Oleana's side as her champion.

Kaia and Jaric converged at back of the chamber. She inspected the wall, scrutinizing every inch until she came across a small rune embossed in the stone, much like in the Devil's Canopy. She depressed it, and the door swung open in the same manner as her comrade's had done. Looking over her shoulder, she motioned with a flick of her head for her companions to follow.

No soothing lavender light greeted them. The air was dank and fetid, the stench of decay infiltrating the entire party's nostrils. Kaia carefully felt her way around the walls, the only light entering the chamber being the now-dim illumination from the outside room. Finding a crystal wall sconce, she knocked the gem out of the holder. "Anyone have cloth they're willing to part with?"

"Aye, that I do." Grildi set his club against the wall and reached into his knapsack. He pulled out a tea towel. Jaric immediately gave him a confused look.

"What in Oleana's grace did you bring a dishtowel for?"

"To wash dishes!" Grildi eyed him incredulously as he handed the fabric to Kaia. "I suppose I'm not gettin' it back, right Lass?"

"Unfortunately not."

Grildi nodded knowingly. "Good thing I brought two."

Kaia produced flames on her palm. Grildi didn't seem to mind her magic use so much this time. Within seconds the towel was engulfed in fire, and she set it back in the sconce. It wasn't much, but the flaming cloth did enough. In the low light, Jaric was able to find a discarded torch. He lit it on the burning rag and held it high above his head.

The sight that greeted them was horrific.

Bookshelves lay toppled on the floor, their tomes scattered on the stone pavers. Potion bottles were smashed, weapons racks destroyed. Most of the sconces had been torn from the walls. The cabinet that once held Ealsig's prized helmet lay in ruins, the glass shattered, the helm cleaved in half. Kaia picked up one of the pieces and sighed.

Using his torch as guidance, Jaric approached Ealsig's sarcophagus. The lid had been smashed in, the mechanism at the foot long since dark. No soothing hum permeated the room. As the rest of the party approached, Kaia sucked in a shocked breath.

A rusted shortsword, spattered with dried blood, stuck out of the bed. Inside, the skeletal remains of the once-proud warrior laid in death, the blade lodged between her ribs. The skull turned at an awkward angle, Ryris noted that her jaw was wrenched open—frozen in a death scream. He hung his head and said a silent prayer.

"Poor lass…" Grildi removed his fur hat and held it in front of his body solemnly.

Kaia yanked the sword from the corpse. The sound it made as it scraped against the withered skeleton and cracked crystal armor was awful, and Ryris fought the urge to clap his hands over his ears. Dropping the feral weapon to the ground, she leaned over and ran her hand over the few remaining strands of red hair attached to the skull.

"Ealsig…I'm sorry."

Jaric joined her at the side of the coffin, and they both stood in silence. Grildi and Ryris stayed back out of respect. After a few minutes, Kaia took a deep breath, straightened her posture, and turned around. Jaric lingered longer, peering down at his deceased comrade. He ran his hand over the hole in Ealsig's armor, stopping his palm just above where her heart had been. After a few moments, he too joined the rest of the group. His eyes were glistening.

Kaia pointed to the side wall. "Grildi, can you move that shelf? It should slide to the side."

"Aye!" He cracked his knuckles and approached the shelving unit, giving it a forceful shove. It protested with a groaning creak before finally budging. Dust flew up from all sides, causing the large man to splutter in a coughing fit. After the dust cleared, he looked back to his companions hopefully. "Did I do it right?"

Kaia smiled in thanks. "You most certainly did. Will you bring me the parcel in the alcove?" Grildi did as he was told, gently picking up the satchel and cradling it in his giant hands. He gave the package to Kaia with a proud grin. She opened it, ensuring that Ealsig's shard was still intact. When she was satisfied of the condition, she re-wrapped it and handed it to Jaric, who stowed it in his knapsack. Looking back at the skeleton in the sarcophagus, Kaia sighed heavily.

"I need your help. All of you."

~~~

Ryris stared at the mound of fresh dirt, flanked on all sides by pure, white snow.

A small pile of black rocks lay carefully arranged at the head of the grave, nestled under a towering old-growth tree. He wished he had a fresh flower to place on top. Taking note of his surroundings, even though the daunting fog and foreboding feeling had disappeared from the forest, Ryris knew it would be years until any signs of blossoms would grace the plants of this place. He uttered a prayer with a bowed head before leaving the gravesite in peace.

Ryris plopped down next to Kaia on a fallen tree trunk. "How's the arm?"

"Smarts, but the wound closed. Thanks for the potion."

"It's what I do." He handed her another vial. "Pour another one over tonight before you go to sleep and in the morning you should be as good as new."

She accepted the bottle. "Thank you—and not just for this." She looked over her shoulder at Ealsig's grave. "She deserved better than that haunted tomb."

"I'm honored we could give her a proper place to rest." He sighed tiredly, and rubbed his hands over his arms to warm himself.

"What you did back there was incredible. Thank you for saving us…for saving *her*."

Ryris glanced down at his hands, no longer covered in soot. If he stared at them hard enough, he could almost see the lightning crackling over his palms. Incredible didn't even begin to describe what he had experienced. He looked at her, dumbfounded. "How did I do it?"

Kaia shrugged and shivered. "Beats me. You just stopped. It was like time slowed down."

"So I wasn't the only one who felt that?"

"I guess not. You glowed, you know. I could see your amulet burning bright under your clothes."

Ryris shivered again, and decided to take a chance. He was cold, and Kaia seemed like she was freezing too. Perhaps they could keep each other warm. He scooted closer, and she immediately curled into his side. He wrapped his arm around her shoulders and instantly felt warmer.

"I've never experienced anything like that before. There was this voice, but I didn't understand it. It echoed inside my head. I think it was encouraging me, but I don't know how." He shook his head in confused disbelief and furrowed his eyebrows. "The power just shot from my hands, I couldn't control it. And when it was over, the voice left and my amulet dimmed. I don't think I'll ever be able to do that again."

"Why not?" Kaia sat forward and turned to face him. Ryris immediately missed her warmth. "You've already proven you can."

"But I don't even know *how* I did it."

Kaia pondered his response for a moment before offering one of her own. "I think you're subconsciously learning to control your power."

"I don't feel any more in control now than I did when I killed the saberstrike. I've learned to aim better and concentrate my fire, but I'm still scared to death every time flames leap from my hands. If I feel anything—it's *out* of control."

"Being afraid is part of every warrior's thoughts. I'm constantly afraid, but I work past it and push on. People die if you don't. I think you need to give yourself more credit." Her eyes twinkled along with a proud smile. "Whether you realize it or not, your skill is rising every time you light up your hands. Your mind, your body— they're both becoming accustomed to the sensations and power surges that accompany your ability. As a child, you were taught to hide your gift. You were shunned, and that's a shame. Had you grown up in Farnfoss, your abilities would have been nurtured from a very young age; you would have been schooled in your arts.

"You don't need books or instructors. Everything you require is right here." She leaned over and tapped her finger against his temple. "Your inherent power is incredible. In my time, you would have been a teacher, not the pupil. Yes, it's true that you don't have the advantage of a classically trained wizard to guide you through the trials and tribulations of magical growth, but something tells me you don't need it anyway. Your pedigree ensures that."

"But it still doesn't explain how I made it happen. I wasn't in control...at all." Ryris sighed.

"It just keeps surprising you, doesn't it?" She tapped his shirt atop his amulet. "That thing is full of history—and mystery. Phia said so herself, the stone had powers even before it was enchanted. I don't think we were meant to understand it."

"I guess..." Ryris exhaled deeply, his breath fogging on the chilled forest air. "So now what?"

"Camp here for the night, then move on in the morning."

"To where?"

Kaia laughed tiredly, her eyes crinkling at the corners. She motioned randomly with her arm. "I haven't the slightest idea. Over there somewhere?"

~~~

Grildi sat alone, his back up against a giant boulder.

Ryris approached, a few morsels of chocolate from the baker in his hand. Yes, he was buttering up the hulking man with sweets, but he had to make amends. He thought back to the hurt in Grildi's eyes as he revealed his magic. Not the place he wanted to do it, surely. Truth be told, he hadn't really thought about *when* he would show his friend his power, and that was his regret to bear, not Grildi's. Ryris just hoped Grildi would forgive him. Grildi had been brave during their escapade within the complex, but had become uncharacteristically silent as they left the temples, and laid Ealsig to rest. After her burial, he had slipped off into the forest alone.

"Hey, Grildi?"

The man turned and mustered a smile at the young alchemist. "Boss..."

"Can I join you? I brought you a treat."

Grildi patted the ground beside him. He had cleared a spot in the snow. Ryris sat, depositing the candies in his friend's massive hand. They sat in silence for a few minutes, Grildi nibbling on his sweets. After a few minutes, Grildi put his arm around the alchemist.

Ryris sighed and rested his head against his friend's shoulder. "I'm sorry I never told you…"

CHAPTER TWENTY-EIGHT

From this day forth, 33rd Summer, YG 675, I hereby declare the dungeons in the Palace of Keld to be shuttered. No longer do we have the need for corporal punishment in our peaceful nation.

--Royal decree from Emperor Welland Vrelin

Dust fluttered down from the gaping hole in the ceiling.

Lyrax grumbled, brushing the offending particles from his velvet-covered shoulders. He sat on the listing throne of the former king, the seat cushion tattered and blotched with mold. The once regal accoutrements of the royal chamber now sat broken and dingy. Generations of monarch's portraits graced the walls, their canvases faded and cracked. The carpets were frayed, the stained glass windows shattered to the ground. The entire room stunk of mildew.

Hardly the place for the next king of the entire world to hold court.

Standing with an irritated sigh, he took note of his surroundings and decided that this place was no longer sufficient. He needed a new palace, and a new seat of power from which to rule unconditionally. Concentrating his mental energy, Lyrax sent a message to his protégé. Several minutes later, Roann appeared in front of him, rising out of a cloud of red smoke. Annoyance washed over the necromancer at the late arrival of the young man.

"Keeping your master waiting, are we?"

Roann frowned as he walked forward through the clearing mist. He moved with vigor, any sign of his untimely death weeks before unseen in the present. "I was in a meeting with the Duke of Dungannon. You can't expect me to abandon my royal duties in a heartbeat."

"I expect you to come when called." A crackle of lightning rippled threateningly across his fingertips.

"My apologies, Master." Roann bowed deeply, hoping he had avoided Lyrax' wrath.

"See to it that you stay in line." Lyrax rose and spread his arms wide. "This place no longer suits my needs. I know I enjoy decay and death, but what do you think is missing here?"

Roann shrugged. "I realize it's not a proper palace, but…"

"Not a proper palace? Where's the gold? The opulence? The *subjects?*" His smile broadened. "You can't be an emperor without people to do with as you please. I wish—to have Keld."

Roann straightened his posture, trying to hide his irritation. He was flustered by the fact that Lyrax would insinuate Keld would be his and not theirs. After all, *he* was the rightful heir to the throne. Roann carefully considered his next words before replying. "With all due respect, Master, are you sure you're ready for such a move? You've only been earthside less than a month, and—"

Lyrax was at his side in less than a second, grabbing him by the hair. He wrenched Roann's head back with a heaving grunt. "Never question me. Just do as I command." He yanked the young man's neck awkwardly. "Clear?"

"Yes…I'm sorry…"

Lyrax released his hold. "You would be wise not to question me again."

"Yes, Master." Roann nodded submissively as Lyrax backed away from him.

The necromancer took a deep breath, a red aura flaring brightly around him. "Soon I will be in power, with you at my side. We will rule Keld—and your father's precious empire. Those who oppose me will fall, and will rise up against their brethren at my word. Those who comply—their fate I have yet to decide."

"Keld will be *ours*, I assure you." He was relieved when Lyrax didn't seem to notice his subtle insubordination.

"And what of your mother? Surely she will not allow such behavior from her precious son?"

"Leave her to me. I'll ensure she complies."

"Are you certain?" Lyrax sat once again on the rickety throne.

"She won't be of any concern." Roann bowed. "I have much to take care of before you arrive in Keld."

Lyrax extended a gracious hand. "Of course you do. I'm confident you'll make my arrival as grand as it deserves to be. Go."

Roann flashed from existence, leaving the necromancer to once again pout at his bleak surroundings.

~~~

"Back from the trade talks already?" Empress Eilith glanced up from her needlepoint project; thin wire-rimmed glasses perched on her delicate nose. She motioned to her son to have a seat beside her on the velvet sofa.

Roann sat across from her in a plush chair, his mother scowling at his disrespect. "Something's come up."

"Oh? Did you find a wife in Dungannon? The Duke's daughter is stunning."

"No, mother." Roann rolled his eyes. His back began to hurt.

"Pity…" She focused her attention back to her work, not bothering to look at her son while she spoke. "Do you want some lunch? It's late, but I'm sure the staff would bring you something."

"I'm not hungry." Roann shifted uncomfortably in his seat.

"Well, you look gaunt." She smiled lovingly. "I'll see to it that dinner tonight is enough to get some meat back on your bones."

"I don't need you to police my eating habits."

"Touchy, touchy…I was only trying to help." She huffed at his moodiness, causing herself to prick her finger absentmindedly with her needle. She hissed sharply as a small bubble of blood welled up on her fingertip. "Damn. Hand me that handkerchief, would you, dear? I don't want to stain my project."

Roann obliged, handing the cloth to his mother with a suddenly shaky hand. The sight of her blood made him flush. He wiped a hand across his forehead.

Eilith peered over the tops of her lenses at him as she accepted the handkerchief, suspicion crossing her face. She dabbed her finger. "Something's bothering you."

"It's hot in here."

She motioned to the windows. "You can open them. Maybe that would help?"

Roann shook his head. In reality, he relished in the heat, it reminded him of Lyrax' volcanic lair. In that place, he had felt safe. In this place—he felt stifled. "That won't be necessary."

"As you wish." She removed the handkerchief from her fingertip and set it aside. The bleeding had stopped.

Roann clenched his hand in his lap. There was an internal war being waged within his mind—one that he intended to win. No longer would he allow his mother or his conscience to reign supreme. He was a new man, a powerful man. Or so he thought. The little voice in his head, moments away from being snuffed out completely, had to have the last word. And so, he sat there, watching his mother stitch the image of a rose onto silk, wishing she would just shut up so he wouldn't have to hurt her. Trying to keep his cool, he exhaled sharply through his nose and decided not to respond. His chest began to feel tight, and his muscles burned.

Eilith kept pushing her thin needle through the delicate fabric resting in a wooden hoop on her lap, unaware of the turmoil her son was experiencing. She let out a humming breath as she completed her final stitch with that particular color, finally looking up to meet his eyes with a satisfied smile. She turned the piece around to show him.

"Do you think Casmit will like this? It's for her birthday next month."

"I don't care about Casmit!" Roann's voice boomed off of the rich tandlewood wall panels of his mother's sitting room.

Eilith flinched. "What's come over you? I thought you were past all this brooding nonsense!"

And instantly, the voice in his head died.

Lightning-quick, Roann lunged at his mother over the coffee table and grabbed her by the shoulders. Lifting her off the sofa, he pulled her close to his body, her long gown swishing the books off the table, her needlepoint circle clattering to the floor. She yelped, but did not call for help. He dangled her in the air, his face centimeters from her own. The scent of her floral perfume wafted into his nostrils, giving him fleeting, nostalgic respite from the rage that poured from his soul.

Her eyes bulged in horror, tears forming in the corners. "Roann...please..."

The emperor snarled with sinister intent, narrowing his eyes as he resisted the urge to snap her neck. His voice, when it finally came, was gravelly and low.

"You dare insult the emperor? You have no idea of my power. But, your eyes are about to be opened, mother. Everyone's eyes are."

Eilith whimpered in her son's mighty grip. "I don't understand..."

"You will." He tightened his hold on her shoulders. She cried out as his fingers dug into the satiny capped sleeves of her dress, pressing painfully into her flesh. He whirled her around like a doll, facing her toward the door of her reading room, left slightly ajar. With a deliberate nod of his head, it slammed shut and locked on its own. Eilith gasped in shock. The window drapes soon followed, falling shut with no assistance. Every oil lamp and candle in the room suddenly flared with intense light, bathing the entire chamber in a yellow glow.

Manhandling her back to face him, Roann focused his gaze directly at hers. Knowing the blackness was overtaking the emerald eyes his mother always loved, he smirked as all the color drained from the empress' face. No longer able to control her emotions, she openly wept, sobs shaking her entire body. Roann watched silently, relieved that the plaguing pain from before had left him. Now, all he felt was raw, unadulterated power.

"I've been given the most incredible gift. And, dear mother, you were the one who made it happen." Eilith's eyes saddened she processed the information. He could pinpoint the exact moment in which she understood—her lips quivered, and her body began to shake. "Yes…it was because of you that I have limitless power. Because of *you*—Lyrax has returned. And now this empire belongs to *us*."

"Lyrax? That's a…fairytale."

"Naiveté isn't flattering on you." He released her, and she tumbled to the floor.

"I should have never let you live…" Her expression changed from sadness to regretful anger.

"And that's a burden you'll have to live with for the rest of your life."

"All these years I thought you had been cured. All these years…" Eilith stood, legs wobbling. Without warning, she raised her hand and tried to slap Roann across the cheek. With the reflexes of a saberstrike, he grabbed her wrist and twisted. Defiant, she spit in his face before unleashing a mother's wrath. "I'll tell the people about you. I'll tell them the truth!"

Roann pushed her, and she tumbled backwards over an end table, knocking an oil lamp over as she fell. The carpet, now wet with fuel, caught fire. He shot the flames a stern glance, and they extinguished. Eilith scrambled away from him, backing herself up against the bookcases. She frantically searched for something to strike him with. Grabbing a crystal decanter from one of the shelves, she heaved it at her son. He simply flicked his wrist and the bottle flew off in the opposite direction, crashing against the far wall. It shattered as it impacted, spraying shards of glass and aged whiskey in all directions.

"Throwing things?" Roann shook his head sympathetically, pity in his eyes. "Telling the people won't matter. I'm in control now."

"You're a worthless pawn."

"We shall see…as you shall *see.*" He moved toward her, knowing she had nowhere to flee. She pressed herself into a corner, cowering like a child, hiding her face behind her hands. He towered over her. "Do you wish to see what a 'worthless pawn' looks like?"

He stood tall, head held high. Feeling familiar energy pulsate around him, his body began to grow, his skin changing to black scales. What had been a painful experience as a child had grown into one of the most pleasurable feelings he knew. Shifting his form was euphoric, as the raw power surged over him. Wings sprouted from his back, and his blonde hair disappeared, replaced by sharp horns.

Eilith screamed in horror, crying at the appearance of her lost child.

Flapping his leathery wings, Roann stood proud, as his mother sobbed in the corner. "Isn't this what you've always wanted for me? Power. Success. Respect."

"No one will respect you, Roann." Her tone bit through her tears.

"I thought my own mother would be more supportive…" He quickly changed back, his velvet doublet and leather pants appearing on his human body once again. Smoothing down his hair, he knelt in front of her, reaching out to caress her face. She flinched back, away from his touch. "You'll come around. You'll realize this is what the people need. Father was a coward, and where he failed—I will succeed. Lyrax has assured me of that."

"I no longer have a son." Eilith lowered her eyes sadly. "I will not allow you to sully Artol's legacy with such filthy talk. You'll have to kill me to keep me quiet."

"No…you'll remain alive. After all, it's every mother's wish to see their child fulfill their potential, is it not?" He waved his hand in front of his body and Eilith disappeared into a cloud of red mist.

~~~

The empress sat alone in the darkness, dust tickling her nose. She shivered, the damp, musty air surrounding her like a cocoon. Something skittered across the stone floor in the distance, causing her to jump in surprise.

She knew exactly where she was—and she was certain not a single soul would come looking for her.

No one came to the dungeons anymore. There was no need. She couldn't think of a time in Artol's reign where they had ever been used. Not since his father had there been a prisoner housed inside its walls. And now, here she was—a prisoner of her own son.

He would lie, of course, if anyone asked about her. On a trip, perhaps? Or fallen ill? No one would question him. She considered screaming, but soon realized that no one would hear her. The dungeons were in the bowels of the palace. True, there were some areas still used, like the fighting arena—but Eilith knew she was nowhere close to that part of the complex.

No, she was in the oubliette. A dungeon within a dungeon. Once a place of heinous torture and despair, it had laid abandoned for over a century. Hidden and scorned, this place held secrets—and she was now one of them. Down the hall, crypts filled with the bones of the less fortunate souls who met their end at the torture master's hand silently waited for their next resident. She knew, above her in the castle proper, workers went on with their daily happenings, oblivious that their empress was incarcerated in a prison under a trap door.

Suddenly wishing for Artol's company, she sighed and wrapped a musty burlap blanket—no doubt belonging to the last unfortunate inhabitant of her cell—around her shoulders. She winced as the rough fabric scratched her skin.

CHAPTER TWENTY-NINE

While Ealsig shows great promise with her weapon and magic skills, her temperament leaves little to be desired. I feel she may be a loose cannon, one that we may not be able to control. We will have to keep an eye on this one...

--Excerpt from instructor's report on Ealsig, year unknown.

Several small children gathered around Grildi's massive legs, mouths agape at his sheer size.

They squealed and laughed, comparing their height to his and shrieking with delight as he picked them up one-by-one and gave them the bird's eye view from his lofty vantage point. Some admired the fur on his boots, while others tried in vain to lift his heavy club from the ground. The rest of the party sat across square of Murnal Village, chuckling at the giddy kids' reaction to their hulking friend.

"The children have never met such a man before." The elder offered the companions a small bowl of local nuts. "He's so kindhearted to give them all that attention."

Ryris smiled and palmed a handful of the snack. "He loves kids. And, as you can see, they always love him."

"You have a wonderful friend, Mr. Bren." The old man smiled thankfully. "You have made such a wonderful, lasting impact on our village in just a short amount of time. The children are happier than I've ever seen them, and your strength..." He looked to Kaia and Jaric. "...in helping right the grain-grinding stone was most appreciated. We're honored to help you with whatever you need."

Kaia put her hand over her heart with gratitude. "Thank you, Zorendun. We appreciate your hospitality. And, in fact, there is something I'd like to ask you."

"Please do!" The elder smoothed his long beard with a wrinkled hand.

"We noticed the entrance to a mine in our travels, about ten miles down the road, and off the main trail. Do you know anything about it?"

"Ah, yes. Onyx Caverns. It's abandoned; the chambers began to collapse due to over mining." He sighed sadly. "It brought a great deal of income to the surrounding area. Many people moved away after it closed."

"How long has it been neglected?"

"Fifty years, maybe more. You're free to explore it, if that's what you're getting at. It's not owned by anyone anymore." The old man winked knowingly. "Just be warned that it is very unstable and probably full of bugs."

"Bugs?" Jaric's eyes bulged.

"Oh, hush." Kaia shot her friend a stern glance. "We'd gladly bring back any onyx we salvage for your coffers in return for your permission to explore."

Zorendun waved his hands dismissively in front of his body. "No need, young lady. If you do find anything there, it won't be of much value. The gem veins had been greatly depleted by the time the mine closed. All you're liable to find in there is rusty pickaxes and creepy-crawlies. Any treasure you uncover will be rightfully yours."

Jaric shuddered at the mention of bugs, trying to covertly hide his discomfort.

The old man glanced to the horizon. "It's getting dark. I do hope you're not planning to leave us tonight. I can't offer you much in accommodations, but there's a barn at the village edge that has a loft with plenty of dry hay. There are lanterns hanging on the wall if you need light, and a fire pit behind the building. You're welcome to stay the night."

Ryris shivered in the chill dusk air, hopeful that Kaia would accept the charity. The less time they didn't have to sleep in tents, the better.

"Thank you for the offer. I think we'll take you up on it." Kaia knowingly eyed her companions. "It's been a long time since we've had someplace indoors to lay our heads for the night."

The elder rose, extending a hand to each member of the party. "Please feel free to take water from the well to fill your canteens and refresh your horse. My wife will be serving dinner soon, and I hope you'll join us in our home."

"We don't want to be a burden."

"Nonsense! A warm meal will do you good—and she has a pie on the hearth that I've been eyeing all day."

"Pie?" Grildi approached, the children reluctantly having gone back to their homes to clean up for supper. "I like pie!"

"Good!" Zorendun smiled broadly. "It's settled then. Make yourselves comfortable in the barn, and come for dinner in an hour."

The old man left, tottering back to his small house. Grildi sat with a lumbering sigh and stretched his legs out toward the fire. "What'd I miss?"

"We're spending the night, and in the morning we'll backtrack to that mine we saw. That is, of course, if Jaric isn't too scared." Kaia's eyes twinkled with mischief.

"Watch it, Quick..."

"Don't be a baby." She turned to Ryris. "What do you think? Sound like a place to hide something? A shard perhaps?"

Ryris took a moment to ponder. "Maybe? It depends on how long the mine's been there. Zorendun did say it's old. But..."

"But what?"

"...it sounds really dangerous. If we get caught in a collapse, we're done for."

"Risk is part of our everyday life, especially now." Kaia rested a comforting hand on his shoulder. "I think we have to try."

Ryris nervously scratched the back of his head. "I suppose. How about this? We go tomorrow and you get your tiara out. If it reacts—even slightly—we go in. If not, we move on."

"Fair enough."

Ryris nodded his acceptance of the plan. Part of him hoped there wouldn't be any signs from Kaia's crown—he really didn't feel like spelunking in a dilapidated mine. But, he'd never tell her that. After a moment more of warming their hands on the crackling fire, they unhitched Ass of the East and made their way to the barn. Jaric couldn't help but reminisce about the previous conversation.

"So Kaia, about those bugs..."

~~~

The cacophony of snores coming from the loft was enough to wake the dead.

Locked in a battle they didn't know they were participating in, Grildi and Jaric serenaded each other—and their two companions—with thunderous noise. Having had enough, Kaia and Ryris climbed down from their perch and took refuge outside, around a small fire. Kaia poked at the logs with a hefty stick, the flames illuminating the exposed skin of her arm. A thick scar was gradually beginning to fade.

"Looks like your arm's doing better. I can give you something to hopefully get rid of that for good." Ryris pointed to his friend's limb.

Kaia looked down at her battle wound. "What's one more?"

"Suit yourself." He dug through his knapsack, producing several ingredients and a field alchemy kit. Crumbling some dried moss into a small beaker, he added a few splashes of base fluid. Giving the liquid a stir with a thin metal spoon, the specks of moss soon disintegrated. After a moment, he squeezed a thick paste from a leather pouch into the solution, and the beaker began to glow. Kaia watched in awe as he worked. Stirring it once more, he finally set the vessel on a flat log within the fire and allowed the mixture to come to a boil. Ryris sat back and admired his handiwork.

"What did you make?"

"Antiseptic. I figured it couldn't hurt, seeing as though we've been getting our fair share of battle wounds."

"Good idea."

They sat in silence for several moments, Ryris stirring his churning potion every few minutes. Night birds chattered high above in the treetops. When he was satisfied the tincture had cooked sufficiently, the alchemist grabbed the beaker with a towel and quickly deposited the burning-hot glass vessel in the dirt beside him. In a few hours he could store it in a bottle, ready for use to clean wounds. Turning to his companion, he noticed she was staring into the fire, lost in her daydreams. He was reluctant to interrupt her. "Kaia?"

"Hmm?" She seemed mesmerized by the flames.

"Can I ask you something? Something kind of personal?"

She looked over at him with tired eyes. "I suppose. I can't guarantee I'll answer, though."

"Fair enough." Ryris scooted closer. "About what happened with Ealsig…"

Kaia sighed sadly. "She was a good friend. A true warrior."

"Do you want to talk about it?"

"Not really."

Although disappointed, Ryris decided not to push the subject. He sat quietly, hoping he hadn't offended her. He nervously repositioned his cooling potion. After a few minutes, she surprised him with an unexpected admission.

"I'm a soldier, Ryris. I need to keep my emotions in check. The only thing sadness brings on the battlefield is more death." She sniffled in the waning firelight. Ryris wasn't certain, but it sounded as if she were crying. He didn't want to make her feel uncomfortable by turning his head to confirm his suspicions.

"Kaia, you don't ever have to hide anything from me. I won't think any less of you for showing emotion. I'm not a soldier, remember?" He took a chance and reached out, grasping her hand. He half-expected her to scoff and pull it away. When she didn't, he felt warmth creep up his arm and flow straight into his cheeks. "I think it might do you good to get this off your chest."

Kaia squeezed his hand before pulling hers away to rest on her lap. A great, heaving breath blew from her lips. "No one deserves to die like she did. Unable to

291

defend herself. Unable to—fight that incredible power that took her over. A soldier expects death to come valiantly on the battlefield. Not at the hands of spectral cowards."

Ryris leaned in and put his arm around his companion in her time of need. His stomach immediately fluttered when she didn't move away. She laid her head on his shoulder.

"She wasn't that much younger than me, but joined at a later age. When she came into our ranks, the elder soldiers were extremely wary. No one knew much about her, other than her parents had disowned her for being a problem case. She was—very misunderstood." Kaia paused for a moment, shifting her body on the ground. She curled up more into Ryris' embrace. "She was passed from one mentor to the next. They were ready to relegate her to the quartermaster, and that would ensure she would never see battle. But I saw something in her…"

"You've got a very kind heart."

"Perhaps." She sighed. "We couldn't have been more different, and we butted heads a lot in the beginning. But she had the potential to be a great warrior. Her ambition proved she was meant for something grander than sharpening swords. I volunteered to assist with her training. She needed guidance.

"It took a long time to instill a warrior's temperament, and she was furious with me more than once. But I think she realized I was her last chance. If she didn't learn anything from me—or refused to—there was nothing else. She would either be taking inventory for the rest of her life, or be out on the street."

"Was she always good with an axe?"

"Thankfully, yes. She needed training on battle technique, but her skill was inherent. And her magical ability was impressive…as you saw earlier." Kaia let out a long sigh.

"How old was she when she joined?"

"Sixteen. She already had a…*personality* all her own. I don't think she liked the fact that someone close to her age was bossing her around. I think she felt threatened by me. But then everything changed."

"What happened?" A sudden chill overcame Ryris, the wind picking up and blowing glowing embers close to their feet. He quickly stomped them out.

"She had been out at a pub, got drunk, and ended up mouthing off to a patron. They got into a verbal tussle, and he didn't care much for this strong-willed young woman getting in his face—and he hit her. So naturally she fought back, knocked the guy out cold, and ordered another drink. Someone in the tavern alerted the Guard and she was brought back to the barracks and told to pack her things. The Crystal Guard had a reputation to uphold, and that kind of behavior was unacceptable."

"But somehow she was allowed to stay…" Ryris could already feel pride for his friend welling in his chest.

"Word got back to me just in time. The elders wanted her gone, but I convinced them she deserved a second chance. She was allowed to stay, under my direct and constant supervision. The council warned me that it wasn't just her reputation that was on the line—but mine as well.

"They had her waiting in a small windowless room in the barracks tower. All her belongings were stuffed into two duffels, her crystal axe nowhere to be seen. The quartermaster had confiscated it since it still belonged to the Guard. She looked so helpless." Kaia paused, staring up to the sky for a moment. "I told her to grab her bags and follow me to my private quarters. Later, when she asked why she was being allowed back, I congratulated her for cold-cocking the loudmouth in the pub before telling her never to do it again.

"She was astounded someone would stand up for her. No one had ever shown her an ounce of mercy or compassion—until she met me. Our relationship changed that day, and she blossomed into the fierce warrior—and friend—that I knew from that day forward."

"At least you can cherish those memories, right?"

"Yes. It doesn't make it hurt any less, though. My heart is broken, and I fear that part will never mend." She wistfully looked up toward the barn loft. "And Jaric…it must have been horrible for him to come to grips with her death, although if you think getting me to admit my feelings was hard…"

"I don't understand."

"Relationships were forbidden within the Guard. Never mind the age difference."

Ryris was absolutely shocked. He had always thought there was a—sometimes spoken, sometimes not—rule about fraternization within military ranks. It made battle hard, made emotions flare up. He looked to Kaia; her head slumped between her shoulders, her fingers picking at the stitches on her pants. All of a sudden, he had a revelation about her—about Jaric. When they had arrived at his tomb, Ryris had alluded to whether or not they had been involved. Her reply had been curt—and now he knew why. Hearing her speak, seeing her body language—it was suddenly obvious that Kaia had once harbored feelings for Jaric that he did not share. Ealsig's death just became much more devastating.

"Ryris?"

Kaia's voice snapped him from his thoughts. "Yes?"

"You can never tell Jaric I've confided in you about his relationship with Ealsig. Promise me?"

"Pinky swear." He held out his little finger, and she hooked her own around it in solidarity. "Did she have a title, like you and Jaric?"

"Of course. All members were given special monikers, usually by comrades. I chose hers." Kaia smiled at the memory. "She was Ealsig the Intrepid. Fearless, adventurous. She never backed away from exploration or adventure. She'd be chomping at the bit to get into that mine."

"Thank you for sharing her story with me, I know it was difficult."

"She deserves to be remembered, faults and all. It makes us who we are."

Ryris nodded knowingly. "Do you think we'll be remembered? When this is all over?"

"Only time will tell."

~~~

The army arena was cramped, hot, and smelled of sweat and steel.

Almost a thousand soldiers stood in rank, awaiting an inspection from their emperor. Not the entire army's force, for some three-hundred warriors were stationed in the far reaches of the empire. Some finished final checks of their armor, others polished weapons to a mirror sheen. The commanding officers ensured their garrisons were in perfect order before the monarch arrived.

Located far north from the city of Keld, the complex was well away from the eyes of the everyday citizens, and the residents seemed to keep their distance without being told. The stagecoach arrived, the setting sun just beginning to dip below the horizon. Emperor Roann disembarked, his always-present assistant nowhere to be seen.

When the sovereign entered the stadium, the military trumpeters blared their klaxons, heralding his arrival. All soldiers snapped to attention, weapons and shields held high in the air. As Roann walked down the center aisle, each row of warriors turned to face him, their clanking armor thundering through the cavernous hall. The doors at the back of the arena slammed closed, the soldiers unable to hear the telltale sound of the locks over their noisy chainmail.

As he ascended the stairs of the stage, Roann shook hands with the general before turning to face the crowd. The soldiers whooped in unison as the emperor raised his fist in solidarity. After a moment of cheers, he quieted them with a gesture of his hands.

"Thank you, General Rayl, and thank you soldiers of the Vrelin army! You're in fine form today!"

Cheers once again erupted, prompting Roann to wait until the general calmed the soldiers down. He finally spoke again.

"You are the pride of the empire, the protectors of all we hold dear. Your unmatched bravery is known to the far reaches of the land!"

The garrisons replied with thunderous applause.

"Time and time again, you have fulfilled your duties, never once flinching in the face of danger."

A soldier in the front row snorted, knowing his job was anything but dangerous. There was no war, no enemies that required complicated sorties or advanced tactics. Yes, the soldiers of the Vrelin army were there to protect should the need arise—but when had that ever happened? They all enjoyed the good things the military life had to offer: great pay, travel, and the respect of the nation. Everywhere they went, soldiers were greeted with open arms, broad smiles, and more free meals than they could ever ask for.

Roann continued to smother his troops with praise, ensuring that each and every one of them was completely enthralled by his charismatic words. The soldiers allowed themselves to be drawn in, eagerly accepting the accolades heaped upon them. He went on about duty, privilege, and loyalty. About the common man looking up to the powerful soldier, and the honor that warriors lived with and abided by.

"… and we know not what the future holds, my good men and women," Roann gestured wide with his arms, "but the nation is lucky to have you to uphold our ideals no matter what the cost!"

The crowd cheered loudly, some banging their weapons against their shields in celebratory clatter.

No one noticed the emperor's eyes turn black.

The air in the coliseum took on a deathly chill as the back doors blew open, seemingly of their own accord, a red fog whirling in on a torrent of wind. It surrounded the soldiers, prompting them to draw their weapons to defend themselves at a moment's notice. It seeped into their noses and down their throats. They were too busy trying to escape the wretched fog to notice anything else.

In the midst of the chaos, Roann pulled a dagger from his doublet and slit General Rayl's throat.

Moments later, the soldiers' destiny came full circle, as an ominous figure appeared beside their possessed emperor.

The warriors didn't have time to react.

~~~

"The quicker you help me pull up this chest, the quicker you can be away from the centipedes!" Kaia's voice was irritated.

Jaric shrieked as a centipede skittered down his armored leg, his hands feverishly brushing it away before stomping on it. Ryris and Grildi stood watch, holding torches to illuminate the dark alcove off one of the crumbling mine shafts. They didn't try and hide their laughter.

"Shut up, or you'll both be permanent residents of this mine!" Jaric's voice was both angry and terrified at the same time. He cautiously slunk beside the hole Kaia was in, poring over every inch of the mine's surfaces before settling in to help.

The ground was muddy, rainwater dripping in from cracks lining the walls. Murky water pooled at their feet, and the musty smell of stagnation surrounded them. Every so often, small rumbles would rattle the shaft, a stark reminder of the unstable nature of the entire mine.

"Grab it by the handle and yank!" Kaia's face was flushed as she commanded her partner to heave the container upwards. Her hair stuck to her face, her armor splattered with mud and debris.

"I'm trying! The...handle's...stu—" Jaric yelped, dropped the case, and frantically wiped at his neck. It would seem there had been an intruder in his personal space of the hundred-legged variety.

"Damn it, Jaric!" Kaia's voice was strained as she struggled to keep hold of the chest. It started to slip from her wet hands.

"They bite!" Jaric flailed as the insect went flying away from him, cast aside by a fearful toss. He reached into the pit to liberate their prize and pulled with a mighty grunt. Jaric ended up on his backside, armor splashing in a cloudy puddle. The chest teetered precariously on the edge of the hole, threatening to plummet back down and squash Kaia. Grildi noticed, dashed forward, and gave the box one more giant tug, ensuring his friend was out of harm's way. Then he leaned down and extended a hand to the filthy subterranean warrior.

When Kaia was safely out of the hole, she took a moment to catch her breath before trying the locked latch. It stuck steadfast, and she scowled at her lack of progress. Offering his assistance, Grildi knelt down and smashed the lock with his fist, a prideful smile gracing his lips. With a grateful chuckle, Kaia lifted the lid, exposing a glittering crystal shard.

"That's five." She retrieved the piece from the chest and handed it to Jaric.

296

Wrapping it in a swatch of linen and mindful of the jagged edge, he placed it in his knapsack. After helping Kaia to her feet, he slung the pack over his back and turned to his friends. All three sets of eyes were locked on him, widening in surprise. Grildi brought a hand up to cover his mouth.

"What?"

Ryris gingerly pointed at the soldier, his finger trembling. "Ummm...Jaric?"

"*What?*" His voice wavered.

"So, don't panic or anything, but…"

The formerly brave warrior screamed like a small child as a dozen centipedes scurried out of the knapsack and skittered down his chest plate.

CHAPTER THIRTY

*"Harvest only that which will bring life, leaving the dregs to rot in the fields.
For you will reap a bigger bounty with proper fertilizer than should you go
without."*

-- Philosopher's saying, pre-Old War. Source unknown.

The crisp winter air kissed Keld.

Leaves, having finally changed their colors weeks prior, had begun to fall from their treetop homes, fluttering to the ground on wispy currents. The sun glared, reflecting off the fountain pools dotting the city. The threat of snow, already blanketing much of the northern portions of the Vrelin Empire, wouldn't rear its ugly head for months still. Being located in the southern part of the central plains had its advantages.

A festival was in full swing, the citizens enjoying themselves to the fullest. Residents milled about in the central park, the aroma of roasted nuts and grilling meats wafting around the promenade. Children shrieked with delight as a band of roving jesters did acrobatics. Onlookers gawked in awe at a caged saberstrike on display.

High above, Roann watched from his private balcony, thinking to himself that they had no idea what was about to happen. Blissfully unaware. The antique clock on his desk chimed, and he smirked. In an hours' time, the people of his city would be called to order, with the promise of an address from their beloved emperor. The culmination of a weekend of parties celebrating winter's arrival, Roann's speech would usher in a new era for Keld—and his empire.

Today he would make the people see the truth—and they would cower before him and his master. The very last shred of decency and morals had left Roann the moment he struck his mother. His transformation was complete. He felt alive, reborn. No longer would his conscience get in the way of glory.

Taking one more look down upon his city, Roann finally went back inside, his eyes flashing black for a split second.

~~~

The royal trumpeters sounded and the citizens of Keld filled the square in front of the palace. Thousands filed in joyously, with pleasantly full bellies from a day of eating, warmed from the inside-out from celebratory drinking. Children rode atop their fathers' shoulders to get a better view of their emperor, residents assisted the elderly and made sure they could see around the crowd. They waited patiently for their monarch to appear, excitement bubbling through their ranks. Every year, at the end of the winter

298

carnival, Roann would make a glorious speech about prosperity and peace, and proclaim the city of Keld ready for the changing seasons.

The sun was setting in the western sky, casting a brilliant red hue across thin, wispy clouds. A brisk wind blew up; carrying the chilled air from the mountains with it, and the citizens collectively huddled together for warmth. Palace guards came out of their barracks towers and surrounded the crowd. In their excitement, no one seemed to notice.

The massive bronze bell in the clock tower rang, and the crowd immediately hushed. Moments later, the castle doors opened, producing their beloved emperor. Arms raised high to greet his subjects, Roann smiled broadly as he exited the palace. The citizens kneeled. Coming to a halt just before the grand staircase that had seen his coronation several months prior, he took a moment to gaze out at the people. He closed his eyes for a few seconds and inhaled purposefully, a wave of calm washing over him. Soon, there would be panic—beautiful, satisfying panic.

He finally bid his citizens to rise and they cheered with thunderous applause. He allowed them to shower him with their love and attention before quieting them with a simple hand gesture. No one seemed to find it odd that both Eilith and Father Morigar were absent.

"It's a perfect day to celebrate a successful harvest, wouldn't you agree?" Roann's voice boomed across the square. The citizens cheered in response, clapping and whistling. "This year has seen the most incredible bounty in recent history from our fields and orchards. The harbor filled our nets to the brim to ensure that we have enough for our winter stockpiles!"

The crowd erupted in jubilant celebration. Flags waved and balloons floated up toward the Gentle Reach.

"My father wanted what's best for this city and the empire, and I am no different! I see great potential in our community, and if we work together and continue on this path, Keld will grow and prosper tenfold!" Roann spread his arms wide as he continued. "You've given the city a great gift: self-sufficiency. Keld does not need to rely on any outside influences to survive. Our successes come from within, our strength in numbers. We look out to the rest of the world and see hidden potential, for those who live outside our walls have yet to experience the glory that is Keld! This nation has been divided, even though you don't realize it. I feel I have failed in that regard, that the upper class and nobility have lost sight of their roots, become out of touch with the more common folk. And, in reverse, the average person has become so far-removed from the rich that they feel no connection with their fellow countrymen! I am ashamed, as you should be as well. We must all be united together, for we all have the same blood in our veins. Ignorance and obliviousness has impacted the world—much more than you will ever know."

299

The crowd began to murmur, never before hearing their emperor speak ill of any of them or their empire. But still, they held their attention on his every word, knowing—hoping—that whatever he was getting at would make sense in the end. For their entire lives, the citizens of Keld, and the Vrelin Empire, had lived under the notion that they were prosperous, tolerant, and obedient. Everyone in the nation did their duty to home and country, and only wanted to make their emperor proud. And yet—he was telling them it wasn't enough. That he wasn't satisfied with them, or their hard work. The residents began to feel uneasy.

"We are on the precipice of a new Keld, a new empire! My father would have resisted outside help. Balked had anyone dared to suggest another hand stirring the pot could be anything more than an unwelcome intrusion. Well—" Roann's voice deepened, his face falling slack with a stern expression. "...I am not my father."

Silence fell over the crowd, flags no longer waving. Parents took their children down from their shoulders as their emperor's voice took on a dark undertone. Their attention went to the skies, where the vibrant pinks and purples of the sunset had been replaced with shadowy, ominous clouds seemingly out of nowhere. When they turned their attention back to Roann a moment later, his eyes had gone black.

"Keld! Embrace this change which is presented before you! Relish in the fact that you bear witness to the rebirth of the empire! Never again will I be compared to my father! Today we fulfill our collective destiny!"

Lightning crackled from the swirling clouds above the square, thunder boomed seconds later. With the sun blotted out, an eerie twilight fell over the city. The wind shrieked as it tore banners from their poles high above. The ground trembled. People screamed and tried to run. The guards, unsure of whether to run themselves, or stay and do their sworn job, reluctantly tried to keep the panicky crowd in line.

"My loyal subjects, do not be afraid!" Roann reassured his terrified citizens. His hair whipped around his face. "Dawn is upon us!"

A guard, fiercely protective of his emperor, ran up the staircase to ensure the sovereign would remain unharmed by the whirling wind and erratic lightning. Halfway up the stairs, he was struck down by a swoop of Roann's hand, electricity fanning out from his fingertips. The guard's body, smoking and sizzling, his flesh charred beneath his armor, clattered down the staircase and came to a gruesome halt at the bottom. Horrified citizens backed away, unable to move more than a few feet in any direction. The remaining guards, suddenly fearful for their lives if they were to run, tried to calm the residents. A man vomited on the cobblestones.

A spectral gale howled across the promenade, energy crackling through the air. A red-tinged aura lingered as the wind died down. The hairs on the necks of all in attendance stood on end. The air temperature soared to furnace-like heat before plummeting seconds later to near freezing. A crimson cloud flew above their heads, blowing their hair and hats alike. The square was bathed in a haunting red illumination, seemingly emanating from nowhere and everywhere at the same time. A giant fireball exploded beside the emperor, the young man never flinching. Left in its wake, a humanoid form appeared from within the smoke.

The crowd's collective heavy, panic-stricken breathing was music to Roann's ears as Lyrax revealed himself. The euphoric energy was almost orgasmic. Waves of pleasure coursed through his veins and washed over his body. Relishing in the discomfort of his subjects, he couldn't wait to see how they reacted next. He puffed his chest out with pride and moved to introduce his master to his people. Lyrax said nothing as he glided right past the young man without a second glance. Roann's ecstasy was abruptly cut off as Lyrax ignored him. He scowled, his black eyes boring into the necromancer's back as he approached the crowd.

They cowered before him, too terrified to run, too terrified to stay. Frozen in place, they watched in horror as an unfamiliar man with the skin pallor of death and the aura of undeserving royalty stood at the crest of the staircase. Red mist swirled around him, licking his bald head and fluttering the royal robes of the late Emperor Artol resting on his shoulders. He smoothed them down when he came to a halt, a sickening smirk gracing his lips as he did so. Lyrax knew he had arrived.

"People of Keld...*my* people! Mine is a name that you know, yet do not— sullied as those who hated me worked to expunge my memory from existence. My tale bastardized as history forgot me! Your reluctance to remember the misgivings of the past has resulted in my resurgence!" He walked from side to side, the royal vestments billowing around his thin body. He used his hands as he talked, gesturing wildly as he became more and more fervent. "The former king of Ashal refused to see the light, refused to accept his fate—and paid for it with his life. As did his people. If you value the hearts that beat in your chests, you will not be as foolish. I am here to rightfully reclaim what was taken from me centuries ago! My life—extinguished because of ignorance! Taken by magic users!"

The crowd gasped at the utterance of the forbidden art.

"Yes, magic! You are right to fear magic—just as you will fear *me*. And my young protégé as well." He gestured to Roann, who found new pride within his former scorn. His disdain for Lyrax' earlier disrespect disappeared. "You've spent your lives in fear of the unknown, fear of the magical monsters you were forced to believe in! Look upon me! Look upon Roann! See that which you feared, and realize you were correct! Your nightmares shall unfold before your very eyes!"

Lyrax raised his hands high into the air, the blue robes of the Keld monarchy sliding down his emaciated limbs. He shot lightning into the sky. "You will bow to me— or face my wrath! No one will ever forget the name Lyrax again!"

People, men and women alike, sobbed in the crowd. Children begged their parents to make the scary man go away. Realizing retrospectively that their fates were sealed the moment Roann took his father's crown; some took matters into their own hands. A group of men, no more than ten-deep, had been huddling within the masses, plotting their act of heroism. With a hearty battle cry, they burst through the wall of people and raced up the stairs, daggers pulled and at the ready.

Lyrax sighed in irritation and struck them down with a mere flick of his wrist. They fell in place, their bodies bursting into flames. Smoldering at the foot of the staircase, close to the deceased guard Roann had dispatched, they lay as a stark warning against revolution.

"Death comes quickly to those who disobey. Glorious, dishonorable death."

With a silent nod to his young pawn, the necromancer commanded him to bring forth their next surprise. Roann concentrated his mental energy and, cocooned within twin wisps of smoke, summoned both his mother and Morigar from the dungeons. Chained and terrified, they appeared before the crowd, magically plucked from their prison cells and dragged through the chaos of the inner dimension.

Eilith instantly collapsed as she materialized, Morigar rushing to her side despite shackled feet. He tried to wrap a comforting arm around her only to find himself being torn away by a strong-armed emperor. She screamed as her son forced his body between them, knocking her down in the process. Roann's eyes flared, Morigar becoming lost in their ebony depths as he was flung aside. Landing awkwardly on his side, he was unable to move before his emperor was on him again, shoving him in front of Lyrax and commanding him to kneel. Morigar immediately pleaded with the crowd to pray for the lost soul of their once-beloved monarch.

"Kneel! Beg the Goddess to help this misguided man! He is no longer our emperor!" The crowd did as Morigar had done and fell to their knees. Eilith pressed her hands together, shackle chains clanking, and immediately began to mutter her own pleas. She refused to look at her son. The cleric continued, "He has betrayed us all!" He stared up, past Lyrax, to the sky. "Oleana! Please show mercy upon Roann! Save his soul and restore order! Banish this devil," he motioned with chained hands to Lyrax, "and allow us the peace you desire!"

Lyrax laughed, a menacing smirk crossing his gray lips. "So, you want to pray? Wonderful! See what your prayers can do!" Lyrax telepathically sent Roann the command to change his shape. Sensing his master's order, Roann obeyed in the most spectacular of fashions.

Standing at the apex of the grand staircase, Roann began his transformation. Mist swirled around him and his human features disappeared. Growing another foot over his six-foot frame, his body changed from human to monster with smooth ease.

As leathery wings erupted from his scaled back, a woman in the front of the crowd fainted, her husband barely catching her before her head hit the paving stones. An elderly man screamed *'demon!'* as razor sharp fangs began to emerge from his beastly mouth. Women shrieked at the new appearance of their emperor, shielding their children's eyes. When the transformation was complete, he stood proud, hot puffs of air shooting from his devilish nostrils. He tapped his toe talons on the marble staircase.

Morigar looked on the man he had once known and loved like a son with betrayed eyes. He clasped his hands together in front of his body and rose, the monster towering over him. He craned his neck upwards in an attempt to make eye contact. "What have you become, my child? Why have you abandoned yourself? History surely would have remembered you for your purity and valor, and now all that will be writ—"

Without a second thought, Roann took Morigar's head off with one swipe of a clawed hand. His body limp, it fell to the ground, blood spilling from his neck and pooling underneath his white robes. The head rolled down the staircase, coming to rest alongside the rest of the carnage.

"Oswin!" Eilith screamed, the crowd following suit. Children cried out, burying their faces in the gowns of their mothers. Roann defiantly kicked the lifeless decapitated body of Father Morigar. Lyrax moved on the hysterical empress, grabbing her roughly by the arm and dragging her to her feet.

"Which fate do you prefer? I am offering you your lives in exchange for your loyalty. The choice is this—" He shook Eilith forcefully, eliciting a pained gasp from her trembling lips. "...or *that.*" He pointed to Morigar's corpse. "You may view death as the easy way out. But I assure you it is not."

He released Eilith, and she crumpled to the ground, sobbing. Moving beside Morigar's body, he closed his eyes and spread his hands wide. Mumbling an ancient incantation, Lyrax trembled as red tendrils of mist ebbed from his fingertips. Morigar's fingers twitched as forbidden energy soaked into his pores. A moment later, his corpse rose from the ground and stood, headless and shaky. It took a few shuffling steps at Lyrax' command. The citizens of Keld wailed at the sight.

"Death is not eternal. Death is my ally. For those who seek it, shall have it granted to them—only to serve me for eternity. I have embraced death, surrounded myself in its bliss. You would be wise to do the same." Flicking his wrist toward Morigar's bastard zombie, the form crumpled to the ground and turned to dust. "That man was tainted. His service to his bitch goddess made him worthless to me. But do not fear—your pitiful beliefs in Oleana will not hinder your ability to be my underlings. For I know, deep down, you're all sinners. And I like sinners..." Lyrax laughed maniacally.

As the wind blew Morigar's charred, ashy remains into the square, Lyrax once again stood at the center of the staircase. The same mist shot from his fingertips, and like a cascading chain, engulfed each guard he had struck down upon his arrival. The smoke even floated down to the soldier Roann had eliminated in a fiery display. In succession, as the spectral miasma penetrated their lifeless bodies, they rose. Their flesh was charred and peeling, their eyes haunting and black. They took in no breaths and experienced no heartbeats. Shuffling and swaying in their zombified stupor, they mindlessly picked up their fallen weapons and moved to surround the crowd.

Roann stood behind Lyrax, his statuesque wings flapping languidly. The crowd was silent, their cries having long since been squelched. They no longer had anything to cry about. They understood that no amount of fighting could save them. Citizens looked on blankly, surrendering their will.

"Now you choose, dear people of Keld! Obey me and live—or revolt and be doomed to walk the land as undead until I require your service."

The square was silent, no one daring to utter a sound. So, when Eilith's voice cut through the oppressive quiet, the crowd was unwilling to gasp in shock, unknowing as to what might happen to her for her betrayal.

"This is all my fault..."

Lyrax' head snapped in her direction, ready to strike her down for speaking out of turn. Roann slid away from him and moved to his mother's side, still in his beastly form.

"Go ahead, *mother*. Tell the people about...*me*." Roann's inhuman voice hummed in his chest. He grabbed her by the arm, his claw digging into her soft bicep. Blood trickled down and stained her dingy gown. "Let them know the truth."

Eilith shook her head with sadness. "This...*monster* you see before you today, this abomination—should have never seen his first birthday. After so much heartbreak. The loss of so many babies. Artol and I didn't want to admit that our last chance at having a child—an heir—had been destroyed by...*magic.*"

The crowd gasped, their first audible sound since Lyrax had reanimated the garrison of guards. Eilith continued, her voice quivering.

"Yes—my son was born with magic. We tried everything possible to rid him of his evil. His destiny was cemented hours after his birth, when his bassinette caught fire, the surge coming from his tiny body. It devastated me, broke his father. We should have let him wither and die right then and there. But after all we had been through, losing our beautiful baby was not an option. We kept him hidden, assuring the citizens everything was fine—that we were protecting his immune system from the oncoming autumn. We tried everything to stifle and hide his curse: talismans, mantras, alchemy. But in the end, we were left with only one option."

She focused on Lyrax, eyes burning with disdain. "I know it was you who sent that witch doctor." She spat the last two words, pure vitriol accompanying the title. "It was *you* who promised us a 'cure'. It was *you* who took my son from me."

Lyrax smiled boastfully. "You flatter me."

Eilith licked her dry, chapped lips. Her makeup, dull and worn from days of imprisonment, ran in streaks down her face with her tears. "We were given false hope, a promise our darling son would no longer suffer the stigma of forbidden powers. A clean bill of health after only a days' work seemed unbelievable, and yet—it happened. Placed back in my arms, I touched his tiny hand—and was greeted with only silken skin, not fiery flames. Artol and I were forever indebted to the person who saved him. I swear to you all, we never realized what we had done. I envy my husband now, not forced to witness the repercussions of the mistake we made."

She turned to Roann, swallowing hard. "My heart is broken, but it is the burden that I alone must carry. I was a coward and have now doomed my people to damnation." She faced the crowd, her hands clasped in front of her body in a gesture of desperation. "He's not the man you thought he was...the son that I thought I had raised. He is not your emperor—he is evil incarnate. I beg you to stand up and revolt against him! Stop him before it's too late!"

"Are you quite done, little woman?" Lyrax looked down on her with pity in his eyes.

Eilith didn't respond, and instead hung her head in shame, refusing to look at the people she had betrayed thirty-two years ago. She waited for the public execution she was certain was coming.

"You've heard her admission of guilt! She chose a mother's love over an empress' duty." Lyrax clicked his tongue in a scolding manner and shook his head. "This isn't the type of leader you deserve. A cowardly woman with a dead husband, just as much a coward as she was! I will usher in a new destiny for this empire, one that my young protégé here dutifully readied for my arrival. All the prosperity and success he created—it was for me! I was exiled in my past life, forced to hide for my 'crimes'. No more!"

Lyrax stood silent for a long moment, watching the people cower at the base of the staircase, their expressions of terror mixed with acceptance. They knew there wasn't a fight to be had.

Now satisfied that Eilith realized the truth, he took a deep, satisfying breath through his nose before he commanded the attention of the people once more. "I said before that you all had a choice, dear people of Keld. But I lied…"

Lyrax threw his arms wide and unleashed a massive bow of energy, blasting across the square with unimaginable force. The wave crackled, white-hot plasma surging forward. It sought victims, tendrils choosing terrified citizens as they tried desperately to run. Overtaking the people in the front half of the crowd almost instantly, it burned their bodies beyond recognition, their charred corpses falling into gruesome heaps.

The middle of the group watched in dazed horror as the arc came for them, knocking them to their knees. Some prayed to Oleana instead of running, leaving their fates to the goddess. As the wave washed over them, the searing heat covered the crowd, leaving most with horrible burns. The lucky ones died instantly. The unfortunate languished for several minutes as their bodies smoldered.

At the back, were the citizens knocked unconscious by the force of the blast, cascades of blood instantly pouring from their noses, mouths, and ears. In a matter of minutes, they would bleed to death. The sickening stench of singed flesh lingered over the eerily silent promenade. Eilith screamed in horror, cursing her son's name as he sent her back to her prison cell in a cloud of mist.

~~~

When the call to the square had been made, Isum Dran joined the masses, keeping a position near the back of the crowd. He listened to Roann speak, heard his voice as he praised the people for their incredible work on the harvest. But he knew something was amiss. Perhaps it was the years he had trained the boy—then man. Call it a fighter's intuition or a sixth sense, but Dran knew he needed to leave.

He contemplated alerting the citizens, but he more than likely would have been accosted for speaking ill of the sovereign or interrupting an official function. Realizing if he wanted to escape with his life, he would ultimately need to sacrifice theirs. He didn't know what sort of danger they faced, but he was worldly enough to know when his gut told him to go—he went.

Isum slunk down an alley and headed toward the outskirts of town. He hadn't made it more than one-hundred feet when clouds overtook the sun and the citizens began to scream.

He didn't look back.

Taking quick steps, he darted behind buildings in order to avoid anyone's eyes. He figured everyone had gone to the square like good citizens, but he needed to ensure he made it away from the fray safely all the same. Knowing he probably couldn't get out the city gates, he got close enough anyway, just to make sure. And, like he thought, they were locked tight, chained to trap the unsuspecting residents of Keld.

In their tomb.

Making a beeline for the access tunnel he knew led out of the city, he pried open the loose grating and jumped inside, his senses immediately inundated with the stench of sewage. Walking the first dozen or so feet, the pipe ultimately dove underground to exit the city, and Isum found himself on his stomach, fighting to keep his chin and mouth out of the rancid liquids sloshing beneath him. As his shining ring became caked in muck, he was reminded of his duty—a duty bestowed upon him so long ago it was hard to fathom just how much time had actually passed. Isum shuddered at the thought that history appeared to be repeating itself.

The hair on the back of his neck stood on end as a massive pressure wave popped his ears. In an instant, he could no longer hear the din of the crowd.

Pushing on, he finally exited the city far outside the boundaries, where the sewer line flowed into a small tributary. The clouds over Keld were black as night, spreading out to the countryside and casting eerie shadows over the prairie. Knowing he needed to get as far from the city as possible, he ran downstream and into the forest. His clothes dripping with mucky, putrid water, he circled the metropolis around to the north, where he knew there was a small pier—with a boat he kept for pleasure fishing.

Today, it would be his salvation.

He said a quick prayer to Oleana for a safe journey and pushed off for Zaiterra. Using his mighty strength against the barrage of ocean waves, he maneuvered the vessel out into deeper waters, the shoreline drifting further and further away with each stroke.

The clouds over Keld never lifted.

~~~

His legs were burned.

His arms were burned.

His face, chest, and back...all badly burned.

With each excruciating step, the man pushed himself to the brink of collapse. He knew he had to find someone. He had to get away. He had to—tell the world what had happened in Keld.

Pieces of charred flesh dropping from his body, he forced himself onward. He briefly thought back to his wife and daughters, incinerated by the terrifying wave. Crawling over their bodies to escape the horrors. Unable to fathom why he had been spared, he cried out in both agony and despair, cursing the goddess for allowing such heartbreak to befall him.

A whinny in a grove of trees caught his attention. There stood a lone horse, a ratty saddle resting on its back. Looking around and finding no owner, he cautiously approached, forcing his battered body to move. Heaving himself onto the animal's back with an agonized scream, he used his remaining strength to hike the reins. He steered the mare south, hoping he would make it to Dungannon before he perished.

INTERLUDE TWO

The room was dark.

Outside, the morning sun shone brightly, enveloping the city of Keld in a warm, late-summer blanket of illumination. People went about their daily lives on the streets below, still ecstatic that they had a new heir to the throne sleeping peacefully in the rooms above.

Within the dimly-lit chamber, the drapes drawn to blot out the sunlight and dull the din of the city, Empress Eilith wept. A baby's shrill cries echoed from another room, the sound blocked by the heavy wooden door that separated mother and child. Emperor Artol paced nervously, chewing on his thumbnail. Eilith didn't have the fortitude to scold him for his habit today.

The heir to the Vrelin throne, barely six weeks old, had thrust his parents into quite the predicament. When, within hours of his birth, his mother had witnessed his bassinette become engulfed in flames emanating from the baby's own hands, the suddenly grief-stricken parents knew they had very little time in which to act.

Born with magic.

Shunned.

Cursed.

The empress hung talismans from every hook in the royal apartments, draped the nursery with charm scrolls and wards. Emperor Artol chanted mantras gleaned from forbidden texts in the palace library all in an attempt to rid their precious son of his magical stigma.

Nothing had worked.

Left with the horrible decision of whether or not to let their own child die of starvation rather than live a life of ostracism, hope arrived in the form of a letter, literally fluttering in on the wind through an open window.

The so-called 'witch doctor', the letter had claimed, promised to cure the royal child of his magical ailment, under the strictest of secrecy. How this enigmatic man knew of their plight was a mystery, but he nonetheless knew—and made his living ensuring that children born with the stigma were given a chance to have a normal life, should his work succeed. Unfortunately, unbeknownst to his clients, he always failed. Grieving parents would thank the man for attempting the impossible, and move on to mourn babies that never had a chance to begin with. Families were assured their secrets would be safe, for the witch doctor did not want his identity revealed any more than the people that accepted his help.

That morning, before the sun had crested the horizon, the man had arrived at the palace under the cover of extreme secrecy. Snatching the baby from his mother's arms, he dashed into the nursery with strict instructions not to be disturbed. Whatever was meant to happen, would happen.

Now, two hours later, all Empress Eilith could do was clutch a baby quilt in her shaking hands and listen to her infant son cry in the other room.

~~~

The blonde-haired baby feverishly kicked his legs, his face ruddy from wailing. Flickering flames danced in the air around him, the barrier erected by the witch doctor keeping the infant safe from his own creations.

The drapes were pulled shut, the only light enveloping the room coming from a few oil lamps, set to the dimmest flames. Colorful murals covered the walls: fantastical animals from far-off lands, images to enrich a growing young mind. Stars peppered the ceiling, lovingly painted by the emperor himself. In the dim light of the now-melancholy room, it was difficult to see that such happiness even dared to exist. All this room knew now was sadness—disparaging sadness that consumed grieving parents.

In the corner sat the witch doctor, deep in mediation. Contacting his master was hard enough without a screaming child in the background. He had been concentrating since he entered the room and unceremoniously plopped the baby into his crib, trying to make a connection across the continents. Even having been born with magical power himself, it took years of training to be able to reach his mind out to find the one he sought.

A chill finally ran down his spine, and the small hairs on his arms stood on end. A presence invaded his mind.

"…Master…I think this is the one…"

…there have been many…

"…This child is royalty. His powers are incredible, even in his infancy. And…"

…and?…

"…There is a witching stone…"

…splendid…a conduit …could it be that I've finally found what I seek?…

"…I have no misgivings, Master. This child will serve you willingly…"

…we shall see…connect me…

The mysterious man approached the witching stone, keeping an eye on the screaming baby beside him. He picked it up, warmth washing over his body. Moving to the crib, he plunged his arm through the fires and placed his free hand on the child's heaving chest. He curled his fingers around the gem, concentrating all his mental energy into his connection. Never had he attempted such a feat, but he knew he could not fail. After a long moment of deep breaths and intense meditation, the connection flared to life, the stone glowing a vibrant red—much different from its inherent rosy hue. Feeling an unnatural aura envelop him, the witch doctor suddenly became very nervous, and almost accidentally broke the conduit of power. His skin felt as if it were on fire as spectral energy possessed the gem, ensuring that it would always act as a private channel between the child and his new master. The baby convulsed under his hand, his tiny lungs struggling to breathe. He gurgled and contorted his face in pain. The flames surrounding the cradle slowly lost their strength. Several seconds passed, the gem in the man's fingers becoming red-hot. Knowing he'd more than likely be killed if he let go, he forced himself to keep his fingers curled around the stone. Finally, the gem flared brightly, bathing the room in white light, before dimming once more.

The stone sat unassumingly in his palm, having returned to the original pink color, once again cool to the touch. The baby still shrieked, his tiny voice becoming hoarse from hours of distress. The witch doctor waited.

A minute passed, then another. Dim flames still flickered around the bassinette. Just when he was about to reach out to his master to ensure a connection had been made, the room temperature dropped and a thin, white fog enveloped the palace. A tendril of mist seeped in through an unseen crack in a wooden windowpane and made a beeline for the bassinette. As it approached, the fog took on a crimson hue, and enveloped the cradle.

The magic fires produced by the infant prince flashed blue before they disappeared.

The baby immediately stopped crying.

Outside the door, Emperor and Empress knew not if their child lived—or had perished.

~~~

Eilith held her son in her arms, the baby nursing under a silken shawl. She had thrown the curtains open, allowing the summer breeze and beautiful light to enter the now peaceful room. Artol and the man who had saved their son spoke quietly in the corner. The sun had begun to set, bathing the entire chamber in a warm, pink glow. The mysterious man smiled, his fake countenance belying his motives. He knew that this child no longer belonged to his parents. They would live their lives, enjoying their time with their only-born, raising him to be an emperor—completely ignorant of his lofty destiny, believing he had been freed of his magical curse.

Artol paid the man a hefty sum of sparkling gold coins. He took his leave, escorted out by a servant who knew him only as "a noble visitor", and exited the city proper. Once away from the hustle and bustle of Keld, he disappeared into the forest and awaited his true reward.

Days later, hunters would come across the charred remains of a man beneath an oak tree. Burying the bones in a pauper's grave, the marker would never bear a name.

Betrayed by the master who no longer had need of him, he had died frightened and alone, cursing the day he ever agreed to help the man he knew by only one name.

Lyrax.

CHAPTER THIRTY-ONE

"The sky...black. Roann...Lyrax...everyone burned. I pray for...death...to come quickly now..."

--Last words of an unknown Keld survivor, as told to Reina Traevels of Dungannon, at the moment of his death.

"Ryris! Are you in there? It's horrible...!"

Grildi came barreling into the tiny roadside inn, Jaric hot on his heels. Ryris and Kaia sat at a common table, finishing the last of a light lunch the innkeeper's wife had insisted on preparing for them. The companions were always amazed at the hospitality of the people they encountered—and their insistence on cooking for them. They must have been quite charming—or looked severely underfed.

"What's the matter?" Ryris set down his half-eaten sandwich and stood, trying to calm his friend with a passive gesture. Kaia also rose. Grildi's face was red, his breathing erratic from running. "Take a deep breath and calm down."

Jaric came to a stop beside the hulking man, more capable of holding conversation. "A carrier bird just landed..." He furrowed his brow and lowered his voice. "...Keld has fallen."

"What do you mean, *fallen?*" Ryris' lunch immediately bubbled up in his stomach.

Jaric looked to Kaia, his expression regretful. "You were right."

Her voice was hushed as she reluctantly responded. "Lyrax..."

"...and Roann." Grildi bowed his head. "They killed them..."

"How?" Kaia slumped down into her chair, her shoulders sagging in sadness.

"No one really knows." Jaric took a seat beside her. The raucous din of the small community outside hearing the horrible news was becoming louder by the moment. "A few people managed to escape the city and told tales of a winged creature—Roann—doing the bidding of a madman. He named himself as Lyrax. He..." The warrior hesitated, trying to keep his composure. "...Goddess bless us, he...killed Roann's royal guards and brought them back to life right before the crowd's eyes."

"Necromancy." Kaia remained composed, even when faced with her terrifying realization.

"…and shape shifting," Jaric added.

"I told you it was horrible!" Grildi pulled out a seat, turned it backwards, and sat with a great thud. "All those people…"

"But just how did he kill them *all*?" Ryris was morbidly curious, even as his mind thought of poor Mrs. Briarheart and her wife. Never again would he taste her seafood chowder, or have fresh flowers delivered for his table. He'd never hear her voice, scolding but sincere, telling him to keep hydrated and wear a hat in the rain. A wave of intense sadness washed over him, not only for Mrs. Briarheart, but for everyone in Keld.

"No one knows. The few surviving eyewitnesses were too badly burned to speak clearly." Jaric's tone was somber.

"Burned?" Ryris felt sick. What had happened to all those poor, innocent people?

"All we do know is there's no life within those walls anymore. Lyrax and Roann have wiped the city clean."

The party sat in silence for a moment, half-listening to the sobs of the people outside as they processed the news, half-trying to keep calm themselves. When Ryris finally spoke up, his voice trembled. He tried desperately not to cry.

"What do we do?"

"Deep down part of me wanted to be wrong. But…" Kaia let out a defeated sigh. "…we need to accept that this world is now at war. Lyrax and Roann won't stop until we bring them to their knees."

"It's really happening." Ryris pushed his plate away, no longer motivated to finish his lunch. He did drain his ale mug, however, and beckoned to the bartender to bring him another.

"Yes, it is." Kaia briefly laid her hand atop his and paused. "Soon, this world will see chaos and destruction the likes of which haven't been seen since the Old War— and the people are not prepared for what they'll experience. Death will sweep across the land. I only hope we can stop them before it goes too far."

Jaric thumped his fist on the table with a determined grunt. "Then we better get off our asses and find the rest of those shards. We can't be plowing into Keld with half a sword."

Kaia nodded in agreement. "I need to contact Phia." She turned her attention to the alchemist. "Ryris, do you have a sleeping potion in your backpack?"

"I think so. If not, I can easily make one."

313

"Good. The moon is almost new, so cross your fingers I can connect via the witching stone."

"Do you think she'll be able to help?"

"I don't know. She's had some time to think about where the shards could have been hidden; perhaps she's come up with something. If anything, she can lend an encouraging voice." She stood, blowing out a determined breath. "We need to make sure everything is in order before tomorrow. Grildi, head to the mercantile and buy fresh supplies. Ryris, make sure your alchemy kit is well stocked. Make extra potions if you have the time. Jaric and I will begin to strategize. Above all, we need to stay calm. As the world finds out their beloved sovereign has taken league with the devil, morale will fall and people will become disparaged. They'll need something to latch on to, a thin thread of hope. That's us."

"Those are pretty lofty goals, Kaia." Ryris' eyes were sad.

"Who else will accept the challenge? We may not seem like much right now—just the four of us—but believe me when I say that I have the utmost faith in not only ourselves, but the people of the empire."

"Blind faith doesn't always pan out."

"Neither does skepticism. If we're to succeed, we need to believe in ourselves without question. Others will sense our doubt if we're not confident, and we'll end up fighting alone."

Ryris nodded slowly, knowing that Kaia's words were correct. He prayed Oleana would grant them protection and success. Failure was not an option.

Kaia walked toward the door, her commanding voice getting the daydreaming alchemist's attention. "Get a move on. We leave at dawn."

~~~

Kaia lay in her bed at the inn. Sleet pelted her window, and she shivered. Pulling the blankets around her body like a cocoon, she couldn't stop her mind from racing.

What if they failed?

What if Lyrax succeeded this time and wiped the lands clean with his bastard magic?

What if...

...she watched helplessly while those she loved were murdered before her very eyes?

Kaia shuddered at the thought, forcing herself to push those horrible images from her mind. She rolled over and grabbed the small vial from Ryris off of the nightstand. Prying out the cork, she downed the liquid in one gulp, per the alchemist's instructions. The entire team was counting on her to be able to connect with Phia. Quickly feeling her eyelids begin to flutter, she sighed as contentedly as she could despite the current situation the party faced, and allowed sleep to finally overtake her. Her fingers curled around the witching stone she held against her heart.

As she drifted into her dreams, the tiny filaments within the gem began to glow. With the moon not quite new, it would be more difficult to attempt a channel through the night, but she didn't have a choice. Time was of the essence.

A strange pull tugged at her mind. She allowed herself to be taken via dream conduits—somewhere. Feeling weightless as she floated over the currents of time and space, not once did she feel frightened by her experience. It was as if something—or someone—was beckoning her with open arms and a free mind.

At once, her eyes snapped open and she was standing in the swamps, clad in her thin nightgown. Kaia heard Phia's voice before she could see her.

"Well, the witching stones work."

The warrior smiled softly in the dim light. Watching as the giantess shuffled out of the gray mists toting her walking stick, she immediately noticed that Phia's eyes were no longer milky white. As the hulking woman approached, her face morphed into a broad, surprised smile, and she moved faster, her arms out to embrace Kaia.

"I can see you, child!"

Moisture sparkled in the corner of Phia's eyes, now a vibrant blue. She ran her fingertips down Kaia's face before smoothing a hand through her hair. Taking a long moment to inspect every inch of her features, Phia couldn't control her emotions. Tears flowed like a waterfall as she saw Kaia for the very first time.

"You're beautiful, my dear. All this time, all my life without sight—I never wanted it, never needed it. And now, looking at you standing before me, I lament my time in the darkness." She quickly took in the sights around her. "That witching stone gave me a gift here in our dreams, and I selfishly do not want it to end. But…I fear you are here with dire news." Her smile faded, her bright eyes grew concerned. "Tell me what troubles you."

"We were right." Kaia's voice was hushed, her eyes laden with sadness. "About Roann, about Lyrax. They've slaughtered the people of Keld in what can only be a show of force—or insanity."

"It can be both." Phia took her hand and led her to a fallen log. She sat with a tired grunt, encouraging the young woman to do the same. The withered wood sagged underneath her substantial weight. "Mania manifests itself in many ways. Killing the citizens may have been premeditated or spur-of-the-moment, for Lyrax is definitely a madman. Let's pray to Oleana the residents never knew what hit them—although I fear they were wholly terrified long before their demise."

"The war has begun, hasn't it?"

"The war started the moment Lyrax took possession of Roann." Phia furrowed her brows in thought. "You must hurry at once. Working with Jaric and Ealsig is the only way to raise the army you so desperately need."

"Phia…" Kaia sighed sadly. "…Ealsig is dead."

Phia's expression sobered. "What happened?"

"Senseless tragedy, I'll spare you the details. We…freed her from her misery. She's at peace now."

"You did right by her. I know it must have been difficult."

"I feel as if I've lost a sister."

"But you've gained a companion, haven't you?"

Kaia's thoughts turned to Ryris, and what he would surely face going forward. She was a warrior, Jaric was a warrior—and Ryris, he was a simple alchemist. He would see terrible things in the coming times: bloody deaths, citizens fighting for their lives, and villages razed. Months ago, he knew nothing of conflict. He had lived a happily ignorant life in his town, trained in his craft from birth, only spreading his wings to the big city after a long tenure at his father's side.

"He's not ready."

Phia nodded in agreement. "Perhaps. But he hasn't a choice in the matter any longer. There comes a time in a man's life where he must face fears, and learn to take hold of his destiny."

"What if he gets killed? I've been taught all my life to keep my emotions off of the battlefield and now…"

"Sometimes emotion is what keeps you grounded when all seems lost."

"I'm afraid that my attachment to him will hinder me—hinder us."

"Love is a powerful thing, Kaia. Don't fight it."

Kaia waved her hands dismissively in front of her body. "I don't know if I'd go so far as—"

"I may be old and alone now, but I once loved deeply. He was taken from me too soon, before I was able to admit to both of us that my heart belonged to him."

Kaia sat dumbfounded. Up until this point she thought she had done a decent job at keeping her emotions at bay. She barely had enough time in the day to keep the party alive, much less cater to the will of the butterflies in her stomach every time she caught Ryris stealing a glance in her direction.

Ryris.

Kaia sighed deeply as it hit her. She was truly smitten—and she didn't understand why. He was goofy, plain-looking, and had courage that came in inconsistent spurts. He most certainly wasn't the type of man she had been attracted to so long ago. But there was something about him that made her cheeks flush—even when she was annoyed by his slow pace or unwillingness to charge into the unknown.

He comforted her when she needed it.

He made her laugh.

He paid attention to her for her mind—not her prowess with a bow or ample bosom.

She shook her head in disbelief. "Is it that obvious?"

Phia chuckled. "To me, yes. To men? To Ryris? More than likely not. But I can tell you this—he shares your feelings. I can hear it in his voice, sense his body language when he's around you. But he is nervous and very unwilling to admit his emotions—even more so than you. To him, you're a mystery. A woman unlike any he has ever encountered. I'm sure he's equal parts enthralled and terrified."

"I don't have time for love—if that's what this truly is. People get killed when warriors think with their hearts."

"You have to be the one to decide what's best for you. But allow me to give a piece of wisdom and be done with my 'motherly nagging.'" Phia's eyes wrinkled at the sides as she smiled gently. "Don't wait. War is terrible, and you never know what's around the next bend. You'll regret it for the rest of your life if you deny your feelings."

"Thank you, Phia. I'll keep that in mind."

"That's all I ask."

They sat quietly in the humid, dank marsh. The giantess wrapped a comforting arm around the soldier, Kaia leaning her head on her massive shoulder. Her mind raced, images of battles, blood, and magic infiltrating her thoughts. In all the conflicts she had fought, with all the horrific things she had witnessed the last time around, she had never been as frightened as she was right now. She began to doubt her ability as a soldier, as a general. Would she be able to keep her team safe? Could they really band the people together and fight for their lives? Panic began to bubble in her chest, and she needed release.

"I'm scared, Phia." Kaia's tone was desperate as she blurted out into the swamp.

Phia tightened her embrace around the young woman. "To be afraid is to be alive. Fear is what motivates us: fear of the unknown, fear of not being in control, fear of death. The only way to quell those feelings is to face them head on."

Kaia sighed and patted her companion's giant arm before standing, crossing her arms over her chest as she stared out into the swamp. "What do I do now?"

"Finding the remaining shards of your sword is of the utmost importance. They may be your only hope in defeating Lyrax and Roann. You must keep them hidden, and ensure they stay safe, along with the hilt." Phia stood and joined the young lady, leaning her gargantuan hands on the pommel of her walking stick.

"We've been counting on blind luck to find the pieces we already possess. Roann and Lyrax could be doing the same thing."

"You assume they know about them, child. I believe you have an advantage. It's true that Lyrax was in the blast path of the sword and survived, but did he really know what hit him? Did he know where the energy came from?"

"It's possible..."

"If there is even a shred of possibility, then you need to make it your mission to find them first. If they come to possess even one shard..."

"And the army? Ryris is beginning to sound more right every day. How can we possibly raise garrisons of common folk?" Kaia's voice was laden with uncertainty.

"People will follow. They'll see salvation in you. I'd entrust my life to you in a heartbeat."

Kaia chuckled. "But you know me..."

"And soon the people will as well. Your father sealed you away to serve a very important legacy—and your time has come. Do him proud." Her tone turned very serious. "This is a task at which you cannot fail, dear. It's a huge responsibility to bear, but one that I know you can tackle."

"Promise me you'll stay safe."

"No one visits me, not even malicious hordes. I'll be fine. I may be blind, but I'm no pushover." She turned to face the young woman. "I'm forever grateful that you've returned to me, to the world. This is what you were destined to do, Kaia." Phia brushed a stray lock of hair from her cheek with a calloused fingertip. "I'll never forget the day I was able to see you with my own eyes—even if it was for just a few moments."

"I should go..."

Phia nodded. "In a little while. Stay and keep an old woman company for a bit longer? After all, you need your sleep."

The pair walked back to sit on the the mossy log and watched the swamp together.

~~~

Kaia awoke feeling no better than she had when she fell asleep. Yes, she had been able to talk with Phia, and admit her feelings and fears, but in the end, she was still left with nagging doubt and unfulfilled emotions. Unfortunately, Phia's encouraging words had done little to bolster her confidence. Taking a few calming breaths as she sat up and allowed her brain to focus on the new day, she vowed to herself to not falter. The team needed her, the world needed her. She had proven herself time and time again on the field of battle, in the world of tactics and strategy. This war would be no different, right down to the fact that a man named Ryris was fighting alongside her.

Except that it *was* different.

Past Ryris had been groomed for a life of magical service, trained to be a battlemage. He had labored for decades to ensure his skills would be up to par should the need for them arise. Sacrificing his own safety, he charged onto the battlefields and assisted his fellow countrymen until every last enemy had been purged.

Kaia shivered in the chilled room, instinctively looking to the door she knew the current Ryris was sleeping behind.

This new Ryris wasn't a soldier. He wasn't a battlemage. He wasn't even a wizard from a training standpoint. His powers were mostly untested; he didn't yet possess the skill set that his predecessor wielded. She feared for him, for what he was surely to face.

And Phia was right.

She did love him.

And that made everything much more complicated.

Kaia sighed in the dark room, the sun's rays just barely coloring the morning sky a beautiful lavender. Ice crystals flecked the glass panes, refracting the pale light. She glanced over to her crystal bow, leaned in the corner. It glittered, even in the low light. Seeing the weapon made a wave of pride wash over her, a sense of duty.

Throwing the covers aside, she bounded from her bed, jumping as her bare feet touched the cold stone floor. Today was the beginning of a new era. War was on the horizon. Standing in her thin nightclothes in the middle of her small room at the quaint little inn in the middle of nowhere, she vowed to protect the people, her friends— and her heart.

CHAPTER THIRTY-TWO

Born upper-class, Lyrax had all the means to succeed. And succeed he did—just not in the way his parents had hoped.

--Excerpt from journal of Eldrick Baynel, High Scribe of the Crystal Guard, date unknown.

Roann walked the empty streets of Keld.

Storefronts remained closed, the street lights unlit. The sun was setting, casting an eerie red glow on the buildings. Soon the city would be bathed in the low light of the moon, appearing as a razor-thin crescent in the night sky. The wind blew, scattering dried leaves within whirling vortices along the buildings, and causing unlocked shutters to bang against vacant windows.

Fruit in a hand cart rotted without its farmer to attend to it, perfuming the street with a sour-sweet fermented aroma. A few of the softened pieces of produce had fallen to the cobblestones, two tiny skellins munching on the juicy remains. Roann inhaled deeply, relishing in the scent of decay—and not only from the fruit.

He walked a few more blocks until he came to a grand junction of streets, turning his attention toward the palace square. The bodies on the promenade still lay where they fell, some incinerated beyond recognition, some bloating in the southern winter sun. Swarms of flies hovered just above the macabre mass, their buzzing the only sound audible in the silent city, save for the heels of Roann's boots clicking on the paving stones. Taking a moment to savor the result of Lyrax' ultimate power, he eventually moved on, continuing his parade.

A lone dog snuck out from an alleyway, taking a hesitant look at the only human he had seen in over a week. After a cautious moment, it jubilantly ran at Roann, tail wagging feverishly, only to be stopped dead in its tracks—incinerated with a flick of the emperor's wrist. The ashes billowed into the breeze. Roann scowled as some of the debris collected on his velvet doublet. Brushing the offending substance away with a grumble, he walked again, avoiding the smoldering pile of remains. He didn't want to sully his pristine leather boots.

Striding down a quaint street in the once-bustling business district, the emperor happened upon a shop he recognized. An expertly-made sign swung from simple iron hooks, the bolts creaking within the heavy wood. A small placard was nailed into the door, indicating the shop keep was out of town and that some select wares could be purchased down the street from another merchant. The windows were

320

cluttered; bottles and vials having collected what looked to be over a season's worth of dust.

Now, looking at the intricately-carved sign in the window, curiosity got the better of him, despite remembering how he felt the last time he visited this particular place. He decided to snoop in the shop belonging to Ryris Bren. Reaching a hand out to try the door, he was met with a jolt up his arm the moment his fingertips touched the heavy metal handle. Seconds later, Roann's world went black.

He saw crystal.

Magic.

A massive, smiling man.

Two warriors—one male, one female. Both battle hardened and brave.

A young man with stained fingers and a warm, inviting smile.

A velvet parcel, containing…

Roann awoke with a start, slumped up against the outside wall of the alchemy shop. Taking a moment to shake the faeries from his brain, he jumped up and immediately knew he had to report back to his master. He disappeared in a hail of sparks, no longer interested in his leisurely stroll around the dead city.

~~~

"Master?" Roann squinted as rays of light shone through the windows, Lyrax having thrown the regal blue drapes wide open. The square lay below, the open-air graveyard resting in the setting sun. Slowly approaching his former throne, he felt a twinge of jealousy when the necromancer appeared, donning the royal robes of the Vrelin Empire.

"Those are mine," Roann thought.

"Ah, my young protégé." Lyrax smirked, fanning his arms out to billow the heavy fabric around himself. "How do you like my outfit?"

Roann was determined to remain respectful, even though he wanted nothing more than to rip the robes—*his robes*—from Lyrax' body. Yes, the man was his master and power-giver, but those vestments were his, inherited upon his father's death. They belonged to the heir to the empire, not the new conqueror. Lyrax may be using the country as a base of operations, but the empire still very much belonged to Roann. Choosing not to respond to the previous query, the young emperor instead eagerly told his master what he had experienced.

"Master Lyrax, I've had a vision."

The necromancer stopped his parade, and shrugged the robes from his shoulders with a disrespectful huff. They fell to the floor, crumpled and undignified. "A vision? Of what?"

"I'm not sure. Crystal, magic, a group of companions? I...recognized one as the new alchemist from the city."

"Crystal?" Lyrax flew at the young man, grabbing him forcefully by the shoulders.

"M-master?"

"Have you forgotten everything I taught you?" Lyrax zoomed across the room, feet never touching the ground, and slammed Roann into one of the grand pillars supporting the ceiling. "The alchemist? Why do you think he appeared in your mind?"

Roann hesitated, instantly regretting never telling Lyrax about the incident in the shop months prior. At the time, he brushed it off as coincidence, even though his gut told him there was something off about the young man. And now, with Lyrax' thin fingertips digging into the flesh of his shoulders, he realized he was in for a world of hurt.

"I've...had a run-in with him before." The emperor instinctively winced, awaiting the blow he knew was surely coming. When Lyrax said nothing, he hesitantly continued. "I had a reaction to him in his shop the day we met. A handshake—and I was overcome."

Lyrax' lips tightened, the grayish flesh turning white with the pressure of his anger. He slammed Roann again, the emperor's head cracking against the carved stone.

"I didn't think it had any relev—"

The necromancer threw Roann aside like a doll, his body skidding to a halt on the ornate rug in front of the thrones. Unable to move fast enough to dodge out of the way, the young man was instantly tossed into the air by an unseen force, only to be slammed down again seconds later. Blood began to trickle from his ear from the force of the impact. The wind was knocked out of his lungs. Laying on the ground in a stupor, Roann tried to bring himself to his knees. Lyrax moved beside him, kicked him over, and placed a boot on his heaving chest. Roann struggled to catch his breath.

"Next time you feel something isn't relevant—ignore that sensation!" His voice was low and growling as he pressed his foot against Roann's body.

Staring up into Lyrax' black eyes, Roann realized that he had been spared. The necromancer could have easily killed him for his insubordination. He brought his hands up submissively, pleading for leniency. "Master...forgive me. I've made a terrible mistake."

322

Lyrax stared at him for a long moment, his eyes seething. Finally releasing the pressure of his foot from Roann's chest, he moved back and allowed the young man to get up. "Watch yourself."

The emperor swayed slightly as he slowly rose, the dizziness from the blow to his head impact slow to subside.

The necromancer stomped off and up the small set of stairs leading to the thrones. He sank down into the chair once belonging to Roann and stared at him. "Now, tell me of this alchemist."

Roann approached, staying out of Lyrax' striking range. He stood strong, hoping his sudden pounding headache wouldn't interfere. "His name is Bren, a transplant from Blackthorne. I made a cordial visit to welcome him to the city, and was overcome with sickness—a flash of energy that I can't describe—the moment I made contact with him."

"Bren...Blackthorne? That name..." Lyrax contemplated his thoughts for a moment before continuing. "And you're sure he is the one you saw in your vision?"

"Yes. The moment I touched the handle on his door, the same brilliant energy washed over me and I was rendered unconscious."

"And what of the crystal?"

Roann exhaled deeply before replying. "Flashes, really. Two warriors, with crystalline mail. And a large man with a club."

"I know nothing of him, but..." Lyrax rose and slowly strode toward the window as he replied. "...these warriors you speak of? They can only be from one place—one time."

"How?"

"That I don't know. But they are a threat, as is that alchemist. There's got to be a reason for a simple man like him to be allying with soldiers." Lyrax whirled around, his eyes boring straight into the young emperor. "You're sure there was nothing strange about him?"

"Nothing. His work is known throughout the empire, as is that of his father. From what I've heard, their family name goes back generations in the alchemical field."

"If you've had a reaction to him, it's all the evidence I need to prove that he needs to be silenced. And the fact that he's keeping company with a pair of soldiers from *that war*..." Lyrax' words spit like venom from his lips.

"What do you propose we do?"

"Having one or both of those soldiers on our side would be a great victory. The alchemist and the other man are useless, but those warriors…"

Roann hesitantly posed a question he hoped wouldn't get him in trouble. "How do we know they even exist? I may have imagined it. Hit my head on the door?"

"No." Lyrax shook his head. "No, this is not coincidence. That alchemist and those soldiers are out there, and they're going to be coming for us. You'll need to be prepared, of course."

Lyrax approached Roann, forcefully grabbing his arm. His bony fingers pressed into his sleeve and bruised the flesh beneath. He closed his eyes and both men were instantly enveloped in a green haze, static charges arcing across their clothing. Roann's entire body jolted as Lyrax breathed a word in a language he did not recognize. Soon, his hand released and the necromancer backed away.

"That alchemist shouldn't give you any more trouble." Roann rubbed his aching arm and stared at Lyrax questioningly. "When you see him next, you'll be pleasantly surprised. Be sure to rough him up a bit." Lyrax turned back to the window and stared out, the sun just setting behind the spire of Whitehaven. "Even though you have been a naughty boy recently, I think I shall give you another gift."

"Master?" The emperor cocked his head in confusion.

"A man has needs, does he not? Someone to confide in, to share the most…intimate of moments? A companion—who also happens to be a fierce warrior. Someone who will obey and be loyal to us both." Lyrax sighed confidently. He threw his arms wide, motioning to the city below him. "Find her, and bring her back to me. She will become ours—mine to do my bidding and yours…for whatever you want from her."

Roann smirked devilishly in the darkening room, licking his lips. It had been some time since he had enjoyed the company of a woman. "And what of the others?"

"Bring them back as well. A few playthings would be fun, don't you agree?" Lyrax laughed sinisterly.

"How will we turn her?"

"An enchantment. Simple, yet effective. Of course, you will have to consummate your relationship in order for the spell to be rendered complete."

Roann's eyes burned with lust. The thought of this mystery woman in his bed was almost too much for him to bear. A wave of desire washed over him. "We wouldn't want the spell to fail…"

"Ah, to be a young, virile man again. You will no doubt enjoy her." Lyrax sighed in satisfaction. "She will be yours, and in turn, mine."

324

Roann nodded in the darkness, the sun having dipped so far below the horizon that it no longer threw off sufficient light. He moved to stand beside his master, and they both stared out at the dead city of Keld.

~~~

The door to Bren's flew open, the lightning sparks blowing the lock clean out of the heavy wood.

Waiting for the smoke to clear, Roann entered, his senses once again assaulted by the overwhelming aromas of the ingredients. But this time, they did not bother him in the slightest. The shop was dark, and Roann remedied the problem by starting a fire on the hearth with a flick of his wrist. He no longer had to worry about the neighbors seeing him—for they all lay dead in the square.

Working efficiently, he went through the mental list of items Lyrax had bestowed upon him. It took him several moments to gather the necessary ingredients into a basket, but Ryris' handwritten labels were thankfully easy to read. Grabbing an empty bottle from behind the workbench, he wondered what his new plaything would be like. Her image had been misty and somewhat blurred, but her flowing blonde hair stood out. He wanted to run his fingers through her locks and tug in the throes of passion.

Carefully placing the vial that would contain the elixir into the basket, he felt a telltale tickle in his nose. The stench of dried flowers and musky insect thoraces was something he wouldn't miss. Before he could flash out of existence, he sneezed.

CHAPTER THIRTY-THREE

While putrid and gangrenous in appearance, the undead soldier is surprisingly hearty, and unwilling to fall unless the head is destroyed or removed.

--Field notes of unknown scribe, Old War

"If I never see another spider egg sac again, I'll die a happy man."

Ryris shook the webs from his hair as he swatted at his back, ensuring there weren't any hitchhikers on his clothing. He shuddered at the thought of the giant spider mother—and all her babies—they had just encountered. The battle had been fierce and had resulted in Grildi being bitten by one of her many offspring. Charred spider carcasses perfumed the air with an acrid, smoky scent. Thick, green blood splattered both warrior's crystal armor, as well as Grildi's supple tandlewood club. Ryris' shoes caked with sticky goo, he reached down and peeled a spiky leg from his pants.

At least they had been successful in finding their prize—a glittering shard of Kaia's sword. Ryris had to give credit to the people the King Galroy trusted to hide the pieces. Not one time had the hunt been easy. Whether it was bugs, crumbling caverns, or hordes of angry ghosts, they had ensured the shards would stay safe from anyone that shouldn't be looking for them.

Now, with the light of the forest just feet away, Ryris couldn't wait to be out of the cave. Fresh air assaulted his nostrils as they exited, and the entire party took a deep breath as they emerged into the woods.

"That place gave me the willies!" Grildi set his club against a tree and began to inspect the bite on his arm. Ryris, quick to react, fetched a vial of antidote from the wagon and instructed his friend to drink. Kaia and Jaric shed their armor, efficiently stowing it within crates in the back of the cart. Jaric grumbled audibly about not having time to clean the spider blood from the plates. Finally free of their armor and weapons, the two soldiers joined the alchemist and his massive friend. Seated on the forest floor, Grildi offered a small handful of nuts to both of them, which they accepted.

"Well, that's six now, right?" Grildi counted on his fingers.

"With four more still out there somewhere." Kaia tipped her canteen onto a small cloth, moistening it. She wiped it across her face and neck to remove the grime of the cavern. When she was finished, she drew the fabric over the surface of the shard in her lap, restoring it to its former brilliance after centuries of being kept in a spider's den.

"Four isn't so many!" The large man beamed hopefully.

"I like your optimism, Grildi." Kaia smiled warmly. "We could have used someone like you back in my t—"

She stopped suddenly, sniffing the air. Jaric sucked in a hissing breath, his concerned eyes meeting Kaia's. Ryris and Grildi just stared at each other, shrugging their shoulders. Taking a whiff of the air, Ryris didn't immediately know what they had reacted to.

And then it hit him.

Rotten flesh.

Kaia and Jaric jumped up and made a break for their weapons, leaned up against the wagon. Before they could reach them, both soldiers found themselves being blown back by a grand burst of energy. They landed at the other companions' feet, dazed. Kaia sluggishly tucked the sword shard into the back of her waistband.

"Your weapons won't do you any good."

Ryris recognized that voice. As the man emerged from the darkness of the deep forest and into the clearing, long blonde hair billowed around his face. Tall and lean, his attire was regal. A pair of thin katanas were strapped to his back, the crisscrossed hilts poking up just over his shoulders. His head held high, he approached the group.

"Roann..." The alchemist couldn't stop the words from escaping his lips in a hushed whisper. Grildi instinctively moved closer to his friend, shielding him from whatever was coming their way. The soldiers gingerly rose from the ground, Jaric immediately clenching his fists, ready to fight. If he couldn't get to his weapon, he'd go down swinging.

"Don't be rude, Mr. Bren. By all means, introduce me to your friends."

Ryris' amulet heated up, and he tried not to wince. He swallowed hard as the emperor approached. He knew this day was coming, when they'd finally come face-to-face with their enemy. But to have it happen out of the blue, when Ryris was sure their encounter would have been within the walls of Keld—needless to say he was caught off guard. They all were. Roann came to a stop before the small band of adventurers, crossing his arms over his chest.

"Surprised to see me?" When no one replied, he cocked his head confusedly and continued. "Saberstrike got your tongues? It's customary to answer a question that is posed to you, especially when it's asked by royalty."

Jaric snorted, Roann immediately shooting him a disgusted look.

"You're not royalty, you're a joke." Kaia stood tall, her voice matching her stance.

"Such harsh words from such a beautiful creature. You'll learn to watch your mouth." Roann focused his attention on her. He moved closer, leaning forward to smell her hair. "What were you doing in that cave? And just what do you have behind your back?"

Kaia spit in his face, her lips clenched white in defiance.

After wiping the moisture from his skin with a gloved palm, Roann grabbed her and pulled her close, wrapping a hand around her back. His fingertips ghosted over the shard in her waistband, and he removed it carefully. He scolded Kaia with a clicking tongue. "Hiding things from your emperor? Just what do we have here?"

"Nothing your pitiful mind could ever comprehend."

Roann laughed heartily before glancing down at his new prize. It glittered in the sunlight. "You're feisty. You didn't get your fancy little crystal boots dirty for a broken artifact, did you? Are there more pieces?"

Kaia glared at him in defiant silence.

Roann sighed and released her, pushing her unceremoniously to the ground. Jaric, having had enough of Roann's antics, charged at him, fists swinging. While the emperor was momentarily distracted, Kaia dashed for the wagon and liberated her bow. She quickly conjured an arrow of ice, aiming directly for Roann's chest. The projectile screamed through the air, only to be stopped by an invisible barrier. It shattered against the shield, the pieces melting onto the forest floor. Jaric slammed against the shield from the other side, stopping him in his tracks, utterly confused.

"I'm really not worth the trouble, dear. My legion will kill you if I give the word. Is whatever you're hiding really worth dying for? If you perish here, you come back as one of them." Roann pointed to his troop of guards, swaying beside him. Their eyes were vacant, their flesh putrid and gangrenous. Garbled moans periodically escaped their lips. "If you cooperate, you get to live—for now."

Knowing it was a fight they could not win at present, Kaia lowered her bow and dropped it in the wagon. She eyed Jaric, silently commanding him to stand down. Roann released his barrier and kicked Jaric's feet out from underneath him, sending the soldier crashing to the ground. Grildi moved to help him up, but he brushed the giant man off with a stern glance.

"Wise decision." Roann tapped the sword shard against the palm of his hand.

A breeze picked up, and Ryris was thankful that it blew the stench of the soldiers downwind. The canopy above them parted, allowing a shaft of light to trickle down from the sky. The alchemist's eyes bulged as it illuminated the satchel containing the other shards.

Roann's attention went to the shaft of light as well, following it down from the heavens to its destination. A barely visible shard inside glittered, and the emperor smirked. He walked slowly to the backpack, never taking his eyes off of his prisoners.

"My, my…how beautiful—just like you." He smiled at Kaia, who rolled her eyes. "Something tells me my master will be very pleased to have these."

The emperor returned to the group, stopping momentarily to give the knapsack to one of his rotting soldiers. The guard groaned and accepted the pack, holding it loosely in his hands as his weapon fell to the ground.

"Not very smart, are they?" Jaric mumbled under his breath at the soulless abomination. "Looks like they have trouble with priorities."

"I encourage you to attack him while he's disarmed, then. You'll find his priorities are very much intact." Roann began circling the group, his hands clasped behind his back. "My minions may appear mindless, but they'll protect me without hesitation, and defend themselves, even when their limbs have been severed and their eyes gouged out." He continued to walk around the companions, only stopping when he found himself in front of the alchemist.

"And you, Ryris…" Roann eyed him. "Strange place to meet again, wouldn't you agree?"

Ryris refused to answer. The amulet tingled against his chest. His skin was becoming uncomfortably warm. All he wanted to do was burn the smirk from Roann's face.

"I remember that day in your shop. I still don't know exactly what happened, but I do know that it wasn't your stinking inventory that overtook me. And now…" He sized up the rest of the party. "…here you are with warriors that shouldn't even be alive—and I've been sent to fetch you. Why is that?"

"Sent by whom?" Ryris couldn't stop himself as the question bubbled from his lips.

Roann laughed. "Surely you know."

"We want to hear you say it." Kaia stared at him with narrowed, suspicious eyes. "To hear you admit that you're in league with the devil."

"The devil? I'm flattered." He smiled arrogantly, exposing perfect gleaming white teeth. "No, Lyrax isn't the devil—he's the salvation this world so desperately needs."

Ryris couldn't bear hearing the emperor speak ill of his own empire. The young alchemist loved his life, loved his country. Before everything went to pot, there was nothing Ryris could think of that was sullied in his world, except for the rotting oinox carcass. Now, with Roann working for the doom-giver, everything had fallen apart before his eyes. He wanted to scream, to lash out and strike the man in front of him. Ryris felt the ire bubble up his throat before he could stop himself, his anger had exploded from his lips.

"This world was perfect! You're the one who ruined it!" His hands began to heat up, completely out of his control.

Roann grabbed Ryris by the collar and hoisted him to eye-level. He shook him, pleasantly surprised that he was able to touch him without incident. It seemed that whatever Lyrax enchanted him with had done the trick. Ryris' face was close enough that the emperor's snarling teeth threatened to nip the alchemist's nose. Roann's eyes flared with rage, before turning ebony. "This world was ignorant—and tainted!"

Ryris' hands continued to heat up, his fingertips accidentally brushing up against Roann's vest as he pulled the alchemist closer. Roann glanced down between their bodies, eyes gaping in shock as he noticed his prisoner's new trick.

"Just like you're *tainted*." Roann released him and grabbed his wrists, wrenching his hands awkwardly. Ryris yelped in pain as the emperor gazed down at the tiny flames flickering on his fingertips. "So, this is your dirty little secret, eh alchemist?"

Ryris whimpered as Roann applied pressure to his hands, threatening to break both wrists with his extreme strength. He felt the fire go out, replaced by searing pain as bones approached their breaking point.

"I wonder how you slipped under our noses all these years? There were so many of your kind that I eliminated." He pushed Ryris to the ground with an exasperated huff. "No matter. Even if you wanted to use your worthless little flames on me, you'd lose in spectacular fashion. It's a pity, really. I would have loved to have seen you try."

Kaia spat her words. "You might just get your wish."

"Well, then. Now I'm counting on it." Roann smirked arrogantly, his eyes returning to their emerald hue.

Grildi grabbed Ryris under the arms and lifted him back to standing position. He snarled at Roann before talking to his friend. "You okay, Boss? You want me to pound him for makin' fun of you?"

"How precious. The dolt is concerned for his weak friend. And protective, to boot." Roann gently patted Grildi on the bicep, eliciting a furious growl from the massive man. "Such loyalty. I wonder if he'll still follow you when he's a zombie?"

"Nobody's makin' a ghoul of me!" Grildi's face turned bright red, his fists clenching in front of his body.

"We'll see." Roann ran his hands over his arms and shivered. "This forest air has become quite chilly. I invite you all back to Keld as my *distinguished guests.*"

"And if we refuse?" Jaric's defiance was evident.

Roann simply pointed at his troop of undead soldiers, never uttering another word. Jaric grumbled and narrowed his eyes at the monarch. The soldiers moved forward and pushed them toward their wagon. When they were in position, they crowded in tightly around them. The stench was unbearable as they pressed their bodies together to form a circle. Ryris gagged at the foulness of decay. Kaia covertly touched his hand with hers, intertwining their fingers. Ryris welcomed the soothing contact, even though his cheeks flushed instantly at her touch. In an instant, the entire party, ghouls, cart, and all, were enveloped in a red mist and Ryris felt the uncomfortable surge of energy associated with teleportation.

He definitely did not enjoy the sensation.

CHAPTER THIRTY-FOUR

Of all my daughter's skills, I am most impressed with her ability to conjure magic. Fire, frost, lightning...if I were to face her in battle, I would hope against hope she would be quick and merciful with my death.

--Journal entry of King Galroy of Farnfoss

Ryris had always wanted to take a tour of the Vrelin palace.

He daydreamed about the ornate tapestries, grand staircases, and opulent treasures contained within. To be able to see generations of portraits, regal accoutrements, and the literal seats of power. The opportunity to walk the halls of the monarchs, to have his footfalls atop their own well-trodden paths was something he wanted to experience just once in his life. And now, here he was, moments away from stepping into the throne room. But he wasn't on a tour.

He was a prisoner.

The halls were dark, the paintings and statues gathering dust. Mice skittered across the floors, the once-grand ballroom now empty and devoid of life. Where there should have been the bustling action of everyday goings-on of an empire, there was instead eerie quiet. The stench of rotting flesh wafted in from the square outside.

This was not the Keld Ryris remembered.

His Keld was warm and inviting, filled with the delicious aromas of bakeries and flower shops. His Keld was peaceful and full of life. His Keld pulsed with the frenetic activity of a metropolis. *His Keld*—no longer existed.

The undead guards surrounding them shuffled down the corridor, with Roann in the lead. The emperor carried the velvet parcel containing the sword shards in his hands. Ryris glanced at Kaia beside him. She held her head high with a stern face, unwilling to show any fear. Jaric shared her expression and resolve, refusing to let any of the guards manhandle him. He was his own man, and would face his fate on his own terms. Grildi walked behind the alchemist, sticking close to offer whatever protection he could. Ryris was thankful to have his friends at his side, it made the uncertainty of what was about to happen a little less terrifying.

A shudder ran down Ryris' spine. What *was* about to happen? Was he walking to his death? Would he be kept alive to witness more horrors? Was...Lyrax in there? He tried not to vomit.

The grand doors opened, and he was immediately assaulted by a blast of chilled air. Roann's hair billowed around his head as the currents blew past them all. Ryris instinctively shivered, pulling his arms close to his body for warmth. Grildi, sensing his discomfort, put calming hands on his shoulders. The lights beyond were low, as dozens of oil lamps flickered in their wall sconces. On the horizon, just visible through the grand windows, the sun had recently dipped behind the buildings.

As the party crossed the threshold of the throne room, the doors slammed shut behind them, seemingly of their own accord. Cold air surrounded them, a shocking difference from the humid, thick air of the palace proper. Ryris was at least relieved to no longer smell the horrible rotting odor from outside. This room was clear of that stench—but had been replaced by something different. The sickening-sweet aroma of large-scale decay had been overpowered by moldering, disguised foulness. Incense burned in pots surrounding the thrones, attempting to mask a burnt, festering aroma. Like charred flesh that had been soaked to restore it to its former living glory, but fell short of the mark. This smell was unnerving, malicious. Ryris instinctively reached for Kaia's hand, which she accepted without hesitation.

"Master Lyrax!" Roann's voice boomed, echoing off of the gilded walls and buttressed ceiling. "I've brought you visitors!"

Ryris' stomach lurched at the mention of that name, and he squeezed Kaia's hand in response. A figure stepped out from behind a curtain to the side of the royal seats, seemingly gliding across the floor without actually touching it. The azure robes of the monarch draped loosely over his frame, the man was tall, his skin a sickly gray. Dark spots of decay dotted his neck. Roann's jeweled crown rested atop his bald head. He came to a stop in front of the emperor's throne and sat, crossing his legs and throwing his arms over the armrests with a sigh.

"Ah yes, the alchemist and his band of misfits." He smiled, exposing a mouth of rotten teeth. "How lovely of you to join us. I trust my faithful protégé was respectful to you?"

"If you call pushing a woman to the ground respectful, then yes." Jaric's tone was confident and rebellious.

"I've taught him well, then. Such loyalty." Lyrax gazed proudly at Roann. "I suppose you know why you're here?"

"Your *faithful protégé* didn't make us privy to that information. He ambushed us in the woods and brought us here without so much as a handshake." Jaric narrowed his eyes at him.

The necromancer smirked. "Handshakes are only for friends. You're enemies of the state."

Roann motioned backwards toward the companions, all while keeping his attention focused on Lyrax. "They came relatively peacefully. I believe they realized the severity of their situation."

"Only because I couldn't introduce you to the severity of my fist fast enough." Jaric mumbled under his breath, staring the emperor down.

With an annoyed huff and a flick of his wrist, Roann reduced Jaric to a crumpled heap on the floor, clutching his stomach in agony. Grildi immediately dropped to his side, grabbing him by the shoulders to steady him. The warrior groaned as he writhed on the ground, unable to control the sudden convulsions that wracked his body. After a long moment of intense torture at the emperor's hand, Lyrax commanded him to be released. Roann reluctantly obeyed, and Jaric was liberated from the invisible torment.

"What did you learn?" Roann's tone was mocking.

Jaric stared at him through half-closed eyelids, snarling weakly as the pain abated. A moment later, with the waves of agony washing away, he allowed Grildi to help him up, and stood under his own power. He refused to look at Roann.

The young emperor silently approached the throne podium, his guards filling in to surround the prisoners. He set the velvet satchel down on the stairs, posed a question. "Master, did you know we had a magic user among us? Mr. Bren has a habit of setting fire to his fingers."

"Magic?" Lyrax' eyes widened with intrigue, looking at Kaia first, then Ryris. He rose, gliding down the stairs to come face-to-face with the alchemist. Ryris immediately gagged at the stench enveloping the man. "I thought I knew about all of your kind. How is it you managed to evade me?"

Ryris kept silent, his throat getting drier by the minute. The amulet on his chest began to warm, and he mentally begged it to stop. If Lyrax found it—or sensed it—he'd be dead in a heartbeat. The necromancer moved closer, practically touching the tip of his nose to Ryris'. His stinking breath puffed at the younger man's face.

"You don't have to be afraid of me. I'm genuinely curious about you and your secret to staying incognito."

Ryris swallowed hard, staring the old wizard down. He hoped his terror wouldn't bubble over and cause him to shake. The amulet resting against his skin continued to heat up.

"Please, won't you show me?" Lyrax backed away. "I give you my solemn word I won't hurt you because of it."

Jaric snorted, and Lyrax felled him with the same power Roann had. He let him writhe on the ground for a moment before letting him up once again. Lyrax never said a word to him, and cast his attention back to Ryris. The young alchemist steadied himself and conscientiously objected with a determined shake of his head.

"No."

Lyrax raised an eyebrow in surprise, before bellowing out a grand laugh. "You're a brave one, aren't you?" Motioning to Roann, he waited for what he knew was coming. Like lightning, the young pawn was directly in front of Ryris, jabbing him in the stomach with his elbow. He lurched in pain, grabbing his abdomen.

"Do as you're told." Roann grabbed his hands, bending his wrists.

"N...no." Ryris grit his teeth as Roann twisted his arm. He knew what they did to magic users, and he was not going to comply—even if it meant his life.

Roann rolled his eyes and looked to his master, silently asking for permission to hurt his captive further. At Lyrax' nod, Roann pushed Ryris to the ground and planted his boot firmly on his neck. His air supply was immediately cut off, and Ryris' face began to turn blue as he lost oxygen to his brain. He watched in horror as Roann reached out with a strong arm and grabbed Kaia, placing a knife to her throat.

"What say you now, alchemist? Still uncooperative?" Roann pressed the blade into her soft skin, a droplet of crimson blood appearing on the tip of the dagger.

Ryris panicked. He didn't know if it was from the quickly-waning brain function or the fact that Kaia's life was being threatened on account of him, but he suddenly felt compelled to comply. Roann would certainly kill Kaia if he didn't play by their rules. Her eyes were strong and clear, never breaking their contact with Ryris' own. She silently begged him to revolt, a small almost undetectable shake of her head warning him that it wasn't worth it to give them the satisfaction of seeing him crack. But, Ryris wouldn't let her perish—not because of him.

With all the strength left in his body, even when he couldn't breathe, he mustered a few tiny flames on his fingertips. Kaia's eyes lowered in disappointment as Roann let her go. The emperor removed his boot from Ryris' neck and grabbed him by the lapel, dragging him up and planting him gruffly back on his feet. Roann laughed at his measly fire.

"You call that magic?" Lyrax shook his head in disgust, obviously not impressed with his ability. "What a paltry attempt. Just like your mother..."

Ryris' world immediately crashed down around him. He had no words. The mention of his mother brought back all the horrifying memories of her murder.

"You saw it all, didn't you? Tell me, did she scream? Choke on her own blood?" Lyrax narrowed his eyes and stared Ryris down. "I'm sure it was quite painful."

Ryris' fingertips burned and he began to reel out of control. The reality hit him square in the chest—Maxx had been absolutely correct about her murder. He acted on instinct and flung a ball of fire out of sheer fury. It hit Lyrax head-on, setting his robes on fire. The man stood there and burned, all while laughing maniacally. He wasn't being affected at all. Lyrax simply blew out a long breath and the fire threatening to consume him extinguished, his skin showing no signs of burns, his clothing completely un-marred. Ryris stared at him in disbelief and his shoulders sunk. He had nothing left to give, and backed away. Grildi put a hand on his shoulder.

"Keep trying, young Mr. Bren. You'll get it right eventually. Perhaps dear old Mummy will be proud from the Gentle Reach." Lyrax glided halfway up the stairs of the throne podium and threw his arms wide, raging flames appearing almost instantly on his fingertips. They consumed his hands before he meshed them into one gigantic fireball, more than two feet in diameter. He hurled it at the companions, who flinched and waited for their fate. Ryris closed his eyes and prayed to Oleana that his death would be quick and relatively painless.

When the fireball didn't hit them, Ryris opened his eyes and to see it was hovering only feet from their bodies. The heat was incredible, the broiling plasma ebbing and flowing on the surface of the miniature star. He smelled the telltale aroma of singeing hair. Lyrax was visible behind it, the intense heat currents obscuring his image.

"Kaia the Quick, why don't you put out the flames?" Lyrax' voice was condescending. "You are King Galroy's daughter, are you not? The one who commanded his army? Who gave the order to throw me into that wretched volcano?"

"One and the same." Kaia held her head high, paying the blood drying on her skin no mind as she spoke.

"I'd never forget that beautiful face of yours. And even facing certain death, you keep up the regal defiance I so fondly remember from times past. I like that in a woman, in a soldier." He stared at her with his leering eyes before flicking his wrist in her direction. "Put the flames out. I know you're capable of incredible magical feats."

She looked to Ryris, the young alchemist no longer able to hide his fear and sadness. His eyes glistened with the telltale signs of emotional moisture—which he was trying incredibly hard to keep at bay. Silently, Kaia concentrated her mental energy. If Lyrax wanted her to put out the flames, she would do so in spectacular fashion.

Her hair billowed around her head from an unseen wind, and the air temperature dropped within a seemingly invisible bubble that had enveloped the party. No longer did the intense heat from Lyrax' fire threaten them. Ice crystals appeared from thin air, coalescing into a giant frozen spike hovering just above their heads. With a mighty roar, Kaia hurled it at the ball of fire with only her mind, the icicle slamming into the sphere with such force that it shattered the plasma, sending globs of fiery material in all directions. Grildi threw himself in front of his three friends, shielding them from the molten onslaught. But, nothing ever hit them—for Kaia had shielded their group with an icy wall conjured from the same air that produced the crystal blue spike.

Lyrax clapped his hands and bellowed his congratulations, marveling at Kaia's raw power. "Well done, Quick! You've certainly lived up to your reputation. You'll be a great asset."

"Asset?" Kaia laughed out loud. "I'll never join you. I'd rather die."

"Death can be arranged, rest assured." Lyrax stared her down. "But I'd much rather take advantage of your abilities while you're still among the living."

She allowed flames to lick her fingertips once more, readying a molten volley. Jaric screamed, begging her to stop.

"Kaia, no! He's not worth it!" He lunged toward her, grabbing her by the shoulders, effectively breaking her concentration. The fire dissipated from her palms.

Kaia glowered at him, fire seething in her eyes. Jaric knew she was mad at him for stopping her. But, he knew—as did she, deep down—the attack would have been futile.

"You'll get your chance!" Jaric's voice was hushed as he leaned in close to speak.

"Listen to your friend, daughter of Galroy. He's wiser than he seems." Lyrax sighed sadly. "But, I can't have you doing that again, I'm afraid. You're too dangerous if I let you keep your magic."

Instantly, Kaia's hands glowed yellow, her skin illuminating itself from the inside out. She shook her fingertips with a pained wince before looking to the necromancer in confusion.

"No more magic for you, dear. Not until you prove you can behave yourself."

Kaia snarled at him, before looking away with a huff. She curled her fingers into tight fists.

Roann moved toward Ryris, eager to dispatch the young alchemist. He reached behind his head and unsheathed his twin blades. He whirled them in his hands before bringing them to rest at his sides. "She will be an impressive fighter for us, but he's useless, Master. His magic is weak. Let me have him…"

"No, I think I'll keep him for now." Lyrax removed himself back to his throne and sat with a satisfied sigh. "There must be something special about this one to have avoided my keen senses—and I intend to find out what it is."

Roann pouted and put his swords away. He moved toward the velvet parcel he had set on the steps. Picking it up, the emperor untied the silken rope holding the fabric together. Exposing the contents, he made the short climb up the stairs to the throne and offered up the shards.

Lyrax leapt from his seat, kneeling before Roann and the package he bore. He instructed him to set the parcel down, and stared at the glittering contents. His mouth gaped as picked up one of the pieces. "Do you know what this is? What this...was?" Lyrax' voice was hushed in reverence. "I didn't think it existed anymore, not after..." He looked to Kaia. She puffed her chest out with defiant pride.

"Master, they had just found another piece when I arrived to their base camp. I *knew* these had meaning." Roann smiled proudly.

"Indeed. These are shards of a sword—the same sword that brought me to my knees." The necromancer held one of the larger pieces above his head, tilting it to allow the light from the hundreds of lamps to reflect across the surface. "And now it's here before me. If there is one piece, there are more..." He opened the fabric wider to reveal the other five shards the party collected. "...and there most certainly will be a hilt."

The necromancer moved all the pieces out of the way, looking for something more within the package. When he found nothing, he growled with irritation. Lyrax replaced the shard back to its velvety home and approached the party once more. He eyed Kaia with suspicion. "The hilt, my dear. Where is it?"

Kaia answered, her tone defiant. "What hilt?"

Lyrax moved closer, bringing his face within centimeters of her own. Kaia flinched backwards at his intrusion of her personal space. He grabbed her arm with his bony fingers and pulled her closer. "The hilt you're hiding. Tell me where it is right now."

Kaia spit in his face. Lyrax slapped her across the cheek. "I can see you're going to be trouble." The necromancer pushed her toward Roann, who caught her and held her tightly to his body as she tried to wiggle away from him. "Use any means necessary to get the location of that hilt from her."

"Of course, Master."

"And as for the rest of you," Lyrax sighed in irritation. "The dungeon will welcome you with open arms."

338

Roann forced Kaia into a side door of the throne room, her friends unable to help her. Guards surrounded them and instructed them to begin the march to their prison cells.

~~~

The heavy wooden door swung open, and Roann pushed Kaia over the threshold.

Rich wooden paneling covered the walls, bookshelves filled with hundreds of volumes fit nicely into recessed nooks. A few paintings hung around the room, a plush, comfortable couch sitting in the middle, an ornate woven rug underneath its feet. Roann guided her to the sofa and encouraged her to sit. He moved to the windows and threw them open, tying the drapes back with golden tasseled ropes. Stars speckled the heavens. Kaia briefly contemplated running while his back was turned, but soon realized she would have nowhere to go. She was trapped—a prisoner guest.

"Do all the dungeons in Keld look like this?" Kaia sat stiffly on the couch, her inner sass becoming louder by the second.

"That filthy place isn't worthy of your beauty. You deserve better. Your friends on the other hand…" Roann stood before her, unbuckling the swords from his back. He rested them up against an end table. Never taking his eyes off of Kaia, he removed his heavy doublet and threw it on a nearby chair. Underneath, he wore a simple cotton shirt, which he quickly unbuttoned near the top. Kaia caught a glimpse of a geometric pattern peeking out from underneath the fabric, seemingly tattooed onto Roann's skin. With a satisfied sigh, he rolled up the sleeves. "That's better. A long day trapped in those clothes will do a man in."

"I want to be with my friends."

"Well, that's not going to happen. You're much too important to Lyrax—to me—to be locked away in a stinking prison." He motioned to their current surroundings. "This on the other hand, is fit for an emperor—and his empress."

"Wishful thinking." She stared at him, unimpressed.

"All this can be yours, you know. You come from regal blood. You're too good to be traipsing around with rabble, getting your pretty little feet stuck in the mud." He smiled broadly. "You're a princess, and you need to be treated as such."

"If you think you're going to sweet talk me into giving you the information you want, you should probably save your breath and throw me in the dungeon."

Roann laughed, his green eyes twinkling in the low light of the oil lamps. "Come now, Kaia. I'm not Lyrax. You don't need to speak to me like you do him.

We're equals, you and I. I think we can find a middle ground that will make us both happy." He walked to the liquor cabinet and uncorked a green glass bottle. "Wine?"

Kaia crossed her arms over her chest and blew out an annoyed breath.

"Your loss, it's an incredible vintage." Roann sipped at his glass before joining her on the sofa.

"Just get on with it, already."

Roann scolded her with a clicking tongue. "Now, now…being sassy won't get you anywhere. Although I do like a spirited woman."

"You don't stand a chance."

"We'll see." The emperor drained the rosy liquid from his glass and set it on the table in front of them. Draping his arm over the back of the sofa and behind Kaia's shoulders, Roann moved closer and leaned in, looking deep into her eyes. "Tell me where the hilt is."

Kaia pursed her lips in rebellion, inching backwards away from her captor. She suddenly found herself unable to go any further, her back pressing up against the arm of the couch.

Roann rested his palm on her thigh. Kaia immediately re-crossed her legs, forcing his hand away. "Playing hard to get, eh? I tell you what, I'll remove Lyrax' enchantment as a show of good faith."

"Defying master?"

Roann smirked and set his hands atop Kaia's. He traced his index finger along the scar tissue. Bringing her marked hand to her lips, he kissed the permanently inflamed flesh. "Such pain…"

Kaia tried to move her hands away, bur Roann clasped them tightly. He closed his eyes and took in a deep breath. She felt a tickle of energy sizzle down from her shoulders and jolt her fingertips. Suddenly, her magical abilities came flooding back.

"Just remember that I can put it back at any time. So don't do anything stupid."

Kaia rubbed her suddenly-aching hands together, in an attempt to dissipate the pain.

"Aren't you going to thank me?"

The warrior just stared at him.

Roann sighed. "No worry, I know you're grateful. So, let's forget about that hilt for a moment and talk about something else. I want to know what you see in that cowardly alchemist."

"See in him? Nothing."

The emperor narrowed his eyes and sized her up in silence. After a long moment, he finally spoke again. "No, I think you're lying. I think..." He sighed and stared wistfully into her eyes. "...that you care a great deal for him."

"You don't know anything about me." Kaia huffed and turned her head away.

Roann gently grasped her chin and guided her face back in his direction. "I could see it in your eyes in the forest, and when I had my foot inches away from crushing his throat."

Kaia swallowed hard and tried to avert her eyes from Roann's piercing gaze. She didn't need emotions clouding her judgment right now. Not when her fate, and that of her friends, was on the line.

The emperor continued, forcing her to look at him once more. "You feel for him—as does he for you. Dare I say, you love him?"

"Get to your point."

Roann moved even closer to her on the sofa, his body pressing up against hers. He pulled his fingers through her long, wavy locks as he pinned her with his body weight. His voice was low and lusty. "If you tell me where the hilt is, I can make all your dreams come true. I'm a thousand times the man Ryris will ever be, I assure you. You don't have to depend on *him*, when you've got me."

Kaia responded to his advances with fire in her voice. "You're pitiful."

In an instant, Roann's emerald eyes became black voids. "...and you're a bitch."

Before Kaia could react, Roann grabbed her forcefully and ripped her from her seat, throwing her roughly into a nearby chair. He tore the cords from the draperies and bound her arms behind the back. Flying in front of her, he got right in her face, teeth snarling, hair falling across his shoulders. "You want to do this the hard way? Fine." He shook her violently, his voice rising as his anger did the same. "Where's the hilt?"

"You don't scare me."

Roann raised his hand and struck her across the face, his signet ring breaking the smooth skin of her cheek. Blood dribbled from the wound, falling onto Kaia's pants in a splotchy crimson pattern. "The hilt. Now."

341

"Hitting me isn't going to win you any points, either. You're really bad at this." Her defiance was coming to a head.

The emperor, his rage cascading over his body and taking control of his mind, grabbed Kaia by the throat and squeezed. With her hands bound, she was unable to claw at Roann's fingers, and soon began to writhe as fight or flight kicked in. Ever defiant, she narrowed her eyes with resolve, even as she struggled to breathe.

"You *will* tell me." Roann exhaled sharply from his nostrils and stared her down.

Shaking her head 'no', Kaia continued to struggle in his grasp, stars flickering in front of her eyes. She knew she had only moments before she lost consciousness. But she would not give in.

The emperor kept squeezing, his fingers pressing so hard into her throat that they began to turn the skin white. Kaia's eyes rolled back into their sockets as her brain screamed for oxygen. When she was seconds away from succumbing to his onslaught, Roann suddenly let go. Kaia spluttered and gasped as she desperately drew air into her hungry lungs. Wheezing, she narrowed her eyes at her assaulter and asserted herself, still defiant.

"Go ahead, kill me. Your master will have your head."

Roann silently stared her down as he went to his desk and opened a drawer. He drew a dagger from a sheath, ornate and bejeweled. When he returned, he ripped open her blouse, exposing a simple lace brassiere. He straddled her leg, leaning down close to her body. Positioning the tip of the blade directly over her heart, he finally spoke.

"One thrust. That's all it will take."

"Is that a promise?" Kaia cocked an eyebrow. Roann pressed the tip into her soft flesh, just piercing her skin. She hissed at the sensation, but did not cry out. "I don't think you've got the guts to do it, Roann. You're a coward."

Eyes still pools of ebony, he pressed the blade further into her body, the tip disappearing into her breast. He leaned in close and whispered in her ear. "I don't want to do this. You're too beautiful and smart to expire like this."

For the first time that day, Kaia truly feared for her life. Her face was flushed, her body shaking. She could feel the intrusion of the metal within her chest, the searing pain accompanying the blade. Not willing to give up—or give Roann what he wanted— she desperately tried to keep calm, even while she stared death in the eyes.

342

Roann's lips ghosted across the sensitive side of her ear, his breath hot as he spoke. "I want you to beg me to stop. I want you to plead for your life." The blade slid further into her body with ease.

Suddenly, Ryris' face flashed before Kaia's eyes. She realized that if she didn't tell Roann what he wanted to hear, he'd kill her—and then go after the alchemist. He'd be put through hell, and Kaia couldn't bear that thought. He had never been exposed to torture, and the thought of Ryris suffering because of her was too much for her to handle. Beads of perspiration ran down her face, soaking her collar.

"Be a good girl and tell me where the hilt is, and all this pain will go away."

The blade was now a good inch within her bosom, and Kaia was about to black out from the intense agony. Against everything her brain was telling her to do, she finally decided to tell Roann what he wanted to hear. She wanted the pain to stop. She wanted him to get away from her. But most of all, she wanted Ryris to be safe.

"...in the...wagon..." Her eyes fluttered as unrelenting pain washed over her, radiating from the dagger in her chest.

"Where in the wagon, love?" Roann began to slowly remove the blade, savoring every moment of discomfort he caused her.

"...floorboard...underneath..."

The emperor slid the dirk from her flesh completely and wiped the bloody edge on Kaia's torn shirt. He leaned down and kissed the oozing wound on her chest, his lips immediately stained with her blood. Moving up her body, he found her mouth with his own, and kissed her. Her own blood sticking to her lips, Kaia was in too much agony to care. Her consciousness was fading, and this time she could not fight it. Too weak to protest, she reluctantly allowed Roann to press his hungry lips against her own. After a long moment, he pulled back, running a comforting hand through her sweaty hair.

"I knew you'd tell me. It's a pity I had to pierce that perfect breast of yours in order to get what I wanted, though." He reached behind the chair and cut her bindings with his dagger. "But don't despair, you'll be rewarded for your cooperation, Kaia. Such a beautiful name..."

Kaia cracked her eyes open, trying to focus on Roann's face. She could feel his body heat, smell the light scent of his cologne wafting from his hair. As she struggled to keep her gaze on his eyes—his black eyes—she found that his visage morphed and bubbled. Blinking to try and clear her mind, she suddenly found herself staring into Ryris' eyes. Pain-induced dementia overtaking her, she reached a shaky hand up to touch the alchemist's face.

Roann closed his eyes at her touch, bringing his own hand up to cover her trembling one. "That's right…you're mine."

Tears streamed from Kaia's eyes, clearing her field of vision. No longer was she looking at Ryris. Roann's deep ebony eyes peered down at her, boring directly into her very soul. *"I'm not yours…"* she thought. *"I'll never be yours…"*

The emperor reached down, placing his hand over her heaving chest. Pressing strongly on the wound, he closed his eyes and concentrated. The pressure of his ministrations caused Kaia to finally scream out in pain. Blue light enveloped them both, tendrils of smoky fog coalescing around their bodies. Kaia writhed under his weight, praying to Oleana that he'd just kill her and be done with it. She was barely aware of a healing wave washing over her, concentrating its effort on the cut in her breast. After a moment, as the energy seeped into the wound and knit her skin back together, the light dissipated and Roann removed his hand.

"You see? I'm not Lyrax. I can heal—and I can love." He leaned in and kissed her deeply as she fell into a dream state, exhausted from her ordeal. "Let me love you…"

~~~

Roann sifted through the contents of the party's wagon, the scent of the horse stables wafting around him in all directions.

The city was empty and quiet, the only noise being the ever-present din of buzzing flies in the square, and the annoyed whinnying of Ryris' horse. By the light of a lantern, the emperor had removed the tarp from the cart and delved into the companions' lives. Alchemical ingredients and a field alchemy kit, sacks of dried berries and jerky, multiple sets of clothing. Four crates containing shimmering crystal armor. Ornate helmets of the same material lay tucked under blankets, carefully wrapped in linens. He removed the crates containing Kaia's armor and set them against the stable wall. She would most certainly need it later. Small weapons, cooking utensils, and a plethora of books rounded out the inventory. All items needed for everyday life on the road—if you were warriors preparing for battle. He set an alchemist's satchel aside, filled with various brightly-colored vials. Perhaps it would come in handy at some point. Another bag, filled with stinking ingredients, he left alone.

Working efficiently, Roann rearranged the items in the cart, exposing the floor. He methodically tapped on all the boards, listening for a hollow spot. After a few moments, he found his target and pried the nails out with a pair of tongs he found in the party's belongings. Exposing a secret compartment, Roann smirked in the low light. He brought the lantern down in close, shining the flickering light on a velvet-wrapped parcel. He removed and unwrapped it, exposing a brilliant silver hilt. The gem in the pommel, although cracked down the middle, gleamed in the moonlight. It was magnificent, even in its broken state. Another item, shimmering just as bright, caught his attention from inside the recess. He brought out a glittering tiara. Fit for a princess, no doubt.

Standing tall once again, he tucked the hilt into his waistband, grabbed the small satchel containing Ryris' alchemical creations, and sighed in satisfaction. He would send a pair of guards to retrieve Kaia's armor and weapon later. Roann held the delicate tiara in his hands. His breath fogged on the cold night air. Lyrax had predicted, that with this piece of the puzzle, they would gain exponential rise in their power. Should they recover the rest of the shards of Kaia's sword, ultimate power would be within their grasp.

They would be unstoppable.

Roann grabbed his lantern to light his way back to the palace. Yes, he could teleport himself back in an instant, but the night was cool and clear—perfect for a walk. Kaia lay asleep in the castle, exhausted from her ordeal. The prisoners languished in the dungeons, awaiting whatever fate Lyrax had in store for them. Everything was going according to plan, and Roann felt completely content.

He moved beside the horse, running a hand through her mane. Not having any of his contact, she stomped her feet and bucked, trying to get away from him. Snapping her head to the side, she nipped at his arm, her teeth just barely breaking the skin. Immediately irate, the emperor backed away and incinerated her without a second thought.

As smoke rose from the ash pile that was once the flatulent horse, he sighed again, unwilling to let one little incident sully his good evening. He took in a deep breath, filling his lungs almost to their popping point, and headed back toward his home.

CHAPTER THIRTY-FIVE

The prince takes his breakfast at seven o'clock sharp. Eggs, scrambled. Cured ham, don't skimp. Juice, coffee, and two biscuits with honey. Orange melon only, he's allergic to the green variety.

-- Note from the Royal Chef to his apprentice, preparing for his annual vacation.

Kaia awoke with stiff muscles, a stinging cheek, and a gnawing pain in her bosom.

She cracked her eyes open slowly, half expecting to find herself in the dungeon for her unwillingness to cooperate in a timely manner the night before. But, she soon realized she didn't lay on a dirty cot or a stone bier, and she wasn't surrounded by moss-covered walls and insects.

Her head was cradled by a puffy, down-filled pillow and the sheets covering her body were soft, blanketing her with comfort she hadn't felt in centuries. The sun peeked through a crack in heavy maroon drapes, illuminating her face. She squinted for a moment as the light invaded her space, and turned her head sharply to move from its path. Stretching her body after a long night's sleep, it took her a moment before the previous day's memories all came flooding back.

Bringing a hand up to her chest, she snaked her fingers into her shirt to check for evidence of healing trauma. She ran her fingers over her flesh, sucking in a surprised breath when she found absolutely no sign of the wound Roann had inflicted the night before. Sitting bolt upright in the bed, she opened her shirt wider and peered down over her chin at her breasts.

Nothing remained of the previous night's torture.

Her skin was clear, unmarred by the blade's bite. No dried blood, no scar. The only remnant was the ache beside her heart, waning with every passing minute. She let her hand linger as she tried to recall yesterday's events. Her heart sunk as she remembered that she had told Roann the location of the hilt. She had failed her friends, failed her father—failed the world. Now that Roann had his hands on that piece, there was a good possibility he and Lyrax could figure out a way to utilize it. She hung her head and sighed in defeat.

Ryris' face had been the catalyst in her pain-induced admittance. Her unwillingness to bring harm to him had forced her hand. And now, Roann had the hilt.

She cursed her emotions, knowing her growing love for the alchemist had exposed a crack in her warrior's façade.

Love.

Love...

Suddenly very aware of Roann's last words to her, *"Let me love you..."*, she pulled the blankets aside and was relieved to see that she still wore her trousers. Taking a moment to ensure she hadn't been assaulted, she finally brought her knees to her chest as she blew out a long breath and took in her surroundings.

The room was large and inviting. Beautiful tandlewood paneling adorned the walls. The furniture was well-made, the bedposts and dressers crafted from the same material. Grand windows flanked by draperies took up the entire far wall, one of the balcony doors cracked slightly to allow a wisp of fresh air into the chamber. A large wooden wardrobe sat in the corner, a full-length mirror resting beside it.

She was in Roann's bedroom, no doubt. Where he was, she had no idea. Deciding that she couldn't be expected to not snoop around, Kaia slid out of the bed, wincing as her bare feet hit the cool wood floor. Locating her boots by the bureau, she put them on before beginning her reconnaissance. She made quick work of the window shears, throwing them open to let the morning light into the room.

Kaia began at the door, tugging on the ornate knob with slight hope. She figured Roann wouldn't be so stupid as to leave the bolt unlocked, and she was correct. It was fastened tight, and no amount of jiggling would get it to open. She bent down and peered through the keyhole, unable to see anything in the adjacent room. Shrugging her shoulders, she kept moving.

The mirror in the corner caught her eye, and she saw her reflection for the first time in ages. She scowled at her tangled, mussed hair, and dingy clothes. Yes, she washed her linens in rivers and community washbasins in the hamlets they stayed in, but it was a far cry from a good scrubbing with soap. Certainly not befitting of a princess for sure—but she wasn't a princess any longer. She was warrior, nothing more. She moved closer to inspect her face, the red mark on her cheek glaring at her. The small cut from Roann's ring had healed overnight, a scab sticking to her skin. Her cheek was still slightly swollen from the impact. Rubbing the angry area gently, she hoped it wouldn't leave a scar. She had enough already.

Deciding to pry, she opened the wardrobe beside the mirror. Men's clothes hung within: doublets and vests, pants folded neatly on the shelving. A few worn cotton shirts, hardly befitting of an emperor, peeked out of a cracked drawer. The light scent she recognized from Roann's uncomfortable closeness the previous night tickled her nose. Closing the cupboard, her eyes rested on a glittering pink gem sitting on the top of a dresser. She immediately recognized it.

Taking a peek back to the door to make sure she was still alone before picking it up, Kaia held the witching stone in her hands. Even in the marginal morning sunlight of the room, it shimmered from the inside out. Kaia thought to the almost identical stone nestled in the wagon, cradled in a small, unassuming box within their food stores. A shiver ran down her spine as she tilted the gem to get a better look at it. If he had one of these…

Kaia was suddenly struck by a horrifying epiphany.

She was holding in her hands that which had corrupted Roann. It had to be what Lyrax used to gain control of him. More than likely, it had been a staple of the young man's life in his early, formative years. A way for Lyrax to connect without being seen, without being heard. With his young mind perverted by promises of power, Roann never stood a chance against the necromancer. Rebellion wasn't an option, because Lyrax made him an offer he couldn't refuse.

Of course, this was pure speculation on Kaia's part, but standing there with the gem in her hands, she couldn't think of any other explanation. She set it back on its velvet pedestal, careful to ensure it looked as if it hadn't been touched. Walking past the wardrobe and dressers, she spied an open door, no light emanating from the small room behind it. She pushed it open, letting in the light from the open drapes, to reveal a modest bathroom, complete with a porcelain claw-foot tub. Kaia, absentmindedly scratching her dry skin, briefly contemplated taking advantage of Roann's "hospitality" by using his bath. She ultimately decided against it, not wanting to be caught in a compromising position by her captor. All she needed was to give the bastard the wrong idea.

She rounded the bed before moving past a plush chair and small table. An oil lamp and a stack of books sat on top, a leather bookmark poking out of the topmost tome. Kaia leafed through it, purposely moving Roann's bookmark to a different section. A historical reference book about economic strife of centuries past, she rolled her eyes at the dull content.

Kaia finally ended up back at the windows, and decided to explore the balcony. As soon as she left the bedroom, the wind whipped past her face, blowing her hair around in a tangled nest. She grabbed it by the handfuls and tied it in a loose knot at the nape of her neck. The breeze was chilly, reminding her that even though the sun was shining and Keld was in a warmer climate, it was still winter. A glass table and a few chairs sat well-used on the veranda, a tea cup and saucer left haphazardly behind— no servants to remove it after use. The soldier walked forward, bringing herself closer to the railing with each step. The breeze continued, lifting the sickening stench of decay up from below. She stopped, not wanting to witness the horrors of the promenade underneath.

"Beautiful view, isn't it?"

Kaia whirled around to find Roann, toting a cart laden with breakfast foods. Her fists clenched at her sides out of instinct. He wheeled the cart closer, stopping at the table. With a smile, he moved toward her, Kaia inching backwards away from him with each of his steps. He looked at her with confusion.

"Something wrong?"

She stared at him with a blank expression, wondering if he was really that stupid—or just didn't care.

"Cold? Would you like a jacket?" When she didn't respond, he continued, knowingly. "Ahhh, it's about last night, isn't it?"

"You got want you wanted, why am I still up here?"

"You're really determined to get into that dungeon, aren't you? If you're worried about your friends, I can assure you they're just fine. Crabby, but fine." Roann moved back to the table, motioning for her to follow. "Join me?"

Kaia peered over the balcony at the open-air mass grave below them. "How can you eat when your people lay decaying down there?"

"They made the ultimate sacrifice for me, Kaia."

She scowled, crossing her arms over her chest. "You didn't give them a choice."

Roann huffed and rolled his eyes. "I really don't want to get angry with you. You have no idea what you're talking about. You will—in time—but for right now I think we could both use a little breakfast. Morning crankiness is soothed by a cup of coffee and a fruit tart, wouldn't you agree?"

"I'm not hungry." At that exact moment, Kaia's stomach betrayed her, grumbling loudly.

Roann raised an eyebrow at the growling. "Starving yourself won't help your situation. Allow me to be a gracious host."

"Why, so you can stab me again? You have a funny way of showing your hospitality."

"Then allow me to make up for my misgivings." He pulled out a chair for her and waited, a hopeful smile crossing his lips. "Please?"

Kaia blew out a long breath and begrudgingly accepted his invitation. She *was* hungry. She also figured if she played nice, she may be able to get valuable information from the emperor about her friends and Lyrax' plan. If it meant feigning politeness and turning on some female charm to get what she wanted, so be it. The soldier sat, allowing Roann to ease her chair closer to the table. He rounded the cart and placed a few trays of fruit and cured meats on the tabletop. A basket of sweetened bread joined the rest of the foodstuffs as he sat.

"Juice?" He poured the amber liquid into a glass for his guest.

"How'd you manage such a spread when everyone in Keld is either rotting in the square or a mindless ghoul?"

Roann laughed, his smile wide and perfect. "Contrary to popular belief, just because I'm royalty doesn't mean I can't take care of myself."

"You did this?"

Roann nodded his head and put a spoonful of scrambled eggs on her plate. Kaia immediately pushed it away with a grimace. Mildly offended, Roann slid it back toward her, adding a slice of melon to the bounty. "There are no sinister motives at work here. I'm not going to poison you. I'll even eat first, if it'll squelch your fears."

He seductively brought a slice of fruit to his lips, teeth slowly sinking into the soft, orange flesh. His eyes, back to their original emerald hue, never broke contact with her own. He set the melon down on his plate, waited a minute before checking his pulse, and smiled. "I'm still alive. Now won't you do us both a favor and eat before you pass out? I know you must be famished, and I'm fairly certain you haven't eaten off of a proper breakfast set in an eternity."

With her stomach growling again, she relented and sprinkled a bit of pepper on her eggs before lifting a forkful to her mouth.

"Good girl. I can't have you keeling over on me, you're too important."

The soldier said nothing, turning her attention to the Keld skyline. A grand spire rose from across the city, the sunlight glaring off of the small metallic inclusions in the rock. From her vantage point, she could see vast gardens, the the last of the winter blossoms of thousands of flowers peppering every vine. Purposely not looking to the promenade directly below them, she let her eyes wander across the rest of the metropolis, staring at the buildings and fountains, now empty and dry. She wondered where Ryris' shop was. A wistful wave washed over her, and she thought that in another time, in a different situation, she would have very much liked to have seen Keld alive. Roann's voice broke her reverie.

"Tell me about your father's kingdom."

"I'm sure your master could enlighten you about anything you wanted to know." Kaia continued to stare out at the city. "Does he know you're fraternizing with the enemy?"

"I don't answer to him."

She finally turned to look at him, a skeptical expression crossing her face. "Funny, it seems to me that you do."

Roann took a sip of his coffee. "You're awful sure of yourself. There are a lot of men who would feel threatened by your assertiveness."

"Don't pretend to know anything about me." She set her fork down and leaned back in her chair. "We're not here as friends, remember? You took us prisoner. I don't know what you have in store, but I'd appreciate if you'd cut the act and tell me what's going to happen."

The emperor threw his head back and laughed. After a moment to catch his breath, he wiped a finger under his eye and finally turned his attention back to his guest. "It's a pity that alchemist didn't wake you up sooner. My mother was always trying to find me a wife—and it seems like the perfect woman has fallen directly into my lap."

"Keep dreaming. There's no way I'd ever marry you."

"My feelings are hurt, dear. You can't say that you don't find me even a little bit interesting—or attractive."

Kaia's cheeks flushed. She was sitting here with an insane emperor, controlled by a lunatic necromancer brought back to life by his own powers, and yet she found herself fighting his captivating allure. He was handsome, yes, and in another time she may have been attracted to him. But her heart belonged to another—and no amount of prodding would ever change that fact.

"You've yet to realize your potential. At my side, you can be part of history— for a second time. Granted, the first time your name crossed the time currents it was for naught. But now…" He reached across the table and took her hand in his own. Squeezing tightly, there was no way for Kaia to wrench her fingers from his grip. "…you have a chance to witness more than history. You're a part of this whether you like it or not, so why fight it? Why ally with Bren and those idiots? You deserve so much better."

"So you said last night." Kaia wiggled her hand away from him. "Nothing you can say will sway me, Roann. You're the enemy, and I'll do everything in my power to take you down."

He narrowed his eyes seductively. "We'll see how you feel about that later." Roann arched his back and stretched his shoulders, eliciting a sharp pop. "I trust you slept well? I must admit, the couch in my den isn't very comfortable. But, I couldn't let you get your beauty sleep on a sofa, now could I?"

"Opulence isn't my forte."

"My life is far from opulent. I've always prided myself as being a monarch of the people. I never shied away from city life, good honest work, and the simple things

351

Keld had to offer. Just because I was born into royalty, doesn't mean I had to surround myself with diamonds and gold."

"I guess that's the only thing your parents taught you."

"On the contrary. My father instilled in me the confidence to be a great ruler. When I was thrust into this position before most young people have even decided what they want to be 'when they grow up', I knew I had to make a name for myself. And I did—as I shall continue to do."

"Your sense of duty is severely skewed."

Roann huffed in annoyance, his eyebrows furrowing. "I don't want our relationship to be like this."

"Relationship? There's nothing more here than a warden trying to get something from his prisoner. You can't butter me up with meals and comfort. I gave you what you wanted, you should be proud of yourself that you got it out of me at all."

The emperor stared at her. "You know, cooperation is your best ally right now. You may think you can smart off to me, push my buttons because I like you. And yes, I do like you—and I admittedly find you very attractive. But Lyrax..." Roann leaned forward and commanded her attention. "...he'll kill you without a second thought. *I'm* the one keeping you—and your friends—alive right now. You'd be wise not to cross me."

The sudden seriousness in his voice, the way his eyes bore directly into her soul—Kaia knew he was telling the truth. She had to remind herself, sitting here eating off of fine china on the balcony of a palace, that she was still a prisoner. The man sitting across from her might be charming, but he was her enemy and held her life in his hands. Whatever he was trying to do, whatever he hoped to accomplish, she would be wise to allow him his druthers and play along. Making him angry was only going to make her situation much worse. She thought to her friends, somewhere in the bowels of the castle, and hoped they were alright.

"I'd like to change the subject, if I may. I don't want to squabble anymore; it's not good for either of us." Roann pointed to her face. "If you don't mind me asking, where'd you get your scar?"

"Which one? I have two now, remember?" Kaia's inner sass came roaring back. Obviously, she would have a harder time controlling herself than originally thought.

Roann's eyes softened as he put on an apologetic air. "I *am* sorry for that. Marring that beautiful face of yours was a mistake. Chalk it up to the heat of the moment. You must admit, you forced my hand—quite literally."

"That's pretty low, blaming the victim for the abuse. The decision to strike me was yours alone." She narrowed her eyes. "Your mother must be horrified to see what her son has become—or did you kill her too?"

"My mother is very much alive and well."

Kaia's thoughts went to the empress for a second, as she sighed internally with relief. Although they had obviously never met, she felt a twinge of sadness for the woman who had inadvertently given birth to the bane of the planet.

"You'd like her, my mother. She's a kind soul, but has fire in her breath, if you catch my meaning. You and she are very much alike in many ways, although she'd never lift a weapon." He smiled warmly. "And she'd most definitely like you. A strong woman, she always said, was needed for a strong man like her son."

Kaia had several biting responses, all at Roann's expense, waiting in the wings of her brain, but decided not to engage any further. They sat quietly, Roann periodically casting his glance over his city. She wondered if he would talk again, of if he had grown bored with her antics. After all, she hadn't been very polite to him—something she was quite proud of. But, she wanted more information out of him, and decided to pry a little. She really wanted to know about the witching stone and how it came to be in his possession, but quickly decided against asking such a thing. Kaia didn't want him to become suspicious that she even knew the gem was significant, or that she knew its purpose. She wracked her brain for something to present him with, something he couldn't—in his arrogance—deny her an answer to. Kaia knew she had to word her query carefully, to maximize his interest and force him to respond. Perhaps, in a way, he'd admit to the significance of the gem in his bedroom all on his own.

"May I ask *you* a question?"

Roann's eyes perked in surprise, and he leaned forward, resting his elbows on the table. "By all means!"

"I'm curious as to how you knew where we were. It couldn't have been just dumb luck to come across our party."

"Since you're being polite again, I'll be glad to share." Roann stood up and moved around the table, taking a seat right next to Kaia. He draped his arm over the back of his chair and relaxed in the sunlight, the rays bouncing off of his golden locks. "I dreamt about you. About that little alchemist and his massive friend, and that arrogant soldier that blindly follows you. I saw your beautiful face in the mists and knew you were the key to unlocking all the mysteries that plagued me."

"How poetic."

"Indeed." The emperor smiled, lust in his eyes. "Can I tell you a secret?"

"Please do."

"Some of my dreams actually come true. They have since I was a child, for as long as I can remember. And I'm not talking about what I've wished for over the years, or what I hope will happen when I least expect it. No, I'm talking about actual dreams. I see things in my head, and they come true, as simple as that."

"But how exactly did you know our location?" She leaned forward, resting her chin on her fist. "Dreaming about me is all well and good, but as a tactician I'm always interested in how my enemy knows my secrets."

Roann licked his lips and inched closer, his voice lowering to a husky growl. "I know you've seen it. In my bedroom."

Kaia decided to play dumb, even though she knew he was referring to the witching stone. "Seen what?"

"Don't play me for a fool. You know exactly what that glittering gem on my bureau is for."

She tried not to panic, hoping against hope he had no idea she possessed one. Because if he knew, and he found it, he would have a direct link with Phia.

Roann stared at her. "It comes from your time. Surely your father had one as a royal accoutrement. Those stones were used by the nobility as a show of wealth, although few knew what they were capable of."

"He had one, yes. But I never thought it did anything." A wave of relief washed over her. She kept up her naïve play, hopeful he'd educate her.

"What a pity. It allows me to see things others can't, to experience a different plane of existence."

Kaia hung on his words, feigning pure interest. But what Roann didn't know was she couldn't care less about his metaphysical manifestations. She let him continue.

"Perhaps someday, if you'll let me, I'll show you the gem's power firsthand." He leaned forward and tucked an errant strand of hair behind her ear. She shifted uncomfortably at his touch. "I don't want you to be afraid of me, Kaia. We can do great things together if you cooperate."

She sat back, her tongue getting the better of her as she bit back at him. "Great things like murdering your subjects? No thank you."

"I'm very confident you'll have a change of heart." The emperor sighed deeply and pulled a gold watch from his pocket. "I've got to go, love. An emperor's duty never stops."

"Duty? I thought your duty ended the moment your citizens died in the square."

"Your cheekiness knows no bounds, and I absolutely adore that about you—no matter how much you think you're insulting me." Roann stood. "Please, stay out here and eat your fill. Perhaps you'll be able to once I'm gone, for I think I'm quite a distraction, am I not?"

"You *are* distracting…"

"I hope you understand I can't have you snooping around the palace by yourself?"

Kaia cocked her head, a hurt tone to her voice. "You don't trust me?"

"Not in the least. But…" He motioned to the apartments. "You'll have free reign of my quarters. I don't have anything to hide. Read from the library, take a nice warm bath. A set of freshly laundered clothes is laid out on the bed. There's enough food here to last you for days, and if you'd like to partake, I have a full liquor cabinet in the den."

"You do remember that I'm a prisoner, right?"

"Hardly." He leaned down and took her hand in his, kissing his lips lightly to her skin. "I look forward to continuing our conversation tonight over dinner. I trust you'll be here when I get back?"

"I don't have a choice, now do I?"

"Oh but you do. Play nice and you'll get more privileges. Be uncooperative…" His eyes took on a sinister look for a fleeting moment, almost undetectable. Kaia was just glad they had stayed green. "Be a good girl while I'm gone."

He took his leave from the balcony, and Kaia heard a door close and lock a moment later. She sighed and hoped Ryris, Grildi, and Jaric were alright. Feeling very guilty about being pampered while they languished in a dungeon, she had to tell herself they were going to get out of this—somehow. If she didn't allow herself hope, she'd wither and die.

Deciding to take Roann up on his offer, she finished her juice, grabbed a slice of melon and padded into the bathroom. If he wanted her to take a bath, then she would—and she'd use up all of his fancy shampoo.

CHAPTER THIRTY-SIX

Torture can be a valuable tool, if utilized in a proper manner. But one must not be too quick to invite death to the arena. Your subject may beg for it, however.

--Excerpt from torture master's notes to a young apprentice, date unknown

"Everyone please be seated so we can start."

The town hall was full, with bodies crammed into every available space. The elderly and infirm took the first seats, the remainder of the citizens filling in behind them. Those who weren't able to nab a chair stood along the side walls. Babies bounced on their parents' knees, the children sat obliviously in the corner with a pile of toys. A fire blazed within the hearth, frost built up on the windowpanes. The crowd mingled with one another as they tried to figure out why the mayor had called the meeting.

The burly man who led the town appeared from a side door and walked out of his office, fingers nervously tapping together as he refused to look at the audience. He tried to calm his breathing, fearful of his residents' reaction to the terrible news he was about to bestow upon them.

"I know you all saw the carrier bird arrive this afternoon, and I'm sure you're eager to hear the news it brought." Blackthorne's mayor tried to keep his voice calm. His forehead was covered in beads of sweat, and not from the inferno's heat in the fireplace. He blew out a long breath as he dabbed his neck with a handkerchief. "We've received troubling news."

The townsfolk murmured nervously, husbands holding their wives close. An elderly man gripped the pommel of his cane tightly, his knuckles turning white. As their faces turned concerned, the mayor fought to keep his composure. *"If only I could keep them oblivious,"* he thought. *"Their lives are so peaceful and devoid of sorrow. How quickly things change."*

"I don't know how to say what I need to say, so I'll just come out with it. Keld..." He felt vomit threaten to rise in his throat, not believing the words that were about to escape his lips. "...has been wiped clean. The citizens are dead. Killed...by the emperor and another man."

Cries rang out from the people, unwilling to accept what had just been told to them. The mayor saw the sheer disbelief on his residents' faces, and wished he could wake up from this bad dream. All eyes shifted to the old alchemist in the corner, expressions laced with concern and condolences.

Maxxald Bren immediately spoke up to ease their fears. "He wasn't there. He's...travelling indefinitely with his friends."

A man stood in the back, cradling a baby to his chest in a linen wrap. "What do you mean, 'wiped clean'? Surely it's a mistake."

"I'm afraid it's not, Xan."

"But how? I find it hard to believe that the entire population of a city can just disappear."

"They didn't disappear." The mayor hung his head for a moment before making eye contact with his citizens once more. "The people of Keld were lured into the city square under false pretenses and slaughtered. The emperor seems to be in league with another man—by the name of Lyrax. Apparently a great wave of energy mowed the citizens down in their tracks. This information is coming by third party, as only a few survivors were able to escape the city after the massacre."

"Then how can we believe it's true? You said so yourself, it's hearsay." The man with the baby furrowed his eyebrows.

"Would you like to go to Keld to make sure yourself, then?" The mayor couldn't stop the curt remark from leaving his lips. He took a calming breath before continuing. "Please, everyone, hear me out. The letter I received came via Lullin from Dungannon. A survivor made it to the lake city, burned and battered. He was able to give his testimony before perishing from his injuries. No matter how hard we want to trick ourselves into believing that it's not true—it happened."

"But why would Emperor Roann do such a thing?" A woman in the front row spoke up with disbelief in her voice.

"I don't know. I don't think anyone knows." The mayor tried not to weep. The thought of all those innocent people being killed sent shivers down his spine. He hoped their deaths had been quick and painless. Although, after hearing the tale of the survivor whose account he was now relaying to his residents, he wasn't sure that was the case. "But what I do know is that no one is safe in this empire any longer. There is no more news coming from the west. We don't know if the emperor and his devil are staying in the capital, or have plans to move forth. It would be foolish of us to assume that their evils will be contained within Keld's walls."

The baker spoke. "What do we do?"

"The only thing we can do—protect our town." The mayor suddenly found bravado. "Whatever happened in Keld, we must not allow it to come to our home. We will fight if need be. Prepare yourselves, for we may soon be in the battle for our very lives."

~~~

"Jaric, what's that?"

The warrior pulled a long, thin metal rod from inside his boot with a smirk. He held the lockpick up for Grildi to inspect. "Just a little something for emergencies. Careful, it's the only one I have, so don't bend it."

Grildi turned the piece over in his giant hands. "What else you got in those boots?"

"Quit being wise." Jaric accepted the pick back and quietly shuffled over to the cell door. "You never know when you're going to need to liberate some goodies from a locked chest—or escape from prison."

"Well, why didn't you use it last night? The floor is really uncomfortable, you know." Grildi rubbed his aching neck and shoulders.

"In case you forgot, I slept on the floor too—with your arm crushing my chest most of the night."

"I was cold…"

"And how soon you forget about the garrison of zombie soldiers right outside our door? If I tried to get us out then, we'd be one of them right now." He peered down the corridor. "I don't know where they are this morning, but if we don't take this chance, we might not get another."

"You're smart, Jaric." Grildi clapped him on the back with a broad smile.

Jaric forced a weak grin of his own, thinking to himself that there were much worse cellmates to be had than the loveable giant. All night, when they didn't know whether or not they'd see the light of the next morning, Grildi had been by his side, ready to protect him at a moment's notice. He had watched the man do the same thing with Ryris, always at the ready to defend his friend, and he was grateful that Grildi's loyalty seemed to bubble over to him. Thinking of the alchemist sent a worried shiver down Jaric's spine. He hoped he and Kaia were both safe. After she had been led away by Roann, the three men were taken down into the dungeons, where they were immediately separated. Ryris was dragged away to his own prison, far down the corridor from their cell. Jaric and Grildi had both tried to hear any evidence of him all night— but came up empty. There was no way of telling whether or not Ryris was still alive. They would just have to break out and find him. Kneeling, Jaric got to work inspecting the lock that stood between them and freedom.

It was an old tumbler lock, covered in a rich patina. Fortunately, it was one that could be opened from either side. Jaric wasn't sure whether to laugh at the ineptness of the prison builders, or thank Oleana for this small blessing. Taking a deep breath, he inserted the lockpick into the keyhole and hoped he wouldn't break it on the first try. He worked for several minutes, grumbling to himself as the lock refused to budge. His hands gripped the pick tighter as he upped his strength, hoping with every breath that his tool didn't snap.

Grildi shuffled forward, mindful not to block out the meager torchlight from the corridor. "Looks stuck."

Jaric stared up at him, a deadpan expression on his face. "Are there any other important points you'd like to bring to my attention?"

"I'm hungry, too."

Shaking his head with an irritated grumble, Jaric returned to his work. The lock was ancient, but well-made. It was obvious it had spent centuries keeping prisoners contained within the dungeon halls. Jaric surmised it had never been picked—successfully—for the tumblers inside were tight and unwilling to budge. But, he was nothing if not determined, and wasn't willing to give up without a fight. There was no way he'd spend another night in this filthy place. Jiggling the thin metal rod within the mechanism, he could hear the tumblers clicking within the lock. But there was no way to tell whether they were moving toward unlocking—or seconds away from chomping his lockpick in two.

"I could break the door down."

Jaric paused his activity, looking up at the giant man. "I really don't want to have a party with some rotten guards, Grildi. Bust that door and they'll be back faster than lightning."

"Aye." The large man nodded with a slight pout. "I guess I'll just sit and watch, then."

Jaric knew the gentle giant wanted to feel useful, and he was confident he'd get his chance eventually. Their weapons were sticking out of a barrel down the hall, and if they broke out, they'd most definitely need them to find their friends and escape the castle. So, he kept at it, carefully applying just enough pressure to get the tumblers to move without snapping his implement in two. More minutes passed, and the soldier lost confidence that he would ever be able to free himself and his friend.

"You must get out. You have to stop him!"

Jaric stopped dead. He brought his finger to his mouth to shush his friend. The voice wasn't menacing, but he wasn't taking any chances. The two men waited silently, wondering if the whispers would continue, or if they were just a figment of their imagination.

"Please. Stop my son."

The two men looked at each other in shock. Were they really imprisoned with the empress?

"Shhh, you'll get the guards down here." Jaric continued to work on the lock as he whispered. "Have you been there this whole time?"

"I didn't want the soldiers to come after us if I tried to talk to you last night. Where did they go?"

"I don't know. I'm trying to pick the lock, but it's being a bastard. Pardon my language."

"No offense taken." A rustling of fabric indicated that the woman had moved closer to her cell door in order to be heard clearer. *"Perhaps your large friend can break the door? I saw when you came in, I'm fairly confident he could do it."*

The locked popped, breaking the pick in the process. Jaric scowled and threw the pieces to the ground. He swung the cell door open, wincing at the loud squeak coming from the rusty hinges. He hoped the zombie guards didn't hear. Motioning for Grildi to follow quietly, he snuck out of their cell and moved to stand in front of the empress'.

"No need, Ma'am." Jaric bowed in the presence of the monarch, nudging Grildi to do the same. "I'm Jaric and this here is Grildi. Are you hurt?"

"No, just cold. I'm Eilith—and there's no need to bow to me, I'm no longer royalty." She frowned sadly. "Please, take me with you. I'm afraid I'll be killed soon."

Jaric grabbed a torch from a holder on the wall and illuminated her cell. "You don't happen to have an extra lockpick, do you? Otherwise I'm afraid we can't get you out. Ours broke."

Eilith took a moment to think before reaching into her hair. She drew out a long, silver hairpin, encrusted with pearls. "Will this do?"

"Well I'll be damned; you had a lockpick this whole time…and a fancy one at that." Jaric accepted the implement through the bars and inspected it in the flickering flames of the torchlight. He shook his head with a frown. "This'll never work. The metal's too soft, it'll bend straight away."

The empress begged him. "Please try. Roann is insane…"

"I can't promise anything…" Jaric hunched over, Grildi bringing the torch closer to his work area. He inserted the hairpin into the lock, only to have it bend awkwardly within seconds. He threw it to the ground with an exasperated huff. "Damn it!"

Eilith hung her head, and sank back against the wall. Her gown caught on the stones, tearing the fabric. She looked down at the dirty satin and began to cry. "Thank you for trying. You'd better go before they catch you. I'll try to buy you some time."

Jaric couldn't bear the sight of the empress in tears. He had to figure out a way to release her, because he couldn't in good conscience leave her to her fate at Roann's hands. The warrior scanned the cellblock for anything he could use as a pick, or to break the lock. A few stones fallen from the crumbling walls littered the floor, but none were heavy enough to break down a door. He pushed on the bars with the weight of his body, in hopes that they would just give under the pressure. After all, the prison *was* old. As he pressed against the door, dust and pebbles rained down from the jamb, indicating that it might just relent.

"Grildi, give me a hand. Push on that other side with all your might." He pointed to the back of the cell. "Stand back, Your Highness. I don't want you to get hurt."

Eilith pressed her body up against the far wall and covered her face with her hands. The two men heaved their bodies against the bars, the metal groaning under their collective weight. Inch by inch, with every shove, the cell door pulled further and further out from the door frame. The hinges, rusty and old, began to buckle. When they finally gave, the door came crashing down into the cell. Fragments of the wall flew into the small space, eliciting a muffled shriek from the empress. As the dust cleared, Grildi barreled into the prison and extended a hand to the old woman.

Eilith accepted the gesture and gingerly stepped over the rubble and broken bars now lying on the floor. Noise from down the hall—a rusty door being hastily thrown open—caused all three prisoners to snap their heads in the direction of the new commotion. Grildi guided Eilith into their former cell and put a finger to his lips, encouraging her to hide. Jaric swooped toward the barrel and grabbed their weapons, hurling the massive man's club at him with a grunt.

Shuffling footsteps and the unmistakable odor of Roann's undead guards were quickly upon them. As one rounded the corner, Jaric swung his sword in a graceful arc, lobbing the soldier's head clean off his body. The abomination crumpled to the ground in a heap, his weapon clattering to the cobblestones. Eilith gasped and covered her eyes. Another guard soon appeared, only to have his skull smashed by Grildi's brute strength and trusty club. The last two guards came down the hall side-by-side.

With a determined smirk, Grildi set his bludgeon against the wall and waited. Jaric had no idea what he was up to, but there was no time to argue about tactics. He had to trust him. The giant man pressed his body as best he could up against the wall and waited for the final guards to round the corner. As their bodies came into view, he threw his arms wide, grabbed both their heads, one in each hand, and slammed their faces together. Gurgling moans came from their rotten mouths as their flesh and bone intermingled in their final moments of "life."

"That's one way to do it!" Jaric smiled broadly in the dim light and punched Grildi's arm in congratulations.

Grildi puffed his chest out with pride before retrieving his club. Moving into the cell, he held out a giant hand to the empress, who curled her tiny fingers around his own. He guided her around the carnage, moving one of the soldier's decaying hands out of the way with his foot to clear her path.

"Where do we go now, Jaric?"

The warrior looked both ways down the corridor, trying to decide. He pointed up the stairs the soldiers had come down with his sword. "If we go that way, we'll be caught for sure." He looked to the empress. "Do you know anything about this place? We've got one more friend down here somewhere and we're not leaving without him."

"There's no one else with us in this section, I'm afraid. But..." She wracked her brain for a moment, before her face turned sad. "...there is another part to the dungeon. It was used centuries ago...for torture."

"Can you show us?"

"I can try. This is the only time I've been down here, but I was fascinated by the history of this palace when I married Artol. I pored over building plans and the like in my free time." She chuckled in disbelief as she led them the opposite way down the cell block. "Who would have thought a newlywed's obsession with architecture would someday help break her out of prison?"

"Nostalgia's a funny mistress, that's for sure." Jaric followed beside her, lighting their way with the pilfered torch. Grildi brought up the rear, looking back over his shoulder every few seconds to make sure there weren't any more surprises.

~~~

Drip.

Ryris didn't even wince as the cold drop splattered on his forehead. He was unable to summon the strength to do so.

His entire body was freezing, the dampness from the constant sprinkle of water seeping into his very soul. His clothes were soggy, his skin clammy and gray. No longer able to shiver, he begged for death to quickly find him. He didn't know how much longer he would last.

Drip.

He tried to wiggle his hands, restrained high above his head, to encourage circulation to return. The manacles were rubbing his wrists raw. He knew using his magic to try and melt the metal would be futile, and more than likely get Roann back in the chamber in a heartbeat. Besides, he wasn't even sure he had the fortitude for such a feat.

Drip.

Freezing cold and terrified, he found himself wanting his amulet to flare— even if it was just to keep him warm. There was no light in the cell, no heat source. Just stone walls and the constant splashing of water from Roann's torture device.

Drip.

The water was starting to drive him mad, the anticipation of the next drop almost too much to bear. He didn't know what was worse: the slow flow of liquid bouncing off of his forehead, or the restraints. The fact that he couldn't move, that he couldn't get away from the incessant dripping—that he couldn't save himself—was wreaking havoc with his mind. Thoughts, random and terrifying, flew through his brain.

Grildi laying dead at Roann's feet.

Lyrax decapitating Jaric, touting his severed head on a pike.

Kaia in Roann's embrace, sharing a passionate kiss before he strangled her with his bare hands.

Knowing next to nothing about torture, Ryris surmised, even in his ever-waning mental capacity, that being emotionally abused was far worse than physical pain. Roann had left to let the water and the solitude work on his prisoner, hopeful he would get the information he sought from the alchemist.

And now, head soaked to the skull, chilled beyond belief, and questioning his sanity, Ryris felt as if he might just give Roann what he wanted.

After being alone in his cell for hours the night before, Roann had appeared without his guards. The emperor himself had dragged Ryris into the torture room. Ryris had immediately wondered why Roann hadn't been affected by contact with him this time. But being manhandled by a maniac didn't give him much time to ponder. When Ryris had asked about Kaia and his friends, he was greeted with a slap across the face.

Roann had shed his regal attire, donning a simple, thin, short-sleeved shirt and his ever-present leather pants. His hair pulled tightly behind his head, he looked like a man who was ready to work. Gone was the majestic air, replaced by sheer malice. His gaze cut through Ryris like a knife, peering deep into his soul. He had circled the young man, shackled to a chair, in silence for several moments. Not knowing what was coming, Ryris flinched every time Roann purposely got close.

And then it began.

The two men had spent the better part of the evening at odds in a particularly horrifying part of the dungeons. Torture implements, beds of nails, and an iron maiden had made Ryris briefly consider telling Roann anything he wanted to know. He wasn't brave in the least, and he didn't really want to find out just how much pain he could endure before cracking. But, the thought of his friends being subjected to whatever Roann had in store should he die without giving him information made his decision for him. He would survive, string the emperor on as long as possible, and maybe—just maybe—his companions would find a way to break him out.

They had started slow, with Roann promising to be lenient if he just told him about the extent of his magical abilities. Ryris was immediately surprised the man didn't ask him about the hilt Kaia had hidden. He hoped it was safe—and she hadn't given it up. They bantered back and forth, Ryris refusing to give in and show Roann what he was capable of. He knew he could summon some pretty spectacular flames, but decided to keep it to himself. Ryris didn't want to be Lyrax' puppet, and doubted his powers would be satisfactory to the maniac anyway. Flaunting his own powers, Roann had smirked at his show of force, bragging about his abilities while belittling Ryris'. In the end, he had been called a sorry excuse for a wizard and a coward. Staring up at the powerful emperor in front of him, Ryris was starting to believe him.

When Roann had grown bored of his interrogation, he turned to physical means, striking Ryris with his fists until his nose bled and his ribs were bruised. Whatever the emperor had hoped to glean from the young man, he had failed on his first attempt. For a good hour—Ryris had lost track of time after the blows ceased to stop—Roann had pummeled him in the hopes he would crack and tell him something. His questioning became erratic as his fury grew, irritated at the alchemist who refused to cooperate. Ryris had been shaken, struck, kicked, and smothered, but in the end refused to tell Roann anything.

With the emperor growing tired of Ryris' antics, he had upped the ante. Unlocking Ryris from his chair, he had grabbed him by the arms and threw him onto a rack, with Ryris kicking at him the entire way. Roann was much stronger, however, and it just fueled the manic emperor's rage even more. When Ryris was secured in place, Roann simply started the water and left, extinguishing the torches as he locked the door.

Left there in the darkness, he suffered for hours, alone and terrified.

Drip.

Drip.

Drip.

"Ryris? Where are you, boy?"

The alchemist snapped back to reality as Grildi's voice echoed from outside the heavy door. He desperately tried to cry out, but found his voice had left him. The footsteps got closer, the sound of each door being opened in sequence raising his almost-destroyed hopes. Soon, his door began to rattle, the lock holding steadfast. The voices in the corridor were hard to hear, muffled by the surrounding stones and dried blood in his ears.

"I can see him! Boss…I'm comin'!"

"Better watch out, Your Highness. Our friend here wants to practice his battering-ram skills."

The massive grunts and telltale slamming of a body against the door started seconds later. Again and again, Grildi smashed his shoulder into the cell door, the hinges and lock bending with every blow.

"One…more…should…" Grildi slammed the door with all his might. *"…do it!"* The barrier crashed inwards and fell to the ground with a giant thud. The noise jolted right through him.

"Goddess, no! Ryris!"

His vision foggy, he whimpered as three figures stepped into the room, illuminated by hand torches. One of the people ignited a wall sconce, causing Ryris to screw his eyes shut at the blinding new light. Soon, calming hands were touching his body and face, frantic voices urging him to respond.

"Ryris, can you hear me?" Jaric's voice was commanding yet calm as he tried to unlock his shackles. The warrior grumbled when they wouldn't budge. "Grildi, can you…?"

Grildi approached, and Ryris could hear him sniffling with pity. Strong hands encompassed his wrists, their warmth a welcome respite from the frigid metal. Grunting as he pried the cuffs apart, the massive man was eventually successful in wrenching the shackles from the alchemist's hands. Jaric eased his arms down slowly, mindful of his atrophied muscles. The alchemist hissed in pain, an agonized yelp bounding from his lips as his joints protested. Still, he couldn't muster any words. He tried to lock eyes with whoever was beside him, only to find his vision to be very uncooperative. A soft piece of fabric swiped across his forehead and cheeks, removing the torturous moisture from his skin. Blinking rapidly, he finally brought the smiling face of an unknown woman into focus.

"You're safe. We're going to get you out of here." Her voice was soothing and reassuring.

He closed his eyes with a whimper as his other friends helped him to sit up. A strong arm wrapped around his back, enveloping him in a familiar embrace. Ryris melted into what he knew was Grildi's body and allowed the giant man to comfort him.

"I gotcha, Boss. Roann ain't gonna hurt you no more."

Ryris' voice croaked from disuse. "Kaia...where's Kaia?"

"Roann still has her." Jaric helped him to swing his legs over the side of the table. "We've got to move. If we linger, they'll find us. We need to get to her, break her out, and make a run for it."

"I don't know if I can..." Ryris was exhausted, his body burning with pain. Every movement felt like it was threatening to tear him apart.

"You don't have a choice." Jaric helped him stand, Grildi's support never wavering. After a long moment, Ryris felt somewhat confident on his feet and tried to stand on his own.

"I need a minute. Please."

Jaric blew out a long breath from his nostrils before agreeing to the slight respite. He went to the gaping hole where the door once hung and stood watch. Ryris took a few deep, painful breaths. He tried to flush the awful thoughts the torture had forced into his brain out of his mind, reminding himself this was no time for self-pity. His friends had rescued him and, in turn, he would now rescue Kaia. Ready or not, they needed to move on—even if his battered body screamed at him to stop.

"Any idea where she is?" Ryris rubbed his aching shoulder.

"No, but it just so happens we have someone here with us that can help us move through this place with a little more ease." Jaric looked back at the empress. "Ryris, I'd like to introduce you to Empress Eilith Vrelin."

Ryris attempted a feeble bow. "I'm honored, Your Majesty."

"Please, I'm unworthy of that title now. Not after what I brought upon this world by letting Roann live." Her eyes were filled with sadness, her voice meek and defeated.

Ryris felt pity for the woman. It must have been terrible, knowing that your child was in league with a demon and wreaking havoc on the empire. "It's not your fault."

"Oh yes, it is." She hung her head. "But this isn't the time to discuss the matter. If we get out of here alive, I'll tell you anything you want to know."

The party stood silently for a moment before Jaric grabbed Ryris by the arm and placed a shortsword in his hand. "Liberated this from one of those rotting bastards. It might stink a little…" He turned to Eilith. "Lead the way, milady."

Ryris prayed his legs wouldn't give out on him as he stumbled forward.

CHAPTER THIRTY-SEVEN

Consider loss. What will it do to a man? To his very soul? Only he can tell you.

--Wisdom of Grayden Dloss, prophet of Oleana.

There was definitely commotion in the halls beyond Roann's apartments.

Kaia pressed her ear against the heavy wooden door, trying to get a better angle in which to hear. Raised, muffled voices. Scuffling, crashing, and the clanking of metal against metal. Footsteps—some shuffling and slow, some hurried and heavy—ran up and down the corridors. Roann's commanding tone, stern and unwilling to falter, barked orders at his troop of undead soldiers. Lyrax' chilling voice came soon after, although it was unclear to her what had been said. Kaia wanted desperately to be in whatever action was unfolding—either as a combatant, or an escapee. She hoped her friends were behind the fracas. Jiggling the doorknob, even though she knew it to be locked, she hoped that somehow Roann had forgotten to bolt the door.

He hadn't.

She scowled and continued to do the only thing she could—listen through the wood. The ruckus approached at the same pace as before, Kaia hearing vases shattering, tapestries being ripped from the walls. A door slammed shut in the distance, excited voices erupting seconds later. Her hands clenched, and she wished her trusty bow was at her side. That would make quick work of the door. She glanced down to her fingertips, tiny flames beginning to dance on her skin. She smirked at Roann's ignorance, trusting her enough to never re-enchant her hands before leaving. Her female allure had obviously clouded his judgment. *This door is as good as gone,* she thought.

"You think that'll keep us out?"

Kaia immediately recognized the taunting voice as Jaric's. A wave of relief washed over her. Concentrating her mental energy, she brought ice to her palms and grabbed the doorknob. Immediately, the metal crackled and popped as the temperature of the material dropped. Kaia held her hands steady, even when the cold threatened to chill her to the bone. Freezing the lock to the point of shattering seemed like her best option for escape.

The commotion got closer, and Kaia suddenly smelled the unmistakable odor of Roann's ghoulish guards. She wrinkled her nose in disgust. Suddenly, a great blast of heat blew through the crack under the door and the stench disappeared, replaced by that of charred flesh.

"That's the spirit, Ryris! I knew you'd get your strength back!" Jaric's voice was proud and congratulatory, even over the clanking of swords against armor. *"Burn 'em to a crisp!"*

Kaia blew out the breath she hadn't realized she'd been holding at the mention of Ryris' name. Her heart fluttered with relief. The frozen doorknob finally broke in two and fell to the ground, crumbling into hundreds of tiny bits at her feet. She kicked the now-icy lock out of the door and swung it open. Taking a second to peer around the corner of the door, flames readied on her fingertips, she surmised the coast was clear and made a break for it. She dashed through Roann's sitting room and toward the front door of the apartment—just as Jaric burst through in a frenzy. Right behind him was Ryris, the alchemist red-faced from the frenetic battle, tiny wisps of smoke rising from his sooty fingertips. He stooped slightly, exhaustion beginning to take hold. His face was bruised, dried blood caked under his nose. He had the look of a man who had endured incredible pain and emotional abuse. Kaia's heart sunk as she realized he had been subjected to Roann's torturous hand. Grildi followed, an unknown woman hanging on to his massive arm as he led her through the door.

"Lass!" Grildi's face lit up at the sight of her, and he immediately dashed forward, wrapping his arms around her tightly.

Kaia quickly returned the embrace before pushing away and bolting to Ryris' side. She scrutinized him intensely, taking quick inventory of the numerous cuts and bruises. The smell of blood and magic wafting off of him was incredible. His eyes were tired, yet obviously happy to see her. He sighed audibly, lunged forward, and fell into her embrace in exhausted relief. She selfishly didn't want the moment to end.

Their reunion did not last long. Yelling, crashing of weapons, and shuffling feet approached. Roann burst through the remains of the door, flanked by his undead guards.

"Did you really think you could escape so easily?" Roann's nostrils flared as he stared Kaia down. She just raised an eyebrow and stared back in defiance. Grabbing her arm forcefully, he pulled her into the center of the room and shook her.

Ryris didn't think. He couldn't control himself. The sight of Kaia being manhandled by Roann made him seethe. He snarled and brought flames to his hands, even in his exhausted state. But before he could even release his volley at the emperor, Roann sighed in irritation and flicked his hand. The fire on Ryris' palms snuffed out.

"Look at that. Your friends think they're about to be heroes."

Kaia managed to free herself from Roann's grasp while he was distracted, only to find her body bumping into something behind her. The stale stench she associated with meeting Lyrax the day before floated on the air currents, and she turned to find herself face-to-face with the menacing necromancer. She held back a gag at the horrid scent wafting out from his body. His nose was caving in on the side, the telltale signs of putrefaction very obvious. Shuddering at the contact with the horrid man, she instinctively moved away and back to Roann to try and get away. She immediately cursed herself for not thinking.

"Deep down, you know I can protect you. He can't hurt you..." Roann held her close, wrapping his arms protectively around her shoulders. Kaia immediately began to struggle again. She stomped on Roann's foot in an attempt to get away. He still held tight, enjoying the pain. "...I won't let him."

"We can no longer wait." Lyrax' voice was showing signs of exhaustion. His eyelids drooped momentarily before he regained his composure. "She must be turned now."

Kaia felt a wave of panic sweep over her. *Turned?* Her throat went dry and she frantically began to devise a way out of this mess. Roann had a true grip on her, and it wouldn't be easy to wrench herself free. Lyrax stood between her and the window, and even if she did manage to get onto the balcony, the fall from the tower would kill her. Her only chance for salvation lay with her friends.

Jaric, hearing of Kaia's new intended fate, charged forward, with Grildi hot on his heels. With his sword swinging expertly in front of him, he made his attack—only to be stopped dead in his tracks as he hit an invisible barrier. He fell onto his backside with a grunt, his sword clattering to the floor beside him. A blue aura enveloped the group, shimmering around them like a thick bubble.

"Wait there," Lyrax commanded as he lowered his arm.

Grildi moved forward, letting his hand drift over the miasma enclosing them. A small shock tickled his fingers as he tried to penetrate the film, and he pulled his hand back with a yelp. Ryris moved as close as he could to the barrier, his eyes flashing with uncharacteristic anger.

"Let her go!"

Lyrax pointed to the group, and the force field shrunk around them. The friends huddled closely to avoid being zapped. Ryris backed away from the barrier, but kept his eyes firmly glued on his friend and their captors.

"I said let her go!" The alchemist's sooty hand clenched at his sides. His stomach churned at the sight of Kaia's compromised situation.

"Or what? You'll attack me? I don't think so..." Lyrax shook his head in pity. "It's a shame, really, that you won't get your chance. I hoped to research your powers more thoroughly. But, your overzealous actions this afternoon have forced my hand. Your beautiful friend will just have to serve as my pet project now."

Ryris felt his aura leave him. The exhaustion and pain of his ordeal the night before melted away. His vision clouded and he was barely aware of his body slamming against the magical field, not bothered by the electric jolts shooting across his skin every time he made contact. He roared like a wild animal, each unsuccessful crash against the barrier adding to his fury. He had to save her—he had to save them all.

Lyrax laughed at his show of bravado. "You want to kill me, yes?"

Roann held Kaia close and ran a hand seductively through her hair, keeping his sinister gaze trained on the out-of-control alchemist. Ryris growled, baring his teeth.

Lyrax pointed at the emperor. "Look at Roann. He now possesses what you so badly want for yourself. She will be his, and you will watch, unable to fulfill your destiny."

Ryris continued to slam into the barrier, his strength quickly waning. But he wouldn't give up. He would sacrifice his life if he had to, if it meant Kaia would be safe. His brain was screaming at him to stop, that it was futile, and he would just cause everyone to suffer in the end—but his heart wouldn't listen. He bashed his body again and again, his muscles and bones protesting with every crash.

"Perhaps you should challenge him? A duel of men?" Lyrax wrung his hands together.

"He's no match for me. Let him continue to make an ass of himself inside his little shameful bubble." Roann's tone was condescending.

Lyrax raised an eyebrow. "Let's see, shall we? Go ahead, alchemist. Fight him."

The barrier suddenly disappeared, sending Ryris tumbling forward as the momentum of his moving body overtook him. The shield encompassed the remaining friends once again. Ryris came to a stop, sprawled out on all fours, mere feet from Roann and Kaia. Roann huffed in annoyance at the interruption.

"Let's get this over with." Roann shoved Kaia away, Lyrax immediately encasing her feet in magical restraints. Her feet stuck to the floor, blue mist, crackling with spectral power, swirling around her boots. Kaia growled at him, unable to do anything to help Ryris. Her warrior's will bubbled up, but she squelched it. This was something Ryris had to do for himself—and for them…no matter how much it hurt her to watch.

Ryris stood and shook the fog of adrenaline and magical power from his head. He squared his shoulders and puffed out his chest, suddenly filled with courage he had never experienced in his life. His mind told him to stop, apologize, and run away, to hope his death would be quick and painless. But his fists clenched, flames flickering onto his fingertips.

371

Roann, annoyed at the whole play, huffed and changed shape before their eyes. The tall, slender emperor was quickly replaced by the black, scaled beast Lyrax had created. Grildi shrieked and covered his eyes. Jaric's mouth gaped at the sight before him. Eilith hung her head and said nothing.

Ryris stared up at the monster before him. He knew he should be scared—terrified, really—but all he felt was anger. He was actually offended that Roann would take the easy way out by making the fight so one-sided. They both knew there was no way Ryris could best him while he stood in his sickening form. The amulet on his chest, uncomfortably warm since their arrival in the room, reminded him that he indeed had power. It remained to be seen whether or not it would be enough to best the emperor.

"You coward!" The words flew out of Ryris' mouth before he had a chance to stop them. Never in his life had he stood up to anyone like this, not even Maxx. And especially not an insane, brainwashed emperor. But, Kaia was in danger. His friends were in danger. The entire world was in danger—and he'd had enough.

The monster lunged forward at the accusation, only to be stopped by his master's command. "I think our alchemist friend has a point. Be sporting, would you, Roann? Give him a fair chance to defend Kaia's honor."

The beast stared Ryris down before backing away and assuming his original form. Not giving Ryris time to prepare, Roann hit him with a small bolt of lightning, knocking him to the ground.

Stunned, but in no way out of the fight, Ryris scrambled to his feet and shook off the jolt. He knew that if the emperor had intended to kill him, he wouldn't have survived the initial surprise attack. No, Roann was toying with him, trying to get him to fight back. And that's exactly what Ryris intended to do.

Bringing his hands out in front of himself, Ryris quickly conjured a ball of flames and flung it at his opponent. Roann, not even bothering to move out of the way, simply brought a hand up and knocked the sphere out of the air with an invisible force. Undeterred, Ryris grit his teeth and tried again, forming an even larger glowing ball between his hands. With a guttural cry, he lunged at Roann and threw it at him with all his might.

Unimpressed by the effort, the emperor sighed and flicked the projectile back at its caster, Ryris jumping out of the way by the skin of his teeth. The alchemist swore he smelled the ends of his hair singeing. Not about to let Roann get the better of him, and unwilling to let his friends down, Ryris got up again. He snarled as he cracked his knuckles. The bauble underneath his shirt pulsed in warm waves, encouraging him to keep on. His legacy—and that of his ancestor—was at stake. The name he wore, he hoped, would help in some way to ensure his victory. Roann's unwillingness to even fight back properly was infuriating.

With one final volley, Ryris formed an undulating, pulsing sphere of pure plasma, the biggest and strongest he had ever made, and manipulated it in his hands. He sent it flying outwards, speeding toward its intended target.

Roann blew out an irritated breath and encased Ryris' fiery weapon in a block of ice, smashing it to the ground with a flick of his wrist. It shattered into thousands of chilled bits, melting onto the wooden planks of the floor almost instantly.

"This sorry excuse for a wizard impresses you?" Roann approached Kaia and pointed to Ryris. He ran his hand through her hair, even as she tried to pull away. His eyes were filled with lust.

Ryris' blood boiled. If there was ever a time to bring forth tremendous magical power, this was it. He wanted to shut Roann up once and for all. His mind flitted back to their battle with Ealsig. The incredible ability that came from seemingly nowhere would be the perfect ammunition against the cocky emperor. While Roann spent a moment belittling him in front of Kaia, Ryris concentrated all his mental energy, willing himself to tap into whatever his amulet had given him access to previously. He searched his mind for the voice again, mentally begging it to help him.

He was met with stunning silence.

Ryris stared at his palms, desperate for lightning to envelop them. He didn't understand why the mysterious force was unwilling to help. In his distracted state, Ryris didn't even notice Roann charging at him full force, fists in a furious flurry.

Ryris was barely aware of his body being slammed against the far wall of the den. The blows coming from Roann's hands were fierce and precise, knocking the wind from his lungs and breaking thin ribs with horrifying proficiency. The emperor made quick work of his torso before moving to his head and neck, showering Ryris' face with a flurry of cross-jabs before finishing with a swift uppercut to his jaw. His nose bled, his ears rung. Thick blood poured from a split in his lip, leaving a metallic taste in his mouth. Ryris struggled to hold onto what shred of consciousness he had left. Roann swept his legs out from under him without so much as an effort, and the young man crumpled to the ground. He kicked his flank, eliciting a pained yelp from Ryris' bleeding lips.

Kaia, unable to watch the senseless onslaught anymore, brought lightning to her hands and arced it at Roann, hitting the emperor square in the back. The jolt sizzled through his ornate katanas in their scabbards and right into his nervous system, temporarily seizing his muscles. He staggered backwards, momentarily getting him away from Ryris. He fell to the ground in a trembling heap. Kaia narrowed her eyes with defiant pride, already charging her next attack.

"What have we here? You seem to have mysteriously regained your magical ability." Lyrax, stepping over his incapacitated protégé, clicked his tongue in a scolding manner. "Well, we can't have that. Not yet, anyway..." He immediately replaced the enchantment on Kaia's hands.

Her next volley, seconds away from being unleashed, fizzled out of existence on her palms. She screamed an ancient obscenity at Lyrax. A faint tinge of moisture flecked the corners of her eyes. She couldn't watch anymore.

Roann, initially slow to rise to his feet after the electrical attack, finally regained his footing. He spat a mouthful of blood on the floor as he stared Kaia down in defiance. A silent vow to get back at her for her insubordination. He smirked maliciously before flying to Ryris' side once again; crushing his knee into his abdomen with such force that blood spurted from the alchemist's lips. He grabbed Ryris by the left arm and yanked him upwards, dislocating his shoulder. Roann slammed him to the ground with incredible force. Upon impact, an agonized, audible breath bellowed from Ryris' lips.

"Stop it, you'll kill him!" A pleading voice erupted from the behind the barrier, muffled by the magic. Eilith, cheeks red with anger, appeared from behind Grildi and stared her son down. "How can you do this? Haven't I taught you right from wrong?"

Roann rolled his eyes and stopped his attack for a moment. Ryris whimpered at his feet, curling into a ball. The emperor drew one of his thin swords and pointed it at Eilith. "Shut up, woman! I'll be more than happy to make you a martyr at a later date, just be patient."

Eilith scoffed, hot tears rolling down her cheeks. "Your fate is your own now. I can't save you."

"I don't need you to save me." He narrowed his eyes. "I've got someone else to take your place in my heart now." Roann stared directly at his new conquest.

Kaia stiffened at his words. She didn't know what they had in store for her, but she was damn sure she wasn't going to go down without a fight. There was no way she would belong to anyone but herself.

"You're a pathetic man, Roann! You don't deserve to bear Artol's good name!" Eilith screamed at her son, hands clenched in the fabric of her gown.

The emperor laughed, his voice echoing off of the vaulted, beamed ceiling. He sheathed his weapon once more. "You think you can shame me by mentioning him? He was weak, as are you. I'm the salvation this empire requires!"

"There's no hope for you..." Eilith backed away from the barrier and took her place once again behind Grildi's massive frame. She refused to ever look upon her son's face again.

Ryris lay on the ground in a battered, bloody heap. His body shuddered as he tried to breathe, his broken ribs making every breath feel as though a hot knife was being jabbed into his lungs. He desperately struggled to keep his eyes open, to see their fate. Blood pooled under his head, oozing from a deep laceration on his scalp. His brain thumped within his skull. The amulet ceased to burn, and cooled as if it too were giving up. He did the only thing he could to stay in the moment—he focused on Kaia. Her beautiful face, her golden hair—he wished he could hold her hand one more time. He wished—he could tell her how he felt. But he had nothing left to give. He had failed her, failed his friends—and failed himself. Swallowing a mouthful of blood, he gagged as his throat protested the crimson waterfall.

Lyrax released Kaia from her magical shackles and Roann swooped in, his bloodied hands quickly grabbing her by the shoulders. His eyes turned black, staring her down with such fervent intensity that it made her shudder in fear.

"Make her ours," Lyrax impatiently growled. He pulled a parchment charm from his robes and spat on it, the symbol adorning the paper immediately flaring to life. Tossing it into the air, it sped at the pair, coming to a hovering halt directly over their heads. Pulses of energy blasted off of the surface.

Roann leaned in, his lips ghosting over her ear, his voice barely a whisper. "No...not ours. *Mine...*"

He reached into the pocket of his vest and produced a small vial, filled with a bright yellow liquid. Never releasing his grip on the small of Kaia's back, he used his teeth to pluck the stopper from the top, spitting the cork onto the floor. He forced Kaia's lips apart with his finger and held her mouth open. She tried to bite him, but he just laughed at her attempt. He poured the liquid down her throat, Kaia gagging as the potion entered her body. A few drops dribbled onto her lips. With his conquest wriggling in his arms, desperate to get away, he held on tight and leaned as close to her face as possible. As she fought him, he pressed his mouth against hers, and the pair was instantly enveloped in a flaring yellow aura. The charm scroll caught fire, the ash mingling with the mists. Roann pressed his hand to Kaia's chest, heat radiating through the fabric of her shirt. Seconds later, a mark, identical to the symbol on the charm, appeared on her skin.

A single tear fell from Ryris' eye, the saline solution tinged pink by his own blood.

CHAPTER THIRTY-EIGHT

Take this gem to Foyt. Protect it with your life. Ensure it finds itself in the possession of Arch-battlemage Wylmar before he too is killed by the devil himself.

--Orders from King Galroy of Farnfoss to Jaric the Bold, date unknown

Kaia felt like she was floating.

Everything she was, everything she had ever been—was leaving her. Roann's lips were warm against her own, and even though she knew it was wrong, she couldn't help but be drawn in by his power. Their long golden locks billowed up around their heads, mingling together as a spectral wind encompassed them both. She opened her eyes briefly, to see Roann staring back at her, his eyes dark ebony pools. His hand was heavy against her breast. Her vision began to cloud, tendrils of darkness floating into her center of sight from the corners of her eyes. She tried to fight it, fight *him*. Her gaze flitted to Ryris for a brief moment, waves of desperation washing over her. She was betraying him—and had no control over it. Kaia's struggling began to wane, and a final tear fell from her eye. Soon she brought a shaky hand up to Roann's face, stroking the smooth skin of his cheek with a lover's touch.

In a matter of seconds, it was over.

Roann leaned her upright, released his lips from hers, and steadied her with a strong grip. He reached down and cupped her chin in his hand, bringing her face up to his own. He stared at her, ebony eyes meeting ebony eyes. Running his thumb over her lips, he smiled.

"You belong to me."

"I belong to you…" Her voice was calm and determined.

"At long last, a powerful ally." Lyrax' stood suddenly hunched, his voice devoid of prior determination. He focused his attention on Roann and Kaia. His eyes clouded over, and a thin stream of black blood trickled from his nose. "We no longer need the services of these miserable wretches. It's time they met their maker."

Ryris just laid there, his broken body unable to move. Grildi screamed from inside their magical prison. The massive man's voice was cracking with sadness and fear. "Ryris! Get up, boy! You've got to save the lass!"

"Don't just lie there!" Jaric's tone was commanding, certainly befitting of an army general. "Don't let them take her!"

Ryris heard their voices, though muffled due to the head trauma. He looked on helplessly as the woman he loved—the woman he knew he should be protecting—gave her allegiance to another man. An insane man who now controlled her. His fingers twitched, his legs jerked. The muscles in his body spasmed as his brain willed him to move. But it was obvious that no matter how badly he wanted to react, Ryris just didn't have the strength.

The amulet around his neck suddenly glowed bright white under his shirt.

Without warning, a blast of energy swept out from the young man, blowing papers around the room and rattling paintings on the walls. Lyrax brought his arm up to shield his face, while Roann wrapped his arms protectively around Kaia. Ryris felt a familiar burning on his chest, the fabric of his shirt beginning to smolder. He tried to bring his hand up to move it out of the way, not even caring anymore if Roann or Lyrax saw it. Finding himself quite without the strength to even lift his arm, he just lay there, waiting for the fire to consume him and end his pain.

He felt like such a failure.

Flames began to wick through the cotton shirt, licking his skin. Roann flew to the alchemist's side and tore the burning garment from his body, exposing the glittering, glowing amulet. Ryris, too weak to protest, did nothing as the emperor ripped it from his neck, breaking the thin silver chain in the process. Roann brought the bauble close to his face to inspect it. The gem began to lose its brilliant purple hue, replaced by a dark, blood red.

Ryris waited for him to be overcome again; like that day in the shop, but nothing happened. He watched with confusion as the emperor turned it over in his hands, running his fingers over the smooth cabochon.

"What do we have here?"

Ryris whimpered, unable to form words. He didn't have the energy—or the will—to answer. For a fleeting moment, his thoughts went to Gran. He had let her down. Their family heirloom was now in the hands of the enemy.

Roann grabbed him by the shoulders and shook. "Speak up, alchemist! What little secret have you been keeping from me?" Irritated by Ryris' inability to respond, he dropped him back to the ground. Roann stared at the jewel, suddenly overcome with a revelation. He jumped up, amulet in hand, and turned to face his master. "This! This is what kept him from us!"

The necromancer shuffled forward and inspected the talisman, resting in the palm of Roann's hand. "Shimmerbane!" He scolded the injured alchemist. "Shame on you, Bren. Keeping this precious stone from me." He moved to take it from Roann's

377

hand, only to have the young man clasp his fingers tightly around it. Lyrax' eyes seethed and he inhaled a surprised, hissing breath.

Roann spoke before the necromancer could lash out. "Master, I've done everything you've ever asked of me. I deserve to wear this amulet. You have the hilt and shards of Kaia's sword—I deserve a prize too."

Lyrax clenched his fists, his lips quivering with anger. His voice was low and growling. He held his hand out flat. "Give it to me."

Roann nodded and bowed curtly as he handed over the bauble. "Forgive me."

"You will be rewarded further, I assure you." Lyrax quickly mended the broken chain with his magic. He held it in his hands, eyes closed as he concentrated on the stone. Quickly his excited expression changed to concern. "There is something strange about this talisman. Something…fighting me." He clasped his hands around the gem tightly, trying to make sense of what he was feeling. "It's weak…but nonetheless there."

With an exasperated huff, he slipped the necklace over his bald, withered head. Immediately, a crimson cloud enveloped him, sending sparking embers flying out in all directions. The necromancer inhaled deeply within the mist, drinking in the massive power swirling around him. Pained moans escaped his lips as the magic flowed through him. His body trembled, and the waves threatened to bring him to his knees. The rotten spots on his neck pulsated. Several seconds later, the fog dissipated, leaving the amulet glowing a haunting red on his chest. He weakly regained his footing and stood as tall as he was able. Finally, he spoke.

"The stone of your father has come full circle, dear Kaia. Although it does not seem to want to help willingly at the moment, I am confident it will be used once again to grant immeasurable power." He faced Roann and his new mistress. "We will be unstoppable."

He turned to leave, not paying any more attention to the captives or unresponsive alchemist. Roann and Kaia followed, the young emperor posing one final question as they retreated.

"Master Lyrax, what of the prisoners?"

Lyrax flicked his hand and the barrier dissipated. His voice was once again laden with exhaustion, and he leaned on the desk for support as he disappeared into a hidden doorway in the paneling. "Do with them as you wish. I must rest."

"Be a good girl while I'm gone? This will take only moments." Roann grabbed Kaia by the arm and pulled her close, kissing her passionately.

Roann's lips were warm against her own, luring her deeper and deeper into the spell that consumed her. A spark of defiance, weakening with every passing moment, still resided within her, though. A flash of white light appeared before her eyes and she was rewarded with a moment of clarity. The mark on her bosom ached. She tried to get away from the amorous emperor.

Roann dug his fingers into her bicep and held her so tightly it threatened to break her ribs. He put his lips to her ear and whispered forcefully, "Don't fight the charm. Soon I'll make sure you remain mine forever…"

Kaia fought with her mind. With each passing second, she lost more and more control. The last small kernel of determination to get away was moments from being squelched completely. Her gaze drifted to Ryris, barely conscious on the floor. She knew she should save him, protect him—and yet her loyalties had been tainted. In her last lucid moments, she knew she had to get Roann away from him. If she was going to inevitably fall into his clutches, she could at least buy her friends some time to escape.

She finally pulled away. Her eyes turning black once more, she knew she had only seconds before she lost the battle. She ran her hands seductively down Roann's chest. "Forget them…"

A lustful growl rumbled from Roann's throat and he roughly ran his hands through her hair. "You're making this difficult, love."

With the last shred of herself left, Kaia made one final effort to sway him. Her voice was desperately breathless. "Please…"

"You're very determined, aren't you?" He leaned in and kissed her passionately.

With Roann distracted, Grildi raced to Ryris' side, kneeling and pulling the young alchemist's head into his lap. With the barrier down and Lyrax gone, Jaric charged at the emperor. Roann, never releasing his lips from Kaia's, made quick work of the warrior, knocking him to the floor with a gust of magical wind from a hand nonchalantly flicked behind his back. Undeterred, Jaric scrambled to his feet to oppose him once again. Roann let go of Kaia and a second, more powerful burst of air knocked him backwards, flinging him into Grildi's back. Jaric struggled to his feet this time, the impact with the giant man taking its toll.

Roann sighed and rolled his eyes. "I've had quite enough of your pseudo-heroics today. You and your worthless partners," He looked toward his mother, who refused to set eyes on him. "…aren't worth my time." Roann gestured to his rotten guards. "Throw them off the balcony. Make sure my mother joins them."

"Not willing to dirty your pretty little royal hands with our blood, eh? Kaia was right, you really are a coward." Jaric snarled at the emperor.

"You don't have the right to say her name anymore." Roann narrowed his eyes. "In another time you would have been a worthy adversary."

"Come on, then! Show me what you're made of!" Jaric practically foamed at the mouth, eager to teach the arrogant emperor a lesson.

"I'm *wanted* elsewhere. Like a gentleman, I didn't indulge while she was my captive. But now…" Roann took Kaia by the hand.

"Kaia! Dust and bones, remember! Don't let them win! Fight it!" Jaric clenched his fists.

But, the last sparkle was gone. Her eyes were consumed by ebony clouds once more and her voice hardened. She looked down to Ryris, spluttering on the floor. "Pitiful…"

Ryris, utterly devastated and totally defeated at Kaia's words, finally gave in to his exhausted body and slipped into unconsciousness.

Roann swooped his hands beneath Kaia's legs and lifted her into his arms. They disappeared into the same disguised door Lyrax had, Kaia draping her arms around his neck as they walked away. The door closed behind them and the room was suddenly eerily quiet, save only for Ryris' labored breathing and the ghoulish guards' clinking armor.

The soldiers moved on the party, weapons drawn. Grildi grabbed his club, discarded when the barrier enveloped them, jumped up, and swung it wildly at their opponents. One soldier crumpled to the ground as Grildi's bludgeon smashed the putrid brains right out of his skull. The other seven lunged at the group, their swords ready to pierce their bodies and send them to oblivion. Scrambling for his own blade, Jaric's arm caught the edge of one of the soldier's swords, drawing blood. Unable to give his wound any attention, he lunged for his weapon and raised it high above his head, plunging it into the skull of his attacker. Eilith moved back, away from the raging battle, to Ryris' side. She eased him into her lap, running a soothing hand through his blood-matted hair.

The skirmish raged, bodies flying every which way. Careful not to allow any more harm to his fallen friend, Grildi protected Ryris with his own body as he defended them. His club clunked against the armor of their attackers, smashed into their bodies with unimaginable force. One of the horrid beings lunged forward, his axe poised to remove Eilith's head from her petite frame. Grildi blocked the mighty weapon with the shaft of his club, the blade cleaving the wooden end clean off. Angry beyond belief at the destruction of his trusted fighting companion, the giant man screamed in fury and barreled at the remaining troops. He bowled them over with such intensity that they smashed into the door, forcing it clear off the hinges. Jaric rushed to Eilith's side to ensure she was alright, the entire time watching Grildi take out his frustrations on the decaying guards. One by one, he smashed their heads with his bare hands, punched through a rotting rib cage with such force that a festering heart rocketed out from the soldier's back. It splattered onto the floor, Grildi taking a moment to stomp on it for good measure. As the last guard made her final attack on the party, Grildi grabbed the discarded weapon of one of the zombie's comrades—a grand battleaxe—and swung it gracefully, removing her head from her body. As she crumpled to the ground, silence overtook the room. The stench of decaying flesh and fresh blood permeated the air. Grildi immediately ran to Eilith's, ensuring she was unharmed.

"You okay, Your Highness?" He scrutinized every inch of her, making sure she wasn't bleeding.

"Just fine, dear. You were incredible!"

Grildi blushed at the compliment. "Just savin' my friends." He bulged his eyes at the mention of camaraderie, immediately settling his attention on his gravely-injured friend. He gently shook Ryris, but got no response. His stillness caused Grildi to panic, pleading to Jaric with terrified eyes.

"He's not dead. But we need to move. He needs medical attention I can't give him."

"But, Boss! What about Kaia?"

Jaric sighed painfully. "We have to leave her."

"No!" Grildi's face flushed, his voice echoing off the walls. He pointed wildly at the door she had disappeared into with Roann. "She needs us!"

Jaric laid a calming hand on his forearm. "We need to go…now."

Eilith offered an escape plan. "There's a passageway in my apartments, just down the hall. We can use it to get down to the stables. Our stock of horses is plentiful, and we can use them to leave town."

Jaric stood, with Eilith's help, and encouraged Grildi to pick up the unconscious alchemist. The massive man gently eased his friend into his arms and hefted him up, cradling him close to his chest.

"We'll figure out a way to get her back. I swear it." Jaric patted Grildi on the arm. "But right now, we need to get out of here. We're of no use to our cause if we're dead."

"Aye. I trust you, Boss." He nodded sadly before leaning down and whispering into Ryris' ear. "…and I know you trust me. I'll protect you, and get Kaia back."

Eilith poked her head out the door, scanning up and down the hallways. There was no sign of any more undead troops. She beckoned the two men with her dainty hand. "Hurry, we won't have much time!"

The pair followed her out of Roann's apartments and down the hall, mindful of the bodies littering the entryway. They hurried down the corridor and into Eilith's chambers. Not possessing her key, she asked Grildi to kick it open. The door fell inwards, puffs of dust floating out of the old wooden remains. The party rushed in, fearful of the noise attracting more assailants. Eilith scurried to a mundane-looking wall; a bookcase leaned up against the rich wood paneling. She removed a seemingly random tome and the shelf moved, swinging outwards on hidden hinges.

She ushered them into the dark passageway with frantic hands. When they were safely inside, she grabbed an oil lamp from a desk, quickly lit it, and darted into the hidden chamber. Jaric, using all his strength, pulled the bookcase back into position, clicking it shut behind them. The light of the empress' lamp was dim, barely enough to light their way.

"Where now?" Jaric took point, squinting to see in the almost non-existent illumination. Ryris groaned in Grildi's arms.

"Follow the corridor. It leads to a stairwell down to the back of the palace. An escape route built long ago. Never in my life…" Eilith's voice sounded wispy and longing. They ran for what seemed like an eternity, wiping cobwebs from their faces and stepping on the occasional rodent. The companions finally came to a stone spiral staircase, Jaric tentatively taking a few steps down to test its strength. It seemed solid enough, having been constructed of masonry, but it was ancient and he was unsure if it was still structurally sound.

"Careful, it's narrow and if you slip, you'll ride the wave all the way to the bottom." Jaric started down the stairs, grasping Eilith's hand tightly in his own to guide her on the trip. Grildi brought up the rear, careful not to smash Ryris' head against the stone wall. He kept one ear trained upwards, listening intently for any signs of pursuit. They scurried as fast and as carefully as their feet would take them down several flights until they reached the end.

A wooden door opened into a small alcove, a barred gate the only thing keeping them from freedom. Jaric approached the gate, peering through the bars as best he could to get a view of the area. Cool, fresh air blew at his face. Bright sunlight assaulted his eyes. Jaric realized their chances of escape were quite low in the daylight's brilliance. But, they didn't have a choice in the matter. "I don't see anyone. I hear horses, though."

"The stables are just around the corner. If we can get the door open, we can make a break for it." Eilith moved to his side, her now-stained and filthy gown brushing

382

up against his rugged trousers. She reached for the bars, gently rattling them in hopes the gate would just miraculously open.

The lock held tight, centuries of disuse allowing a calcified coating to build up on the surface of the hinges. Jaric eased her back behind Grildi. With the tip of his sword, he pried the door away from the jamb, the hinges popping off soon after. The gate fell inwards, Jaric catching it and setting aside with almost no clatter.

He readied his sword and took a few hesitant steps outside. Jaric crouched as he walked, keeping a keen ear to the air and a sharp eye to the horizon. After a few moments of reconnaissance, he beckoned for his partners to join him. They circled the tower they had just emerged from and made their way toward the stables. The horses grazed in the afternoon sun, a foal bucked and played with its mother. Jaric led the group into the stable, out of the open expanse of the courtyard. They crept through the corral, the horses paying them absolutely no mind. Ryris lay still in Grildi's strong arms, never once uttering a sound.

"See if you can unhitch a couple, and I'll try and find a…" Jaric's tone of voice suddenly rose with glee, as he bounded toward the other side of the stable. "…wagon! It's our cart!"

Grildi and Eilith followed him closely, the giant man smiling broadly at the sight of their wagon. His demeanor suddenly changed as he took a more careful look around.

"Where's East?" Grildi scanned the stable.

Jaric moved away from the wagon, his boots kicking up a cloud of dust. He coughed and inspected the pile—and realized it was ashes. Coming to a sad realization, he dreaded having to tell his lumbering friend. Grildi had become quite attached to the horse.

"I think she's dead…" He pointed to the mound of ash. "I'm sorry, Grildi."

Grildi lowered his head. "She didn't do nothin'…"

"Can't waste time mourning her. We need to move." Jaric's tone was commanding, yet sympathetic.

Grildi nodded his acceptance of the situation. He set Ryris down on a bed of hay before assisting Eilith in attaching the ropes to the bridles of a pair of horses.

"There's quite a bit missing, here." Jaric quickly took half-assed inventory of their belongings, ensuring that his crystal mail was still stowed safely inside. Kaia's armor and bow were nowhere to be found, along with the box that contained the hilt of her sword. He grumbled at the losses. "Roann must've been down here pilfering. Kaia's armor is gone, and…so is the hilt."

"We have to go back! If he has the hilt…" Grildi's voice was panicked.

"We can't! We'll figure it out, I promise. Now get those horses ready!"

Eilith and Grildi brought their two charges forward, with the empress securing hers to the wagon's hitching shaft. She pulled their reins through the eyelets and up to the front seat. Jaric maneuvered some of the cargo to make a space for Ryris. Picking up his battered friend, Grildi carefully laid him on the bed of the wagon, and covered him with a tarp to keep him warm. Blood from his multiple wounds began to seep through the fabric. Once he was confident his companion was secure, he helped Eilith up into the front seat, where Jaric was waiting. Hoisting himself onto the remaining horse, he kicked her to make her move and the team set out. They steered toward a small alley jutting out from the side of the castle.

The wagon's wheels and horse's hooves made an ungodly racket, and soon two undead guards rounded the palace. Jaric threw the reins at Eilith and jumped down, making quick work of the inept soldiers. He decided to run alongside the wagon until they were clear of danger, should he need to defend the party once again. They kept a brisk pace, making it to the outside perimeter of the city in record time. Jaric was shocked they didn't encounter any more guards.

Eilith pointed with a dainty finger toward a rickety gate. "There! The wagon will fit perfectly!"

Jaric helped steer through the portcullis, with Grildi bringing up the rear on his horse. When they were safely through, he hopped up into the driver's seat and accepted the reins. He looked over his shoulder and breathed a sigh of relief. There was no sign of pursuing soldiers.

Grildi rode up next to the wagon, peering over the side at his unconscious friend. "You just hang on, Ryris. We'll get you fixed up." He moved forward, keeping up with Jaric's fast pace. "Where to, Boss?"

Jaric pressed his hand to his forehead in an attempt to block out the blinding sunlight. He scanned the horizon, finally focusing on the crystal clear waters of the ocean. Bringing a finger up, he pointed to the northwest.

"The only place that's still safe. Zaiterra."

EPILOGUE

Isum Dran burst through the doors of the king's court, not caring whether or not he was following proper procedures.

The sovereign rose from his throne, surprised to see his old friend. He bounded down the small set of dais stairs. Running toward his compatriot, he wrapped his arms tightly around the man and hugged him for the first time in decades.

"Isum Dran! That was quite an entrance!"

The weaponmaster pulled back and out of the king's embrace. "Sire, I bring terrible news from the Vrelin Empire."

The king dismissed his attendants and listened intently as his longtime advisor regaled him with the horrors of what had transpired on their sister continent. The monarch's expression saddened as he wrung his hands together.

"...and they all perished. He's gone mad—and Lyrax is at the heart of it." Isum twirled his ring on his finger.

King Symond nodded knowingly, unwilling to show any sign of fear. He knew this was the time to be strong. "Never in my life would I have imagined we'd be having this conversation, old friend."

"I as well. I helped to raise that boy. How could I have missed the signs? How could I have allowed this to happen?"

The monarch grasped Isum tightly by the shoulders, steadying him with a calming touch. "With a maniac such as Lyrax," he shuddered as he uttered the name. "...nothing can be assumed. Nothing can be expected. Roann was likely doomed long before you took him under your wing."

"Sire, is *it* safe?"

Symond silently led his friend from the throne room. They walked through the modest palace of the Zaiterrans; the people milling about unaware of the grave news their sovereign had just been given. Stepping into a small side hallway near the back of the castle, away from prying eyes, the pair ducked into an unassuming room, closing and locking the door behind them. The king activated a hidden passage, and lit a torch before they descended down a dark staircase. At the bottom, they headed down a narrow shaft, supported by sagging wooden ceiling beams. It was barely tall enough to accommodate the two men. They followed the passageway for several minutes, the damp air smelling of dirt.

Finally, the old friends came to an iron door, no visible lock or handle. A brass placard was bolted to the surface, a small geometric indentation no larger than a pea embossed into the metal. Isum Dran approached the door and raised his hand, bringing his ring close to the switch. The crystal shard embedded in the silver glowed, and he pressed the ring against the metal, causing the entire placard to flare brilliantly. Tendrils of energy cascaded over the door. Suddenly, it swung open on its own. Dran motioned for King Symond to cross the threshold.

They emerged into a small, natural chamber, cut from the rock eons ago by rushing water. Symond snuffed the fire from the end of his torch, leaving the two men bathed in shimmering light.

"It's safe, old friend."

Isum Dran felt both relief and dread at the same time. He just stood there with his ally and stared out at the brilliant crystal before them.

Made in United States
North Haven, CT
23 January 2024

47812683R10236